Forgotten Future

At the edge of the world, an impossible relic from the fables of antiquity has risen from the frozen wastelands of Antarctica. Professor Logan and his exploration team rush to investigate this historic find, but this unique discovery puts their lives in peril when they unearth the remnants of a long-forgotten civilization left buried beneath the ice.

Within the twisting labyrinths below the melting glaciers, they uncover an ancient culture which had perished from a mysterious cataclysm. They soon realize it was a polar shift which had caused their destruction and our world was presently facing the same fate.

༄༅

Titles by Michel Savage

Faerylands Series
The Grey Forest
Soulstorm Keep
Sorrowblade
Ivory

Shadoworld Series
Shadow of the Sun
Veil of Shadows
Shadows Gate

Outlaws of Europa
Rebels of Alpha Prime

Hellbot • Battle Planet

A Couple of Zeros

Forgotten Future

Broken Mirror

Project EVE

Witchwood

7

଍ଓଔଓ

Islands
in the Sky

MICHEL SAVAGE

Enter the Grey Forest

www.GreyForest.com

Islands in the Sky

The Grey Forest
P.O. Box 71494
Springfield, OR 97475

www.GreyForest.com

Cover art by Michel Savage

ISBN: 978-09719168-2-1

First Edition: April 2018

Printed in the United States of America

0 9 8 7 6 5 4 3 2 1

The Iron Tree

The bitter cold was biting at my cheeks as we pushed our way through the snow while it crunched beneath our feet. The man in charge of the expedition to this frozen tundra had put up his own money to fund this trip. Six months ago, I was fresh out of the military and fully admit that I had hated every minute of my time in service. After our crew had set sail from the South Shetland Islands to trek the Antarctic shelf, a nagging thought rolled through my mind a dozen times or more as I questioned myself why I had bothered to take this job.

Frankly, I disliked snow and cold weather, and this white frozen hell reminded me of that with every vapor of my breath. The truth was I needed the money, plain and simple. When I enlisted for this adventure, I might have been a little too eager to sign the contract when they showed me the exorbitant pay and the promised bonuses if we met their deadlines. I jumped at it because I owed people money; greedy thugs that were the type of soulless individuals who were nothing more than human filth; morally depraved degenerates who wouldn't think twice about burying someone for the thrill of it, no matter how petty the loan. They were that rare variety of psychologically damaged and ethically corrupted individuals who were bred to be the scum of society. Most people called them Bankers, I called them by what they were: *Vampires* and *Leeches*; and they would bleed you dry if you gave them the chance.

If my years in the military taught me one thing it was that there are some really fucked up individuals running the country. It's the psychological manipulation that goes on behind closed doors that accounts for the rash of suicides by our combat veterans; which is information that is usually censored from the eyes and ears of our public media. After I got out of the service and back into civilian life, I had nothing to show for it but a cheap haircut and enough mental scars to weigh me down until I turned gray. Like most servicemen recently discharged, I found a girl and bought a house just so I could fit in and cling onto that mundane suburban dream which I had fooled myself into believing was the core of everything I had been fighting for. What they don't tell us grunts when we signed up, was that there are no promises in life.

When I couldn't find a dignified job worthy of my lackluster credentials, it wasn't too long before both my personal and intimate relationships went to hell in a hand-basket, and the ruthless banks were after my ass for the house payments. I made loan upon loans to keep up with the daily cost of living; such as the fancy car we owned, which my ex-wife took off with, along with the diamond engagement ring and the shit-ton of clothes which she bought until she managed to max out all my credit cards. The armed forces put food on the table and a roof over our heads, and taught us how to fight and survive foreign aggressors, but absolutely zero coaching on how a soldier was supposed to defend themselves against the drama that comes with civilian life.

Currently, I was in deep financial debt and was looking forward to starting a new life. That's how I ended up here in this frozen wasteland; playing pack-mule and security watchdog for this aging professor and his small team of archaeologists. I was trying not to think about my shattered past, but your mind tends to wander in the frigid gloom of this pale bleak wilderness.

"Logan, the GPS says we're 40 kilometers from the target area. Where the hell are you taking us?" Tom cut in over the radio.

Professor Logan had the transport ship set our team ashore far ahead of our target site that he had logged on the map, and the last 20 kilometers we traveled by motor sled over the ice seemed like the longest trek I've ever known. The radios were strapped inside our coats with wired headsets tucked snugly beneath our furred hoods.

"Trust me, Thomas, I know where I'm going," the weak breath

of the professor called back in response, heavy with exhaustion. Professor Logan was in his elder years, and I was slightly worried if he decided to have a heart attack from the sheer exertion of punching through knee-deep snow, then I might have to haul his lanky ass all the way back to the boat. Luckily, he was far too ornery than to let himself succumb to the frost which bit at the back of your throat whenever you took a breath. He had led us in the opposite direction from where our map coordinates had been logged for this mission, which now left us on the leeward side of a sloped glacier where we had to leave our sleds at the bottom shelf on the packed ice. One slip meant a dangerous tumble down its icy slope and a long climb back up if you were still alive at the end of it.

The small dot in the distance that was the professor disappeared around the edge of the glacier below the shadow of the summit. Tom was in close pursuit; I came in third as Alexander and Walter took up the rear. I could swear the rifle I was carrying got heavier with every step I took, but as the trained marksman in the group, I was the only one armed besides Tom. I sure as hell didn't know what I was supposed to be guarding them from, since there were no polar bears in the Antarctic as far as I knew.

Tom ordered me to wait in step and help the two members lagging behind. They were both in their late 40's, but had spent most of their lives at desk jobs, and had not realized just how physically demanding this journey would be. The professor had surprised us all with this little jaunt off the map but as he was the one who was writing the checks, we had no choice but to follow his lead.

"Alex, Walter, get up here, now!" Tom ordered over the radio, though the demanding tone of his voice seemed off, as though he was distracted by something, "Allen, carry those two up here if you have to, I need them to see this!"

I was glad for the few droll moments of rest as I stood my ground waiting for the two crew-members to catch up to me along the trail. I sure as hell wasn't going to carry them as Tom expected, but I wouldn't mind prodding them with my walking stick, if need be. Looking ahead, I could see through the cloud of my breath that Tom had also cleared the rim of the glacier behind the professor. Walt and Alex trod through the crunching snow and I took their place in the rear; as if that was going to somehow make them quicken their pace, which it didn't in the slightest. With our heads bowed, following in the footsteps in the snow left by our guide, we were too busy staring at our feet as we pushed ahead until we almost bumped into Thomas as he was busy looking through his binoculars.

Here, the glacier had split apart where it opened into a large chasm below. Within this large cavity was a void, which was almost entirely clear of ice down to the barren soil; this sunken hollow was completely hidden from the horizon. Professor Logan had made his way down to the bottom where giant glazed boulders rested in a mix of freshly fallen snow and shattered stone. It was what towered above him that made our eyes widen and our mouths fall open in disbelief. There before us stood a tree nearly a dozen stories high, its thick roots writhing deep into the bedrock. The girth of its trunk was enormous, covered in dark and twisted bark which curled up its way into its thick branches that reached for the open sky, fanning over an area the size of a small stadium. Its branches were bare of any foliage, though covered in sheets of icicles that hung like spears precariously above where the professor dared to tread below its frozen canopy.

We stood there in awe gazing at this impossible thing. It takes a moment for your mind to shake off the shock when you see something that shouldn't exist. I imagined it must have been similar to the same reaction when ancient travelers first saw the great Pyramids of Giza or the Colossus of Rhodes; which were legendary testaments to the skill and ingenuity of mankind. This, however, appeared to be a product of nature sitting smack dab in the middle of someplace it shouldn't be. Our minds reeling in wonder; Walt spat out what we were all thinking in our heads.

"Is that thing real?" Walter stammered.

"This magnificent relic is what I've been waiting to show you," Logan answered back from below, "words would not have explained it properly if I had tried to tell you ...even if you had believed me."

"But, but how is this possible?" Alexander mumbled out loud as he began to scurry down the broken path to get to where Logan now stood at its base.

"And yes, it *is* a real specimen. I took a bark sample back for analysis, of course, to verify my findings. It's not a sculpture nor is it petrified. Apparently, this beauty is dormant," Logan announced.

Huffing as he slipped on his way while scurrying down to the professor's level near the trunk, Alex took immediate attention to the giant writhing roots which dug their way into the solid stone foundation.

"What species is this ...and, and how did it come to be here in the middle of this ice field?" Alexander bumbled over his words in excitement. Walt fumbled with his camera, taking photos from the ledge as Tom carefully skirted his way down the broken shaft to explore the foundation with the other men.

"Allen, stay up top with Walter and keep your eyes open," Tom ordered before his descent. I realized he wanted me to keep the high ground, but I didn't know what he was expecting me to watch out for? There was little chance of anything dangerous besides a colony of wayward penguins making it this far inland, or anything at all for that matter.

"I hired several talented botanists who were experts in their field, and paid top dollar for their silence on this matter," Logan mentioned, "however, there were some anomalous readings within the carbon dating scans and other minor oddities that turned up in the genetic results, which stated this specimen may well be more than a hundred thousand years old."

"How is that possible?" Walt chimed in as he joined them at the base of the gnarled trunk.

"I would imagine being locked in ice could have either altered the DNA of the specimen, which may have led to the erroneous readings or possibly preserved it over the span of hundreds of centuries," the professor surmised.

"How could this have possibly lived through that length of suspension?" Alexander shot back in wonder.

"I'm not sure, but the genetic evaluation was just as puzzling, showing that this particular species of tree contained over nine million chromosomes," Logan answered as he stared up in amazement at the giant looming before him.

"Impossible!" Walt snapped back, "That's simply unheard of."

"I was just as skeptical as you, my friend, but that is why you are here. You are both distinguished professionals in your field, and I wanted to share this finding with you first hand," Logan offered with merit, "it has only been eight months since I first found this site but this basin around this specimen has widened dramatically since that time; abnormally so for this climate.

"What exactly does that mean?" Tom inquired as he approached the trunk, inspecting the deeply grooved bark with his thick mittens.

"I'm not quite sure, and that's why you're here, old friend," Logan replied, "to take measurements and samples for further study, so we can come to a scientific conclusion to this extraordinary find before we release it to the public and academic scrutiny."

"Do you have any idea what may have caused this level of melt-off?" Walter inquired as he scanned the labyrinth of roots weaving in and out of the quarry.

"Not entirely," the professor returned with a noted measure of uncertainty in his voice, "this ice sheet is dated at over twenty million years, though the shelf of this continent has sunk dramatically over the past thirty to forty million years, by conservative estimates."

"The real question is not what caused the exposure of this relic, but perhaps it is better to ask; why now?" Alexander suggested.

"A very astute question, my friend, and that is exactly why I brought equipment to detect magnetic anomalies on this venture," Logan answered as he motioned for Tom to bring over his pack of supplies.

Tom made his way to them and dropped his unwieldy backpack onto the stony ground, and the three of them began setting up monitoring equipment to log the local geomagnetic readings while Walter took additional photographs of the behemoth from various points surrounding the area. Alexander and the professor began taking soil and ice samples from the ground level along with pieces of the bark, which had been shaved off by the glacier ice. Removing a tubular drill, Tom locked together a portable frame to support the machine and secured it against the skin of one of the root systems. With a whir, the contraption began to dig itself into the ancient wood.

A sharp whine filled the air as the drill quickly overheated and the bit suddenly snapped. Tom jumped out of the way as sparks flew from the equipment, while the drill spun wildly after breaking its anchor upon the support.

"Holy Christ!" Tom barked as he got back onto his feet and began to inspect the twisted metal frame, "This outer skin is tougher than iron. We're going to need a better drill."

The incident brought the attention of the professor over to the failed equipment, and it was obvious through his frost-encrusted grimace that he wasn't happy about the unfortunate event.

"Actually, this relic is far older than Christ or any other religious figures in our recorded history," Logan breathed with disappointment as he viewed the broken framework.

"Ah, crap, this drill is shot. We might want to try a laser torch on another return," Tom granted as he held the shattered remains of the tool. He glanced upward for a moment to estimate how they might be able to climb their way to the upper branch supports; then Tom suddenly dropped everything in his hands and took a running dive to tackle the professor just as an enormous icicle broke free from the lattice of branches above and crashed to the ground where the drill was set. Shards of hard ice exploded around them, tearing at their coats.

I jumped to my feet, having just noticed the second before that the scream of the drill reverberated in the cavity, causing the enormous icicles to sway throughout the enormous canopy. Like spears of frozen death, several dozen giant icicles had broken free and came crashing around the team where they stood at the base of the trunk. They quickly scrambled and dove for protective cover among the surrounding boulders.

"Tom! Alex! Report in, do you see Logan or Walt?" I nervously called over the radio as I stared into the plume of fine ice crystals rising from the basin below my perch. After the glittering shards began to settle, I scanned the area for signs of movement. Slowly, a few bodies began to take form out of the shattered debris that covered the rocks below.

"Tom here, I have Logan ...do you have eyes on Alex and Walter from your position?" Thomas coughed through his microphone as he took a cautious glance towards the branches above him before hauling the professor out from underneath a leaning boulder, from where they had found refuge.

"Over here ...I, I'm okay; but I don't see Walter!" Alexander responded nervously as he spat out bits of ice while raising his hand so we could spot his position.

Tom propped the professor up next to the broken stones and looked out across the field. He had just barely caught the shimmer of sunlight from the monstrous shaft of ice as it fell from the limbs above them, before tackling Logan. Looking back over his shoulder, the drill and most of the gear they had set up had been crushed to bits.

"You alright there, Doc?" Tom asked Logan, who was ruffled and shaken, but otherwise unhurt. The professor nodded that he was and waved off Tom, who was his right-hand man on this expedition.

"I'm fine. Go find Walter," he bade towards Thomas.

Tom took off to help Alex brush himself off and checked him for any injuries; then began to check the debris field for their lost comrade.

"Allen, are you there?" Tom barked.

"Yes sir," I called back as I watched him make his way through the hunks of broken ice below.

"Keep an eye out and give me a heads-up if you see anything precarious above my location. Can you see Walt from your position?" he inquired as he began to pull away large piles of shattered ice with his pick.

"No, not yet. I last saw him on the far side of your position before all hell broke loose. Wait! I think I see movement to your 10 o'clock," I snapped over the radio.

Tom jumped from boulder to icy boulder and wove his way under bridges of curled roots surrounding the base of the iron tree. He found Walter under a thick blanket of ice crystals, still lingering in a state of shock and nursing his shoulder.

"Hey, are you alright?" Tom managed to huff with labored breath.

"My arm, I think it's broken..." Walter sighed back, wincing with pain when he moved. Kicking aside the spray of shattered ice, he could see the equipment he had been carrying had been smashed to pieces.

"Aw, for criminy's sake, the magnetometer is completely destroyed," he spouted, but the piercing pain from the movement of his arm caused him to bring his concerns back into perspective.

"It could have been worse, that could have been you lying there instead," Tom nodded towards the smashed gear, "here, let me see your arm," he asked as Tom gingerly inspected Walters left arm. After a few yelps of pain from his patient, Tom confirmed his limb would need to be reset.

"Look, I need you to do something for me, Walter," Tom asked.

"Yeah, what?" he replied.

"Here, take my glove, I need you to bite onto it," Tom answered as he took off one of his mittens, and coaxed Walter to place it in his mouth.

"*Wff, the fkk do I neefm thss frr?*" Walter mumbled through the

mitten as he argued with a quizzical look in his confused eyes.
Tom pointed up at the additional spears of ice hanging
precariously above them as he answered him.

"Whatever you do, keep quiet. Got it?" Tom suggested.

"*Yehh surmf,*" Walt conceded as Tom directed his gaze upward
yet again.

With a single tug, Tom snapped Walt's bone back into place,
and he began to immediately bind the broken arm with his
scarf. It took a slight moment for Walter to feel the pain course
through his limb as he screamed through the fur of the glove
stuffed in his mouth. Tom quickly held Walt's mouth shut to
muffle the noise when his strangled cry began to echo between
the walls of the glacier. The icicles overhead began to gently
sway above them before Tom got Walter to settle down, and he
helped him back to the other team members.

"We've got to move out from under this canopy," Tom ordered
to the three men as small shards of ice began to lightly shower
around them once again. Not wishing to tempt fate twice, Alex
and the Professor made their way to the edge of the ice sheet
and out of range from the frozen spears looming overhead.

"Allen, get down here; you've got the first aid kit in your
pack," Tom ordered over the radio.

I shouldered my rifle in haste and made my way down the side
of the drift and circled around to their position just outside the
break in the glacier. Catching up with the men, I could see that
they were all shaken by the ordeal. Logan attempted to keep
his wits about him, despite his close call. I unpacked the
medical kit for Tom, who skillfully constructed a splint and
sling for Walter's arm.

"Allen, I want you to go back in there and see what equipment
you can salvage. If anything at all survived, we will need those
readings," Logan directed me to search the clusters of shattered
ice for our instruments.

"And, ah, do try not to make any noise," Tom advised as an
afterthought as I made my way back into the cavity.

The melting ice made the footing slippery, while the limbs of the tree reached over me like a looming spider. It was an imposing sight to behold; this once living tree that coiled into the bleak sky above, its twisting branches weaving themselves around my vision as I approached ever closer. Even now, the freshly shattered ice had begun to melt. Whatever forces had exposed this relic from antiquity they were now releasing it from its ancient cage of ice.

The drill was beyond salvage, but Walters meter was worth pocketing as were the few bagged specimens they had gathered thus far. Searching further, I found myself at the base of the giant tree, trying to imagine how its giant trunk had once begun as a tiny sapling that could have fit into the palm of my hand. The deep-set cracks in its bark were nearly a meter thick, snaking its intricate design like armor across its heartwood which lay protected beneath. I was looking for the temperature apparatus Alex had been using to take measurements and found it glinting from a darkened crevice at the base of the trunk; having been flung there by the exploding ice.

Reaching into the crack, I picked the gauge up to wipe it off, only to notice it had been resting on something chiseled into the stone slab beneath where it had lain. Brushing off the slush of ice and snow, I found a figure there etched deep into the ancient stone. Stepping back, I saw that I was standing upon a much larger design that had been hidden under a layer of frost which was encircled by enormous handset stones. I stared for a moment in wonder, but hearing the cracking ice threatening to bring another hail of icicles upon my head, I hurried back to join the others.

"I grabbed what I could," I answered to the professor when I reached him. Walter was looking better now that his arm was secured in a sling.

"Good, good, young man; let us get back to the boat and get some proper medical attention for Sir Walter, shall we," Logan advised as the group of us shuffled back through the snow at the lower part of the glacier.

After we had retreated nearly a kilometer from the site, I

turned to notice that the colossal tree had been enveloped by the surrounding glacier; entirely hidden from sight. It would be easy to miss by air unless you flew directly over it, and impossible to find from the surrounding glacier walls which hid it below the horizon of this frozen windswept expanse.

It was a long haul back to the landing site where we had tethered our small boat. The bitter cold started to bite through our winter jackets as the sun began to set while we made our way back to the anchored ship out at sea. We got Walt into the infirmary where the onboard doctor got him a proper cast and redressed his wounds. Tom got his hands bandaged, while Alex and Logan sought the tender cure of a 30-year-old bottle of scotch. As for me, I was exhausted; having made the hike back carrying twice as much gear as I left with. At least everybody was safe and we considered ourselves fortunate, knowing that this day could have ended much, much worse.

It was late into the evening when our crew gathered in the conference quarters to look over the remnants of our salvaged equipment to see what we could piece back together. At least Walter's camera had survived the ordeal or we wouldn't have had the photos to prove what Logan had found. Alexander promptly began to redraw the charts with the correct location, but when the professor saw what he was doing over his shoulder, he snatched the graph out from beneath his hands. Taken aback, Alex turned to glare at him in shock.

"What are you doing, Logan?" Alex whined, wondering why the professor was pulling a tantrum when he was only doing his job recording the data at hand.

"I would appreciate if you left the mapping up to me, Alexander," Logan scoffed back at the bewildered man, "I can keep track of everything just fine," he granted while pointing to his own head.

"What is going on with you, Professor?" Walter intervened with a suspicious tone, "you invited us to join you on this return expedition and set us ashore a full two days march from the noted GPS coordinates, but then sent us off on a wild jaunt in the opposite direction!"

"Yes, Logan; what is it with all this cloak and dagger misdirection?" Thomas added to the verbal quarrel. I leaned back at the table and quietly poured myself a shot of that prime-scotch behind their backs, to sneak a well-earned drink for my hard day's labor. Honestly, I was just as interested to hear his explanation due to us for having risked our lives.

"You need to understand, gentlemen, that what was revealed to you today must not leave this room; agreed?" Logan demanded. Each of the men nodded; then in unison, they turned to me as I sat there sipping my stolen shot of hooch, which I hastily choked down and nodded back in agreement.

"This is an incredible find, Logan. Your career will be vaulted to the top branch of the Academy of Science, and this magnificent discovery will be chronicled into the history books for all time," Alex offered with cheer. However, the Professor was less than cordial in his response to the dispensed flattery.

"Alexander, if this discovery was made public at this point in time, I can guarantee you that the only *vault* I would experience would be the pit of a tomb!" Logan spat back as he played on Alexander's words, "Be aware that I intentionally recorded false coordinates onto the log chart in an effort to avoid having the artifact fall into the hands of certain unsavory organizations, who are far less principled than you or I."

"I don't understand your conjecture, Professor; the scientific council would protect your findings, especially one of this scale," Walter offered in rebuttal. Logan, however, seemed unimpressed with his naive trust of his peers.

"My friends, I don't think you understand the gravity of the situation, dictated by the very existence of this relic and the dilemma we all now face," he breathed back at us in an unsettling tone, "there are powers that be in our modern world that would thoroughly absorb this find into their folds, and it would be erased from history; never to be seen again," he finished while his finger moved, pointing to each of us; which we took as his cue that we too could disappear along with this rare archaeological discovery.

"So you are trying to protect this ...this iron tree?" Tom asked.

"Undoubtedly so, and ourselves from the fatal consequences which could shake the foundation of our social ties between our international constituents," Logan elaborated.

"What? How does that even come into play?" Walter argued, "You're inflating this all a little too much don't you think?" he finished with a shake of his head.

"It's just some old petrified tree stuck in a glacier..." Alexander started to contend before Logan cut him off.

"No! No, it's not, Alex. The cells of the specimen are active," he related with a stern brow. At that admission, both Alex and Walter shared an astonished stare.

"It's alive?" Tom bargained to translate Logan's claim for us.

"The tests I had performed on the samples prove it so," the professor admitted.

Trying to follow along in the conversation, I too was a bit skeptical that the professor was blowing this situation way out of proportion. I could understand him wanting to protect his find and desiring to get full credit for it; lest an outside agency attempt to seize his discovery, but it was my understanding that no nation could do so under the guidelines of the Antarctic Accord. The articles of the international treaty laid out specific protections for that vast block of ice; essentially labeling it no-mans land. It was an agreement between nations that, in all honesty, seemed a little too good to be true; and could make one wonder if it was truly made in the spirit of peace, or was there a more underhanded and nefarious reason hiding behind its enactment?

Looking through the photographs Sir Walter had taken that day, Logan clarified that this ancient tree was more than just an anomaly. His hypothesis was that it wasn't a freak *of* nature, but one of a specific design *by* nature. He extracted a stack of volumes from his briefcase containing records of ancient cultures from across the planet, from every timeline of antiquity from the Hebrews to Norse mythology; each mentioning the tale of a similar relic known as the World Tree.

"The tree of life ...from which all creatures sprang," Logan suggested, "whether these tales be true or not, there are those that manipulate the strings of human progress from secretive and powerful sects who would do anything to either control or entirely suppress the discovery of such an ancient and iconic symbol," the professor suggested as he motioned to the piles of books now scattered across the table.

"But we saw nothing there that would tie its location to any recorded civilization in recent or ancient past," Alex stated as he thumbed through the books; each bearing duplicate drawings of the same image, of the canopy of a tree and its spread roots in balance with one another, like the figure of an hourglass.

"Well ...not exactly, there was something man-made there alright," I mumbled with a drunken slur from behind the arguing men. They each caught their tongues and turned to me in unison, and I began to regret having spoken out loud. I put down the scotch with a sigh, realizing the liquor had probably done its part to loosen my tongue.

"What was it Allen, what did you see?" Professor Logan prompted his question towards me as the other men drew blank stares of anticipation.

I stood up and went to the table and scanned over the open books, where I recognized several familiar images; those of an entwining snake, which formed in a binding circle surrounding the figure of the central tree.

"I saw what looked to be a large carving in the stone of a serpent, twisting upon itself in looped rings along its outer circumference," I answered as I pointed at one of the images in the pages of the book lying open before me; thinking back to the crude etchings I had seen in the black stone lying beneath the colossal tree. I grabbed a pen and drew it in the corner of the map chart laying on the table; depicting the image as close as I could remember it. Logan snatched it up when I was done and stared at it in a moment of silence, and then began to flip through several volumes laying about the table in excitement.

"The nine circles, the nine worlds of legend..." he mumbled aloud with elation.

"No, no, there were just eight circles that I recall," I corrected as I pointed back to the drawing. In response, the professor marked off each of the loops I had drawn, he then added in the final circle of the entwining serpent itself, encasing them.

"This outer circumference makes nine. According to myth, this is the legendary entrance to the well of souls," Logan revealed as he picked up a volume and began frantically flipping through its leaves until he found the page he was looking for, and held up a similar drawing to mine of an ancient etching in one of his tomes for all of us to see.

The Doorway

While I was recovering from my hangover the next morning, Alex had been busy repairing the smashed magnetometer by salvaging its key internal parts which contained the recorded readings and swapped them out with a spare device. Luckily, its embedded battery had remained attached or the information it held would have been lost. After pumping out the data he showed the results to Walter, who was in the same state as I was; having drunk away most of the scotch to help numb the pain of his broken arm. Logan went over the figures from the device, while trying to determine what they meant.

"This is astounding!" he stated, "It appears this organic specimen is acting as an antenna of sorts, by emanating a tightly woven magnetic field around itself."

"But how would that account for the melting ice around its base?" Tom inquired.

"My theory is that the limbs of the tree are creating a stable field around its circumference, and these micro fluctuations in the strength of the fields are exciting the atoms just enough to warm the area around it ...see these temperature readings here, and how they vary from within the proximity to its trunk," Logan explained as he showed us the notes he had taken.

"So you're saying its acting sort of like a microwave?" Walter questioned, as he worried about the health impacts.

"Well no ...well, okay, maybe, but only in a mild sense," Logan squabbled.

"Alright, let's say that this harebrained theory of yours is substantiated," Alex cut in, "what do you suspect is the energy source creating this field?"

That was a question worth investigating, though there was little doubt that a follow-up expedition was in order. This time we would have to bring equipment which was up to the task, especially in the case of the drill so we could obtain a core sample from the specimen. Logan was reluctant to make an extensive and time-consuming trip all the way back to the mainland and abandon their current proximity of the site, so he ordered the new equipment by radio to be delivered to the ship. The professor wasn't exactly a rich man, and this little endeavor and the cost of this transport vessel and crew was eating a hole in his limited resources.

It would take three more days for the new equipment to arrive by air cargo to be dropped at our location, so we took that time to fine-tune our next approach. My initial interpretation began to sway as I wondered what I had gotten myself into and if I really wanted to stay on board, but Logan seemed preoccupied with charting the next steps in our expedition rather than answering my questions. I was stuck out here at sea with him until the end of my contract term, and thus far, I couldn't sway myself from the fat paycheck I had been promised at the end of this excursion.

"Professor Logan, I would have to inquire as to your rationale for returning to the site so soon, especially since Walter would be unable to accompany us because of his injury. Might I suggest that we attempt another expedition in six months or so, when we have the proper equipment..." Alexander began to argue until Logan interrupted his train of thought mid-sentence.

"Alex, my friend, let me be frank with you," Logan charged while lowering his volume so as not to be overheard by the others, "I have put my entire estate into this trek, and there will be no recovery from this tour unless we return with the evidence I seek," he offered with a wave of exhaustion which suddenly washed over his face, "you must understand that there are others who seek this artifact, and the picture is much larger than you know ...however, for posterity's sake, I will say no more until I have verified my findings."

It was clear Alex had more questions lingering on the tip of his tongue but could see the weariness in Logan's eyes. He instead, took his time to help Walter, who was handicapped for the time being and was struggling to make his data entries in the logs. I had been assigned to help Tom get the additional gear packed since the professor seemed to want us prepped for a full week out in the field. That was a long time to be out in the snow and I was not looking forward to it, so I got some proper rest in the days that followed.

Early one morning, a helicopter arrived with our cargo and we were all mildly surprised to find that another passenger had been dropped off with our new equipment. A slender framed individual barged into the conference room; dusting the frost from their thick jacket. After removing their furred hood and mask, we were all a little startled to see a woman peel her way out of the layers of wool.

"Ah, gentlemen, I would like to introduce you to my star pupil and understudy from the academy, Mica," Logan stated to the four of us, "Mica, this is Walter and Alexander, whom I've worked with for many long years. This is Tom, my guide and crew coordinator; if you need anything, he will get it for you. Oh, and Allen, my security assistant," Logan finished as he pointed to each of us during the introduction.

"Hello," was all she said while tearing off her mittens. Mica was an attractive academic type, with long pale red hair tied up in a ponytail and light freckles sprinkled across her nose; though as frail as she appeared on the outside, she held herself with a hard, if not professional manner.

"Hold on Logan, why is *she* here?" Tom inquired with a harsh tone. He wasn't the type of man who liked surprises in his line of work.

"I'm sorry for failing to notify you earlier Thomas, but it was a last-minute invitation I extended to her, and I wasn't sure that Mica, here, was even going to be able to make it until she arrived," Logan tried to explain, "in light of Walt's unfortunate injury on our last outing, I thought it prudent to get a qualified replacement. Mica here will be my personal assistant, who will be taking over Walters duties in the field," the professor acknowledged.

"Alright, I have no problem with that, just as long as she can handle her own," Tom barked back with a hard look, which won him a sharp glare from Mica.

"I can assure you, sir, that Mica here is quite capable and willing to apply herself to any situation," Logan returned with a gracious nod towards our newest team member.   On that thought, Tom offered a pout of acceptance and asked me to offer my opinion on the matter as their active security.

"Well, uh ...I'm not aware of Miss Mica's background or her ability to work in the field, but I really don't foresee a problem," I replied toward Tom with a shrug of mild confusion; wondering if he was just trying to get someone to jump on his side, or if he was actually a male chauvinist at heart.   At this point, I couldn't tell which.

"Thank you, Allen," Mica nodded with a graceful smile.   Tom, on the other hand, gave a huff and made a petty excuse to remove himself from the room to attend to his duties.   Tom, in my opinion, was acting slightly odd, since being at this conference with the crew *was* one of his duties.   Professor Logan simply reacted with a grunt and a raised brow at the personal slight his logistics officer had shown.

"If I may ask, Miss, what exactly are your skills in this field of research?" Alexander inquired, much to Walter's added interest.

"I've been an understudy for renowned geologist, Vincent Rice, who combined applications of magnetic waves with his background research in helioseismology," she granted.

"I'm, I'm sorry ...who is that?" Alex stuttered with confusion as he adjusted his spectacles.

"Rice was an old friend of mine back when I was a freshman, myself," Logan smiled as he interjected on her behalf, "he is one of the top scientists in his field, regarding; well ...internal fields of solar bodies," he smiled with mild embarrassment to his clumsy analogy.

"Actually," Mica corrected in an effort to stand up for herself, "it is the study of internal wave structures; whether they be seismic, acoustic, or gravitational by nature," she answered.

"I'm a little confused as to what use that will be on this

endeavor," Walter offered in return, which was the same question I would have asked.

"Ah, well that is where my previous decade of research begins to come together, my friend," Logan answered, "Allen, my boy, perhaps you could assist with injecting a fresh viewpoint for us; being one outside the forum of such academic studies," the professor asked as he turned to face me. I was stunned, if not a tad insulted by his question; which sounded like he was calling me a dolt. However, that automated reaction might have just been my ignorance speaking for me in place of reason.

"Yeah, sure; what do you need?" I answered awkwardly.

"Before accepting my employment, if I may ask, what were the major media stories you were aware of before we left the mainland?" Logan inquired.

"Uh, well ...economic downturn and political tensions, which I imagine were primarily linked to the constant threat of international war," I gathered to be the plausible answer he was looking for.

"And has the average mainstream media you've witnessed thus far, rotated around any different subjects of top interest in say, the past 10 or even 20 years?" He tested me.

Truth be told, the answer was no. The foremost news events revolved around war, incursion, invading and occupying foreign countries without provocation; including whispers of wild conspiracies, of which any such motives that might be reported could have been intentionally fabricated in pursuit of a given result; such as creating excuses to engage in war and the public need of a government body to direct the masses. I stood there for an uncomfortable moment trying to analyze what I remembered from outside of the box; and what it suggested troubled me. In all honesty, I had begun giving a measure of credence to those vague, if not fringe claims, of government corruption; especially when it became ever more obvious that our news stories were being scripted. It became commonplace in the public forum that the same stories were being recycled by our national media without any counter viewpoints whatsoever;

even when they were proven to be false, they stuck to their narrative. Having served my time in the military, I can assure you that we weren't always the good guys. In fact, it was common practice just to put on a show of force while we wasted a fortune of taxpayer funds on personnel time, fuel and ammunition on counterproductive and fruitless maneuvers that accomplished nothing of value.

"Alright, now let me ask you another question, Allen," Logan asked again when it became clear that I was struggling for an answer to his first question, "What do you know about polar shifts?"

"Well, I believe I've heard that it may have happened a few times in earth's past," was all I could remember from the sparse nature documentaries I had seen.

"And that's all?" Logan pushed for a more descriptive answer, but the shake of my head told him his efforts were in vain.

"Yep," I shrugged my shoulders, wondering at his point.

"There, you see gentlemen," the professor turned back to his colleagues, "the general public has no idea what is coming, and are completely unprepared for what is ahead."

"You lost me, Logan," Walter intervened as he rubbed his injured arm, "how are polar shifts connected in any way with this wild expedition of yours?" he barked, "Yes, you found an impressive specimen, which was most likely kept frozen from the Mesozoic period; but you've thus far refused to show us the scope of your documentation on this little safari to the far ends of the earth," Sir Walter began to growl, which was out of character for him, bearing the verifiable title as both a gentleman and a British scholar.

"Mica here, as you now know, studies wave fields; and her research with Vincent Rice in the small arena of geomagnetic behaviors were recently repressed and disbanded from the academy," Logan spat.

"Well, yes, but I heard that certain grants had been withdrawn in the ecological labs..." Walter admitted but was cut off mid-sentence by Mica.

"And a concerning degree of censorship was levied upon their research," Mica helped to enlighten the group, "and there is the fact that within the past two months, 4 of the top 5 scientists from this field who had been dismissed, were found deceased; reported as accidents or death by natural causes," she charged.

"If you study the facts, you'll find that our planet's poles have already jumped far off course from their normal regions of variance, and the magnetosphere of this little blue planet of ours has already weakened by a disturbing degree over the past few decades; which I attest, is the forefront of an upcoming polar shift," Logan declared.

"Ah, yes ...but such theories can't be confirmed as they've never been fully recorded; besides, they are reported as rare events taking hundreds of centuries during such reversals," Alex replied as if to brush off the air of concern spouted by Logan and his new associate.

"My studies with Dr. Rice suggested we would witness such an event in our lifetime..." Mica added.

"On a timeline that is much sooner than anyone realizes," Logan inserted his opinion in for hers.

"How soon?" I inquired, as I dared to interrupt the back and forth bantering between Logan and his senior colleagues.

"My calculations won't be complete until we fully audit the site of the anomaly," the professor answered as he pointed towards the stack of books he previously introduced about the fables of the giant tree we had found, "but there is the real possibility that an extinction-level event could occur before the end of the year," he answered as he looked into our glazed eyes; as we were unable to process what he had just claimed.

"Ecological societies and engineers have already logged hundreds of reports of abnormal ocean die-offs, including millions of fish washing ashore. There are the disappearing bee populations and other pollinating insects, and havoc being reported in migrations of wild herds and flocks of birds wandering astray; throwing our entire ecosystem out of balance, and it's only going to get worse," Mica offered to explain the severity of the situation.

"And that giant tree, that unique specimen from antiquity may very well be at the center of it all," Logan sited to our disbelief.

I trusted the professor and his assistant knew what they were talking about, but I couldn't get a grasp at the magnitude of the situation. A polar shift wasn't at the top of my shopping list of things to worry about, as most common folk. Of course, if there was any true cause for worry, the authorities in the government would have warned us; wouldn't they? With a shrug, I realized I already knew the answer to that question.

"So what was it that this Vincent fellow you studied with, actually came up with?" I stumbled over my words as I addressed Mica.

"Are you referring to the concluded hypothesis or our validated findings?" she answered, seemingly confused as to the direction of my question; or, she could have just been acting cheeky to spite me. I couldn't tell which.

"Uh ...both, I guess," was all I could stammer out while trying not to sound like an idiot.

"The naturally occurring artifacts currently affecting our ecosystem are escalating expeditiously," Mica returned without hesitation.

Damn, I sure did hate big words, and this woman was making me feel like I should crawl under the table and hide. I knew I didn't always act like the brightest crayon in the box but I was starting to feel out of my depth here with the high IQ's bouncing around the table. So in a moment of aggravation, I flared with a rant that may have seemed a bit out of line.

"So, basically you're saying that the world is fucked, and there's nothing we can do about it," I blurted as a statement rather than a question. I immediately regretted my crude tongue, especially in front of the lady; but the other men seemed just as unnerved about this troubling news.

"Actually, there may be something we can do to avert this dilemma," Logan answered after the awkward moment of silence following my outburst, "and I will need your help, everyone's help," he offered with a gesture to the rest of us at the table.

Logan's plan was riding on the faith that we had missed something vital during our last outing. If his theory was correct, then the melt-off around the giant tree would have escalated over the past week, and would have exposed more of the site for us to survey and complete his analysis. Now that we had the proper equipment onboard and a viable replacement for our injured colleague, there was nothing stopping us from revisiting the target site. However easy I may have thought that was going to be, it might have jinxed us. It was in the cold dark before the break of dawn when Tom woke me up as I lay in my bunk; ordering me to get dressed.

"Allen, get your ass out of bed! I need you geared up and on the skiff, pronto!" Tom barked as he rudely shook me awake. It was mentally scarring having been ripped from a dream about lying in a hammock on a warm summer beach, only to be pulled back into the reality of my cramped cabin and the unsteady rocking of the ship.

"*Wha...* what the hell? We aren't due for launch until ten o'clock," I whined as I checked my watch.

"There's a squall rolling in from the West, and Logan is afraid a snowstorm will cover the site; so we need to get to the rally site first," Tom answered with a raised voice, "I need you on your feet, now!"

Just for the record, I really ...I mean I *really* hate the cold, and was never fond of snow for that matter. Regardless of how much coffee you drink or how thickly you try to bundle up, the numbing cold seems to seep through it all. Thermal underwear, two sets of wool socks, pants, overalls, anti-frostbite gloves, turtleneck, scarf, head cap, earmuffs, storm jacket, and double-layered mittens. I imagined it took less time for an astronaut to put on a spacesuit.

I made my way up top to the bridge before heading to the storeroom outside the deck and saw the radar track of the storm. The storm front was big but moving slowly. Based on the telemetry data, both Tom and Logan thought it was a risk worth taking. I helped our crew load up the skiff and we hit the water an hour before sunrise. Logan, Alex, Tom, Mica and I, set off towards the inlet where we had first landed several kilometers from our anchored ship.

The glow of sunrise was overshadowed by the enormous clouds rising like a wall above the horizon. At our position on the ice shelf, we were beginning to withdraw from the daylight season, which would leave the sun hanging low above the icy tundra for nearly five more months before entering into a darkened twilight. Personally, I planned on being on a Caribbean beach with a margarita in my hand long before the winter juncture arrived.

This time we hauled out a large motor sled, which Tom and I both shared the burden of riding while the rest of the group kept pace. With a few grumbles from Tom, Mica did manage to keep clip with the rest of us. We attempted a new approach from the bottom edge of the glacier towards our target site, which Logan kept on track by the few sparse flag markers he had left on the upper trail. When we finally arrived, we were perplexed by the recent formation of fresh ice along the lower edge of the field.

On our approach of the iron tree, we could see that a great deal of the surrounding glacier had withdrawn from the limbs of the enormous artifact. The twisted arms of the tree were now nearly bare of the icicles which had been the cause of our last debacle. Approaching the upper platform at the base of the trunk, Mica took a moment to soak in the magnificence of the ancient artifact for the first time. There was a look of disbelief on her face, even though her eyes were hidden by the tinted goggles she wore.

"This is..." she began to say,

"Amazing, isn't it?" Logan interjected.

"I was going to say; beautiful," she corrected him as she took a few snapshots with her camera.

The gale of the approaching storm started to pick up as we

made our way into the protective walls of the melted glacier, which was an area free of ice that spanned like an invisible globe from the center of the tree itself. Tom looked up, and I could tell he wasn't too happy about the amount of overhang above us. A few hundred pounds of ice melt from the limbs was avoidable if you were fleet of foot. However, several tons of compacted snow waiting to collapse was another matter entirely.

"Good gracious," Professor Logan spouted out as he stepped upon the giant platform of hand-carved stone I had mentioned before. Cut within the ancient rock was the chiseled image of several entwined snakes. Alexander grabbed a video camera and began recording the area on his behalf.

"You see here," Logan pointed out to Alex as he recorded the scene, "the eight worlds, tied to the central sphere of our own; entwined within its protective coils," the professor exclaimed.

"Wasn't the serpent considered a messenger of evil, Doc?" Tom queried with a measure of apprehension.

"*Humph*, no lad, only so in younger and less enlightened religious doctrines. In times of antiquity, the mighty serpent was seen as a symbol of fertility and rebirth, even of royalty and divinity itself," Logan responded.

"Are these symbols for other stars in our constellation?" Alex inquired with interest.

"Well ...I'm not quite sure if they have anything to do with astronomy, for the lack of any factual evidence," the professor seemed perplexed at the possibility, "but it could represent another land or society on a more mundane scale."

"Or other kingdoms," Mica offered as an answer, to which Logan nodded in agreement, "or perhaps even astral worlds in the afterlife if viewed from another context."

"Or levels of hell..." Tom smirked back as if to slight her.

"No, no, there are various references to such a purgatory claimed by countless religious zealots and cults from mankind's brutal past," Logan corrected in her defense towards Tom, "if this magnificent artifact was purely a sculpture, I would have an alternate hypothesis; but since it is a living entity, I believe it had a far more sacred purpose."

"It's alive?" Mica breathed as she stared upward into its massive canopy of branches. She touched the hardened bark of the roots in wonder as she saw that it wasn't a man-made artifact, but a work of nature.

"Very much so, and that is why we needed to get a core sample of the heartwood before we leave this expedition, to get a true reading as to its age," Logan granted.

Motioning to Tom, they began to set up the laser drill from the sled, and I helped them clip the equipment into place. Alex collected stone fragments while simultaneously taking soil samples and density readings alongside Mica. Logan explained to her that this relic was entirely encased within the glacier less than a year ago, and he had gone to great lengths to keep this site secret. Upon that revelation, her elated tone turned from excitement towards one of apprehension.

"How secret?" Mica responded in worry.

"Very, my dear. I took great care not to disclose the site location and placed my target coordinates for this expedition far off course to the North-West of us; in case anyone was snooping. Why do you ask?"

"I ah, well," Mica stumbled on her response, "I kind of published a few private drafts you shared with Professor Rice, as supporting notes in my thesis to the academy this past semester," she admitted. The look on Logan's face was one of shock and dismay.

"Ohhh shit, the cats out of the bag," Tom smiled as he finished ratcheting in the last bolt to the frame that held the drill.

"You didn't..." Logan shook his head in disbelief.

"Your messages stated it was personal, not confidential; so I assumed you were in the process of disclosing your data to the Academy of Science before the end of the year ...and considering the chances there might be an expedited end to this term, I chose to include the data," she shrugged innocently.

The wind was picking up and raging gusts began to enter the

small enclosure within the proximity of the tree. Tom radioed the ship but his message was met with pricks of static while he tried to make sense of the crewman's response. The ship's radar had confirmed with satellite imagery that the massive tempest we had seen over the horizon was closing in faster than expected. For the safety of the crew, Tom had to make a call.

"Sir, we need to wrap this up now, and get back to the ship," Tom advised.

"Nonsense, we have far too much data and samples to collect; we will make it back in time," Logan brushed off his misgivings to the seriousness of the situation.

"Even if we left this very second, there is only a slight chance we will make it safely to the ship, sir," Tom corrected Logan's lax demeanor, "otherwise we have to dig in for this storm, and we'll be left snowed in until it passes."

This was unwelcome information that seemed to worry everyone except for the professor, whose concern was that this was his last chance to collect the needed data. He had no more finances for a return trip and there were more crucial matters at hand if he failed to confirm his findings. The rising wind began to curl its way into the breach of the void as fine particles of ice bit at our exposed skin. It was a dilemma that Logan wasn't prepared to face, so he ordered us to continue working in his desperation to not return empty-handed. Another call came over the radio, where Tom deciphered the message through the streams of static overtaking their communications.

"Well, that does it," Tom stated with a grimace, "The ship's captain has raised anchor and moving the vessel to a safer distance. It looks like we're stuck here until the storm is over."

"That settles it then," Logan prompted with resolve, "let's get that core sample before the site is covered with fresh snowfall," he ordered.

"Allen, I need you to get a shelter set up against that exposed wall," Tom pointed towards a stone cliffside which had been recently uncovered by the melt-off surrounding the strange tree.

"Belay that order, Allen," Logan contended, "I need you to

help get this core sample before the equipment is damaged."

Tom looked upset at the professor's counter-order but grunted in aggravation instead of arguing with the old man. Personally, I was getting a little pissed off that we would be stuck here to suffer through the snowstorm but we had to keep Logan happy, lest he dock our paychecks. Alex and Mica put away their recording devices and bagged the few samples they collected, while Tom directed them to take the sled to the far wall and unpack the tents while we screwed around with the drill to get the core sample Logan so desperately desired.

Sharp gusts of wind began to burst through the cavity while smaller icicles pelted the ground around us like brittle daggers. Having locked the drill frame onto the trunk of the tree, Tom cycled on the device which appeared to resist ignition.

"Fucking god-damn battery!" Tom blurted out in aggravation as he kicked the large block case of fragile wiring surrounding the laser. As if by some miracle, that reckless assault caused the device to blink on, and a bright red beam began to bite into the trunk of the tree.

"Temperamental, isn't he?" Mica spouted to Alex as she looked over her shoulder from their position by the cliff wall.

"Ah, don't worry about Tom, he's just concerned about the approaching storm," Alex granted, "I heard he was with an expedition a few years back that got trapped in a drift for eight weeks. They lost over a dozen men during that blizzard, and Tom himself barely made it out alive. Most men would never take that kind of chance again, but he's still here in this godforsaken place."

Mica understood then that Tom wasn't just being a prick, but that he had seen the face of death in this frozen world, and been left scarred by its frigid gaze. He had their well being at heart and didn't wish to see anyone suffer such a cruel fate ever again. Perhaps he stayed to help others explorers of this icy wasteland from meeting the same misfortune; or that he could no longer live with himself if they did. There was a sense of guilt trickling through his veins, a chill far colder than the glacier ice upon which we stood. He was a changed man; and whether that was for better or for worse, who was to say? I tended the laser bore with Tom as he calibrated the device after advising me to keep my tinted goggles on while it was in operation. The beam was cutting a small circular pattern from the outer skin of the hardened bark. After a few minutes, light wisps of smoke began to spew from the aperture, which was expected when using a burning tool on a wooden material. Logan kept a watchful eye on our progress, having readied the specimen tube where we were to lay the core sample when it was extracted.

"Something's wrong," Tom stated abruptly as he fiddled with the controls on the device. I sure as hell didn't know how it worked, so I was relying on his skill with the cutter.

"Is the battery freezing up?" I surmised, considering his difficulties of getting the thing to start and why the beam was beginning to flicker.

"No," Tom flashed back with concern, "...it's almost as if something is deflecting it," he referred to the laser cutter.

"What's the problem?" Logan stepped in to oversee the progress but noting that the power of the drill was oddly ebbing away on the power bar.

"Do you think this antenna-like magnetic wave thing you were talking about earlier might be interfering with the electronics?" I suggested as I pointed up at the tree, trying not to sound like a moron.

"Hmm, that's a very astute possibility I had not foreseen," Logan responded; saving me from my embarrassment, "turn up the power and see if that helps," the professor suggested.

With a shrug, Tom complied and maxed the output on the device. A few minutes later, the shell of the casing began to rattle; softly at first, until it escalated into a violent shudder as it was locked within the outer support frame. The equipment began to whine, and Tom jumped in to try to turn the thing off when the air around us was suddenly congested with a high shrill. At first, it was impossible to tell what it was, or even if it was the sound of the wind rushing through the limbs above. Alex and Mica jumped aside as the rocky cliff face they had leaned the sled and gear against, began to displace; which went entirely unnoticed by the three of us fiddling with the laser as we tried to turn off the machine.

"I say, what the hell is going on over there?" Alex shouted to us over the rising wind.

Grappling with the device, Tom managed to yank the power cord from the battery; snapping off the frozen wires which had grown frail from the excessive cold. This equipment simply wasn't built to be used in such extreme environments.

"Well, fuck me..." Tom blurted as he looked at the stripped wires, "Allen, get me the pliers, I can fix this."

It was then, that all five of us slowly turned our gaze up towards the canopy of the colossal tree; for after the sound of the drill had died, it became clear that the sharp shrill was not from the wind, but coming from the tree itself. The piercing noise rose in tone until it dampened out the sound of the storm and became deafening. The buzz became so strong that it permeated through our earmuffs and hoods as we grasped our heads with our mittens to protect us from the earsplitting pain.

The tree itself was vibrating as the upper limbs shook; creating the high frequency. Logan wondered if it was the sharp wind blasting through the limbs above that was causing this strange anomaly, but my gut told me it was reacting to the cutting laser. The large blocks of stone near Alex and Mica began to move with greater intensity until a pair of square panels folded back into the cliffside. A sudden blast of snow and ice began to shoot into the open cavity, and Tom grabbed the professor to protect him from the falling shards flying around us.

We snatched our gear and scurried into the opening in the cliff to seek protection from the storm and escape the deafening frequency emanating from the colossal tree. Alex searched around in his backpack and eventually popped on a flashlight while handing another to Tom and Mica. Following suit, I put on my headlamp which I kept in my pouch. A long hallway opened up within the deep fissure before us, and we were left speechless as we gazed upon the carvings within. This hidden cavity was man-made.

"What the hell..." Tom queried as he stepped further into the darkness, his mouth gaping open in wonder as he looked around the vaulted corridor.

Logan took an emergency lamp from Alex and held it aloft, inspecting the engraved runes and various symbols decorating the walls. Surrounding us were several pillars carved from the surrounding bedrock. Elaborate etchings of leaves and tree limbs adorned the upper heights of the corridor, which rose before us as the shallow steps below our feet led further down into the darkness.

From outside, we could hear the glacier groaning and cracking as its integrity was compromised by the high winds and the vibration of the giant tree. With a final creak, the massive overhang broke loose and cascaded onto the barren stone base below. With a sudden boom, the avalanche of hardened snow smashed the equipment outside and sent a plume of ice bursting into the open shaft as it collapsed over the doorway. Everything we had failed to salvage moments before, was now crushed under solid blocks of ice.

"Well ...that can't be good," Alex blurted aloud as we brushed ourselves off, while sharing a worried look of concern that washed across our frosted faces as we gazed back at the wall of frozen rubble.

Below the Ice

In a vain attempt to clear the blockage, Tom and I made the effort to dig out some of the debris. It shortly became clear that without the proper tools that there was no way in hell we were going to make any meaningful scratch displacing the mountain of compacted ice which had choked the entrance. Logan seemed to have lost any shared distress we felt about our given situation as he became enthralled with the various glyph's and carvings decorating the entrance walls.

"Ah, there's no way we're going to claw our way out of here," Tom sighed with heavy breath from lugging large blocks of ice, "whatever this place is, we had better hope there's another way out that isn't locked within this glacier."

Alex, Mica and the Professor, were preoccupied with taking photographs of the interior, which had widened dramatically as it led towards a steep descending stairway while the height of the ceiling continued to rise above. The numerous sculptures of trees, with their intertwining branches, thickened the farther these designs progressed down the hall that was littered with debris from the broken carvings which had fallen to the floor from the lattice of stony limbs hanging above.

"This is fascinating..." Mica breathed as she continued to capture photos of the carvings.

"Are you getting all of this, Alex?" Logan motioned to his colleague to an area of the wall of particular interest, "This text here is oddly similar to a mixture of both Nordic runes and Sumerian, in parts ...here, you see?" He pointed.

"Sir, I need you to consider the seriousness of this situation," Tom instructed the professor, who was too busy sightseeing to be worried about their life-threatening dilemma.

"There's nothing we can do at the moment about that, Tom," Logan mentioned calmly as he continued his inspection of the intricate cuneiform, "I believe we have rations enough to last us a week, and if the artifact outside continues radiating energy waves as it has been doing, then I theorize that it should melt off that blockage within the given time period to accompany our safe return," he offered as rationale for his lack of such heightened concern, "besides, what we have found here is of far greater consequence!"

Tom gave a grunt of disgust which went entirely unnoticed by the professor. Personally, I could understand his doubts, since no decorated stonework was worth giving my life for; but it appeared the Professor thought differently. Alex and Mica jumped at the chance when Logan suggested that we continue to explore these ancient ruins to search for another exit. It didn't take much convincing to get Tom to agree, since any radio communication to the ship was being blocked by the storm and the wall of ice covering the entrance.

Beside the point, no one else on the ship was privy to our exact location, which was erroneously logged to be nearly 60 kilometers from our charted position. I was hoping that Logan's paranoia wasn't eventually going to end up getting us killed. We had to find a way out of this frozen monument or face becoming a permanent part of the grim scenery should we find ourselves entombed in this frozen crypt.

Deep racing cracks evident along the walls and the broken chunks of debris scattered about told us this ancient structure had seen its share of seismic activity and succumbed to the pressure of the glacier above. Ice poked through large breaks in the ceiling where sunlight gleamed in from the refraction of ice crystals, which allowed us to conserve the batteries in our lanterns. It wasn't too long before we came upon a platform where there stood an enormous stone door. The steep passage downward in the dark abyss continued on either side of the narrow ledge where we found ourselves. Thankfully, Logan chose to try the door rather than continue the descent.

"Well, this certainly looks promising," he noted with a smile.

I noticed Tom flick his eyebrows in mild annoyance to the professor's childish attitude. Given his prior experience with the team members he had lost during his career, anyone could understand the source of his thinning patience. The door before us was massive and consisted of additional tree designs within its woven limbs which encompassed its frame. At its center was a ring of bright metal, inset with various glyph's held tightly against the stone surface.

"How does it open?" Alex wondered.

"Are you sure you want to?" I shot back, though Mica gave me a look of utter fatigue. I wasn't a coward, I was just overly cautious. Like Tom, I didn't like the idea of opening a locked door when there was no other exit. Point was, we really didn't have a choice unless we wanted to continue further down the darkened stairwell.

Logan took his time inspecting the metal ring, which was the only part of the door which seemed like it didn't belong. Conferring with his assistant Mica, they tried to decipher these symbols inscribed upon it. I was close enough to overhear them say something about a trap, which caused me to speak out.

"What did you say about a trap?" I shot a worried glance their way. Mica turned towards me as she kept her light on the metal hoop set upon the door.

"I was just assuming that it could be a combination lock of some sort, or could spring some type of trap if we got it wrong," she answered with mild annoyance.

"Well, that's a good reason not to screw with it then," I jolted back. I was really looking forward to enjoying that sunny beach in my not too distant future instead of having that snatched from me by some ancient booby-trap. I had seen enough adventure movies to know that things don't go well for trespassers on sacred grounds.

"I admit, it's an enigma," the professor exclaimed, "but we won't learn anything if we don't try."

"Can you make heads or tails of these inscriptions?" Mica asked.

"Alex, do let me know if you have any suggestions that might aid us," Logan inquired to his friend. Taking a step forward,

Alexander adjusted his wire-frame spectacles as he tried to bring their details into focus.

"Hmm..." he offered to the pair, "The writing here is highly decorative, though it does bear a resemblance to ancient cryptic text from areas of the Far East. You see this symbol here? I believe it might represent the token for 'Power or Glory' and this one here beside it is similar to either 'Wealth or Abundance' the tree emblem, of course, means 'Life' and this last design is a very old representation of 'Death', from what I recall," Alex granted.

Logan began to fiddle with the metal ring to test how it operated and discovered that it spun in place. Once he figured it out, he wondered aloud what the combination might mean.

"Ah, so is it Power and Abundance or Life and Death as a cycle, if that's what this ring represents?" he offered in speculation.

"What if it's a combination of four that we need to put in the correct order?" Mica suggested,

"It could be more or less, there is no way of knowing," Logan granted as to the logic of the device.

"Look you three; I don't think you should be playing around with any of this. It's probably sealed for a reason," Tom cut in, though his opinion was dismissed by the Professor.

"What if it's simply one symbol, like a signpost?" I suggested out of the blue. Logan turned towards me with a glare in his eyes but an idea suddenly popped into his head.

"Hmm, yes, yes. That could very well be, Allen," he offered.

"Try the tree symbol first, that makes the most sense," Mica proposed.

"How so?" the professor shrugged.

"The symbolism of the world tree is all around us," she stated as she waved her flashlight around the walls and ceiling, "wealth, glory or death itself, is redundant without life," she offered as a logical explanation, "thus, I would assume it is the first combination key."

Logan looked perplexed but for a moment, then flashed a nod

of agreement her way. Without hesitation, he spun the ring into place. When nothing occurred, Logan's furry eyebrows furled in frustration. There was an odd silence that fell over the group as we stood there waiting for something to happen. With a shrug, the Professor offered another spin on the dial.

"Well, perhaps it is a longer combination," Logan chided as he glanced my way, "...let's see, which one is next?" he began to rub his chin in contemplation. A half-second later, the stone platform beneath us suddenly shifted. Mica screamed as Alex yelped, while I gasped in fright as Tom lost his footing and fell on his rump. Logan was the only one among us left on his feet as the platform dropped a hands width; revealing the sill of the door. It was a unique way to keep the lock secure, one which we would have never discovered otherwise.

"Or, maybe your hunch was correct after all," Logan smirked, "I guess these old gears must be a little rusty, given its age," he offered in mirth. The rest of us were still a little shaken by the movement of the floor shifting beneath our feet and we weren't in the mood for jokes. With surprising grace, the giant door spun on a central axis, pivoting in place.

"Interesting," Alex offered in amazement, "I must say this is very precise engineering," he granted as the giant heavy door swung open to allow us entry into the chamber beyond. What we saw there took our breath away.

A large gallery opened up before us, lined with immense pillars to either side. Between each of them rested large massive bells; each one of the cylindrical chimes was covered with a mottled patina graced by age. This enormous corridor extended along a pathway lined with stone tiles inset into the flooring; their borders caulked with strips of a metal that appeared to be made of lead.

"This is certainly intriguing..." Logan breathed aloud, losing himself mid-sentence.

"I wonder what function these cylinders might have had." Alexander inquired as he walked up to one while examining its exterior. Giving it a slight nudge with his hand to test its weight, he was surprised how easily it moved, "The balance of this device is astonishing..." he started to proclaim, when the giant bell he had shoved began to toll.

A deafening sound reverberated throughout the hallway, sending echoes ringing through each of the tall bells. The entire party was overtaken by the noise as bits of stone and ice began to shower down from the ceiling around them. Slowly, the ringing began to fade, while Tom jumped forward and attempted to muffle the bells by trying to ease their sway. It took several minutes before the resonance faded to a level where we could hear ourselves talk once again.

"What the hell did you do that for?" Tom yelled towards Alex as we picked up the gear we had dropped in our haste to cover our ears. Alexander only offered a shrug of foolish apology.

"It would be my guess that these simple devices were used to warn the inhabitants of earthquakes or aftershocks," Mica offered, "or something as simple as a ritualistic procession."

"But why is the flooring lined with lead?" I asked as I touched the thick grout embedded between the tiles. Mica gave an empty glance towards me as she mentally searched for an answer.

"I don't know, but the real question is; how did all of this get here?" she inquired.

There were a great many theories floating around about the age of the continent of Antarctica, and how long it had been left entombed under kilometers of ice. Some estimates claimed the timeline to be well over a hundred thousand years, if not in the millions; but then there existed anomalies such as seafaring maps from the early 1500's, which closely charted the coastline of the land which had been locked under a vast ice sheet and disguised from view without the aid of modern satellite technology. This put into question just how old the ice covering the coasts of Antarctica might actually be?

That was the reason Professor Logan was here. He had delved into studies of antiquity and lost civilizations since he was a young lad, and made it a subject of personal interest throughout his long career. He had retired years ago with a modest nest egg from his decades of research spent at various universities and institutions, and had placed every last dime of his savings into pursuing his dream. He believed the source of myths and legends from countless ancient and forgotten civilizations across the world had all led here, and now fate had led him upon this wonderful discovery buried deep within the ice.

"Look ahead!" Logan cried aloud as he made his way past the inset pillars at the end of the path.

Upon a great cleft stood a broken archway standing above a path which led down in a vast cavern of ice. Like stonewashed ornaments tossed about the open grotto below were several standing ruins of an ancient city. We stood there in awe looking down upon this hidden metropolis; wondering how something so impossible could exist. Alexander gave out a huff of laughter from the sheer shock of it.

"Wondrous!" breathed the Professor as he cautiously made his way down the slippery steps. Great stalactites of ice hung from various open breaches in a hollowed dome covering the metropolis. The center of which had once been open to the sky but was now covered in a thick sheet of glacier ice, making it look as though a giant crystal sun hung over the city, casting a soft blue light into the chilled air.

"How is it this cavity is still free of ice after all this time left buried beneath the glacier?" Mica inquired towards Logan.

"It may very well be the same abnormality which radiates from the iron tree at the entrance," he exclaimed as they made their first steps into the ruined city, "let us collect some samples for carbon dating. Alex, don't dally; capture some photos of this place!"

It took a moment for Alexander to stop gawking and to pull the camera out of his bag. Mica grabbed some small jars and plastic bags from her side pack and began choosing small bits from the scattered debris to secure for testing, once they got back to the mainland.

"Taking samples is all great and dandy, but they're not going to do us any good if we can't find a way out of this place," Tom stated in a harsh tone.

"Ah, good point Thomas," Logan spouted in response, "why don't you and Allen scout the edges of these ruins and search for a way out of here."

Tom nodded to the logic of that decision and motioned for me to tag along. We dropped our packs in the central square and agreed to meet back there in twenty minutes. Tom took one side of the complex while he directed me towards the other so we could cover more ground. I tried to be excited about exploring an ancient city, but still felt a sense of dread creeping upon me; wondering if we would end up buried and forgotten among these ruins if we couldn't find a way back to the surface.

I soon found myself distracted by the wide array of simplistic to intricate designs that were etched into the architecture. However, there seemed to be a lack of sculptures of any kind which weren't thoroughly demolished beyond recognition. It was almost as if they had been intentionally vandalized. Here or there, you could find the broken base of such an elaborate carving, only to find its remnants shattered to pieces and left scattered about the floor. It made me wonder what chaos might have reigned in the last days of this long lost civilization.

Making my way through an antechamber, I searched several nooks and crannies hidden within the shadows beyond a group of pillars. One room after another seemed to blur together as I kept my quickened pace to explore the outer edges of the entombed city to find a passage out. Each one either came to a dead-end or was blocked by a wall of solid ice. I found little in the way of explanation to who these people might have been, since there were neither bones nor bodies to be found left mummified by the numbing cold.

After searching in vain, I turned around to make my way back and noticed something peculiar. I observed a triangle carved into the ceiling of the doorway high above, through which streamed in a ray of bright blue light from the central dome into the room where I now stood. In curiosity, I backtracked to each of the buildings I had entered before and found the same pyramid shape drilled through the stone structures in roughly the same place; all facing the central opening of the dome above. Unable to assess their function, I continued to scout the edge of the ruins until I once again ran into Tom.

"Did you find anything?" Tom asked with a tired huff as he climbed down from a rooftop onto the edge of a broken pillar to my level upon the landing.

"There is no way out as far as I could find," I conveyed, "however, there were a few passages blocked with ice which could possibly be concealing a viable route."

"Dammit!" Tom barked, "It seems like this section is a dead end. We better find the others," he ordered.

Weaving our way back through the ruins and broken statues, we found Logan and Mica studying a circular structure at the center of the metropolis. Looking up, I took note that it was located directly beneath the opening in the dome high above us.

"If you would Mica, please go find Alexander and bring him back here," Logan asked his assistant. Mica placed down her pack and scurried off in search of Alex, while trying not to make too much noise by calling out to him, for fear of the precarious formation of ice above our position.

"We couldn't locate an exit," Tom mentioned to the professor.

"That's unfortunate, but perhaps we can find another way, or backtrack to take the stairway outside the doorway to another level," Logan mentioned with a mild lack of concern, "however, Mica and I suspect there is a chamber below this structure that seems worthy of investigation."

The entire circumference of the flattened formation appeared as if it might fit into the slot of the dome straight above us, like a plug. Why it was located on the ground was a mystery. If it had fallen from that height, then it certainly would have been shattered into a thousand pieces, but it was nearly unblemished except by age. Beyond the outer edge of its rim, there we found another series of tiles embedded with a silvery metal. Outside of that border were several interlinking blocks that appeared to serve no purpose beyond their odd design.

Logan traced one path cut in the stonework back to a podium which sat below a broken archway. Within its center sat a ring, deeply engraved upon the image of a tree. Logan seemed to be enthralled by this find and brought our attention to the figure.

"Hmm, there must be a device that would operate this. A large ring or cylinder which acts like a key," Logan exclaimed.

"What are you talking about, it's just a decorative carving," Tom answered back, wondering what Logan had meant by his reference to a device.

"I suspect that this dome in front of us is a type of ancient mechanism, which might help us discover a way out of here," Logan proclaimed, "Did you happen to notice anything that might fit into this casting while you were exploring the ruins?"

Tom and I shook our heads that we had not, while we turned to see Mica and Alex as they made their way to our location.

"Professor, there is a trove of jewelry and relics back there!" Alex spouted as Mica dragged him along in his reluctance to leave the treasure behind.

"They were more like curious artifacts rather than jewelry," Mica corrected, "most were damaged remnants."

"Did you bring any of them with you?" Logan asked with intrigue.

"No, no, I wouldn't disturb a find like that without fully photographing and cataloging their placement before moving a single artifact," Alex explained. Alexander Beaumont was a former study of archaeology and he held a high regard for the handling of antiquities.

Bringing his camera over, he showed Logan the digital images he had taken. Agreeing that it was worth further investigation, he led the team up to the temple where Mica had found him. Once inside, we found the floor littered with the debris of what were once intricate statues, now reduced down to their shattered bases. I held up one fragment showing the broken face and eye of a woman with a beaded headdress. Beyond this chamber, we found an adjacent circular room littered with bits of metal and strange artifacts of curious design. None of which we could decipher their possible use or function.

"Perhaps these are parts to some type of machine?" I offered to suggest as I began to pick one of the fragments up. However, Alex slapped my hand away just as I picked up a metal trinket, causing it to fall from my grasp while it clattered to the floor.

"Don't touch anything until we catalog it!" Alex demanded. I just gazed at him in stupid dismay of his reaction.

"Hate to tell you, bud, but all this precious junk will be worthless if we die down here and nobody ever hears about it," I snapped back to attack his sense of logic. I could see regret in his eyes as my perspective sank in and he began to realize that we could actually perish down here among this pile of broken trinkets. If there was something useful here, then we would have to find it quickly.

"Yes, okay. Sorry about that lad," he apologized, "Just let me take a few more photographs and we can see what we have here," Alex added humbly.

Agreeing with that assessment, the team stood back while Alex turned on his camera flash and began taking photos for the records before we disturbed their placement. After he was done, Mica began sifting through the bits and pieces of metal while Thomas made it clear that he couldn't make heads or tails from the scrap around us. Fumbling through the odd devices and ornaments, something glinted out of the mound that caught my eye. Brushing away the frost covering the thick layer of dust, I found a circular burnished ring.

The item was large enough to fit over my entire hand and appeared as if it could fit the etched section on the podium. A part of it had a dull glow to it, which intrigued me. Placing the ring in the shadows, it displayed a noticeable luminescence on a small part of it. After I turned on my flashlight to get a better look at the ring on all sides to inspect its details, I noticed that it had absorbed the light and was glowing on its own after I switched off my lamp.

Showing this to Logan, he determined it a most curious find.

After testing the rest of the room with direct light from the beams of our lanterns; we found no other similar luminescent devices within the pile. Mica collected a few of the smaller trinkets as samples for her collection bag while Logan directed us back to the podium in the courtyard. With high expectations, he placed the thick circlet within the central depression encompassing the image of the sacred tree. When nothing happened, he gave a scowl of disappointment.

"Well, what do we do now?" Tom asked Logan with a sarcastic edge in his voice.

"This metal ring fits within the cavity perfectly, I don't understand it," the professor whined while he scratched his head as he twisted the ring in various positions.

"Ring ...a ring," Mica thought out loud, "perhaps it is some sort of a tonal device activated by the frequencies of the ringing bells!" She suggested.

Even though the large bells were located within the hallway far above them, Mica was adamant that it was the most plausible conclusion she could come up with at the moment. Tom accompanied her as they made their way back up the steep path to the hall of bells while the rest of the team remained below to see if they could operate the device. Personally, I was skeptical that whatever mechanism the professor suspected drove the apparatus might be frozen or damage from age. Regardless, with her embedded knowledge as a geologist, Mica wanted to test her theory.

"Here, take these," Tom offered as he tore out wads of cotton from his undershirt, "stuff these in your ears."

Mica complied and tightened her hood over her head after fitting in the makeshift earplugs. Starting from the rear, they positioned themselves on either side of the corridor. With a nod, they began rocking the first set of bells. In unison, the giant chimes began to ring. With their ears muffled, they moved to the next pair and gently pushed the bells into motion. The reverberation could be felt under their feet as the second set fell in tune; strengthening the percussion.

Even as the noise pierced through the bindings around their ears, they advanced to the third row and set them in motion. A rumble began to shake the floor and they both gave each other worried looks if they should dare to trigger the last row. The frequency created by the enormous chimes began to shake the very foundations and they dodged blocks of stone and ice which came loose and began raining down from the high ceiling of the chamber. The rising noise became too painful to bear, and they reconsidered their choice to start any more bells in motion.

Stumbling through the doorway, they pulled off their hoods to find the cotton swabs they had stuffed into their ears were now dabbed with blood. Looking to the dome above the ruins, the vibration they had triggered had begun to send showers of ice raining from the frozen canopy above. Alex, Logan and I turned our heads skyward when a loud boom echoed through the ruins as an enormous crack split through the plate of thick ice covering the section of the open dome. We gazed at one another in a moment of worry, wondering what a reckless idea it might have been to pull this stunt while we were standing directly beneath untold tons of glacier ice.

A thin shard broke free and came tumbling down like a spear the size of a bus; crashing into the buildings below. A strong shaft of sunlight glinted through as the crack widened around it. I glanced around to see several more shafts of light streaming through the ruins; now focused by prisms of glass which had been inset within the triangular cuttings in each of the buildings facing inward towards the courtyard. When direct sunlight splashed upon us where we stood around the podium, the silver band we had placed there began to shimmer brightly.

The metal ring twisted in place as a green light poured from it to fill the inset tree enclosed within its rim. We stepped back as the chain of silver metal embedded within the floor around us began to glow brightly, and the partial dome set on the ground before us slowly started to rise. We jumped away as another large chunk of ice the size of a small house, fell free; smashing upon the stone shell rising slowly above where we stood. The debris cracked into smaller pieces and crushed several buildings after tumbling off the thick canopy overhead. Thankfully, the ascending dome acted as a shield against the barrage of falling debris raining down around us.

Tom and Mica stood their ground seeing the dangers befalling us in the grotto below, and began to feel an ache of regret for triggering this carnage. Alex huddled under the broken arch which provided little if any protection, while Logan and I moved closer to the rising cap of the dome where it ascended to plug the gap in the ceiling above. As more ice fell free, it served to clear the breach, sending in rays of light streaming throughout the frigid cavern. We could now observe that the dome-cap was supported by several stone pillars, spinning like corkscrews as the cap rose ever higher.

In a dreadful moment, we heard a deafening crunch as the umbrella of stone broke through the lodged ice and sealed the cavern. We gritted our teeth as bits of broken ice and rock showered down around us until the barrage finally slowed to a stop. The glowing silver metal inset within the floor began to fade and we could now see a spiral staircase which had been concealed beneath the lifted dome. Tom and Mica quickly made their way down the path to our position once the falling debris had ceased.

Alexander was the worse for wear, as his spectacles were drenched in frosted tears; the trauma of the destruction having overcome his sensibilities.

"Oh my, well this looks encouraging," the professor breathed with excitement as he peered into the darkened depths of the staircase. He took his first steps upon it even before Mica and Tom had arrived to check on our condition as though he had entirely forgotten about the rest of us.

Logan's sudden advance inspired us to follow, so we quickly grabbed our packs and equipment and started the descent into the open well behind him; coming to a landing only a few stories below. Once there, we found a large circular slab eight meters wide and a full meter thick, leveling off at chest height.

Shining our flashlights from around its circumference, we peered below it to discover to our astonishment, that the enormous stone slab was firmly floating midair a half meter off the floor. We stood there gawking at this impossible artifact; wondering about the true nature of this strange and forgotten civilization we had stumbled upon.

Nine Kingdoms

Logan was just as astounded as the rest of us, concerning what appeared to be a several-ton block of solid stone and how it could resist gravity. Upon further examination, the upper edge of the circular block was covered with lines of script etched within its surface. The text appeared to be the same ancient cuneiform which included several decorative embellishments equally spaced along its rim. Being of shorter stature than the rest of us in our group, Alexander stood on his tiptoes while adjusting his spectacles to get a better look at the text.

"These circular decorations here seem to contain some sort of metal inlay," Alex proclaimed as he felt the smooth surface.

"This text is beyond any conversion of dialect I am familiar with," Logan concurred as he inspected the area Alex had mentioned.

"What do you think it's for?" Mica inquired as she circled the stone slab, "I mean, what function does it serve?"

After encircling its entire circumference, Logan reached Mica's side of the slab and tested its weight by giving it a forceful nudge. The stone gave a slight resistance at first, but required notably less effort the faster he turned it.

"Amazing, I might guess that this device might be achieving levitation by magnets embedded within its structure," Logan presumed, "but I concur that I am at a loss to its function," he granted to his assistant.

As for myself, I could not fathom the reason for this floating monstrosity which spun in place as if it were some child's toy. Perhaps I was puzzled by the simplicity of its operation, which became apparent when the dome cap above us began to quickly descend. The spiral-shaped columns untwisted like screws, lowering the giant cap back into the place where it once sat undisturbed until our arrival. Tom tried to race back up the stairway, but Mica surpassed him, as she jumped outside to the podium and quickly snatched the metal ring from its setting.

In a daring move, she slid back under the stone cap; barely missing being crushed under its immense weight. With a boom, the capstone had sealed us within the dark chamber and a feeling of foreboding fell over us. At least topside in the ruins we had natural light but here we were imprisoned like rats in a dark cellar. Alexander helped Professor Logan to cease the spin of the floating stone wheel, and they tried to reverse its course in hopes of reopening the stairwell above; however, their attempts were in vain.

Mica slipped the large metallic ring over her wrist like a bracelet to keep from losing it among the jumble of bags and equipment she carried. It was only then that Tom had realized that he had left his own equipment pack topside in the ruins when he went to help Mica activate the bells. Cursing to himself, he had left the radio and a significant portion of our rations within his bag; now lost beyond reach between several cubic tons of solid stone. Without much choice, we were left to explore the strange alcove we had entrapped ourselves in.

The floating slab continued to rotate slowly in the opposite direction that Alex and Logan had set it upon in their attempt to open the stairwell. As it spun silently in place, we searched the outer edges of the chamber for a way out. The cavity itself was also circular in shape but we found nothing of interest except smooth walls. Unfortunately, it appeared to be a dead end.

"We are righteously screwed," Tom breathed with a mix of anger and exasperation.

"This doesn't make any sense," Mica chimed in with mild agreement, "this stone mechanism, or whatever it is, would be controlled by operators down here, yet they would be entombed in this chamber just as we are.

"Yet, doesn't it seem odd, that for its supposed age, that this area appears to be completely free of dust or ice particles," Alexander added. We all looked around and began to notice for ourselves that he was correct.

"He's right, and the air down here isn't cold either," I

mentioned as I pointed out that we could no longer see the vapor of our own breath as I pulled back my hood.

It was of interest that there was no layer of moisture or frost within this lower room below the surface of the city, yet there still appeared to be no clear exit from this cell. The metallic ring we had used at the podium had raised the capstone but there was no such device to set it within to activate the pillars it controlled. Thinking there might have been something they missed on the floating slab, Logan asked me to crawl up upon its surface to make a closer inspection towards the center of its diameter for any clues as to its function.

Honestly, I was a bit leery about crawling upon it; but they slowly brought its spin to a halt so that I wouldn't get nauseous from its rotation. I expected the giant slab to sink under my weight, but it didn't budge a centimeter. Scouring the topside for a hint of any sign, all I found were several hair-thin splices in the stone; as if it had been pieced together by separate sections like segments of a puzzle. However, I did discover a slot that looked suspiciously close to the size of the large metal ring Mica had sequestered.

Asking to borrow it from her, Mica removed it from her wrist and attempted to slide it across the expanse of the floating slab towards me. However, it spun back on its own and secured its place upon one of the decorative embellishments. Noting this, Logan made his way over to where the ring now stuck fast upon the stone emblem.

"Astonishing, this metallic device we found appears to have multiple functions," Logan began to theorize just before the giant slab started to spin once again on its own accord.

I was just as startled myself, and scooted my butt off to the edge and hopped off onto the floor as the stone wheel began to oscillate ever faster; then without warning, it came to a sudden halt. Across the room from where the edge of the slab with the ring had pointed, a secret door slowly opened with the grinding of stone. Thomas cautiously peered into the opening with his flashlight and issued his own advice.

"Well, this leads somewhere; and its better than being trapped in this tomb, so I suggest we'd better take it," he added.

Tom's optimism was contagious and it didn't take the rest of the team long to barter for a better solution to our dilemma. Alex and Logan jumped through first, while Mica backtracked for a moment to snatch the ring from atop the slab. I followed her through the newly opened corridor while Tom took up the rear. Unseen by us moments after we left the chamber, the giant floating slab began to rotate once again on its own and the hidden doorway sealed the exit behind us.

The farther we progressed down the narrow corridor we began to notice the sound of moving water. The wet droplets soon turned into cascading brooks of fast-moving water which echoed up through the narrow hall. Intermittent cracks could be seen in the stone which had opened up over the passage of time. We knew we were on a one-way trip and the anxiety of it was etched upon our worried faces. Logan alone, held a look of childish glee and wonderment in his eyes, regardless of the danger we were in.

Coming to a sudden halt, the slender corridor was replaced by an open cavern which had been split asunder from some ancient upheaval eons ago. We stood there gazing into the depths from the end of the passageway, which left us stranded several stories above the cavern floor lying below.

"Huh ...did ah, anyone happen to bring any rope?" Alexander inquired as he peered through his glasses over the edge.

We had, in fact, brought that particular item, but Tom had lost his pack topside in the ruins before the capstone closed upon us. The only equipment on hand was the length of heavy-duty paracord meant to tether our packs together on the glacier for safety. It was a good thing I was carrying it, or we would have been screwed. Tom shuffled himself to the forward edge and double knotted the cord for strength; which, unfortunately, also halved its usable length.

Tom and Alex acted as anchor after I had volunteered to be the first one down to search for a safe route along the edge of the cliff wall. I was a terrible mountaineer, though I fibbed about it on my application for this job; not realizing that I would actually be doing any climbing of this sort. Grabbing onto the icy rock face was close to impossible wearing mittens, so I made the mistake of removing my gloves. The numbness quickly bit into my hands, affecting my dexterity and making my position on the cliffside even more precarious than it needed to be.

Once I reached a small plateau, I untied the end and released the slack to help Alex and Mica descend, along with the Professor. Thomas tossed the woven paracord to us after Logan set down so he could attempt to free climb to our position on the slender rim. The ledge we rested upon had become too crowded for Tom to proceed safely, so we repeated the same procedure by getting Alexander, Mica, and Logan down to ground level. After the rest of the party was safely on the cavern floor, I tossed the thin rope back up to Tom as a safety line so I could anchor him as he climbed down.

Not knowing what the hell I was doing; I failed to secure the straps properly with the cord tied around my waist. Tom couldn't see this from his position above, but my mistake became clear the moment he lost his grip on the icy rock face just below the lip of the passage. He fell silently, grabbing wildly at the slick rock; in the split second that followed, I leaned back onto the outcropping in anticipation of catching his weight. He slipped by me in the air as I reached out my hand to grab him; barely missing one another. The full weight of him yanked the thin rope out of my numbed hands, cutting open my cold exposed flesh as the tether snapped taught.

I watched in horror as I spun my head down and saw the loose bindings of the knots slip loose as Tom's dead weight tore at the spare rope I had around my waist; nearly pulling me over the edge with him. Tom bounced hard against the rock wall, hitting his head. Bleeding from the concussion, he floundered helplessly as he tried to gain a better hold on the rope, but lacking the strength to do so.

"Tom, Tom! Grab onto something!" I yelled in pain as the last remnants of the line began to slip through my bleeding hands.

The team below watched in dread as the mishap unfolded. Their gasps of panic went unnoticed as I could only hear my own heartbeat pounding like a drum. The line felt as if Tom had managed to find a foothold, but he slipped once again; tugging the rope from my grasp. The end of the line held beneath my foot was ripped from beneath me, flipping me hard onto my back; knocking the breath from my lungs.

Thomas went tumbling down and landed with a thud. Logan and Alexander climbed over several frozen boulders to find his limp broken body lying on a jagged stone slate; the bloodied paracord coiled about his twisted frame. I could tell by the reaction of their voices over the sound of my heaving breath, that Tom was gone. I laid there on the ledge, cursing to myself as I stared at the cavern ceiling far above. I had killed him through my own incompetence.

Time itself seemed to slow, as if it too had begun to freeze in this frigid underworld. I struggled not to look but eventually had to crawl to the side to view the carnage I had wrought. My red and teary eyes found Alex and the professor kneeling over what was left of Tom's contorted body. They saw what had happened, and that Tom's fall wasn't truly my fault but there would be no way that I could accept that.

Alexander collected the coil and tossed the cord back up to the outcropping where I was left stranded. I made my way off the ledge by using the bound rope to loop around several small crags on my way down. Slipping to the bottom, I had lost the last of the paracord on a crack high above. Mica came to me to see if I was okay, but I just brushed her off in my shock as I slowly stepped beside the other men while we peered down upon the still corpse crumbled at our feet.

"There was nothing you could have done, lad," Logan consoled, "don't take it too hard ...these things happen."

Any other time his words would have been comforting, but I just couldn't let go of the aching guilt floating in the back of my mind. I felt sick to the pit of my stomach.

"We have to search him," I whispered, "...for any supplies that might help us."

Alex nodded in agreement, realizing the logic of my statement. We found a chart map for the ship, an automatic pistol, and a single food pack. His canteen was ruptured by the fall, but that was to be expected. In his boot I found a knife with some foreign insignia on its hilt I didn't recognize. Unfortunately, most of his gear had been lost on the upper level.

Logan was heartbroken with grief since he had known Tom the longest, but the professor hid it well. His many years on the field had told him there were no guarantees in life. Right now we had to save ourselves. There was no way of carrying his remains, so we left Tom's body where it lay, after we shared a silent moment of prayer.

Making our way down a steep embankment towards a source of light, we turned the edge of the cavern wall, which had hidden a vast grotto filled with flowing waterfalls blended with formations of ice among a braid of broken bedrock. The ceiling itself consisted of a thick ice sheet that spread a glow of soft lighting upon the tranquil scene. Cascading brooks weaved through the cavern where we spotted exposed remnants of ancient architecture.

Mica was keen on extracting fresh samples which had been left buried deep beneath the ice for untold millennia, while Alex captured photographs whenever he could. The Professor referenced data from his notebook which he kept in his breast pocket while scribbling additional notes. We made our way through the landscape of the cavern, which also appeared to be far warmer than we would have expected.

"How is it possible that the temperature in here is being maintained above freezing?" Alexander inquired.

"Well, it could be geothermal venting, which might be heating the water from below and sustaining this delicate environment," Mica offered as a theory.

"If that's so, then what is keeping that mountain of ice hanging above us in place?" I added with skepticism, "I would rather we not risk a collapse of that degree."

"From our departure of that first set of ruins, I speculate that there might be several ancient kingdoms spread across this frozen continent." Logan spouted as he penciled comments into his pocketbook.

"Kingdoms?" I blurted in dismay.

"Yes, and I presume there may be seven more domains to find that may hold far more grandeur than the small desolate city we stumbled upon back there," Logan granted as he referred to the domed plaza we had discovered hours before.

"What brought you to that conclusion, Logan?" Alexander queried his long-time friend. More often than not, Logan kept his projects to himself and preferred to keep the details secretive to avoid ridicule from his peers. Alexander had learned from the past, that an invitation to join any one of the professor's numerous outings, was almost always full of surprises. Personally, finding myself locked under a polar ice sheet, with no chance of rescue or way of escape, was not what I would consider a *pleasant* surprise. I just wanted to get home and forget all this ever happened. After the incident with losing my team member, I didn't even care about the paycheck anymore.

"We set down on the eastern shores of the Weddell Sea, and I suspect that there are several civilization centers located along the Trans-antarctic mountain range, which rise in elevation high above west Antarctica, acting as a natural barrier separating the two territories," Logan advised his comrade, "I took the liberty of combining the various volumes I had shown you back at the ship and recorded their findings into one chart, which frankly, were fairly useless in their individual state if they had been left compartmentalized as separate editions."

"Are you saying that you're expecting to find more lost civilizations left hidden under the ice across this continent, Professor?" Mica added into the fray.

"I can only hope, Mica," Logan answered, "but there are

limitations with exploring what was once a fertile plain in the times of antiquity, but are now veiled by several kilometers of ice resting upon it like a death mask."

"May I?" I inquired to the Professor as he scrutinized the scribbled notes in his pocketbook. With mild apprehension, he agreed to let me view it.

As their security backup, it was my duty to take Tom's place and help guide the team to safety. However, what I saw in Logan's notebook was nothing less than confusing. There were charts and way-lines folded upon sketched diagrams, and references to races I had never heard of. I wasn't the most learned fellow, but the chaos I saw scrawled within his notebook was nothing less than an incomprehensible mess. Then again, the translation of it might have gone entirely over my head. That was when Mica snatched the booklet from my grasp as I was trying to make sense of it all.

"These are geography lines of the Antarctic plates prior to the last ice age," Mica gasped as she studied the penciled notations, "how did you come into possession of these without special satellite imagery?"

"Old maps and tomes from the shelf's of ancient libraries and the salt-crusted desks of seafarers from ages past," Logan admitted, "I fully believe that the last ice age didn't last for millions of years, but instead, the world has experienced several such mini-storms that span a dozen millennium, accompanied by a shifting axis deep within the Earths core," he mentioned, "completely refacing the geography of the continents, including the upset and displacement of plant and animal species alike."

Mica seemed to be stumped on his proposal, considering her own background on global tectonics. It was feasible that the entire Antarctica plate was receiving converging pressure from all sides, keeping it intact. It was the only summary that could explain the jagged mountain range which had bloomed between the two territories, creating the immense rift cutting through the entire frozen continent.

"Oh, my..." Logan's attention swayed from the conversation as he took notice of something which was nothing less than a miracle. Sitting next to several glazed rocks, nestled by the running waters, sat a small flowering plant sprouting from the coarse soil. He brought its presence to Mica's attention and she bagged a few of the seeds lying around it, and got Alex to take some photographs so she could log the design of its leaves.

"How could that possibly grow down here?" I petitioned to Mica, who had gathered the few samples she could find.

"The ambient temperature in this grotto is high enough for a hearty species to survive. The seeds were frozen and somehow endured in a state of dormancy all these ages. This is likely a specimen not seen in millions of years," Mica responded.

"Or, perhaps even less than a hundred millennium," Logan attempted to correct her, according to his theories.

While those two were arguing about his hypothesis, I wandered off to follow the channel of the running melt-off to see where it led. Following rivers was a part of any survivalist handbook. Behind a collapsed part of the cavern wall, I found a fair-sized opening into the rock where the small river emptied into the darkness beyond. There, I discovered a multitude of tiny plants and moss growing around its mouth and thought it was worth investigating, so I returned to tell the others where I was going before running off into some uncharted chasm.

We had to pull Mica away from her obsession with collecting additional rock and plant samples, and we followed the outgoing stream back to the break where it exited the cavern.

"Ah, this likely leads to an underground river; I wouldn't chance it," Alexander warned. Alex also admitted that he was not very fond of confined spaces.

"I've looked around, and there are no other exits from this cavern," I tried to persuade the three of them; "This channel has to lead somewhere, assuming it might reach the sea."

"What are your thoughts, Mica?" Logan begged to ask after taking a moment to rub his chin in thought.

"Based on the strata in this area, it would be safe to assume the bedrock will be stable enough to explore the course of this river, Mica added.

"Fine then," Logan looked around, noting we had no other logical choice in the matter. We had no climbing equipment for us to reach the high inlets of the waterfalls pouring into the chamber from the ledges above; so there was only one way to go from this point.

We made our way into the passage, where several streams converged on the watercourse the farther we went. We had been following the snaking canal for several hours until we stumbled upon something quite unexpected. Half buried in chunks of ice, we found what appeared to be the remnants of a dock, along with old wooden scraps of boats. Logan was drawn to a monolith standing nearby which was covered with the same quasi-Sumerian etchings we had found before.

"Most interesting; from what I can tell by this script, this was once a marina used along a vast trade route," the professor exclaimed, "there are several mentions here to additional ferry harbors along this course," he finished.

"This tributary must have been much larger many eons ago," Mica mentioned as she peered downstream trying to imagine what it must have been like, "Does it say were this waterway might lead?"

"There's a reference to something which appears to be called '*Jotu*' and '*Svar*' or something of that sort, but due to the syntax, I may be pronouncing it wrong," Logan answered.

"Those names ring a bell, but I can't place it..." Alexander trailed off while fiddling with his round spectacles.

We all climbed up the frozen dock to get a better look downriver and noted areas of rapids ahead. These were caused by the added volume to the waterway from the converging streams. Unfortunately, the trail we had been using came to an abrupt end; leaving us no other means to continue.

"Well, we can't continue by foot; anyone up for a swim?" Alex joked, although none of us were laughing at his remark.

Alexander's self-bemused smirk quickly faded when we heard a disturbing crack beneath our feet. We lost our balance as the dock shifted below us and we were sent grasping for one another as the ancient pier began to fail under our combined weight. The securing edge fractured behind us, and the dock dropped below; falling into the stream of ice-melt. We frantically grabbed for Alex when he nearly slid off the raft, which our severed pier had become.

The dock floated down the river with us clinging upon it, spinning as the edges bumped into the ice and rock of the banks; whittling our craft ever smaller as it careened down the icy shaft. Once we had passed through the coarse rapids, our precarious craft finally began to settle to a gentle rocking.

"Did we lose anybody?" I asked as I got on my knees, looking around. At one point I had thought that Alex had slid off and into the drink, but we found him clenching for dear life on one of the exposed supports left upon the broken pier.

"Help him over here, lad," Logan directed, "we need to keep a center of gravity on this flotation."

It was no small feat of balance to reach Alex where he was left stranded, although he seemed equally desperate to reach out for me, as was his effort to keep his death-grip upon the slippery post to which he had attached himself. All things aside, thankfully the water wasn't icy cold but had become warmed to a mild degree, either by geothermal activity or the theoretical geomagnetic properties within this area Logan had spoken of. Either way, we were lucky we hadn't all slipped off the raft and drowned in the rapids. Our heavy coats and insulated bibs would have swiftly dragged us to the bottom of the riverbed.

"Well, that takes care of our transportation problem," Mica offered offhand.

"I wouldn't count our blessings just yet," the professor cried, "keep in mind those inlets from the cavern were the product of waterfalls..." he trailed off with a worried look in his eyes.

His reminder of that fact didn't sit well with us; for we were struggling in a helpless situation which dramatically sapped our morale as it was. With great care, we centered ourselves on the raft; sitting back to back for support. The speed of the river slowed as the channel widened and our anxiety began to wane with the ease of the swaying waters. Each of us sat there in silence for several long minutes, concerned about our fate.

Like a sign from heaven, we peered up in wonder as glowing spores began illuminating the ceiling above us. Tentacles of blue and aqua-greens lighted our course; created by the mosaic of plants growing from the ice. Mica peered over the edge of the raft as something caught her eye. Below the crystal clear waters, we noticed the large leaves of several bright pink plants waving in the current from the bottom of the riverbed, fluttering like seaweed below the tide.

Mica wanted to get a sample, but I had to convince her to sit down before she capsized us. The course of the river widened where the flow of the stream subsided to a crawl. Glowing colors of turquoise and marine spotted the entire structure above, while the pool before us reflected a colorful river of rose and magenta forests swaying beneath the cool waters; appearing like something out of a fairy tale.

"It's so beautiful," Mica whispered as her colleagues agreed with her observation.

I was equally captivated, though finding myself both emotionally drained and physically tired at this point, and still lamenting about Tom's unfortunate death whenever my thoughts began to wander. Guilt can be a dungeon of the mind and I didn't have a key to escape the chains I had wrought upon myself from his passing.

"Look, up ahead!" Logan nearly shouted as he pointed towards an outcropping of stone; one of which was similar to the signage we had found at the previous dock.

We placed ourselves two to either side of the craft and frantically paddled our way towards the harbor with our thick mittens. As we approached the dock, we saw several more outcroppings of broken stone; all tilted askew, which led down several pathways into the mountain. Each of us hopped onto the shore, and we almost lost Alexander again as we reached out to catch him while he jumped from the raft, which began to drift away from the bank where we had come ashore.

"What is that?" Alex inquired as he perked his ears. There was a strange low roar in the air which we couldn't quite pinpoint, until we looked back towards the river where the raft had been caught in its flow. There, on the floating craft sat Alexander's camera, left abandoned like some unwanted stepchild. Alex gave a groan of grief, as did Mica, for the lost images it held as record of this expedition.

As if to accentuate the loss, a moment later, the craft suddenly tilted upward half out of the water and disappeared from view. We had not seen the crest of the steep waterfall in the distance due to the strange ambient light. We counted ourselves lucky for having chosen to put an end to the joyride when we did.

"Oh my, that's quite unfortunate..." Logan sighed as he noted the loss of the photographic equipment, "let that be a lesson, Mica, to keep your camera safe; we can't afford to come out of this empty-handed," he advised.

Mica nodded in agreement and we turned towards the crumbling corridors spanning before us. They all appeared to be leading in the same direction, so we chose one at random.

"Is there anything you can decipher upon that central column by the river?" I suggested to Logan before we left the area.

"Hmm, I believe it says this is the way to the Jotu," he frowned while reading the text, "but there also seems to be an ominous warning scribbled here in haste; cautioning about something I can't seem to make out ...bah, I have no idea what this means," the professor admitted, being unable to translate the last of it.

With exasperation, Logan turned and left us to take the lead down the central hall; which we chose since it seemed less cluttered with debris than the adjacent passages. Unfortunately, none of us saw the sinister icon hidden beneath the thin sheet of ice which fell away as we left, revealing a demonic creature etched below the ancient warning. One that may have very well led us to favor another avenue than the one we had chosen.

The Sunken City

The aroma within the tight corridor was unusually musty. We had become accustomed to the crisp clean air of the glacier ice but that atmosphere quickly faded once we had entered the damaged passages leading away from the river. Mica suggested it was the lack of airflow through this area combined with an abundance of mold leaking from the melting ice. Alex found no comfort in that fact since it was common knowledge in the scientific field that ancient spores were known to hold bacteria and viruses, for which our modern world had no immunities or defenses.

Mica realized that she would have to handle her specimen samples with greater care after Alexander designated them as a potential biohazard. Whatever dangers we might now face from contamination on this journey were unavoidable, so we tried not to think of our situation getting worse in case any one of us fell ill from the effects of some ancient disease. After their short discussion on the fact, I made it a point to cover my nose and mouth with my scarf to filter out the bad air. It didn't take long thereafter that the other team members chose to follow my example in kind.

We made our way through the tunnel, climbing over broken and shattered support columns decorated with deeply embedded swirls and articulate designs. The corridor finally widened into a vast chamber with high walls where we discovered remnants of a city complex half-submerged by water. We were left baffled as to how this chamber had also been left untouched by the thick ice when Logan came up with an explanation.

"This is seawater," the professor exclaimed as he took a taste after dipping his finger into the pool, "I imagine this entire chamber was once filled with salt water, which kept the ice sheet above from penetrating into this cove."

"It appears to be draining somewhere at the moment," Mica

noted the obvious; "we better hope that the roof above retains its integrity while we're here."

"It might be best not to ring any large bells in the area," Alex suggested to Mica, regarding their hairy experience in the last set of ruins they had visited.

Looking behind us, we realized that the adjacent passages beside our corridor at the dock had disappeared. Apparently, each one of the tunnels led to some other destination within the subterranean complex. It was worth noting that at one point in history these ancient cities were once open to the sky, but were now locked under thick sheets of ice. Logan said that it was believed that this area of the globe had retained a tropical climate and that the previous location of Antarctica, had once been positioned near the edge of the equator. This theory, of course, was based on the assertion that the magnetic poles were fixed in a different location than they were in our present era.

The water below us was clear but colored with a dark bluish hue as it sank into the depths below. The dripping water was relatively cool but not entirely unpleasant as one might suspect. There was certainly something strange going on in this hidden civilization which I could not explain; even though the professor tried his best to educate us on his personal philosophy on the matter.

"There is a curious similarity in the design of these buildings," the professor noted, "perhaps my theory about the effects of the saltwater was wrong. It appears each of the structures are rimmed with a sort of metallic substance which may be emanating a type of field that keeps the ice at bay."

We could see what he meant as we observed the preserved city jutting out of the blue lake before us. The edges of the roofs were gilded with the same dark metal alloy we saw being used before. Logan suggested that it was being utilized somehow as an amplifier to direct the magnetic fields. If so, it was an ingenious way to harness natural forces. Logan's theory also proposed that the intensified field was what kept these sections so well preserved despite their age.

I could grasp the concept Logan was trying to weave into his explanation, which he could have helped to prove had we not lost our scanning equipment. Simply put, this strange alloy was applied to critical areas around the dwellings to redirect and concentrate geomagnetic waves. Keeping the encroaching ice at bay was just a beneficial side effect for whatever it had been originally designed for. Since the continent of Antarctica was once a region of temperate climate in the distant past, the true function of this arcane device was still a mystery.

A precarious sky-bridge connected the tops of these buildings that jutted out from the water; though the lower levels were entirely submerged. Making our way across the crumbling stone catwalks was a risk in itself, for any fall could leave us to drown in the turquoise waters below. Looking over the edge, I thought I saw something momentarily disturb the surface of the waters, only to swiftly disappear from view. Strange shadows of large bodies flitted beneath the surface, though their outlines were left blurred and undefined.

I brought this to Logan's attention but he seemed unconcerned about it. Neither Mica nor Alex saw what I had seen and soon lost interest in my sighting. Feeling like a fool, I brought up the back of the group while frequently peering into the water below. The scaffolding was an intricate highway connected like a maze above the sunken city; one which eventually brought us to an abrupt halt.

"Well, now what?" Mica shrugged as the passage we had chosen ended at a broken section of the walkway. The other side continued onward towards a large temple-like structure, but it would take a dangerous jump to make it across. It was more than three meters wide, which was easy enough for me, but I doubted Alex or the Professor would be so nimble as to span the length of the void. Without any safety rope, our choices were limited. We could head back and choose another route from the river, or we would have to risk the vault across.

It took a great deal of arguing to convince Alexander that the distance was not as far as it seemed, but being weighed down by equipment and our winter coats would make it a challenge, to say the least. Since it was my idea to risk it, they voted that I should go first. I took several strides back as they cleared the way, and after building up my courage, I took a running leap.

I landed with a tumble on the other side and nearly skidded off the edge and into the water. The stone walkway groaned under my body as if it objected to the harsh treatment of my landing. Mica dared to take the jump after me, and barely covered the length as she had misjudged her steps. Alex was showing signs of fear and even took off his spectacles to secure in his shirt pocket. He made several false starts before psyching himself into taking the leap.

Mica and I were there to catch him, but he stumbled at the tip of the bridge and barely caught the lip of the edge on our side. He struggled there, kicking his legs in the empty air with a desperate look of fear growing in his eyes.

"Whoa there, stop struggling; let me take your arm, I've got you!" I advised Alex as he continued to claw for a grip. I laid myself down upon the cracking walkway and edged myself towards him as Logan stood watching helplessly from the other side of the rift. Alex said something unintelligible as he gasped for breath in a moment of panic. I grabbed his glove to get a secure hold of him, and his scared eyes shifted towards mine in the split second before he slipped free and off the edge. I laid there with his empty glove still grasped tightly in my hands.

There was a splash below, and we had thought we had lost him. Sputtering and gagging, Alex resurfaced a moment later and began yelling for help. We looked over the edge to see him kicking in the water to keep afloat. He had slipped out of his waterlogged jacket and thermal overalls in an attempt to keep from sinking from their weight.

There were several shorter buildings near him, but most were too high out of the water for Alex to climb. Logan spotted a building farther away from them, of a rooftop just cresting the waterline that he could reach and wait for us to rescue him. Unfortunately, Alex had taken a good chunk of the edge of the walkway with him when he fell from our side of the rift, leaving the professor uncertain that he could clear the extended distance.

"Keep going onward and find a way to reach Alexander, I will find you ...somehow," Logan called across to us.

I tried to direct Alex where to go, but it became clear he wasn't a world-class swimmer by any means as he began dog-paddling his way over in the general area I was pointing. As I peered down, I could again see several strange translucent shadows darting through the waters below; apparently drawn to the disturbance Alex had created as he fought to keep his head above the surface.

Logan backtracked in his attempt to find another way through the maze of catwalks which connected the buildings, while Mica and I tried to find a path to get down to the water level to aid Alexander. Mica noted a sealed shaft atop of one of the buildings and we smashed it open with our boots. The thin stone cap cracked and fell inward, where we found several rows of handles carved into the structure. I wasn't too confident about the slanted angle of the stone ladder built within the shaft, which had rungs that were placed abnormally far apart; making each step hard to reach.

There was a thick layer of slimy algae that coated the surface of the building within, making our grip even more precarious. Even after climbing down several floors and almost slipping to our deaths along the way, I was surprised to see that Mica couldn't help herself from collecting specimen samples from the slick residue growing upon the walls, once we reached the landing. Turning on our lights, we could make out decorative carvings upon the walls which were now blurred and obscured by the thick layer of slime which had been growing in the darkened structure. We found a staircase circling around the inner edge, but even the steps themselves seemed oddly out of proportion.

We eventually made it down to the waterline and found a series of pillars that opened into the blue lake outside the building. Catching my balance on the edge of the window, I called out to Alex as I looked around for signs of him. We finally found him poised upon a rooftop which was barely under the waterline; leaving him standing in chilly water up to his ankles. Instead of answering us, he appeared mesmerized by something within the water, lurking just off the edge of his sunken oasis.

"Alex, swim over to us, we'll help you up!" I shouted to him, but we only got a short worried glance from him in reply, "What are you doing? We're right here!" I waved my arms to grab his attention.

"There, there is something in the water..." Alex muttered back through his chattering teeth. He had lost his thermal gear somewhere in the lake, so it was important to dry him off as soon as possible. Even mild hypothermia could be fatal if it wasn't remedied.

"What the hell are you talking about?" Mica called out to him over my shoulder. From our position near the level of the pool, the reflections in the water masked whatever was lurking beneath its surface.

"I, I don't know, but it's big!" Alexander mumbled back as he clung to himself, rubbing his shoulders for warmth.

"What is he talking about?" Mica repeated towards me, but his testimony had confirmed what I had suspected. I *had* actually seen something moving through the basin.

Half a dozen meters from him, something disturbed the surface of the still lake. It had no real form I could characterize except that it appeared like a semi-transparent balloon. Slowly, it submerged back under the surface to disappear once again.

"What the hell was that?" Mica whispered.

Something that looked like a translucent tentacle made of seaweed swashed across the surface of the water an arms-length from Alexander's legs. He stepped back as far as he could with his back against a sheer wall of the attached building; its summit looming far above his reach.

"Do you have anything you can throw?" I called out to him.

Alex shot a desperate glance towards the two of us as we stood safely between the pillars a meter above the water level. Alex clarified that everything he had was within the pockets of his thermal coat, which, unfortunately, he had to discard when he fell into the lake to keep from sinking.

"Mica, what do you have?" I asked her in response to Alexander's dilemma, "have you got anything small that you don't need."

I had a pistol and Tom's knife, but there was no way I was going to sacrifice the only weapons we had. We only had our water bottles and a few food rations, but Mica turned defensive when I suggested we toss one of the specimen sample tubes to try to distract the creature away from our trapped team member.

"No way, these are irreplaceable!" Mica snapped back as she held her specimen bag protectively.

"You might want to argue that with Alex over there, just how irreplaceable *he* might be; just to see who wins that debate," I snapped back as I motioned towards our friend who was shivering in ankle-deep water. Another tentacle appeared above the surface and slowly washed its way towards him ,while Alex jumped in fright to escape its reach.

"Okay, well, how about the camera then?" I suggested hastily, only having her respond with a look of horror in her eyes.

"We can't..." was all she stammered, but she glanced back towards Alex who was in fear for his life, and Mica realized the ethical dilemma she had walked into, "okay, okay! Here, just try to save this one, and this one, and maybe this one..." she spouted, trying to cherry-pick her favored specimen jars as I opened the bag and started lobbing them as far as I could to the opposite side of the lake, away from Alex.

"Alex, stand still and don't move. We're going to try and distract it," I called to him. He turned and nodded to me that he understood, while the vials I tossed began splashing in the distance, skipping across the water.

The creature slowly submerged once again and the movement of the surface water seemed to show that it was pursuing the source of this new disturbance.

"Quickly, get over here!" Mica shouted over to Alexander while trying to snatch her precious vials out of my grasp while she held them to her chest as though she were sheltering a child.

"And try not to break the water tension by splashing around!" I advised as an afterthought while Alex noted the aquatic beast had left his proximity. He edged his way into the water with care from the submerged ledge of the building and began stroking his way towards us in a self-restrained frenzy. Without warning, his head bobbed underneath the surface and he disappeared entirely from view.

"Holy hell!" I blurted, "Did it grab him?"

Realizing that I may have made a fatal mistake by getting Alex to trust me on my tactics, I had forgotten that I had seen several of the ghostly shadows darting about underneath the calm waters. Alexander was gone, and we poised there for several anxious moments as grief began to knot in our throats. What seemed like minutes later, bubbles escaped to the surface and we feared he had been dragged under by another one of the creatures hidden within the watery depths.

Mica gasped in horror with a reflex of remorse as she realized that Alex had drowned. Half a moment later, a loud yelp escaped her lips as she jumped in surprise when something broke the surface of the water directly beneath us. It was Alex; his eyes were wide with fear as he choked for air.

"Help me up!" he sputtered to keep the water out of his mouth.

I lowered down my canteen strap for him to grasp and we pulled him up onto the sill that supported the pillars just as the creature began to make its way back towards our location.

"Are you alright ...what happened to you?" Mica inquired.

"Why yes, just a wee soaked and with a bit of a chill, but I'm uninjured," he spouted back.

"We thought one of those things had grabbed you and dragged you under," I stated with a tone of surprise.

"I don't know what you mean," Alex replied in utter dismay to my question, "you were quite direct when you instructed me not to splash around; thus, I elected to dip below and covered the distance between us by swimming underwater so as not to disturb the surface."

We climbed our way back to the upper platform and tried to locate Logan by radio but there was far too much static on the line. He was nowhere in sight at the moment and we didn't want to make too much noise shouting for him; as such a disturbance could likely bring several metric tons of ice down upon our heads as we had experienced before.

Alex was notably cold as his teeth began to chatter, having lost his thermal outer gear but we had nothing to spare save a thin emergency blanket from the first aid kit. From his own observation of the aquatic creatures that attacked him, Alex could only conclude that they were a large mutated species of jellyfish, which readily explained their strange appearance. He considered himself lucky for having not come into contact with their tentacles, which likely would have severely injured or paralyzed him with their reputed neurotoxins. There was a large building near the back of the ruins that stood above the others which we considered a good place to spot the professor if he was lost among the catwalks.

We navigated our way to the central temple, only to find our way cut short by a wide moat between us and the structure. Somewhere down below the waterline was a pathway through the outer wall which surrounded the building before us. Skirting the edges proved to be a useless endeavor, which only led to a dead end on either side. The multitude of catwalks that connected the massive sunken city proceeded around the central shrine, and Logan could have gotten lost along any one of them.

"We have to get higher if we are going to have any chance of spotting him," Mica acknowledged as we stared into the depths below us.

There were clear ways of entry into the central building, but they weren't accessible by any other means except by making a swim for it. None of us were fond of that idea.

"We have to climb down closer to the waterline and swim

across," I suggested, "diving in at any distance will likely bring those monstrous jellyfish to our location."

"We can wrap up our coats and try to ferry them across to keep them dry," Mica added as a precaution, noting that Alex had nearly drowned when his thermal coat became soaked; which was why he had to ditch it into the lake in the first place.

Mica and I removed our outer jackets and carefully wrapped them around our gear to protect them from getting soaked, and shimmied our way down a broken section along the wall. Unable to spot any of the creatures lurking in the clear waters, Alex made his way into the pool first and we lowered our bundles down to him. We eased ourselves into the cool lake, trying to tread our way across the open space between the outer wall and the massive stone temple at its center; cautiously pausing whenever we saw movement in the waters around us.

Peering beneath, there was still a good 30 meters of water depth to the ground floor of the temple. We paddled our way in through one of the open windows set within the architecture. Alexander was the first one to find a ledge where we could reach dry ground and he helped us to safety. The three of us sat there for a while; cold and tired from the crossing.

Having lost the emergency blanket during the swim over, Alex accepted the offer to take my coat for the moment; since after putting on my thermal overalls we had noticed that the temperature was fairly warmer within this great structure, unlike the chilled climate of the caverns where we had ventured before. Finding a series of stairwells, we began our ascent to the upper levels. During the climb, it slowly dawned upon us that the pillars which supported this massive structure had been carved to represent giant man-like beings; each of them draped in various forms of ceremonial apparel.

"How long do you think it will be before the water fully drains from this place?" I inquired towards the two scientists as I peered over the edge and into the dark blue depths of the tower.

"From the intact ice sheet above this cavern, I would guess this melt-off has been draining for the past century or more, give or take a few decades," Mica answered as she eyed the dry sections of the ruins.

"That roughly correlates with the peak of the industrial revolution, when CO_2 emissions and pollutants began circulating into the atmosphere at an unprecedented rate," Alex added in response.

"So, you're saying global climate had a hand in the recent exposure of this place?" I asked with curiosity.

"Not caused by it directly per se, but more like it could have triggered a secondary response by the geomagnetic shift which Professor Logan has been proposing," Mica answered as she tied up her hair before putting on her coat.

"I don't understand," I admitted, dumbfounded.

"Think of it more like a chemical reaction, where there is a response of imbalance from the composition of the stratosphere and solar winds," Alex explained, "both of which affect the climate of our planet on such an enormous scale that it goes relatively unnoticed."

"But that unbalance has been tipping ever more rapidly the farther it gets past the cusp and may have somehow affected the magnetic flux of the Earth itself," Mica responded.

"But I thought Logan said that these polar shifts, or whatever he called it, happened on a fairly regular basis in Earth's past," I began to argue.

"That's true, but that natural cycle could have been hastened by man's tinkering with the composition of the planet's atmosphere through excessive pollution," Alexander countered.

"So, you're saying that climate change is real?" I queried with a hint of doubt.

"Actually, the political argument about it is entirely invalid," Alex snapped, "because fundamentally, it really doesn't matter if *'human-engineered'* climate change is real or not; because mankind should be acting more responsibly, regardless!"

Mica nodded in agreement, and I couldn't help but admit the little man had a point. A majority of our modern populations spread across the globe were burning up natural resources at an astronomical rate without a care as to the mess we were leaving the generations that followed. Forest lands were being razed into deserts while the oceans were being clogged with unfathomable levels of pollution as the human race progressively produced mountains of garbage and waste year after year, with nowhere to put it. Mankind was busy poisoning the land, the sea, and the air, while pretending that everything was fine; even when we choked on our own breath from the rotting foulness of it.

If earth's natural cycle of change was every dozen millennia or so, then it was very likely that our careless disregard for the health of the planet was acting as a catalyst to quicken the pace of what might become an extinction-level event. Unfortunately, our nations had become so reliant on such fragile technology and infrastructure as supports to our economy, that mankind would implode upon itself if a sizable portion of it failed. I used to think of how hard life had been centuries ago, and how most people living in our pampered societies today lacked any valuable survival skills if you stripped them of their modern toys. It was a real enigma to consider that the very technology we had created to extend our lives, would likely be the very source of causing our untimely end.

It was Mica who pointed out that the oversized steps and general architecture of the buildings here, appeared to have been designed for a race of people who were much taller than our current scale. A modest guess would have placed the natives here to be three to four meters tall. The steps and handholds were of a much greater proportion, so much so that we felt like children walking in a world designed for adults. Checking to make sure her camera still worked, Mica took a few snapshots of our surroundings from the upper level.

"Look, down there!" Alex pointed below while he adjusted his glasses. Along an outer causeway, we saw the beam of the professor's headlamp swinging wildly about.

"Quick; grab your flashlight and signal to him, but don't do any shouting!" I ordered towards Alex in a hushed tone.

Alexander noted my concern as he took a glance up at the layer of creaking ice capping the cavern above us. He hurried towards the edge of the balcony and waved his flashlight for a few minutes towards our lost teammate, which we finally got a response from Logan far below who was using his own light.

We had to find a way to get down to the Professor's level on this side of the complex but found ourselves running into a series of dead ends. The deeper we went into the interior of the temple, the darker it became. I took out one of my emergency flares from my vest pocket and aimed it into the darkened void of the sunken sanctuary.

"Step back," I warned as I aimed the aerial device. Alex and Mica stood back as I pulled the trigger, and the bright red flare shot out into the darkness beyond the reach of our weak headlamps. The crimson glow illuminated several tall columns of carved stone bodies as it slowly arched and made its way down into the levels below. We were trying to find another access to a lower section and spotted several open archways a few floors below us. The hot ball of light from the flare bounced off the far wall and plummeted downward; eventually landing on a solitary ledge. In its flicker, the light played tricks on my eyes as I thought I had seen something strange stir just within the sphere of its fiery glow.

"Mica, come over here," I asked, "can you see anything moving down there?"

Alex came up behind Mica, and the three of us stood there peering into the darkness at the glowing ruby light as it began to fade. There, within the edge of its illumination, a shadow moved, then another. Soon, those small handfuls of shaded flecks, quickly became dozens, as the walls surrounding the dying flare began to flutter as a strange sound filled the air.

Eventually, the flare sputtered out, shrouding whatever we might have seen; leaving us standing there with our flashlights grasping at the enveloping darkness. Like winter ghosts, cruel fanged faces began to appear out of the gloom; their tight snouts and sharp teeth curved up towards their enormous ears.

Their stretched skin was as pale as death, pulled taught over their muscular frame; attached to wide featherless wings. Most horrible of all were their pink glazed eyes, devoid of any iris.

We tried to scatter, though there was nowhere to run. Jumping towards an outer window, we lodged ourselves against the inner wall as a mass of flying creatures soared past us, screaming like banshees. We had disturbed a colony of large albino bats, and like everything else in this accursed place, they were giant in dimension. Most of them had bodies the size of a wolf, though there were several that were far larger; and the breadth of their wingspan was frightening. They screeched like ivory demons as they cut through the air and swarmed into the open expanse above the city ruins.

"What the hell are those things?" Alex mumbled in terror.

"Ice bats or something ...I don't know. Keep your voice down!" I hissed in return as we held our backs to the wall.

The creatures appeared to be blind, but if they were true to their species, then they more than made up for it with their sensitivity to sound.

"Holy hell; Logan is down there!" Mica spouted, as I realized that I had just released a horde of giant bats upon the unwitting professor.

Giants in the Earth

The cloud of giant bats began to disperse throughout the cavern as they tested the heights of the ceiling and skirted their way around the cavern walls. At one point in history, this ancient port, surrounded by its protective cliff walls, had once been exposed to the open sky, but over the countless millennia it had become buried under the encroaching ice. The mammoth jellyfish were not as shocking a find as were these enormous flying mammals, for it was speculated that the inner continent of Antarctica was entirely devoid of life.

A dozen thoughts ran through Mica's mind as she wondered how these bats could have survived here through the ages. There were no records of insects or plant life they could have possibly survived upon after all these centuries; so the only conclusion she could come up with, was that these were carnivores which had either fed off of the aquatic life, or upon the weak members of their own colony. Seeing how they had been woken from their sleep, there was also the possibility this species had the ability to hibernate for extended periods. As fascinating as that theory was, saving the Professor was a far more pressing matter at the moment.

On the positive side, the lower stairwell was now clear of the flying creatures, so we hustled our way down through the labyrinth of stairs until we reached an exposed antechamber that opened to a broad balcony overlooking the entrance to the temple. Upon the high rail were the remnant growths of dying plants which appeared to be the same pinkish seaweed we had found growing in the bottom of the river. Now exposed to the air, their strands had grown taught and lifeless. Upon testing their strength, I was impressed by their resilience.

"Logan, up here!" Mica yelled over to the Professor, who had scurried towards the edge of the surrounding wall. Logan became alarmed when the swarm of giant bats had poured into the grotto and were now spreading throughout the sunken cavern like a screeching fog.

Mica had shouted a bit louder than I would have liked, and the creaking of the ice roof above us argued to that fact. Cracks appeared above in the frozen ceiling as her voice echoed throughout the cavern; though our salvation was that the reverb was mostly absorbed by the lake below us. I begged her not to tempt fate twice.

"Keep your voice down or you'll send the roof down on our heads!" I pressed in a hushed tone. She caught herself in her blunder and shrugged in apology.

Logan had seen our headlamps and made his way towards us but came just short of diving into the water mere meters below where he stood. I motioned for him to grab onto the lengths of dead vegetation but he flashed a look of despair as elongated shadows of the jellyfish could be seen coursing just below the water's surface. The giant albino bats were soaring close overhead, bearing down upon his position, so Logan gathered his courage and took a leap of faith. Gauging himself, Logan hesitated for but a moment before he plunged into the water just as one of the winged mammals honed in on where he had stood.

A few seconds after he hit the water, the professor could be seen dog paddling towards the hanging vegetation along the wall. Mica called out to the Professor in alarm as one of the bats dove for him as he splashed around in the cold lake. The creature flared its wings to slow its descent to snatch at him with its clawed feet, but suddenly, an array of transparent tentacles lashed out from beneath the creature where it's beating wings was disturbing the water. The beast screeched in a mixture of fear and anger as it was dragged under the glassy waters.

Several other jellyfish were drawn to the disturbance it made as the albino bat fought for its life; far from where Logan had reached the outer wall directly below us. Scrambling up the aquatic vines, the shaken professor grabbed our hands as we leaned over the balcony to help him up.

"Holy hell! That was close!" the stunned professor spouted as he pulled off his thin jacket. He was lucky that his thermal underwear was of a lighter layer and he had only a short way to swim before he reached the wall, or he would have likely drowned.

"Are you alright?" Mica flared with concern as she helped Logan get his wet coat off, and wring it dry.

"I do say, I was starting to feel a bit of despair after losing sight of you, and got myself lost among that maze of bridges," Logan responded.

"We found an inner walkway and made the mistake of awakening that swarm of bats," Alexander breathed as he motioned to the shrieking creatures darting about the cavern.

"Bats you say?" Logan snapped back in astonishment, "This species is enormous; but how could they have survived in this enclosed environment for such a length of time?"

Mica filled him in on her own theories on the contained ecosystem, but there were too many missing pieces to the puzzle to be sure of anything. I tried to remind them that there were more pressing issues at hand and that their debating the evolution of these flying vermin would be better contemplated after we had found a way out of this place and back to the safety of our ship.

We struggled our way down to the lower level just a floor above the waterline, and pushed our way through the interior of the gigantic temple. Logan mumbled remarks about an odd reference of an ancient myth about something called Yggdrasil; which was an old legend derived from northern European legends. Noting the several giant steps and doorways, he tried to tie the locations of their origins together from all sides of the globe. Whatever he was saying didn't make a lick of sense to me, but it rang a bell with his assistant.

"Ancient earth and its continents were forged from the landmass that was once Pangaea, which split into the northern and southern hemispheres, what we call Laurasia and Gondwana," Mica commented.

"...The what?" I stumbled on my words, trying to pronounce the names she had uttered.

"They are based on the theories of landmass distribution across the surface of the earth, and how it relates to the migration of their residing species before the shifting continental plates were separated by the open seas," Mica tried to explain; although I wasn't following her line of thought.

"As I mentioned at the exterior site with the giant tree, the numerous fables tied a series of nine realms together," Logan affirmed, "the massive circle of eight surrounding a single inner circle at the base of the tree may very well refer to eight lost civilizations locked under the ice of Antarctica."

"You mean these ruins and the ones we had crossed before?" I blurted with dismay.

"Yes, these may be the lost worlds of gods and elves of dark and light, including the hidden realms of trolls and dwarves, from the tales of old Norse mythology." Logan began to spew with wonderment.

"And of giants," Mica added, as she motioned to the enormous stature of the architecture within the ancient temple.

I just gave a scoff of laughter but caught myself when I could tell the three of them didn't consider it a joke, "Elves and giants ...come on, really?"

"Consider that the Mammoths of old earth were enormous creatures in their own right," Mica granted as I nodded in agreement, "which diminished to a mere 1/5th of their size over the generations of their species during the bleak era of the ice age when food became evermore scarce."

"It is a common fact that species evolve into smaller or larger body sizes due to the availability of food and the influence of their habitat," Alexander interjected.

The way these scholars related their knowledge on the subject, it began to make sense that there was a correlation between what we called Dwarves and giants, were likely just products of evolution at that given time in history, originating from the same biological strains. Their reference to 'elves' was a little fanciful but not when placed in the context of the many races and skin colors presented in modern humanity. It wasn't a far stretch to add physical exaggerations to that mix of large eyes and pointed ears which were usually features of feral animals that relied on their sense of sight and hearing for survival.

Delving our way deeper into the interior of the temple, we began to hear a low hum that could be felt through the walls. As we descended farther into the complex, I couldn't help but realize that we should have hit the waterline by now if the entire facility was actually flooded. It wasn't until we dropped several more stories in our descent that I was positive we were now below the water table and that this section had been somehow sealed off from the floodwaters. We followed the source of the noise until we came upon a long bridge reaching out into the darkness.

"Hmm, what's this?" Logan whispered as he inspected the architecture. The structure of the bridge was of particular interest to him as it seemed almost mechanical in the precision of its construction. The pathway beneath our feet turned to a type of solid black plate that appeared to be seamless and retained a vertical rail to either side a mere 20 centimeters tall. These rails were lined with a smooth silvery metal which had been inlaid within its surface. This narrow path led down through a corridor where it came to an abrupt end among a strange cobweb composed of what appeared to be wet leather.

"What do you think this is?" Alex inquired as he began to test the strands but withdrew his hand when Mica snapped at him.

"I wouldn't go handling that until I can test a sample," Mica warned, "this looks like some sort of organic animal secretion, so it would be best not to touch it with your bare hands," she noted towards Alexander who had lost his gloves.

Mica took out a small test kit from her bag and applied a few drops of an alkaline substance onto a piece of the sticky material she had removed. The skin immediately turned a deep blue, then began to give off a green fizzle.

"Oh my, well that's certainly not good," she frowned.

"Uh, what ...what was that?" I inquired towards the little chemistry test she had performed.

"Its toxicity is elevated, but I can't determine what species it might be from..." Mica trailed off in wonder as she poked at the elastic web of leathery strands with her tweezers, "maybe some kind of arachnid or aquatic animal we haven't yet seen."

"But this area is dry," Logan noted to his assistant.

"Sea turtles are aquatic a vast portion of their life, but come to dry land to lay their eggs," she responded as an objective example.

"Well, we've got to get through to the other side, so I suggest everyone get behind me," I ordered as I reloaded the flare gun.

"Wait, this is a rare biological find, we can't just destroy it," Mica spat in defense as Alex and the Professor shuffled behind me. I tried waving Mica out of the way, but she was persistent.

"What are you doing? We have to go through!" I noted as I made it clear there was no other passage we had the luxury of choosing from.

"But if you burn this, you may release the toxins within it and kill us all," she warned, which partially explained her hysterics.

"Aye, I agree that's a pretty good reason there not to fire that thing, Allen," Logan muttered over my shoulder. So I lowered the flare pistol as a response to his basic logic.

Mica cooled down once I realized she was right and began to follow the motives behind her precaution. As the tension subsided, it was quickly replaced by a raking screech that echoed through the hallway behind us. All four of us turned back towards the light funneling down the hallway to see the silhouette of something very large and unfriendly climbing its way towards us along the walls.

"Oh my..." Alex sputtered as he adjusted his glasses to get a better glimpse of the creature.

"Ah, fuck this," I muttered out loud as I turned back towards the webbing and ushered Mica out of the way. I don't know whether it was the menace of the approaching monster, or the serious look in my eyes that convinced her to step out of the way, but I'm glad she did.

"Cover your mouths!" I warned as we pulled our scarves up over our noses, and I fired the flare.

Flares guns weren't exactly meant to be used at such close range, so the jettisoned ammo took a moment before it burst into a fiery red ball after it struck the web. A cloud of thick black smoke began to bellow from the threads of poisoned skin as it crackled and withered while being consumed by the growing flames. A hole opened up large enough for us to pass through as the material fell away, and I stood back while my crew members scurried through. Pulling my firearm, I aimed my pistol at the creature bearing down upon us and fired; missing once as the bullet glanced off the wall near it. The beast paused for a moment and gave a horrid hiss, which made my stomach drop with fear.

Partially blinded by the glare of the brighter light behind it, I took a second shot, and the creature lurched. With a pause of confidence, I stood upright, thinking I had done it in. That moment of satisfaction drained away into stark panic as the spidery beast gave off a blood-curdling growl of anger and lurched towards us with added haste. Jumping back, I dashed through the burning strands and caught up with my comrades farther down the hallway.

"Did you get it?" Mica asked in despair as she looked past my shoulder. I turned with a glint of dread in my eyes to see where the creature was.

"The flames are keeping it at bay for the moment, but I fear that won't last long," I informed the two men who were standing before a barrier comprised of a series of thick crisscrossed bars, of what looked to be tubes of glass.

"Well, this is a dilemma," Alexander admitted as he tested the temperament of the translucent bars.

"This appears to be made from a natural crystal of some sort, I would assume," Logan added, "but I don't see any mechanism to operate this barrier."

"Yeah, guys ...we don't have much time; so figure this out," I prompted them to hurry as Mica and I watched the flames eating away at the web behind us as they began to dwindle. The creature hissed its outrage for being injured and scurried in circles with furious anticipation of catching its fleeing prey.

"Here, let me try something..." Logan offered as he pulled out a tuning fork from his breast pocket. Tapping it on the side of the crystal, he set the base of it on one of the bars. As the frequency of the small device began to fade, the bluish crystal turned a pure opaque white and pulled up into the recess in the ceiling.

"Astonishing!" Alexander whispered aloud in wonder, as the professor continued the same process on the other crystal bars.

"What kind of oddball carries a tuning fork?" I muttered under my breath in confusion.

Logan worked as fast as he could with the tuning fork by removing several bars to create a small opening in the cell wall just wide enough so that we could slip through; which was quite literally barely in the nick of time before the multi-legged beast scrambled its way past the smoldering debris in its attempt to snare us. Mica fell back upon Alex as she dodged a claw coming through the opening in the bars; which were still too tightly spaced to allow the large beast to follow us. I aimed the gun back up at the creature, but Logan placed a hand to my shoulder to settle me down.

"If you miss, you could break the crystal bars and let it through," he warned.

I was hesitant to take his advice as the creature continued to hiss, but after a moment it slowly turned away, yielding to the fact it had lost a fresh meal just beyond its reach. We watched the horrid creature as it scurried back up the corridor just past the smoking shards and began adhering a fresh layer of web material between the surrounding walls.

"That must have been its deathtrap," Alexander noted, "and used the hallway to funnel its prey towards the web, in order to catch it."

We collected ourselves and continued down the dark corridor

while following the source of the strange hum which permeated the air. As we progressed, the ceiling above us began to flare ever higher until we saw a soft blue glow beckoned to us from a room at the end of the long passage. The light from it shone upward high into the vaulted ceiling, reaching into the unfathomable darkness floating above. The definition of the object set within the center of the chamber came into focus as we drew closer.

Before us sat a large stand composed of pale pitted stone, curving in a complete circle with a flattened top. Within this bowl spun an enormous sphere. The simple construct of it resembled a replica of an old-style globe one might find in a mansion full of antiques. The orb itself was pewter in color, decorated with streaks of deep scratches upon its surface. It turned upon itself slowly while emitting the low hum we had followed to its source.

"Oh my," Logan uttered, breathless at this unique find, "this is amazing, just amazing. Mica, get some photographs of this mechanism," he directed her to get shots of it from all angles.

Mica fumbled for her camera, as she too, was caught staring at this enormous object in wonder. The sphere was spinning gently with such grace and fluidity that the sight of it was mesmerizing.

"Professor, do you think this is the magnetic amplifier you mentioned in your notes?" Alexander wondered as he adjusted his glasses.

"I cannot tell, but it does appear to be held aloft and stabilized by magnetic energies," Logan affirmed, "this very object might be the core that is generating the energy waves which are being drawn by the iron tree and causing the ice to retract from its location, including the various points around these ancient ruins."

Looking at the floor, it was clear that we were now standing at the center of a hub that connected to several other hallways lined with identical railings and blackened tiles, which led off in equal directions around us. It was almost like a giant circuit board that was directing the power emitted by this massive device. It was a type of energy we could neither see nor feel until Mica noticed something strange.

"My camera won't activate," she complained while gently shaking the casing.

"What's wrong with it?" Alex asked.

"It turns on for a second, and then shuts down," she answered.

"It's drawing the power from the batteries perhaps, or I would rather assume that this giant sphere is impeding or interrupting its functions," Logan explained. After several moments, Mica gave up on trying to get her digital camera to work.

"Well that's a shame, nobody is going to believe this," Alex remarked on her inability to capture any photographs.

"What exactly is this thing, Doc?" I prompted my question towards Logan.

"What I assume we have here is a converter of sorts, which is harnessing the natural energy waves of the earth itself. Transforming them into usable power that can be directed towards specific uses ...whatever they might be."

"So, it's a giant defroster?" I half-joked.

"...Of sorts," Logan admitted, though any humor I had found in my remark had entirely escaped him.

Shining our flashlights around, the lights began to fail as the bulbs flickered then began to die one by one; leaving us to bask in the soft blue aura radiating from the enormous sphere.

"Well, that certainly puts us in a pickle," Logan voiced as we stood there in the veil of indigo light radiating throughout the room. Alex did note that the light emanating from it seemed warm and tingly, and actually not all too unpleasant since he and Logan were still standing in their soaked clothes. The ambient temperature did appear to rise the closer we stepped towards the strange orb, but I did wonder what we would do about providing proper clothing for Alexander, once we breached the surface again. Whenever that came to pass he would be hard-pressed to fight off the effects of hypothermia. Logan could manage if we were able to dry out his gear properly; however, standing this close to the source of heat, that issue didn't seem to be a problem at the moment.

"Ah yeah, I enjoy a sunbath and all, but did anyone stop to think that the reason this light feels warm, is that it might be radioactive?" I inquired with a raised brow, although my concerns were genuine.

Both Alex and Mica took a notable step back from the device as Logan began to rub his chin in contemplation. He seemed perplexed as he looked around the chamber and took interest in the silver rails that led out in all directions from the stand that held the turning sphere. Counting, he noted there were six spokes that led out into the darkness from the central hub.

"What if we could spin that orb a little faster, do you think it might help melt the ice any quicker?" Alex dared to ask. I thought it was a reasonable question but Logan just gave him a hard glare.

"I'm not too entirely keen on playing with ancient devices I don't fully understand, my friend," the professor advised, "as this apparatus is obviously drawing power, the consequences of fiddling with it could be dangerous, if not catastrophic."

Alexander nodded in agreement like a dolt, though I didn't share his level of humility. I wanted to get the hell out of here as soon as possible and this circular engine, or whatever it was, might be the key to our getting out of here alive.

"Well, why not test it somehow and figure out what this thing really is?" I offered, "Maybe Alex is right and we should give it a go since there's little chance we will be returning back to this spot," I noted, adding that we were only carrying a few days of food at most if we rationed it out since Alex had lost his own personal share of our supplies when he fell into the lake.

After walking the entire circumference of the orb, Logan noted that there were no markings or controls of any kind that he could see around it, nor were there any present upon the odd pedestal. We would have to hoist someone on top of the platform which supported the floating orb. Grasping onto one another, Logan and I helped Alex crawl onto our shoulders since he was smaller than either of us. Mica, however, was the lightest, so we made a rudimentary human stairway to boost her up to the edge of the rim which was well over a meter above our standing reach.

Kicking and groaning her way up, Mica finally managed to pull herself upon the wide rim that held the spinning silver orb. After a moment, she came back to the outer ledge to address us after her visual assessment of the apparatus.

"The sphere is levitating about half a meter above the base, but it's not connected to it or anything else that I can see. However, I did notice some small point of light directly beneath it, though it's difficult to view it clearly at this angle," she noted.

"Do you want to try and turn it?" Logan asked his protegee.

"Well ...I guess so," she shrugged, since that was the purpose she had climbed up there. Logan was just being polite about asking her to risk herself, and let Mica know she had a choice to decline if she thought the task was too dangerous.

Mica approached the sphere which loomed before her, watching the streaks in the fine metal encompass her vision. Merely staring at it produced a strange feeling she found both hypnotic and intoxicating. Mica held out her hand, then paused a brief moment to take off her mittens which had started to become a little too warm to wear from the passive heat radiating from it. She reached out slowly to the surface of the sphere as tiny fingers of electricity reached back to meet her bare touch. There was no pain from the sparks, feeling only a slight tingle, so she dared to make contact with its surface.

The three men below passed each other nervous glances as they tried to step back far enough to see Mica where she stood high upon the platform, so they could tell what was going on as the tiny arcs of electricity flashed into the heavy gloom above them. She gently caressed the skins outer edge as a buffer of electricity began to accumulate under her palm, giving her a slight tickle which brought a smile to her face. It was a magical moment to connect with a part of antiquity lost among the ages.

She pressed another centimeter further, but the moment her

hand made contact with the metallic surface, the rotation of the sphere came to a sudden halt. The hum flowing from within it died away and the light emanating from its surface faded dramatically. Thinking she had broken it somehow, Mica jerked her hand back in confusion as the room became swamped in darkness. A moment of silence passed as the team wondered what they should do next, and Mica crouched to the floor of the pedestal for fear of falling off the high ledge.

Slowly, a high-pitched whine began to rise from deep within the silver orb which suddenly began to rotate in the opposite direction from its preceding course. The pace of its orbit quickened to the point Mica was afraid of being near it. Her fears were soon justified as hot strings of electricity began to lash out farther from the orb the faster it turned. We ran over to catch Mica while she tried to scramble down from the pedestal to save herself from the electrical strikes that pushed her further towards the ledge. Logan and I caught her and placed her beside us on the ground.

"What did I do?" Mica breathed in fear, wondering what calamity she had brought upon them.

Forest of Light

The glow from the orb transformed into an olive hue while we were forced to step further away as dangerous arcs of electricity struck out like miniature bolts of lightning, which connected with a number of the silver rails spaced upon the floor. These pathways lit up, coursing down the corridors as the power sped through the conduit. Three of the six paths were now illuminated with energy from the rotating orb, which was spinning violently in place. Whatever affect Mica's touch had done to trigger it, the device was now far too dangerous to approach for us to attempt to reverse the process.

Recoiling from the hot arcs of light, we backed away to the far wall where the multiple passages spanned outward from the central chamber. We looked towards Logan for a hint at what we should do next.

"It's not safe to stay here; we've got to choose one of these shafts!" I called over the crackling electricity.

"We should take one of the lit pathways," the professor suggested to our utter dismay.

"Are you crazy, we will get fried! Those rails are electrified now," I spat back while Alex and Mica also contemplated our compromised situation.

"It doesn't make sense that these conduits would be exposed like this if they were truly dangerous, and I propose that whatever Mica triggered would be activated at the end of one of these illuminated routes," Logan noted in the defense of his wild suggestion that we follow the transmission path of the flowing energy.

"Why, what is it that you hope to find?" Mica inquired as she shielded her eyes from the flashing bolts of electricity dancing around them.

"I propose that the power this thing is kicking out is being directed towards one of the multiple domains recorded within the archives I've studied," he concluded, and we noted that only three of the lanes were being allocated for the transmission of the mysterious energy.

"There's a sense of logic in that," Alexander granted, "if this device is harnessing geomagnetic energies then it is plausible that whatever is at the ends of those conduit tunnels would be a viable way to extract ourselves to the surface."

As insane as it sounded for him to suggest that we hop down a conductive pathway, what the professor said made a scrap of sense. It would be far better to stumble across another ruin which had power running through it, rather than one left dead in the dark. Listening to the way I was thinking, I realized I had compared this ancient civilization to a modern city. Here was proof beyond any doubt that an advanced society had once ruled this continent; one which had tapped and controlled natural energies with such linear design in its architecture that it baffled the mind.

This frozen city from antiquity carved from the solid bedrock had once been a flourishing metropolis that utilized powers and technologies far beyond our own crude understanding. Thinking about it, these dwellings were built with the grace which our modern urban cities paled in contrast as they were littered with noise, pollution, and errant waste. This machine had lasted thousands of years, if the professor's calculations were to be believed. The only thing that disturbed me was the continuous worry throbbing at the back of my mind; hoping that the technology we discovered wouldn't be exploited by our military' minds, rather than for the benefit our general population as a whole.

I wasn't a nutty conspiracy theorist, but I wasn't stupid either. During my time in the military, I had personally witnessed far too many occurrences when governments ran afoul of their oath towards the public good. That twisted frame of mind seemed to have become more pronounced and contagious between many of the powerful countries of our modern world. There was no logic in their thinking while wars and violent excursions erupted across the globe. Citizens rose up to voice their disapproval, but an unfortunate fact of our world was that it's usually those who hold the guns who make the rules. It made me wonder if this ancient society had actually fallen into its frozen silence by some unavoidable curse of nature, or if by some evil plight fashioned by their own hands.

"Well, if you're going to choose one, choose quickly!" I stammered as the violent electrical arcs began to lash ever closer to where we crouched.

Logan got up and made his way towards the lit pathway nearest him, and dared to use himself as a guinea pig while taking a timid step into the black tiled path as the energy lit the rails surrounding it. Several small fingers of electricity slipped from his feet as he made contact with the floor, but they were nothing more dangerous than static. Motioning to us that it was safe, we gingerly followed in his footsteps behind him while being careful not to directly touch the small rails lining the corridor on either side. We were soon ushered farther down the path as the chamber containing the orb began to light up like a Christmas tree.

"Where is this one heading?" Alex asked curiously from behind Logan, who had taken the lead down the narrow corridor.

"Honestly, I don't have a clue," the professor admitted curtly.

"Ah ...okay," Alexander sniffled in bland bewilderment.

The rails retained their dim glow down the length of the straight tunnel. As the pathways looked so similar, for a brief moment I had feared we had returned down the same path we had entered, since we lost our sense of direction when the sphere had activated. However, the end of this particular tunnel was much farther than the previous; and fortunately, our flashlights and electronics began to work once again the further we withdrew from the power core at the center of the chamber. Mica played with her camera once again to make sure it was working properly. Luckily, the batteries in our flashlights hadn't been drained or we all would have been out of luck.

Our path led us directly to a deep pit which opened into a large circular shaft several meters wide. Shining our lights down into it, we could not see the bottom. The rails which ran along the floor tipped over the sharp edge and continued into the abyss. Looking above us, we noticed that the shaft extended upward where there awaited only the murky gloom of darkness mirroring what we saw below.

"Well, this path was a dead end. Best we go back and try another way," I suggested to Logan, who appeared just as disappointed in crossing this impassable obstacle.

"Very well, I suppose we have no choice," he granted.

Backtracking our way to the central chamber left us coming up short as the leading edge of the passage was now engulfed by hot streaks of electricity, which had inflated from the orb and crept their way into each of the conduit passages. We were stuck with nowhere to turn.

"Oh bugger!" Logan breathed.

"Holy Hell, we better hope that field of electricity doesn't keep growing or we'll be backed up against that pit," I warned with a mark of dread in my voice. On a personal note, I wasn't very fond of heights.

We contemplated for a moment as we watched the surge of electricity course further towards us along the causeway; defeating our hopes that it would recede back into the chamber so we could choose another route. We hurried our way back to the pit while Mica took some measurements from her watch.

"At its rate of expansion, I calculate we have about 15 to 20 minutes before that field reaches us," Mica estimated.

"The rail just dives down into this hole, what do we do now?" Alex whined, feeling his own mortality creeping upon him, giving a shallow squeak to his voice.

"Allen, hand me your flare gun, if you would please," Logan requested, but I took it out and checked the barrel, noticing I had already used the only two shells it came with.

"I'm out," I blurted, trying to find any spare shells stashed in my pockets that might have gone unnoticed.

"Hmm," Logan contemplated as he rubbed his chin while looking down at the illuminated rails, "have you got anything like wires on you?"

"I, I think I have a connector for my camera for downloading images," Mica noted as she searched through her bag, but Logan seemed discouraged by her offer.

"No, no, we need something more substantial than that ...like a metal rod or a cane," he suggested.

"Oh, well then I have this mini tripod for the camera; I think it is mostly metal," Mica answered as she whipped out the small apparatus.

Logan snatched it out of her hand and extended it as far as it could reach, then he measured it against the rails on either side at their feet. Unfortunately, it came up mere centimeters too short.

"What are you trying to do?" I inquired, not understanding his objective.

"There might be a chance we can short out this conduit and create a temporary back surge," Logan hoped, "then we could backtrack to that central chamber and choose another path out of here," he added as if trying to convince himself on the logic of his plan.

I quickly grabbed the tripod from him as I unsheathed Tom's knife, and pried away the rubber feet on its tips and unscrewed the plastic handle which controlled the pivoting head, and tilted it straight up. Now it would reach. Logan gave me a smile, thoroughly impressed by my quick thinking.

"Fantastic," he noted, "...but, you should all take a step back," he cautioned after a moment of reflection to the risk he was about to undertake, and ushered us away from where he stood.

With a measure of apprehension, the Professor carefully placed the aluminum rod on one side of the track, and then began to set it down on the opposite rail. Centimeters away, sparks fingered out towards the staff as he dropped it into place. For a moment, the lit rails dimmed dramatically; seconds later, the tripod linking both connections began to glow white-hot.

Its brilliance became blinding as a sudden flash of light illuminated the tunnel, and Mica's tripod rapidly melted into a pile of scorched slag.

The stench of ozone lingered in the air as an acrid white smoked flowed from the pool of scalded metal. A tense moment later, a grating 'clack' issued from the pit beneath us; followed by a rising wave of air that pushed up from the shaft with such force that it nearly knocked us to the ground. After seeing what happened to the tripod, I was careful not to touch both rails at the same time lest I get cooked by the volatile energy flowing through them.

Staggered by the surge of air that swept upon us, we finally caught our feet when the wind fell away and was replaced by a soft hum. From the darkness of the pit rose a platform that spanned the entire circumference of the well. The landing was composed of a bright blue metal mottled with streaks of dulled silver and gold, flecked within its surface like marbled stone. It rose to the level of our passageway and came to a gentle stop. We glanced at one another as we took our first steps towards this miraculous lift.

"Do you think this is an elevator?" Alex questioned the obvious explanation but neither Logan nor Mica bothered to answer him.

We crept up to its edge, where Logan took a cautious step upon its surface. Noting it seemed solid enough to take our weight; we escaped from the electrified tunnel and began to make our way across to the opposite side where a continuing tunnel awaited. Halfway across, we noticed a large shallow bowl made of crystal which was set upon the floor at the very center of the platform. Its edges were precisely cut and it appeared to be of exquisite design.

Mica approached it, and urged us for a spare moment so she could take a photograph of the object. Taking her camera out of her bag, she adjusted it for a few shots and bent down to touch the edge of the rim to see if she could lift the bowl; however, it seemed to be firmly attached to the floor in some manner she couldn't identify. Feeling its surface with the tips of her bare fingers, residual static which she had absorbed into her body from her contact with the energized orb, clicked a small spark. That tiny flicker was all it took to reactivate the strange lift.

As we nearly reached the passage on the other side, a soft whir erupted from beneath our feet. Turning around, we gazed back at Mica as a look of guilt washed over her face. The platform began to rise, cutting us off from the passage we were trying to acquire. Its speed of ascent increased to a point where we were forced to steady our footing. Logan stepped forward and rushed to his assistant's side.

"What exactly did you do?" Logan pressed.

"I was just seeing if this glass dish moved, and there was a spark from my fingers when I touched it," Mica snapped in her defense. She appeared just as worried as everyone else, and with a quick inspection of the object there didn't appear to be any type of physical controls upon the smooth crystal container that she might have accidentally shifted.

The platform was rising at a fair pace, which passed by several more levels containing open passages and doorways as it continued to ascend ever higher. Logan carefully touched the crystal bowl in an attempt to duplicate what his assistant had done to activate the lift in his attempt to stop it, but his efforts were in vain. I tried to judge our chances at leaping into one of the open passages as they passed us by, but there was no way in hell we could all fit into one narrow corridor even if we tried; and the rim of the platform was so close that it would be far to easy to lose a limb if the timing wasn't perfect. Scratching that reckless thought, I turned back to the professor for answers. At least we were going upward and in the right direction to the surface, which I admit was far better than the alternative.

"It would be safe to assume that this conveyor is electrically activated. Mica, try touching it again," Logan instructed.

Leaning back over towards the half-sphere bowl, she lightly touched the edge. This time a rush of electricity streamed from the tips of her fingers across the flattened rim of the basin. The lift quickly decelerated, followed by a series of 'whooping' sound from underneath the platform, and it slowly came to a gentle stop several dozen meters from the very top of the shaft. There was a long moment of silence shared between us as we stared at one another, wondering what to do next, then suddenly a hidden section of the wall surrounding us slid open.

Just as quickly, a semi-transparent wall erected up around our platform, which began moving horizontally through a large corridor littered with shafts of light. We were all a little stunned by the technology of an elevator being transformed into a monorail; with no clue as to how the platform was being suspended, as there wasn't any obvious track it was set upon. The ancient tram sped through what appeared to be a natural cavern braced with carved support columns sporadically placed along the route. We all felt the way Logan had expressed in his words that followed.

"This is truly astounding!" he muttered while trying to peer through the mottled glass encompassing the platform.

"How do you think it's able to traverse like this?" Alex wondered as he tested his footing while daring to stand beside Logan, who was on the leading edge of the deck as we swept through the tunnel.

"Magnetic levitation, perhaps; maybe something akin to our bullet trains; applied in some unconventional way we have yet to dream up," Logan answered, seeming to be quite sure of himself.

"That's great and all," I beamed with cynicism, "but you do realize this is taking us much farther away from the shoreline where we docked our boat, don't you?" I added with flare.

I was not too terribly happy about being taxied so far from our port, because that meant a long fucking way to be hiking back on foot through the frigid Antarctica weather and deep snow once we breached the surface. Furthermore, without his thermal gear, Alex didn't stand a chance of surviving once we got topside; nor any of us for that matter if we were left lost somewhere among the frozen wastelands with only a few days rations left between the four of us.

Mica was still crouching near the bowl, afraid to touch it again. Apparently, her physical contact with the giant generator had left residual energy coursing through her body. There was a sudden gleam in her eyes as she had a wild thought, and she pulled up her sleeve to look at the metal artifact still hanging upon her wrist.

"Ah, well now this makes a bit of sense," Logan turned to see the large silver ring she had retrieved from the ruins which she wore upon her arm, "that, little lady, is likely what is responsible for retaining the electrical field from the orb; storing its energy like a battery," he announced as he pointed towards the ancient silver bracelet she held.

Mica removed the ring she had secured under her sleeve and took a closer look at it. Apparently, it was some sort of key that allowed it to operate multiple devices. This tram system was taking us somewhere; hopefully, it wasn't to a place we didn't want to be. A loud *swoosh* of air passed above us as the open platform slid under a low hanging column of ice jutting from the ceiling. As we progressed, we noted several more of these enormous icicles scattered along the way, their placement becoming evermore dense by the minute.

We all backed away from the glass screen in alarm as we approached a far larger stalactite of condensed ice, which snapped in two when it was clipped by the edge of the transparent shield surrounding the platform; sending sharp shards of blue ice spraying across the smooth floor of the lift. Alex adjusted his spectacles and pointed ahead as we all turned in dread just as another large block of ice crossed our path in the distance. We gathered at the back end of the platform, expecting the worst. Moments later, the platform clipped the encroaching ice and began to spin wildly as we were flung towards the retaining walls by the centrifugal force.

Without slowing, the unbalanced tram hit another sliver of ice which had infringed into the transport tunnel, which sent our lift skidding off to one side of the passage. We tried to brace ourselves as the spinning top hurled us about within the walled enclosure while sliding across the rough floor of the tunnel, until it hit a pair of ice boulders blocking the passageway. What followed next was a blur of motion filled with screams and hollers of panic as the platform careened to a halt. In a state of shock, we slowly got to our feet, helping one another check their aches and bruises for signs of serious injury.

"Is everyone accounted for?" I ushered to the rest of the crew as I struggled to stand. I found Logan and Alex intertwined like a pretzel, while Mica ended up in a pile wedged between the floor and the retaining wall. My foot was sore and I had somehow twisted my wrist in the chaos, but everyone else seemed fine, though we were all a little worse for wear. Stumbling over the retaining wall which was sharply tilted, we looked around to see where we had been left stranded. We could clearly see that further down the way that the path had become choked with ancient ice which had intruded into the causeway over the passage of time. The density of the formations stacked before our route was far too dangerous to scale given our current lack of climbing gear.

"Well, I must say this puts us in yet another pickle," Logan chimed in as he looked around the area, and even peeked under the platform in a vain attempt to ascertain a clue as to how the device operated.

"We can try to walk back to the entrance from here, but that would only leave us at the edge of that pit yet again," Mica added into the conversation of our dilemma, "I would suggest that we press on and see where this leads," she pointed ahead.

"We aren't going to get very far," I responded with a sigh as I surveyed the tunnel before us, "but I guess it would be worth the effort to find where this glacier ice had managed to creep in and search for a breach to the surface," I concluded with a shrug of my shoulders as I glanced back towards her.

Alex fiddled with his glasses, trying to clean a cracked lens as we began to weave our way in and out around busted pillars of ice and over its slippery flows, searching for a way to continue.

Nearly an hour later, the Professor continued to lead us onward as we struggled to keep a steady pace, though I could tell the old man was losing steam. We were all a little tired and stressed from recent events and were in dire need of rest, so I took a post and offered to keep watch just in case a swarm of albino bats or any other unpleasant surprises might show up while the others took a break.

Logan found himself a small cranny to lie down in, as did Alexander, who tried to pull his legs up into the long coat I had let him borrow. I was sitting next to Mica while I was playing guard duty, as everyone was getting a few moments of peace.

"What's on your mind, Allen?" Mica whispered low enough so as not to disturb Alex and Logan; although, I didn't think anything would wake Alexander, especially with the way he was starting to snore.

"Anyone would be worried. Aren't you?" I sighed, realizing I was zoning off while wondering how we were going to get out of this mess.

"Archaeology has its risks; I knew that before I went into this field," she admitted, "I believe discovering the lost knowledge from mankind's past helps not only to guide but can even dictate our future."

"That sounds ...pretty enigmatic," I joked, trying to sound smart, even though I didn't fully understand what that word meant. Mica took it in stride, regardless.

"There are many of us in certain scientific circles who are trying to reveal the mysteries of our past, because all too often it is intentionally buried and hidden from us," Mica noted, being quite literal.

"Well, that's certainly an admirable goal," I admitted with a shrug, "but the truth is, it doesn't seem like many people in our modern world seem to give a damn, from what I've seen."

"It may appear that way, Allen," Mica whispered back with a tone of confidence in her voice, "but I hope we can sway you into understanding our motives one day," she ended with a sad smile. A moment later, we heard Logan calling for us, who came barreling around the corner from the shattered pillar of ice where we had been taking shelter.

"Everyone, come quickly, I found something!" he chattered with excitement, though there was still a tired look in his aged eyes. Apparently, he hadn't gotten much sleep but instead, chose to go exploring on his own. Shaking Alexander awake, we grabbed our sparse belongings and followed Logan's lead. We hadn't gone a hundred steps until we crossed a large crack in the ice which had been hidden from view behind a giant column. Logan needed our help to get a boost up to the rocky outcropping where he could reach the opening. We all went up in tandem, hoping we had found a way out of this maze.

The entrance was quite large and expanded as we progressed; the presence of ice fading the further we advanced down the passage. It appeared to be a natural cave formation, likely created ages ago by a vast underground river. What was remarkable about this particular passage was that it was lined by spheres of light, not unlike the wisps we had seen before in the ceiling of the icy river. I had heard of glowing mushrooms but these were tall plants with illuminated stems and translucent leaves of every shape. They were truly unusual.

"They're beautiful," Alex breathed aloud before Mica could; who of course was eager to gather a few specimen samples to bag for her collection.

"Bio-luminescence within plant chemistry like this, is extremely rare," Mica noted with a slight frown after the light faded from a plant sample she had cut free and stuffed inside a test tube.

In a strange way, the unique vegetation seemed to have a symbiotic relationship by feeding off of the illumination from the adjacent plants around them. Their translucent leaves appeared to be positioned to direct the surrounding available light towards their core stems in a curious arrangement to attain photosynthesis. The plants themselves, even seemed to react to our flashlights as Mica noted when she drew near to inspect them. Turning a winding zigzag of corners, we were stunned to find the corridor ahead of us was lit up like a holiday market. It was a forest of light beaming in every color. Bushes and tall organic structures as tall as trees were lining every section of the walls and ceiling. Oddly though, the plants lining the floors were sparse. While walking through the open trail, I shared my wonder about this curiosity to which Mica responded.

"With the ice melt-off, any water flowing through here might freeze the plants and harm their delicate roots; so they cling to the walls instead," Mica theorized as she inspected several long vines laced with glowing webs. It was an enchanting scene of color and light we found eerily beautiful.

The cavern opened up wider still until the ceiling loomed far overhead, blooming with an aurora of gentle hues. The cascade of light drifted over the high walls and washed down to hug the barren riverbed where we stood. There was moisture in the air here and plumes of mist drifted lazily among the grotto. We found the temperature within the cave far more agreeable, so we tied our coats around our waists since we were beginning to work up a sweat from the exertion.

The four of us followed the open trail along the riverbed until we reached a series of inlets to the main cavern. Still tired and hungry, we voted to resume our interrupted break from the hour before and get some much-needed rest. Alex appeared grateful to not be suffering from the cold as he lay down upon his coat, while the Professor chose to wander off with Mica to capture photographs of this amazing realm. I couldn't deny I was fatigued, and found a spot of my own to lay down my head on a patch of soft sand along the riverbed.

Any concern I had about what dangerous and unfriendly critters might be lurking in this shimmering cavern among its delicate flora, soon faded away as exhaustion caught up with my tired body. I drifted off into a heavy sleep with dreams filled with flying monsters and electrical storms while enveloped by a white wasteland of ice. I was shaken from my restless nightmare by a heavy odor and a low roar which I recognized as the sound of rushing water. I woke up to the painful sensation of my legs starting to scald from a flow of acrid water reeking of sulfur; which was now flowing around where I had lain at the edge of the riverbed.

I jumped up, cursing as I did while trying to shake off the boiling water from my pants. Hot steam wafted from where it had soaked into my coat and gloves, and I checked to see where I had left my pack and unceremoniously yanked it up into the higher level of the flora where it landed with a thud. Looking around in a panic, I couldn't see Alex or the others as thick impenetrable steam began to fill the cavern. My shouts were soon drowned out by the heavy flow of water gushing from the surrounding geysers as they discharged from the numerous inlets embedded along the cavern walls.

I gagged on the thick mist as I retreated back into the foliage, which glowed ever brighter with the rising heat. I tried calling out again and again to locate my comrades, but they were lost among the hiss and clouds of blistering steam that filled the cave. I had found myself abandoned.

The Golden Hall

It was clear to me now why the riverbed had been barren of vegetation, for any overgrowth or seedlings would only be scorched by the thermal springs. Apparently, the release of the scalding waters was infrequent enough where the riverbed would run dry. The entire cavern was now filled with a thick mist, creating a brooding atmosphere like something out of a horror movie. I grabbed my pack and made my way further up the cavern walls in an attempt to escape the heat of the boiling river coursing below.

I took shelter in an outcropping while wondering which direction I should go to find my associates. Several of the glowing plants near me started to sear brightly and began popping from the extreme heat like burned-out light bulbs. A wisp of glowing spores released into the rising air from their corpses, carried by the currents of hot air churning about the chamber. Nearly an hour had passed until the flow of the springs began to wane and the water level started to drain from the cavern floor.

My breathing had become heavy as I gasped in the thick mineral-laden air and soon found myself drinking the last of the water from my canteen to quench my thirst. The hot mist began to thin, and I dared to explore the rest of the cave as the noise from the geysers lessened until I was able to hear my own voice over the roar of the surging waters. The radios we carried weren't working so I shouted for the Professor and the others every few steps until a shower of rocks began to tumble upon me from above. Looking up, I could see beams of light cutting through the mist as they waved back and forth. Logan called out to me from overhead as I backed away far enough to see them where they stood upon a high rocky shelf.

"Allen, up here lad!" the professor yelled down, "over there, you can make your way up and over to us," he advised while pointing to the far cavern wall.

I hiked my way through the glowing undergrowth as swirls of glowing spores whirled around me until I finally approached what appeared to be a rudimentary staircase. The steps themselves were unusually small but climbable, as they curled their way up along the cliff wall in an unrealistic and dangerous route. I was a little afraid of heights myself and didn't like the idea of free climbing in the clunky snow boots I was wearing. The rock face was still slick from the hot moisture lingering in the air, so I used the plant roots as a handhold wherever I could find them entrenched upon the walls.

I slipped more times than I could count and nearly took a tumble into the glowing foliage below. Finally reaching the group, I was wondering how little Alexander could have made it up this far over such a treacherous course. Mica reached out to take my hand as she helped me onto the exposed platform.

"We thought you were a goner," Logan chimed in as I brushed off my hands, "we found ourselves trapped between spouts on the far side of the cavern and shimmied our way up here."

"Alex tried to find you, but he got lost in the thick steam," Mica confessed as Alexander shrugged an apologetic look in response for failing in his attempt to locate me.

"Glad you're alright," Alex admitted with a friendly pat on my shoulder. I could see now that with his smaller frame and foot size that he would've have had a much easier time than I had while climbing the steps that led along the wall.

"So, what is this here?" I asked while noting the bright metal surface pronouncing itself from under the thick foliage where we stood. While I was climbing up to them, Logan had been busy ripping the vegetation from a section of a column that appeared to be made of burnished copper. Hidden beneath the thick woven vines we could make out the frame of an immense doorway before us. Peeling away the remaining plants obscuring the lower part of the enormous door, we stood back to get the full scope of its structure.

"It's a door ...a door is good, right?" I stammered, trying to make logical sense of its placement set unusually high upon the cavern wall.

"Unless it might be some sort of mechanical valve holding back more boiling water," Alex remarked.

"Don't be so pessimistic," Logan rang back, "sometimes a door ...is just a door," he grinned with tired enthusiasm.

"Did you see any other route out of this vast cavern?" I tried to inquire with an ounce of hope in my voice, but Mica remarked that they had not.

"Logan noticed this platform as it stood out from the rest of the cave, and we were looking for a higher ground anyways to try to see if we could spot you in the foliage below," Mica stated with a grin; grateful they had found him once again.

Alexander and the Professor found themselves busy trying to translate the chicken-scratch text they discovered lining a horizontal seam scrawled across the door.

"Svar ...Svarta?" Alex sounded out as he read a certain line.

"Ah, it might be connected to the Nidavallir, from the text of old Norse mythology which was either home of the Dwarves or the Dark Elves, which were considered one and the same in most legends of their time," Logan educated us on the cult history of the ancient Norse.

"Sounds like a pretty big difference to be confused about," I muttered to make conversation as I glanced up at the tall doorway.

"Not necessarily," Logan corrected, "they are both beings of the underworld or *under-earth*, so to speak. The tales mention a race of short dark-skinned creatures that preferred to reside underground in the shadows rather than the light of day. Thus, the men of that age saw anything different than their own kinsmen as another race entirely, and it was quite common during the times of antiquity for colorful yarns to be elaborated upon each time such stories were retold."

I wasn't buying his fanciful tale, but I wasn't such a bookworm as the Professor had proven himself to be. It seemed to me that history books were always being rewritten, and that the original versions had been either twisted beyond recognition, or forgotten entirely. In a way, that made me feel self-conscious, and I began to wonder about my own lack of insight.

Some people care too much for the future, and some of us dwell far too much on the past, and it was usually a difficult task to find a comfortable balance between the two if you were only concerned with trying to live in the moment. Most people lose sight of what's important in their lives because of such self-inflicted dilemma. I was just as guilty as the next person to feel the emptiness in mankind's currently established social order and the dark direction our world was heading. In a way, it made me feel a measure of envy towards Mica and the other scientists for recognizing their sense of direction so clearly, and having found a measure of their own immortality by being able to touch these distant voices from the past.

Mica was searching for a place where the large ring she retained might fit into the door, but there was no such recess they could recognize. Grim faces had been sculpted into the decor, each filled with glares of contempt. Unfortunately, there were no rubies or precious gemstones present in their design, despite what every adventure movie I've seen had groomed me to expect. After taking a gander at the behemoth archway, I came up with a stupid idea.

"What if it's not actually a doorway, Professor," I shrugged, and each of them turned to me with a gaunt look of disbelief.

"What do you mean, exactly?" Logan responded with a huff.

"I mean, look at where it's located," I turned and motioned to the fact that this outcropping was situated far off the cavern floor, "what would be the purpose of placing it so high?"

"Maybe it was put here at a safe distance above the geyser flows which pour through this cavern," Alexander suggested while adjusting his glasses, though clearly irritated with the damaged lens he continued to endure.

"Or, maybe it's just a monument or sign of some kind," I offered back in response, "try banging on the surface to see if it sounds hollow," I finally suggested.

Logan looked a bit miffed as he didn't agree with my analogy but looked around for a loose rock that he could strike the door with to test my theory. He rapped a large stone against the entry several times with a dull thud. Apparently, it was either very thick, or there was nothing on the other side.

"*Humph*, maybe Allen's right," the professor concluded as he dropped the stone. Logan looked around to the three of us for additional options. If this piece of architecture wasn't designed as a means for access in or out of this place, it didn't make much sense to position it here.

"What if it's a valve of some sort?" Alex offered innocently as he was reaching for ideas, "that would mean that it could control something else, like the geyser spouts."

"Eh, I'm not so convinced," Logan breathed as he scratched his head in confusion, "there are no controls here that I can find," he finished. Mica was scanning the distant walls to see if she could spot any similar structures which might give a clue as to the purpose of this strange edifice, but most of the details were blurred by the lingering fog rising from the chamber floor. After close scrutiny, I noticed something odd hanging from the cavern ceiling far above.

"What do you think that thing is up there?" I nudged at Mica's shoulder while pointing to a loop of vines hanging in a bizarre formation. A closer look revealed that the object appeared to be a set of bars or chains, almost completely disguised by the overgrowth from the abundant plant life growing throughout the cavern. Whatever it was, it didn't look natural.

"Who knows, but it's up too high for us to reach," Mica admitted as we scanned the walls for a way to access it.

"Well, it looks like we'll have to withdraw back to the previous passage and try to make our way through that debris field of encroaching ice," Alexander sighed as he sat back against the metal structure overhead. After a moment, we noticed that the tiny glowing spores released from the multiple plant blooms were concentrating into illuminated clouds, which appeared to coalesce together near the strange structure stationed overhead.

Several more clouds of colorful spores also rose to the ceiling above and drifted towards the center of the chamber as they followed the draw of hot air to that point.

Logan, Mica and I, were watching the light show while Alexander sat on the ground behind us; stretching his arms as he leaned against the faux doorway. Looking down, he noticed a metallic crossbar protruding from the wall which was poking into his back. Turning around, he brushed aside the thin foliage covering it; wondering what it was. Grasping it with his hands, Alex innocently tried to see if he could move it, finding that the lever turned with relative ease. There was a sharp 'click' as it locked into place and he pulled his hand away in mild surprise as the lever slowly spun itself to complete a full rotation.

Alex jumped to his feet in shock as a loud whirring sound began to beat to life from behind the metal wall. We all turned around to see him stumbling back towards us as the stone platform beneath our feet began to tremble. Mica screamed aloud as the massive metal wall began ripping apart the frail vines veiled over it and started folding itself down upon us where we stood. The four of us jumped to either side of the narrow outcropping to avoid being crushed by its immense weight.

The bronze wall fell outward and stopped at a slight angle, revealing a thick set of plates stacked within. The interior behind it was filled with an odd assortment of strange gears and swinging pendulums that squeaked and complained as they performed their various functions. Once the wall jolted into place, the next section of it extended outwards in succession. One after the other, the plates connected together until they reached ever higher towards the metal harness we had seen attached to the cavern ceiling.

"Well now, that's certainly impressive," Logan sputtered in mixed surprise at the ingenuity at the mechanical bridge.

Testing its edge, it seemed solid enough to place our weight upon. High above us, the last plate fell into place and latched itself to the tackle, which was securely affixed to the ceiling.

The pressure of its connection triggered another device that lowered itself from the hanger onto the last plate accompanied by a rush of air. The colorful clouds of glowing spores floating about the ceiling began rushing towards this outlet and were sucked up through the open shaft. We glanced at one another in a moment of warm surprise; perceiving that we had just found our way out.

"Come on, let's go!" I ushered to the rest of them.

"Any guess as to where this goes?" Alex asked nervously.

"How the hell would I know, it's a way out of this place," I responded to the irrational question.

"We at least have to see where it leads," Mica offered kindly towards Alexander, who was clearly worried, "we can always backtrack if it doesn't go anywhere."

"Have faith old friend," Logan offered, "the way that spore cloud evacuated from the chamber means there is likely an air draft to the surface," he concluded. With a shrug, Alexander yielded to our combined encouragement and we cautiously climbed aboard the bridge and ascended to the landing above.

"It sure is a long way down," I breathed as I carefully peered over the side while questioning the structural integrity of the platform as we gained altitude.

The bridged swayed slightly with the combined weight of us moving upon it and I wondered if we should have chosen to make the ascent one at a time, for safety's sake. Logan seemed far beyond confident in its design, although I couldn't figure out why. Perhaps he had no fear of death at his ripe old age, or that he considered meeting his demise in the bowels of a long lost civilization was a good way to die. Either way, I didn't fancy joining him on such a fateful quest into the afterlife.

Numerous clouds of spores, glittering with a rainbow of colors, swept their way around us towards the inlet. When we finally reached the support hanger, we could see how it interconnected with the bridge which led towards a long circular tube made from the same type of bronze material. The wide cylinder had a horizontal opening that flared outward from its side but appeared to be stuck in a cycle of circulation while it clanked in place repeatedly.

"Seems like its gears have seized," I stated while trying to figure where it connected above, while the large opening was sucking air into its funnel.

"What do you think this contraption is?" Alexander asked the professor as he examined the strange device.

"Well logically, it seems to be drawing up hot air from this chamber and redirecting it somewhere," Logan trailed off.

"Like a heat-exchange system?" I blurted in wonder.

"It would make sense if that was so," the professor responded, "by using the natural geothermal heat, this mechanism might be part of some sort of temperature regulation system."

"That's all fine and dandy, but now what?" Mica proclaimed as they all stood on the upper platform while tiny illuminated spores were drifting around them and sticking onto their hair and clothes.

"Maybe we should take a look inside," I offered as an answer.

Logan nodded in agreement as Mica followed in suit. Alex was a little skittish about that idea, but he didn't want to leave his companions or take the chance of having the sky bridge retract; which would leave us stranded high off the ground in case the funnel withdrew back into the ceiling. We climbed into the large orifice to see what we could find, and we were slightly surprised by the design of it. Once inside, we found several rotating flaps that either seemed to direct the airflow or were measuring it in some fashion.

Shining our flashlights around the darkened interior, the only other light source was the stream of glowing spores that were being sucked up into a funnel far above our head. We couldn't detect any ladders or a way to climb the smooth chute, so it appeared we had reached another impasse. Our only option was to climb back down to the forest of light and search for another way out of this cavern. Surrendering to that option, we were making our way towards the egress when we suddenly heard a loud 'snap' and the sound of metal grinding on metal.

Looking through the opening, we could see that the bridge had disengaged and was currently retracting away from us. Now we were trapped high above in this unlikely nest.

"Ahhh, that's not good," I breathed with a sigh of worry as Alex began to pace back and forth in the small circular room with noted anguish. Just as suddenly, we were thrown to the floor as the telescopic pipe withdrew into its former placement within the roof of the cavern.

Before it sealed, there was an immense pressure of air that lifted us off our feet and sent us tumbling through the ductwork. I could even hear Mica cursing while Alexander screamed like a little girl as we were sucked up into the ventilation shaft. Rings of light swam past us as we were inhaled through the tubing and were siphoned through its length. I lost all sense of direction of which way was up or down and started to feel like I was going to vomit from the constant spinning. Clearly, this duct system wasn't meant to be occupied in any fashion, but I was too busy feeling sick and dizzy to be worrying about where we might end up. Like the others, I just wanted this unbearable joyride to come to an end.

Our unfortunate transit through the ductwork ended up spewing us into a basin of warm water. We grabbed Alexander, who was flopping about like a fish as he struggle to keep his head above water. Logan himself, looked as ruffled as the rest of us while we waded to the edge of the pool to climb out. Stripping ourselves as much as we could of our soaked clothing, we got the chance to look around at our surroundings.

"What is this place?" Alex grumbled curiously as he spit up more liquid from his lungs. Directly above us was what appeared to be a giant sieve, made of the same bronze material situated directly above the spout from which we were ejected.

"This pool must be a collection point for condensation of the water vapor," Logan speculated as he inspected the strange contraption. As we stepped away from the obscuring steam of the watershed we were amazed at what we saw before us.

Towering structures of brass and bronze lined an entire

causeway for as far as we could see. The details of the cavern roof were lost in the dark shadows beyond the reach of our weakening lamps. There was a churning sound like gears and pumps that brought us to the outer edge of a walkway, which was lined with rows of dim lights. Mica tapped at the thick glass of these lamps, which appeared to be encased in a type of crystal.

"This is incredible, I wonder how they work?" Mica beamed as she searched for any sign that might reveal how they were put together.

"What is it, Allen?" Logan asked as he came to put his hand upon my shoulder. He could see the worn look on my face as I glared into the darkness of the metal city.

"Ah ...I, I just can't help but feel that we're getting ever more lost the farther we go and we'll never find a way out, Professor," I admitted with a heavy sigh, "we're running pretty thin here boss. We're all tired and hungry and nearly out of fresh water."

Logan's face washed with a mix of sympathy and guilt as he realized that he was the sole reason we were all here facing this dilemma. Logan had felt a great deal of remorse for Tom's death, and began to doubt his own principles for having brought us on this expedition into the frozen wilderness, and eventually conceded how reckless it was of him to risk the lives of others. The professor wasn't usually the kind of man who would second-guess himself, but there would be no recognition of his life's work if we all remained trapped beneath the ice and his expedition party became the next permanent residence amongst this lost realm.

"You're right Allen, we should keep moving," Logan agreed while swallowing his guilt, "maybe we can find a vent shaft to the exterior and call for help on the radio."

We set off through the open causeway that led between the towering metal pillars and strange machinery powered by the rising steam. Farther down the walkway, we began to find bones lying in scattered piles; their texture was so brittle that they decayed into dust when handled. The skeletal fragments were small, almost the size of a child, but far thicker in diameter than that of a normal human. Mica gathered a few biological samples as Alexander investigated what was left of the cadavers.

"This is strange indeed," Alex declared, "they appear to be the thickness of full-grown adults, but stunted in stature."

"Dwarves, they must be dwarves," I blurted out loud.

"Dwarfism is a rare genetic condition," Alex responded in defense, "but here, it seems like an inherent trait," he noted as he motioned to the few dozen bodies lying about the pathway.

"Is it normal for the skeletal structure to disintegrate like that?" I had to ask, not wishing to touch any of them.

"No, we do digs all the time, and depending on their age, they might be fragile but they don't crumble apart like this," Mica added as she put away her collection bag and attempted to take a few photographs; only to notice that her camera was acting belligerent and refusing to work properly after its recent dunk in the water.

"Professor, what do you think that is?" I asked as I stood upon the highest edge of the path and pointed out towards the end of the causeway.

There appeared to be several softly glowing vein-like tubes running from the machinery at the edge walkway, which led out into an open field. We approached this exposed area while following the nearest conduit, which was slowly pulsating with an internal light. At the edge of the clearing, we found what appeared to be a type of nursery. Within this vast field, was strewn a mix of strange crystal formations growing within large circular enclosures. Each of these closed pens was cut into four triangle-shaped compartments; within their centers stood spouts which released a fine mist of water vapor several minutes apart.

A great number of the devices which fed the nozzles were now clogged and broken, and where those tubs sat, the crystals within were dissolving in a state of decay. Many of the minerals appeared like something you might find within a geode, while others were enormous samples of crystalline growths. These beautiful structures glinted in our flashlights as we walked among the scattered field.

"This is incredible," Logan proclaimed, "this field of crystals must be used as some type of conservatory."

"A what?" I asked, completely confused.

"It's like a greenhouse, but instead of plants, it appears they were growing minerals instead," Mica replied.

"You mean all this equipment is a mineral farm?" I responded while daring to touch some of the colorful formations, "for what reason would they do that?"

"Their form of technology might rely on it, in place of fossil fuels like our own modern civilization," Logan answered, "it's quite ingenious actually, as it would be an entirely renewable source of material. The microscopic substances that form these minerals are naturally filtered and collected from the deep geothermal springs below us."

"But what would they use them for?" I shrugged; not having a clue to the complexities of this lost culture.

"It could be anybody's guess. These could be source material for construction or a type of resource material which helped supplement their dietary needs in this environment," Logan suggested.

"So they grew their minerals and base ores, rather than digging them from the earth?" I asked, trying to understand the process.

"Maybe so; instead of having to waste time and energy on excavating the soil, they had learned to extract such resources through a much simpler means," the professor offered in return.

Progressing onward, we came upon a foreboding structure located in the middle of the mineral field. Connected to it were several of the same feeding tubes fanning outwards from its base and into the crop of mineral baths, but they didn't appear to be functioning. It held a clump of large beehive-shaped tanks stacked upon one another, which surrounded a series of central antennas that reached straight up into the darkness. Alexander was the first to mount the deck, to examining how it might work or any clue as to its function.

Alex had a bad habit of recklessly experimenting with things he didn't fully understand, which was probably due to his overly curious nature. Near the center of the formation, he found a tall cone made of the same bronze metal as the rest of the machinery we had seen.

"Mica, if I may borrow that ring of yours," Alex inquired as he turned to the professor's assistant.

Mica removed the large silver bracelet and handed it over while she glanced over her shoulder to receive a nod of approval from Logan. Alexander took the ring and gently slid it upon the sharpened cone which pointed vertically among the array of antenna-like structures. Once the thick ring slid down to a section where it fit snugly and came to rest upon the shaft, several glowing characters began to appear upon the cone's surface.

"What does it say?" I asked in surprise, wondering what he had discovered.

"It's not Sumerian or any of the dialects I'm familiar with. Why don't you take a look, Logan," he offered for the professor to take his place in front of the mysterious device.

Logan strode over and inspected the strange characters with interest as he rubbed his chin in thought. I dared to peer over his shoulder to see what they were. The glowing red symbols appeared to be an odd combination of old Norse runes all jumbled about like complicated Chinese characters. I had no clue as to what they meant, so I nudged the professor to tell us what he thought. That inquisitive nudge was a mistake.

I bumped his shoulder as he was tracing one of the characters with his finger, which he accidentally came into contact with when I bumped his shoulder. The symbol he unwittingly pressed, immediately turned a bright green, while several of the other characters sporadically faded to a dull orange. Logan glared at me over his shoulder for my clumsiness.

"Oops ...sorry about that," I apologized with a guilty shrug as I backed away a step. Just as I did, the silver ring we used began to spin in place upon the cone, vibrating ever faster.

More green lights shot through the tubes at our feet around us and fanned out through the mineral field. We jumped back as we heard loud pops and explosions of what sounded like water tanks bursting, and the group of us stood there stunned when the distant walls surrounding the open field began to burn brightly with strings of lights. Within their illumination, a city of golden metal beamed to life; the habitats stacked upon one another like intricate cliff dwellings from some old forgotten age. Around them stood tall effigies of bearded men with gaunt faces; the moisture upon these formidable metal figures glistening in the hard light.

"*Holy shit* ...a real Dwarven city," I blurted aloud in my astonishment, as the rest of my companions turned in unison to gaze upon this incredible spectacle while our mouths fell open in awe.

The Catacombs

The clanging of old and broken machinery echoed from within the central spire which Alex had initially activated, leading us to wonder if we were in danger in case this thing decided to explode. Wary of the risk, we backed away from the device until Mica dared to dash back to grab the metal ring they had left there. She gingerly lifted it off the spike, wondering if doing so would disable the device. After removing it from the cone, the machinery within the spire remained working, which allowed the surrounding spotlights to keep the city illuminated.

"What's the plan, Logan?" Alexander inquired as we gazed upon the glittering city while Mica slipped the ring safely back upon her wrist for safekeeping.

"We came here to explore, so we might as well take a look and see what we find," the professor muttered with mild jubilation.

It was amazing to see how the old man's eyes would light up every time we tripped across a new discovery. I wanted to say he looked like a kid in a candy store but the thought of that made my stomach grumble. Thus far, we had already gone nearly a full day without eating and the strain was starting to wear on us.

We approached the largest statue made of the familiar burnished bronze commonly used in the construction of the dwellings stacked upon the walls, and marveled at its design. It was not pieced together by rivets nor welds as we might have expected from an older civilization but was instead, compromised of tightly interlocking seams. Alex noted that it was similar to the ingenuity of the ancient Inca's, who were known for their masonry and fine stonework by which they pieced together great blocks of rock without the use of mortar. This advanced technology was from a different era and would take several decades to reverse-engineer for us to understand it properly.

However, that was time that we did not have, as Mica had informed us before we left our vessel. The dark brooding shadow of global war arose like a serpent of death across several rival nations throughout the world, in the midst of civil unrest. These uneasy tensions were caused by political turmoil which had matured during the past several decades between such adversaries. Many governments had become ever more militarized to protect their individual interests and personal agendas. It was a dangerous time for everyone in the modern world, as the threat of thermonuclear war was ever-present in our lives.

It made me wonder if this culture hadn't met a similar fate by its own hand. Logan's personal theory was based on decades of study he had gathered about such lost civilizations from the annals of antiquity. There were certainly wars of a massive scale between tribes and empires in Earth's recent past; which were usually primed from differences between social casts or what was considered the lower class and their ruling nobility. I would've liked to suggest that our modern world had grown beyond such pettiness, but saying so would be a lie.

A narrow staircase led into the building directly beside the enormous effigy of a sculpted face. We entered the structure, which was lit by rows of amber lights embedded within the walls. We found the passage within to be cramped in many areas which would lead off into several antechambers, as were the shortened height of the doorways. It became obvious that the previous inhabitants were much smaller in stature than average, as was confirmed by the scattered physical remains we had seen earlier.

We also crossed several stairways that were exceptionally steep and narrow, making them a challenge to ascend. It wasn't until we reached the upper levels where we found something of particular interest, which is where Logan and Alex began contemplating the purpose of their eerie find. Stacked three high atop one another, were endless rows of corpses, held in miniature open coffins; their skeletons facing the hall as if they were a part of some grisly display.

"Well, that's not creepy," I half-joked as we entered the vast hall. The three scholars were used to dealing with the bones of the dead during archaeological digs but the sight of this was downright chilling. The bodies were situated in little tombs with their bodies embedded in some type of solidified substance, like an insect caught in amber.

"Allen, can I borrow your knife?" Mica inquired as I gave her a sideways glance.

"What for?" I answered her question with a question; though knowing full well what she was going to do with it.

"I have to get a sample of this material that these remains are encased in," Mica noted as she tapped on the hardened extract.

"Do you think that is some sort of preservative?" I noted as I handed her Tom's old boot knife.

"Maybe, maybe not; I'll know when I'm able to test a skin sample," she answered promptly.

"Do you think this is some sort of weird crypt?" I inquired trying not to ask the obvious, but failing horribly, "I mean, why would they set their dead out like this?

"It could be some type of ancestral catacomb; a place where their deceased relatives or warriors were left to be honored and preserved for the afterlife," Mica suggested, "you should try asking the Professor what he thinks," she offered as if to bait my curiosity, so I strode over to Logan and Alex as they were inspecting the unique design work within the architecture while searching for any runes or scripted text that might reveal the purpose behind this ghoulish exhibit.

"Did you two find anything?" I inquired to them both as they were scrutinizing one particular crypt with a flashlight.

"Ah, Allen, glad that you are taking an academic interest," the professor grinned as he turned to me, "You see here, what this person..."

"The Dwarve," I interrupted a little rudely.

"...Yes, the Dwarve, or dwarvish, per se;" he acknowledged, "and what this device is that he ...or she, has hanging around their neck?" he noted.

I peered closely into the dried amber in which the corpse was embedded and could make an outline of a brassy neckband adorned with several large gemstones.

"Ah, it's jewelry. Do you think they plastered them in there like that to keep treasure hunters from snatching their valuables?" I suggested to the two scientists. Alex just gave me a quirky smile, as if I had said something childish. Logan, though, offered to correct me.

"We're not grave robbers, my boy," the professor coached me on archival etiquette, "there is something about the basic design of it that makes us believe it is more than just a mere trinket," he answered as he moved the beam of the flashlight to each of the surrounding cadavers. Sure enough, each one of the crinkled bodies wore a similar necklace bound around their necks. It appeared the only difference between them were what type of precious stones they were set with.

"We think they might be either some sort of control device or maybe even the token badge of a servant class," Alexander explained.

"You mean like a slave collar?" I asked, noting how the choker could resemble one, although their inclusion of gemstones made little sense to me; unless they were servants to some sort of royalty.

"We were hoping to remove one of the collars so we can take a closer look at it," Alex offered as he turned to see Logan's assistant jabbing at the solidified material for a sample, although, not having much luck in her task. Mica finally gave up and had to satisfy herself with a small chip of the amber which eventually cracked loose from the struggle.

"Eh, well that might be a problem," I noted, hoping that Mica hadn't bent the tip of the knife during her wild antics chipping away at the cadaver.

"Yes, so it seems," Logan concurred as he realized they weren't having much progress from their effort, "so I suggest that we try exploring the rest of these vaults, for they might contain preparation chambers where the dead were encased, and hopefully discover what we are searching for therein."

"Like directions out of this place," I stated.

"Exactly," Logan agreed as Alex turned with him, while motioning for Mica to join us.

The length of this ancient mausoleum seemed endless. The Passages encircled the full length of the outer walls surrounding the mineral field below. We eventually stumbled upon a thin stairwell which led into a large gallery. Within this chamber we found what Logan had been looking for.

"Ah, this might provide some answers," Logan exclaimed as we approached a wide panoramic mural comprised of deeply etched metal that encompassed the entire room.

The style of artwork was notably blocky in areas but made up for it in finely etched details in others. It displayed a story of their past, showing a great transition of their people's plight.

"Ah, little do people know that it is usually the work of artisans that last throughout the ages, which tells us about our past." Logan smiled as he began viewing the figures in the illustration.

"What do you mean?" I asked innocently, not comprehending his statement.

"Well, let's say that our modern world is destroyed either by fire, plague, or some other disaster," Mica explained, "and imagine for a moment what items that might survive such a calamity if they were left to rot or ended up buried for thousands of years. What could archaeologists from a future civilization derive from what they found if they did not know our spoken language or anything about us if our entire history was lost?"

"Well, there are countless movies and libraries and videos, and..." I began to blabber until Mica cut me off.

"But those are items of a particular technology that would have vanished, if the paper in our books decays into dust and anything recorded on digital media is unreadable," she explained, "the only thing left after all those lost centuries would be preserved in metal or stone, such as shown by the Egyptians, the Mayans, the Aztecs, Olmecs, or Babylonians..." she began to count off a series of ancient cultures whose mysterious histories had also been lost to the tides of time.

"We learned cuneiform from the Sumerians, which was left on little more than fragile clay tablets," Alex added into our conversation.

"Let's say, what meager use this flashlight would be a hundred thousand years from now," Logan entered the fray while holding up his lamp, "long after the batteries had decayed and all that was left was some bits of metal or rotted plastic; there would be no clue as to what it was used for or how it worked. Duplicating these mysteries from the tiniest clues are what draws archaeologist to discover our lost past; to make an account of all the lives before us and to learn of them, and from their mistakes."

Logan's analogy made sense. Even if something from our era was perfectly preserved, there would be no way to use them; like listening to music from a radio if there were no broadcast towers, or audio recordings if there were no devices to play them on, or even the right type of power source to operate them. It made me start to think just how very finite and temporary the things we used in our daily lives actually were. The simplest of tools made much more sense to utilize; but unfortunately, our own modern culture had evolved to become far more wasteful beyond any of our predecessors before us.

Would some future humanity misinterpret our entire culture based on scant clues if there were no spoken or written language left to decipher; leaving the true history of our society to be nothing more than a guessing game? I felt a touch embarrassed amongst the three of them for never having thought about the world around me in that context. Where they saw the past, present, and future as one; people like me only conceived of the here and now, not really caring about tomorrow or the legacy we left for future generations.

I felt a twinge of guilt, but I couldn't quite place why. Maybe it was because I had lived most of my life in blissful ignorance of the world around me; which made me wonder what it was that I would leave behind for others to know what I had done to make my mark, be it for better or worse. I started to feel like a real prick for not caring about it before and wondering what it was I was really doing with my life? Here we were, in the middle of the most incredible discovery of our time, yet I still felt detached from what Logan and his team were trying to achieve. They weren't here for money or glory, but for something far more relevant.

The mural was organized in a strange fashion, as Logan pointed out that it began on both sides of the entrance going from left to right, then right to left on the other side of the chamber; meeting a central point in the middle of the room.

"I've never seen a layout of this fashion," Logan admitted, "this appears to comprise of two separate eras which conjoin here at the middle, to describe what could be perceived as same closure to a saga expressed towards those viewing it," he noted as he took the left mural while Alex took the right-hand side. I tried to get a good look at the images portrayed within the carving, but they made little sense to me.

"It appears that there was a group of six tribes which had experienced fierce internal struggles across their borders with one another, until they managed to attain some common treaty or alliance together," Alex called out from his side of the chamber.

"On this side, it shows there were three great kingdoms of seafarers from a small sliver of joined islands who sought conquest beyond a great wall of mountains," Logan announced from the opposite side of the room as Alex continued with the narrative from his part of the panorama.

"The six tribes of the people on this section, collaborated to defend themselves from a great invader, depicted here as to what appears to be a Triad," Alex announced.

"Ah, a trinity of foes, that would very well correspond with the three dynasties depicted over here!" Logan affirmed, "Although from what I'm viewing on this section, there appears to have been a feud among these three companions whereupon one body of their forces chose to separate from its allies, leaving the two other dynasties to battle against a great army of six tribes."

"It's hard to tell here, but I would presume that these images illustrate the toppling of some great wall or mountain, in their effort to resist the invaders," Alex added from his section of the large mural.

"It's starting to make sense now. Here it explains that after the trinity was broken, they created a powerful magic that could shake the walls of the great mountain asunder and invade the lands of their enemy," Logan continued as he advanced further alongside the mural.

"I see," Alexander intervened, while we listened as Mica approached the central figure where the two sides met, "...here, the six tribes combined into one force and captured what appears to be a great prismatic orb from the Triad, and used it against these invaders who had brought it to their lands," Alex stated as both he and the professor began to close in on Mica, who stood at the center of the elaborate scene.

"In the aftermath of their battle, the great walls of the mountain arose and the stars spun above them as their lush green lands withered and died from frost, and the white shadow of death swept upon them," Mica announced as the two scientists came to stand beside her as they traced their stories to the midpoint of the great mural.

"What the hell does all of that mean?" I asked bluntly as the three of them stood gazing upon the central image, sculpted in larger proportion as its dazzling centerpiece, where it displayed the sun and the moon changing places in the sky.

"Three kingdoms against six, separated by a great wall; which I would presume are the vast mountain range that divides East and West Antarctica," Mica proposed to the agreeing nods of her comrades beside her, "West Antarctica has a great peninsula that stretches out from the south Pacific to the Atlantic Ocean, which had actually once connected a narrow land path to South

America, back when the ocean levels were far lower than they are today."

"That would account for the seafaring kingdoms seen here, if the sea levels rose and such a passage evolved into a string of islands," Logan suggested in kind.

"With six empires spread across the far larger eastern side of Antarctica!" Alex proclaimed.

"So, if I got this straight, six rival clans joined to fight off a group of three invaders at this mountain range, and stole their prize weapon and used it against them?" I shrugged as I attempted to piece the story together.

"Exactly Allen," Logan replied, "but something went drastically wrong when the stars in the heavens fled; which might very well mean they experienced a massive tectonic shift or some other cataclysm that was significantly worse."

"Do you think this flashy orb thing they used might have caused that?" I offered as I inspected the area were Alexander had pointed out the carved circle in the center.

"I surmise that may very well depict the electrified sphere we discovered," Logan interjected while I gave him a look of surprise, "which was some massive power source that harnessed the natural harmonics of the earth. However, they were experiencing a polar shift at this epic time in their history, and I would dare to suggest that the device they used only managed to amplify the destruction."

"Which likely spun the earth's crust into a new axis," Mica added while pretending to hold a ball in her hands and twisting it sideways.

"As the Earth's equator realigned, tropical and temperate climates suddenly shifted into a new place on the map, where they transformed into respective arid or polar regions," Alex explained.

"In their eyes upon the ground, the stars swayed above them and the solar bodies fell away; while across the world, jungles turned into deserts as forest ranges transformed into wastelands of ice ...or the '*white shadow of death*', thus portrayed herein,"

Logan tutored as he pointed towards the central image.

It was a cataclysm so enormous that I had a hard time wrapping my head around it. The magnetic fields of the earth swapped places but not in perfect opposition or alignment; which sent the angle of the entire earth askew. I had remembered reading an article many years ago that claimed the Arabian deserts were once home to a tropical region covered with vast jungles in our ancient past, but was now nothing but a vast ocean of barren dunes and hot sand. Even now, we had no technology in our modern era to stop a tragedy of this nature, and if such a catastrophe of that magnitude happened today, our world would be annihilated.

"In all respects, we would be drawn back into the dark ages, or beyond," Logan cautioned.

"As the Professor mentioned, from data that's been gathered over the past half-century, we now have scientific proof to support that the Earth's core has been tipping towards yet another historic shift of our magnetic poles; which, if the calculations are correct, has been predicted to be due by the end of this year," Mica reminded me.

"And how long does one of these magnetic shifts, last?" I shot back with a worried tone.

"Nobody knows," Alexander responded, "it could be as short as a few weeks, or as long as months or years, or longer, for such a cycle to complete. Hopefully, we will be able to acquire some clues to answer that question if we're able to translate these scripts."

"Do you think that giant electrical ball-thing we found might be able to control, or even stop it, somehow?" I asked with a measure of hope; for I had several nice beaches in mind I wanted to retire on, but that dream was being dashed to pieces with every word they spoke about this approaching calamity.

"I can imagine that would be doubtful, Allen," Logan answered, "for I believe that device was only able to harness or transform energy, and wasn't employed at the scale that would be needed for such a colossal task. For the moment, I believe these people were the victims of an immense climate shift that overcame them so rapidly that they were unable to adapt."

"Except for the single ally of the Triad, which fled the region," Mica corrected as Logan considered her summary.

"By Jove, that's it!" the professor exclaimed, "Eight domains circled by a ninth. The surviving ancestry of modern man could very well have been the one dynasty which fled the fight and retreated across the straight to the Americas, and extended across the vast reaches to Europe in that lost era."

"And those survivors of the seafaring domains could have sailed the oceans to find other lands upon which to settle. So why didn't these folks do the same?" Alexander inquired.

"Perhaps they were landlocked, or these dwarves were a subservient race which had no ability to escape their bondage," I suggested to their raised brows.

It made sense to me that a race of giants could easily bully a smaller pygmy race into servitude. Unfortunately, slavery had persevered across our planet for a long time. It was one of those peculiar curses of mankind which separated us from other beasts and cast us in a bad light. Subjugation was even present in our modern world, which went neglected and overlooked by many countries.

No one could disagree that the social ethics and principles of our species were a horrid mess, and our governments didn't like facing them. In fact, governmental bodies were usually the prime culprits of such moral lapses and did a lousy job of presenting themselves as symbols of virtue and morality in the public eye. In this current day and age, it seemed like everyone in authority or power around the world was either crooked or corrupt on one level or another behind the vast political facade which protected their kind. It made me wonder if most of humanity was as blind as I had been to the blatant exploitation and abuse of position by our officials.

"To be frank with you, Doc," I replied, "I think this whole thing is much bigger than us, and we should get some high tech personnel in here to decipher what it was that happened to these people and learn how we can avoid facing their fate."

"That is where you are dead wrong, my boy," Logan snapped back, "our own national governments and those abroad would wrap this discovery up tighter than a drum! Mind you, they would suppress and censor this site in order to exploit it to fit their own prescribed narrative of our world history."

"Why would they do that?" I slipped before thinking.

"Power," Mica answered in a snap, "knowledge is power; always has been, and always will be. Every government is a dictatorship in one form or another and the very thing they fear most is a free society. For in such a society, they would have less purpose, and thus..."

"Less power," Alexander finished for her.

"Look, I don't want to argue conspiracies with you guys, but this is an entire continent of architecture and technology that we've never seen before, and if there is any chance we can get that big electric ball to..." I began to rant until Mica interrupted.

"The geomagnetic sphere," she corrected.

"...Yeah, the *whatever*; and use it to abate this pole shift you keep talking about and save the world, then I think we should give it our best shot, starting with getting a lot more feet on the ground out here!" I pressed with a note of anxiety in my tone.

"We will cross that bridge when we get to it, Allen," Logan answered firmly with a hand to my shoulder to calm me down, "first we need to find our way out of here, and I promise you I will do the right thing when the time comes to pass ...alright?"

Logan gave me a look of assurance as though I were a small child who had dropped his ice cream on the ground, and being promised a replacement treat. As a recipient of his attitude, it was wholly embarrassing, to say the least. Until now, there were no records from past civilizations which had survived a global shift. It was our obligation to find the clues we needed to solve this mystery and find a way to avert the looming catastrophe, while we were trapped within a continent of ice.

Forest of Stone

We had been on a one-way trip since we entered this underground labyrinth while exploring these ancient ruins forgotten by time. For now, our trail had seemed to end at these Dwarven ruins. The bedrock appeared to be capped by a massive roof that hung high over this cavernous chamber. The protection that it once offered in the distant past, now served as our prison.

"Mica, I have an idea," I mentioned as Logan and Alex appeared intrigued by my suggestion, "that ring bracelet gizmo that you held onto looks like it might fit into the image of that sphere in the center of the mural."

Certainly enough, it was designed to appear like an undersized eclipse, with both the sun and moon stacked on top of the other, making it appear like a doughnut that roughly resembled the ring she held. Stepping forward to touch the engraving, she found it was gently recessed. Mica removed the silver band from her wrist and carefully placed it within the depression, when it suddenly pulled from her grasp and snapped into place. Both Alex and the professor's eyebrows curled in mixed astonishment that I had detected such an obvious clue which they had overlooked.

The large ring began to turn slowly as the four of us watched with anticipation until it clicked into place, and the shallow recess engulfed the device while the bangle became flush with the wall. Mica attempted to retrieve it, but there was no way to get a grip upon the ring in its current position.

"It's stuck!" Mica announced in alarm, and a moment later the floor beneath us seemed to move.

However, that was purely a visual effect which momentarily confused us as the walls around us began to slowly rise. Looking behind us towards the entrance I could see the stairway by which we had entered was still visible as the walls of the chamber rose; revealing former details in the enormous mural which had previously been hidden below the level of the floor. The rising walls lifted the ring far out of our reach and was replaced by detailed scenery within the exposed carvings that emerged. Once the ascending walls ground to a halt, they unveiled six elaborately carved panels characterizing each of the individual empires which once ruled the great lands of Eastern Antarctica. Above them were several scripts written in assorted languages, one of which Alexander recognized as resembling ancient Sumerian.

"Can you understand that, good fellow?" Logan asked his companion as Alex stepped forward to inspect the glyphs.

"Those Nordic-looking runes there are much older than elder Futhark, and these markings here are too confused to be true Akkadian," Alex muttered as he adjusted his cracked spectacles while reading various sections, "but it appears to give the names of the six major dynasties you formerly proposed which had once ruled the eastern lands."

"Those there," Mica pointed towards a carving of a warrior depicted larger than the others, "I recognize seeing those symbols before."

"Ah, the Jotu, where the giants dwell," Alex responded, "which appears to be the sunken city overtaken by jellyfish and those vicious bats," he noted.

Next to it was another panel depicting crystal towers standing upon a scene of ice and snow, which Alexander noted was the frozen underworld of the 'Nif'. Next to that panel was the desert people of the 'Mus', who ruled vast deserts and wastelands upon a landscape littered with active volcanoes. On the opposite side was the wild forest tribes of the 'Alf'; which he suggested might have translated to what we know today from fanciful legends as the Elf race, or Elves, depicted within glowing woodlands. In addition, there were the familiar designs of the 'Nida', known as the underworld of the Dwarves, portrayed by their short stature while surrounded by clusters of minerals. The carved portraits of their race also showed them wearing the same neck pieces we had seen upon their dead, displayed within the surrounding crypts.

"And what about this one?" I inquired to Alex about a panel which was far more intricate in its design than the rest of the portraits on display.

"The 'Asga'," Alexander stumbled on his words as if he was unsure of its pronunciation.

"Otherwise known as the Asgardians," Logan whispered as a correction, "...which were the sacred lands of the old gods," he breathed with elation.

The professor related his knowledge on the old Norse legends and the lands of their deities, where their dead warriors would go to feast in the afterlife. Of course, if it was a real location then it would be the first place any scholar would want to visit. As Logan approached the panel to get a better look, an array of bright amber lights lit up from below the edge of the floor. The walls suddenly lifted another level around us, stretching the panels far above our heads while revealing a previously hidden chamber that opened before us.

We immediately noticed a small figure huddled in the corner of the room where there stood a simple stone dais. Upon it appeared a series of notches set in a half-circle with a narrow teardrop-shaped recess; its overall layout resembling that of a sundial. Mica turned on her flashlight to get a look at the figure which revealed the bones of a long-dead Dwarven citizen wrapped within a decorative robe. By the elaborate design of its clothes, she deduced it must have been a high priest or other such figurehead of position. Around the body lay several small sticks that drew her attention.

Picking one up, she discovered it operated like a fold-able fan. Though she carefully tried to open it, the paper-like material within it fell away to dust before her; its recorded contents forever lost. One after the other, they decayed into powder as she tried to examine them until she finally found one within the bony grasp of the dead priest. The panel of this particular fan was made of a thin sheet of the same bronze metal that the

Dwarfish race of the Nida preferred in their construction. Gently opening the instrument, it revealed intricate writings placed within each of its folds.

It was certainly an interesting way to preserve writing, which didn't curl and damage the pages like a scroll nor did it possess the clumsiness of a heavy tome. The items on the paper-like material had decayed but the embellished metal had survived these long eons. Turning over the body, she discovered the corpse was wearing one of the golden neck-pieces they had seen adorned by the other cadavers within the catacombs. Gently removing the heavy necklace from the body, the brittle bones fell away as she lifted up the metallic mantle.

Though tarnished by age, it was clear that the ornament was not merely cosmetic but had served some type of function. She handed it to Logan for him to examine.

"Look here, inside the chest piece," the professor motioned towards the jeweled artifact, "embedded within the metal are several disks," he noted while showing Alexander and I. They were shaped like small thick coins stacked upon one another. They seemed to serve no decorative purpose because they were on the underside of the neck plate.

"What do you suppose those are?" Alex wondered.

Logan took out his tuning fork to test a theory, but when he attempted to tap it gently, the small steel fork snapped out of his hands and attached itself to the disks. A look of surprise lit up his eyes as he turned to us.

"Whatever this is for, it appears to be highly magnetic," the professor granted as he tried to wrestle his tuning fork back. The attraction was extremely strong, considering how difficult it was for him to pry it off the neck-piece.

"It must be a type of rare-earth magnet," Mica stated.

"Like a refrigerator magnet, I get it," I added, trying to sound crafty.

"Not exactly," she brushed back, while taking a small key out of her pocket and testing it on each of the disks, "The strength of each of these appears to be significantly different ...see here," she noted while she could pull her key away from one with measured ease but had to put great effort on another to get the same result.

"That doesn't follow physics," Alex barked, "fundamentally; magnetic stacking of that fashion would naturally attain its relative field strength in balance between the others!"

"Apparently they have found a way to counter that," Logan noted on Mica's observations, "what purpose do you think this mantle serves?" he asked his assistant.

"My best guess is that it performs the same purpose as this," she stated while holding up the locker key she had used to test their field strength.

"What, a magnetic key?" Logan marveled at her theory.

"Are you able to translate these markings?" Mica asked Alexander while handing him the metallic fan. Adjusting his glasses, he took the fan over to the podium to set it down so he could use his flashlight with one hand and take notes on the other to decipher the script. He was mildly bewildered when he saw that the metal fan fit perfectly into the pie-shaped holder carved upon the stone pedestal.

"Most interesting..." Alexander stated as the fan slipped into place and he began to decipher the text engraved upon it, "this cuneiform appears wrong somehow; like its formation is jumbled out of context," he related, "it's just not making any sense."

"Here, try putting this on," Mica suggested as he handed Alex the gilded neck-piece from the dead priest. Fumbling with it, he was finally able to get the mantle over his head and resting upon his shoulders. The latch in the rear was loose enough to attach to his smaller frame, and after getting it on, Alex made another attempt at reading the text.

"There's no difference ...I just don't see how this is supposed to help," Alexander sputtered while trying to wiggle the large metal mantle into a more comfortable position upon his shoulders as he scratched at it.

"Hmm, try squatting lower," I suggested, realizing that even as short as he was, Alex still stood a good height above the heads of these dwarfish people who once resided here. Following my suggestion, Alexander awkwardly stooped until he finally surrendered to the idea I was hinting at and got down upon his knees before the short pedestal; which now brought the dais up to the level of his chest.

Looking down, he leaned forward and jerked back abruptly when the metal fan suddenly flinched and folded upon itself until only four particular leaves appeared.

"Are you doing that?" Logan queried his friend, but Alex just gazed at him in dismay.

"No, I, I was just..." he stammered for a moment until a glowing red aura appeared over the dais, emitting a shimmer like a fountain of light from the teardrop-shaped depression. Alexander sat there on his knees staring at us as if wondering what to do next.

"Search the body again; there appears to be something missing," I suggested to Mica as I pointed at the priests decomposed body where it lay in a heap upon the floor.

Rifling through its tattered clothes, Mica finally found a small leather bag and shook off the pale dust of decomposed bone. Tearing it open, she found a large smooth jewel carved in the shape of a teardrop. The opal glimmered in the light as she handed it to Alex, who gently placed it within the depression on the base before him. The delicate rose-colored light streaming from its center intensified as it flowed through the translucent gem.

We stepped back in alarm as the carved panel that represented the Asgardian domain began to slide forward, grinding roughly upon the stone floor; revealing a passage beyond. Logan cautiously peered through the cavity and into the hall behind the massive masonry block.

"Come on everyone, let's not dally," Logan cried as he ushered us to follow him into the corridor. Mica and I hopped through but turned back to see a look of worry creep across Alexander's face who thought he might be left behind. He had tried to stand up to join us but the stone doorway began to slide shut as he did so, and opened once again when he resumed his position at the pedestal.

"Hey, ah, guys ...what am I supposed to do?" Alex's voice quivered as he knelt back at the podium, afraid to move lest the doorway close and separate him from the team. We could see that he was afraid of being left abandoned there. Mica turned back to give him some advice.

"Get up slowly, and come to us," she offered with assurance.

"I tried that already," Alex yelped as he stood once again to take a step towards us and Mica jumped back into the narrow passage as the heavy stone door, once again, began to slide shut across the entrance.

"Oh my, well it appears there is a reason behind the discovery of our lone priest here within the chamber; he must have been a gatekeeper of sorts," Logan whispered to me and Mica privately behind the great slab.

"Uh, wait a moment ...try taking off that neck-piece and lay it upon the pedestal," Mica suggested, which seemed like a plausible plan.

Alexander struggled with the awkward mantle and tried to shimmy his way out of it while keeping the magnetic key in place atop the podium. He gently set it down in various positions, but each way he tried only managed to sever the source of light emanating from the gemstone; causing the doorway to slide back and forth as he fiddled with it. We jumped back each time the slab moved for fear of being crushed, while wondering what he was doing.

"What the hell Alex, just put it down and get over here!" I snapped; while I became worried about one of us getting injured during his antics.

Alex gave us a squeamish glance, and hastily fumbled with the large mantle and left it lying on the pedestal in the middle of the room, then took several clumsy strides forward and stopped halfway when the weight of the neck-piece caused it to slip, and it fell from the podium, knocking the opal gemstone from its setting in the process. He froze mid-step and turned around with a look of dread creeping upon his face as the pile of jewelry clattered to the floor. The rays of light holding the portal open extinguished and the stone doorway once again began to grind closed.

We yelled at Alex to hurry as the gap between the stone panel and the passage began to shrink. He made the poor split-second decision of trying to jump back to the pedestal to rearrange the apparatus, but suddenly chose to abandon that idea and lurched back towards us, but by then, it was too late. The gap closed as we saw the look of utter fear in Alexander's wide eyes before the stone barrier ground back into place with a final jolt. We remained there for over an hour calling through the stone block as we waited for Alexander to open it once again, but our efforts were in vain.

"It appears the gateway has cycled shut and he is unable to reopen it," Logan surmised with a look of despair at losing his friend, as we were unable to detect any noise through the slab.

"Perhaps he can find another way to reach us, but it does us no good to wait here," Mica finally admitted, while Logan and I conceded that we had to press on. I felt an uncomfortable pit in my stomach as we left the corridor; leaving Alexander Beaumont to his fate in that quiet chamber beyond our reach.

We each had a look of unmistakable weariness worn upon our faces as we slumped forward into a wide hall, decorated with bold carvings. We had discovered so many unbelievable and fantastic things, but our team had paid a heavy price along the way. The corridor we now traveled was adorned with empty vats situated among several sculptures that lined the passage, where tall effigies of warriors and priests stood towering over us in their silent gaze.

I could understand how the seeds of ancient Norse mythology could have taken root in our past as we walked here among these great statues. I lacked the appreciation that Logan and his ilk had for they're craft of studying our ancient past. Earth's ancient history hadn't really mattered to me until now but seeing what we had thus far, sparked something in my conscience which I couldn't deny. Perhaps it was the sullen guilt of how frivolous and irresponsible I had lived my life until this moment, a murky sense of shame which I felt eating away at my conscience.

The joy of exploration seemed to have been sapped from the Professor and his assistant, and I couldn't blame them. We were tired and hungry, and worn from the stress. I just wanted to get back to my bunk on the ship with a bottle of liquor, so I could drink my weariness away and pretend like this whole expedition never happened.

At this point, my flashlight was beginning to fail, so I gazed into one of the torch basins which appeared to be rimmed with a coagulated sludge. I wasn't exactly thinking straight when I fumbled for my lighter to see if I could get it to ignite, in hopes to illuminate the chamber so we could get a better glimpse of our surroundings and a chance to fix my flashlight. Logan and Mica had shambled on ahead, searching where the hallways had branched out. Thus, I was left alone to entertain myself.

A few sparks from the lighter and I was able to get a dull flame going within the basin near the wall, and took off my gloves to warm my hands as the flame slowly grew brighter. What I didn't expect was the suction of an air tube hidden within the mounted canister, which collected the flame and transferred it to the next closest wall torch. One after the other they lit, as a system of fine duct-work transferred the flame between the other canisters inserted within the grand hall. Logan and his assistant turned their heads in shock as the entire chamber came alive when wicks of yellow flame illuminated the room as though by some ancient magic.

Mica strolled over with a stern look on her face, and I was fully expecting to be scolded on my reckless behavior but our attention was turned towards a great creaking from the wall across from us. An aperture began to open in the facade, and we spun to hear a similar argument from the stonework on the opposite wall from where we stood. We both glanced towards

Logan for an answer to this mystery, but he appeared equally perplexed.

The combustible muck, which had been lining the numerous holders, began to burn away, and were replaced by a much more potent mixture which had been kept sealed from the open air in their reservoirs over these countless millennia; from which various torches began to produce a fierce blue flame. Dust fell from the ceiling, exposing a fine silver drapery of woven metal mesh which lined the entire room above our heads. This netting had been adhered to the material, and began to gently rise like wisps of clouds billowing in a summer breeze; surging ever higher above our heads.

"What's going on?" Mica breathed, baffled by what she was witnessing.

"It's these flames," Logan began with a gleam of thought twinkling in his eye, as he rubbed his chin while looking about the chamber, "...the hot air is rising and inflating the decorative drapery attached to the walls."

At first, his comment didn't make any sense, until the entire section of the roof above us unclipped from their posts and the chamber itself began to sway. Stumbling to keep our balance, we looked up to see the net-laced canopy was rising ever higher over our heads. It reminded me of a...

"It's a hot air balloon!" I finally stammered.

We lurched to one side of the narrow corridor and fell to our knees as the sound of a defiant creak ripped at our ears, while the airship tore away from its ancient moors. The hallway we had been standing in separated itself from the causeway, where it was resting, and the narrow section with the flaming braziers broke free of its anchors. The extended gondola swayed at first, leaving us desperately grasping for a handhold while the ship lifted ever higher as the envelope fully inflated and began to rise with increasing speed. Within moments, we found ourselves being lifted through a cavern of ice towards a narrow chasm high above.

"This is utterly astounding!" Logan uttered as we got to our feet and carefully plodded our way to the forward end of the walkway, which was left suspended underneath the mushroom-shaped balloon.

"How is this possible?" I uttered to myself, not realizing I was being overheard by my companions.

"That appears to be a weave of metallic mesh supported by a net of interlocking couplings," Logan noted as he pointed above into the underside of the balloon's envelope, "and that strange smell coming from the flame canisters tells me they were using some exotic mixture of fuel to create the gas necessary to attain lift for this ancient zeppelin."

"Yeah ...uh, that's great and all, but what happens when we hit the ceiling?" I urged with growing concern as I pointed upwards towards the roof of the icy cavern.

We peered into the direction we were heading, and began to feel a rising sense of panic the closer we drifted to the jagged icicles hanging above.

"Oh, this isn't going to end well..." I whispered to the others.

The ship ascended quickly up towards the cold spikes where we feared they would puncture the mesh and send us plummeting to our deaths below. The silver material of the metallic balloon brushed the bottom-most layer of ice, snapping off several pieces which sent a shower of shards cascading over the edge of the umbrella above us. Suddenly, the gondola tilted sharply and the airship was brought to a level altitude. We had no idea what was controlling its course.

The floating ship began to move forward through a narrow chasm within the glacier; its fringe frequently rubbing along the inner edges of the crevasse, leaving a glittering trail of ice particles in its wake.

"Look, over there!" Mica exclaimed with excitement as a gleam of sunlight burst through the fissure before us.

Our path took us into a passage of sparkling shards that crossed to interlock overhead, forming a wide passage for the airship to travel. Beyond these massive translucent shards were walls of blue ice and compacted snow, which gave way to open sunlight gleaming in through their panes, as if it were some type of mythical cathedral made entirely of glass.

"That's not ice, that's rock crystal!" Logan announced as Mica stepped forward as they examined the formations which created the protective barrier for the corridor, "The people of this lost world were able to grow minerals into any form they required, such as this highway for their airships..." Logan led off with his errant thoughts about this advanced society, but was unable to finish his sentence.

Ahead of us, there was a breach in the crystal passage where the cold wind howled in the morning light, and a fresh breeze now entered the great corridor. There was a look of mixed excitement and worry in Mica's eyes as we approached the open breach. It took a moment to appreciate the danger that would be upon us within the next few minutes, as the course of the airship itself would become a slave to the direction of the surface winds. If the burning flames of the braziers were to be blown out by the arctic gale, we could be sent crashing to the ground and lost among a vast continent of snow and ice, even if we somehow survived the fall.

"Allen, use your radio and see if you can contact our ship!" the professor ordered as he turned to me.

Realizing we had finally reached the surface, I fumbled for my radio to check the open frequencies.

"Mayday, mayday, this is Allen. Is anyone on this channel?" I blurted while hearing nothing but broken static in the wake of the call, "Ah, we might be too far from the ship," I began to whine to the others as I changed to our backup frequency, "Walter, are you there? This is the Logan Expedition; we are requesting a rescue team for an emergency evacuation."

We gave one another a look of despair, realizing that we may have either traveled far out of radio range or were suffering interference from the inclement weather. The storm clouds we had encountered back at our base site by the giant tree were now distant upon the horizon, but there was no guarantee the blizzard wouldn't turn our way and sweep the airship deeper into the Antarctic wilderness. There was a sudden click of static from the radio and Walter's voice came over the air, garbled as it was.

"This is Sir Walter, do you read me?"

"Yes, Walter! This is Allen, I'm here with Mica and the Professor; we need to be retrieved immediately, over," I cried through the heavy static.

"What are your coordinates?" Walter inquired as he sat in the radio room of the ship scanning over layers of charts spread before him.

"Uh, yeah ...we aren't quite sure about that," I shrugged as I looked to Logan for advice. We were rapidly closing in on the breach in the passage but couldn't see any familiar landmarks across the vast plain of broken ice.

"Turn on your transponder and it will give us your GPS coordinates," Walter remarked as he leaned over to flip on the receiver at his console, "Alexander has it in his bag, it's the black and yellow striped box," he noted as a reminder.

All three of us looked at one another in despair, knowing that Alex had dropped all of his equipment into the half-sunken city of the giants where it still laid on the murky bottom of that cold lake. There was no way for the crew to triangulate our signal between the ship and ...well, wherever the hell we were. The fact was, we could only guess that we were somewhere on the vast eastern windswept plains of Antarctica. We had lost most of our equipment and had no way of giving our exact position; especially with the thick storm clouds veiling the horizon.

"Unfortunately, we kind of misplaced the transponder," I clicked back over the radio, trying not to sound so disappointed but failing miserably in my effort.

"Can you see the shoreline, or any mountain ranges from your position that you can describe?" Walter begged, feeling hopeless as he sat in the radio room, where he had bunked for the past several days without a wink of sleep since his comrades went missing in action.

I tried to see what I could outside the walls, but the thick crystal structures warped the field of view beyond the tunnel. As we got within several dozen meters of the breach in the passage, the ship was captured in a suction of cool air, which started to quicken our pace towards the rift. The gondola began to sway violently and I almost lost my grip on the radio and nearly dropped it over the edge. We each grabbed onto something solid and held on for dear life as the airship was drawn through the break and out into the open weather, where we were buffeted by high winds.

Expecting the worst, we grabbed onto one another and used our straps to clip a short safety harness between us, in case one of us slipped overboard. The balloon rose ever higher above the whitewashed terrain until the winds eased and the ship started to level off. We glanced at the decorative burning canisters, hoping they would last a while longer until we could find a familiar shore. Our luck didn't last, as we encountered brutal wind sheers from the storm that began to toss the airship about as it glided through the open sky, far beyond its protective crystal highway left below.

When the ship finally began to settle, I looked down to notice that we seemed to still be heading in the same direction of the crystal passage directly below us, evidence of which eventually sunk once again beneath the thick cover of ice and snow. Our pace appeared steady, and it soon became clear to us that we were no longer drifting freely with the wind but that our airship appeared to be set on a defined course.

"I would swear that this vessel is actually going against the direction of the wind," Logan declared in astonishment. We each took a glance at the storm and realized he was right. The airship was actively countering the heavy gale.

The gondola swayed erratically from time to time, sending us tumbling for a handhold, and being tossed about like rag dolls did nothing good for our stomachs. We eventually secured seats to keep from losing our footing each time the ship began to sway, and we sat there huddling in the cold winds for what seemed like hours. I tried to reach Walter back on the ship several more times by radio but finally gave up on the effort so as not to entirely drain the battery. Eventually, our airship entered calm winds, and Logan unstrapped his harness. He stood up from our group and stumbled slowly towards the edge of the ship, in an effort to scrutinize something of interest on the horizon which had grabbed his attention. Staring through his frost-caked hood, his old worn eyes opened in wonder.

"Look, look over there!" Logan cried with his cracked voice, made dry from the biting cold.

Mica and I rose to our feet to reach his side to see what the professor was babbling about. Standing out from the bleak horizon was a mountain of ice, like a colossal spike piercing the cloudy sky. Nightfall was fast approaching, and stars glimmered through the dancing curtains of aurora lights which fluttered like veils of untethered rainbows above us. It was a beautiful sight to behold but what had drawn the professor's attention was even more amazing.

The closer our airship approached the spire, a strange formation of blue crystal towers began to appear poking above the mountain ahead. It looked as though a giant crystalline castle had once been consumed by snow and ice, which had formed over its structure; masking it from view. It now lay partially exposed to the world once again; uncovered like the iron tree which had freed itself from its icy veil, where it had been entombed for countless centuries.

"It's a castle!" Mica exclaimed as the breath from her tired lungs condensed in the cool air.

The ship steered directly towards this spire, as if some hidden mechanism guided its course. Logan presumed it must be some sort of magnetic technology that had been lost to the ages which directed the airship and guided our way. He assumed the crystal passage still existed somewhere below us, now veiled by untold layers of compacted snow. As I scanned the horizon, I began to wonder how many other towers like this might be hidden within the surrounding glaciers.

The airship slowed and came to berth within an enclosure on

the uppermost tower. Pockets of ice shattered as the gondola docked with the icy decking which surrounded the high turret. We stepped off the ship, glad to have found solid ground beneath our feet once again. A moment after we disembarked, the docking clamp began to deflate the collapsing canopy and pulled the ship down into the enclosure hidden between the tightly woven towers, leaving us standing precariously high above upon the tower balcony.

The material of the building appeared to be made of something hard like glass but was thick and crystalline in its composition, and it made me wonder if this fortress could possibly be a product of the mineral farms we had seen.

"Allen, come help me, lad," Logan grunted as he struggled with a doorway he had found, "this hatch is frozen shut."

I took out Tom's old knife and chipped away at the encrusted ice around the seams of the doors, and we gave it another try. After a few minutes of effort, we were able to crack the entry and forced it open wide enough for us to gain access. The condensed vapor that expelled from the opening revealed that the interior environment was a great deal warmer than the freezing temperatures outside. After several minutes inside, it soon became warm enough that we had to open our jackets just to cool off.

"Do you think this citadel might be that Asgard place you were talking about?" I asked Logan as we circled the main room while admiring the strange architecture and decor.

"I would imagine so, Allen," the professor answered, "but there is no way to tell at the moment."

"What do you make of this?" Mica inquired as we were drawn to her side of the chamber. She was standing in front of an elaborate carving of a tree engraved upon one of the depressed panels along the wall.

"Ah, the symbol of the world tree," Logan cited, "and quite an exquisite design at that," he admired the motif.

Mica ran her hands down the trail of the carving while looking for any clues the pattern might reveal. When she touched an emblem at the center of the tree where they branched apart, the lines of the engraving began to glow, growing outward from the source of the emblem until the light reached the outermost tips of the sculpture. We jumped back when the room began to hum and the ground shifted below our feet. Retreating to the center of the room, the floor began to slowly spin; winding its way down through the tower, similar to the way we had seen the capstone function within the first set of ruins.

The levels of the citadel disappeared above us as we were drawn deeper into the fortress, however, where we eventually ended up was a place so astounding that even Logan was at a loss for words. The platform came to rest in the middle of a great chamber lit by several fissures in the compacted snow, which was now high above our heads. A ring of steps led us off the circular lift and into the opening of a great forest residing beneath the castle.

We stepped off the platform and into the woodland, noticing something peculiar. Their branches were all dead, twisted and intertwined as they stretched unnaturally along the walls like vines but were bare of any leaves, which gave them the appearance of roots seeking out the inner depths. Several stems lay broken among the ground, shattered into pieces. Mica gathered one to take a sample, and it was then that she noticed a most peculiar detail.

"These trees are petrified," she exclaimed as she dropped the branch of stone to her feet. She went from tree to tree, feeling the grain of the bark which had solidified. The forest of stone was as silent as death; their cold bare branches reaching out through the shadows like dark fingers. The fable Logan had sought to find had been left here, buried and forgotten. The forest of the old gods was dead, but there were still the mysteries of this crystal keep to explore.

The Fallen

It was a riddle as to why there was a forest located beneath the crystal castle. Logan himself, was at a loss to explain its presence, given his thorough studies on the ancient lore which surrounded this place. The field wasn't entirely underground, for sunlight could have made its way into the grove through the crystalline walls which were now covered with ice and snow. It must have been quite a garden during the era of this unique culture when their community was alive and thriving.

Now all that was left was dust and bones, and the musty ghost of death which filled the air with its stale perfume among these scattered ruins. There was no escaping that this civilization may have once rivaled our own and it was humbling to realize, that despite all their great achievements, that they were now long forgotten. The very existence of these people and their great accomplishments opened a great void in our recorded history, which was what worried the professor so.

"One of the challenges the scientific community faces is the release of hard evidence, such as this, into the public arena because of the subjective social and religious ramifications, and the scrutiny we would face," Logan contended with the realities they would cope with once they got back to the mainland, "there are many powerful governments around the globe, which are either restrained or swayed in some part by those secretive foundations, who care not about fact-based education but rely instead, on fabrications and propaganda as a means to control the general populace."

What the professor suggested made more sense than naught; for even I could imagine a handful of modern religious institutions that would outright deny any discovery of an ancient civilization that predates or counters their biblical text and sacred doctrines, and would declare such findings as outright blasphemy. Including the fact, that those governments which relied on the continuance of their citizens to believe in a certain faith or political viewpoints, might lose face when their populous starts asking questions they don't wish to comment upon. For such unscrupulous regimes, it was always far easier to bury the truth than it was to answer to it.

Mica fully understood Logan's viewpoint, for she too had seen how a vast majority of researchers and experts in their fields would readily turned a blind eye and took a stance of silence whenever their jobs or funding was put at risk by a higher power. They cared more about their careers and reputation rather than holding to their principles as scientists. Logan was not one of those who were weak of heart, and neither was his assistant. Their moral fiber gave me the incentive to reconcile my own beliefs and to take a stand for what I knew was right.

"Well, you won't be facing any community of scientists or the glaring spotlight of their scrutiny if we don't make it out of this place alive," I begged for the professor to consider.

"True Allen, very true," Logan remarked, "Let us see where this path might lead and try to take our chances to reach the ship again," he offered.

The twisting path along the dead grove was littered with dust and debris, some of which I found partially disturbed. Leaning down, I could see fresh prints in the thick powder from some type of animal I could not identify.

"What is it, Allen?" Mica asked as she passed me by, noticing my momentary distraction.

"I don't know ...it might be nothing," I answered as I brushed my hands clean of the dry soil while we followed in Logan's shadow.

At the far end of the grove, we approached a massive structure that appeared to be a grand tree made of a coarse white crystal. Its branches filled the space above us in its canopy as its thick limbs seemed to penetrate into the roof which supported the castle above. It looked oddly familiar to the iron tree we had seen above ground at our first base camp; mimicking the design of every branch and twig of its larger counterpart. At its base was a small sphere of red marble which sat in stark contrast to the pale ivory trunk before us. Logan was the first to approach the strange artifact.

"There are runes carved into this! Mica, come take a few pictures for the record," he ordered to his assistant.

Mica stepped forward and took several shots with her camera from different angles of the blood-red sphere, which was vaguely the diameter of a beach ball. Fine symbols were engraved into its surface. It sat in a shallow glass-like bowl, very similar to the one we had found on the elevator lift that crashed within the ice-filled channel. Mica examined the bowl while Logan attempted to decipher the symbols on the rose-colored stone.

"I no longer have that bracelet key which activated the lift, and this orb doesn't seem to want to shift very easily," Mica admitted as she attempted to roll the stone ball in place to get a look at its underside.

"Let me take a look," I offered to the two of them as I glanced at the setup. I had worked on machines before and this appeared to function as a simple ball bearing, but one which had lost its lubricant to function properly, "this is only a guess, but it looks to me like its conductor has all dried up." I noted off the top of my head.

"Allen, give me your canteen," Mica pressed as her eyes widened at my suggestion. I was thinking that some sort of grease would be needed to move the sphere in its socket but she apparently wanted to try using water in its place.

I handed her my nearly empty canteen, and she gently poured the last of its contents around the edge of the crimson sphere where the water seeped into the recesses of the basin. Taking her flashlight from her pocket, she unscrewed the end cap and removed the batteries within. With a note of caution, she touched one of the ends to the stone, but nothing happened.

"Maybe try putting the positive end of one battery on that side and a negative end on the other," I blurted as a suggestion.

It was a crude approach to the problem, but I could see what she was trying to do. Mica only needed a spark to jumpstart the device. There was a click as the batteries touched the water in which the stone sphere rested and the orb lit up like a neon light. The symbols began to glow a searing white as the orb spun freely in place as it floated in the shallow pool of water, and came to rest with a ring of three circles at its top.

"Well, that's certainly interesting," Logan exclaimed, but he couldn't help himself from touching the central ring. When his finger made contact with it, a woman's face made from fine beads of light, appeared above the crimson sphere within the recess of the tree. In shock, Logan withdrew his hand as a voice emanated from the glowing mask.

"Jotunn, modir o'jord..." it began to announce in a tranquil feminine voice which held an underlying tone of authority. The words that followed didn't make as much sense as the first incantation, so Logan tried his hand at adjusting the device to see what it would do if he touched the other rings. However, as he did so, the words she spoke became clear to him. Withdrawing his hand in surprise, the words again returned to an ancient gibberish until he once again placed his hand upon the vibrant sphere.

"...and so it was the beginning of the end of our people and our way of life because we could not see with our eyes, nor hear with our ears, the sacred voice of nature calling to us." The strange image finished its chant.

"Hmm, I wonder how this works," Logan spat as he fiddled with the orb as he tried to turn it, "I can hear the words clearly when I'm in physical contact with this device."

"What did it say?" Mica leaned forward and touched the red sphere at his side, trying to hear what the avatar said.

"I will repeat myself, young one..." the glowing image of the woman answered to her and Logan's utter surprise, "The life-giver and mother of the earth called forth to her people and warned of a time of change and reckoning, but we did not heed these omens, and so it was the beginning of the end of our people and our way of life because we could not see with our eyes, nor hear with our ears, the sacred voice of nature calling to us." The voice finished its mantra once again.

"She, I mean, *it*, heard me?" Mica blundered aloud in shock as she turned to Logan who was equally amazed.

"I did, young one," the image answered.

"How is it that we can understand their dialect?" Mica again spoke to herself in wonder, still in disbelief of this ancient technology which was thousands of centuries old could match, if not surpass, their modern computers. This device appeared to be comprised of little more than water, crystal, and stone, yet it struck them as nothing less than pure magic. Mica turned back and ushered me over to touch the marbled orb beside them since I couldn't understand what they were hearing.

"You now touch the heart stone, a source of both learning, and healing, and understanding amongst our many races and tribes," the woman spoke, "as long as you touch the stone, the wisdom of our elders can be passed through the third eye to translate and share our knowledge among the tongues of many peoples, from those of distant lands beyond the sea and sky."

"This device must use some form of psychic interface for communication, which relies on bio-physical contact with this apparatus in front of us to fulfill that function," Logan surmised as his assistant concurred with his hypothesis. His statement went unnoticed by the interactive image of the woman.

"Well, this is your chance, Doc; ask it something," I urged while I nudged his shoulder.

"We have traveled through many of your great cities which now lie in ruin. Tell us what this place is and what became of your once-thriving civilization?" Logan inquired. However, there followed a moment of awkward silence before it spoke again, but we all kept our hands touching the device so we wouldn't miss the answer.

"Many moons ago, before the time of bitter winds and ice, it is true that our green lands were once lush with life and our people were prosperous. However, the six domains of the great lands were threatened by the Trinity," the voice mentioned as six broken semi-circles appeared around the three rings Logan had touched on the orb, "during the conflict that arose, in our efforts to defend our frontiers, we seized the great weapon of the Trinity which had split apart as hostilities reached their climax."

Logan had remembered the tale which the great mural had foretold of this event, and here it was being confirmed. These vast lands had once seen great violence which engulfed the entire continent, but the cost of peace had come in the form of a perpetual winter which had stolen all life and ravaged everything from its mountain peaks to its quiet shores.

"We understood as much, but what happened after that great battle?" The professor inquired, eager for an answer.

"We used our enemies own weapon to fell the great wall of earth and stone against the vanquished; who then fled back across the bitter seas from whence they came. However, after the conflict was abated, tensions rose between the remaining domains as the dreadful weapon we had acquired was deemed too powerful for any single clan to possess; so the great sphere was split apart and shared equally among them."

The image of the woman's face was replaced by a circle of six rings, which displayed spheres within spheres that were separated into half a dozen sections.

"But these weapons were cursed, as their very presence fed suspicion and strife, and created rivalries where peace and balance had once existed before. Thus it was declared that the energy these weapons harvested would be better served as a resource of creation rather than that of destruction. Although, the wisdom which gave birth to this age of freedom soon passed, and in its place were bred the seeds of conflict," the face within the tree delivered, "brothers and sisters of our lands pitted against one another, and those that were vanquished, were condemned to servitude."

"But everyone is dead now, we have seen their tombs. How was it that these thriving lands are now locked in a perpetual season of ice?" Mica asked the mystical interface, while the professor appeared to support her question with an eager nod.

"The great weapon we captured from our adversaries was repurposed to serve the six ruling domains, but the danger of their use was never diminished. There came a time when this divided artifact was once again synchronized to operate within the boundaries of its original design," the glowing face remarked, "as this device harnessed the soul of the earth, there came an era when the bleeding of these sacred energies began to awaken great powers we had not foreseen, and our folly caused the beginning of a great catastrophe to displace the islands in the sky."

"She means the stars," Mica noted, "She might very well be speaking of the polar shift, which caused the equator to reposition eons ago when the continents were not yet divided into their current global positions as we see them today."

"Did anyone survive this great cataclysm when the position of the stars changed?" Logan inquired regarding their rather mundane perspective of the massive continental shift. Again, awkward silence followed his question as if it was gathering data until the interface responded once again.

"During the time of the terrible war between the nine known domains and the great wall was shaken to fall upon our enemies; it was within these blocks of ancient earth and stone where our scholars discovered evidence of a civilization that predated our own by countless millennia," the voice of the device revealed much to Logan's sheer surprise, "These voices from the past told of a cycle of change upon our world from which the many races of men must begin anew as children. These same signs and portents revealed themselves once more, warning us of the dangers we were to face in our era, but to our shame, the words of our elders fell upon deaf ears."

"Astounding!" Logan cried, "This ancient society uncovered evidence of an even older civilization which existed before their own which had also fallen victim to the polar shift."

"Are you saying it was those magnetic spheres ...those orb devices which siphoned the energies of the earth itself, that caused the catastrophe which decimated your people?" Mica asked the glowing interface.

"Although the great weapon was split among each of the domains and was thought to have been rendered harmless, we did not expect the soul of the earth would awaken it once again. The wisdom of those who came before us had laid buried beneath our feet, but their lost voices had remained silent far too long before we finally realized what we had done," the glowing maiden confessed, "The warmth of the sun fled us to rest upon the horizon, and cold winds stripped the trees of our lush jungles and forest. Those of us that survived escaped underground and used the living earth to protect ourselves during this time of tragedy and strife. The sacred tree is a symbol of equilibrium to the Asga; for what is above is also below, which bears the fruit of life. Fire and wind above as water and earth below; all parts which cradle the element of life. With no place to turn, our people abandoned this sanctuary to find another home where they could hope to flourish once again," the woman finished.

Upon hearing that revelation we each removed our hands from the red orb to contemplate what we had learned. These ancient people had used the captured science of a foreign enemy against themselves, which in turn, had exposed an even older culture predating them from beneath the ruins of that great battle when the mountainside collapsed. They had then divided the captured weapon among their peoples believing they had disarmed it, but when the cycle of polar shifts commenced once again, the results were disastrous. The parted weapon they had seized forged a resonance within the geomagnetic poles, which had spun the earth into an unstable position and cast the continents into a new bearing.

Mica knew there were geologic anomalies around the world that still remained unexplained even to this day, but this revelation shed new light upon those unanswered mysteries. Great forests withered into desert dunes swept by oceans of sand while snow and ice befell once parched lands; sterilizing them in its cold embrace. The world itself had tumbled out of alignment, killing off countless species in a great extinction event. But in their wisdom, this ancient culture sought balance in the turmoil, for the great tree was the representation of life which bound all other elements as one.

Their core theology wasn't based on the acts of men nor of nature, but they had found divinity in the creation of life itself. It was a profound thought that took a while to sink in. The giant iron tree topside, this crystal tree before us, and the various symbols thereof we had seen; we had taken far too absolute. The tree wasn't a deity to them; it was simply a symbol of hope.

The problem we were facing now was evident and stretched far beyond our own survival upon this continent of ice. Once again, a polar shift had been creeping upon the age of men and we had inadvertently triggered the device that harnessed the geomagnetic fields; accelerating the conversion. It was that realization which sent us reeling with regret. In our efforts to escape the icy tomb of this forgotten world we had nudged the day of reckoning ever closer, putting billions of lives at risk.

"Logan, ask that thing if there is a way we can turn off the electric sphere we activated!" I spat at the professor.

Once again, Logan placed his hand upon the crimson stone and pressed the central ring, but nothing happened. Trying several more times, he became aggravated that it wouldn't activate the interface we had spoken with moments before.

"Well criminy!" Logan barked, "I can't get this thing to turn back on!"

Mica looked through her pack and found a spare set of batteries, but the process she had used before to jump-start the device failed to work a second time. Clearly vexed by this change of events, Logan tried to spin the red stone ball and began tracing the symbols in an attempt to activate anything that could get the device working again. Unfortunately, the only thing that happened was that a crystal slate on the far wall lifted to expose a doorway, so Logan forced himself to be satisfied with that outcome.

"Well, that's better than nothing I suppose..." I whispered.

We were all suffering from exhaustion at this point and couldn't endure much more of this strain pushing ourselves. Mica had used the last of our water to activate the AI device within the crystal tree, making me wonder if we had only days or mere hours left before we eventually succumbed to fatigue.

As we passed into the newly exposed corridor, I noticed the sound of something scampering through the petrified grove behind us but passed it off as ambient noise grating at my nerves. Beyond the breach the passage came up short, leaving us in a chamber with a spiral staircase that hugged the outer wall of the spire. Each of the levels we passed through were filled with an assortment of oddities that appeared to be items of studies and research. It wasn't until we hit the uppermost floor where we stumbled across something which spiked Logan's interest.

Sitting on the edge of a crescent-shaped table stood the model of an orb with several cross-sections removed. It sat within an exact replica of the holding base we had seen supporting the first rotating sphere we encountered.

"Most fascinating," Logan exclaimed as he began to remove the inner pieces, which fit together like a puzzle box, "these spheres appear to nestle within one another and were separated into nearly equal parts," he noted, seeing how they fit like a globe within a globe, each one getting progressively smaller.

"This resembles the theoretical model of the inner core of the Earth," Mica gestured towards the device which floated within the bowl-shaped support.

"I see ...now that would make sense. If each of these layers spun freely from one another they would create the effects of a dynamo, which would generate a magnetic wave," Logan added, "what if our planet is not merely an iron core spinning in a pool of magma as geologist speculate, but instead, resembles this intricate model here?"

Mica took a close study of the inner pieces and how they

merged as one and realized what she had been missing all along.

"Take a cube, its top, bottom, and four sides, right?" She proclaimed, "Now take that fundamental six-sided shape and smooth it into a circle," she pointed towards the individual globes which nestled into one another, "each side is needed to correspond to a place or coordinates in a three-dimensional space. However, in a sphere shape like our own or any other planet, they are interlocked in motion, acting like a gyroscope. Yet sometimes these points fall in and out of sync; much like our own Sun's solar maximum and minimum, but on a much greater scale of time."

I wasn't keen on the scientific data Mica was referring to, so I just nodded my head in agreement like an idiot; pretending as if I understood what she was saying. Logan, on the other hand, seemed quite absorbed with her hypothesis. It made sense to him, for the fact that there was a visual model in front of them to confirm her deduction.

"A geomagnetic collector and energy distributor in one elegant design..." Logan postulated the idea of it as his eyes went glassy with the mental strain of calculating the possibilities.

"So let me get this straight," I interrupted the two researchers, "this model with all these hollow metals spheres within it, might be a replica of this acclaimed 'great weapon' that glowing woman out there was spouting off about, and it was parted out for use as some sort of energy source for each of the six kingdoms across the Antarctic?"

"Well, she noted them as 'domains' instead of kingdoms; but that's pretty much accurate," the professor granted.

"And even though they were separated, each part continued to serve the same function by creating some sort of sympathetic or electromagnetic resonance," Mica added.

"So that thing you ...I mean, that 'we' activated," I corrected to not sound like a pretentious dick, "will eventually trigger the other five energy orbs?"

"That's the theory," Logan admitted, "from what I understood from that interface down in the grove."

Looking around the room for more information on this artifact, Mica found a map of the Antarctic shelf which displayed the way it had appeared in days long past. Great forests and valleys encompassed the central mountain peaks and coastal ranges to the north surrounded by large rolling plains to either side. The high ridge mountain range the interface had referred to during its dialog as the 'Great Wall' stretched the entire expanse, leaving east Antarctica as a large kidney-shaped continent with several large island masses snaking into the oceans off to the west. This, apparently, was from whence their adversaries titled as the Trinity, had emerged.

The locations of each of the six energy orbs were shown upon the map before us, where she pointed at one in the territory called the Jotu.

"Come over here and take a look at this!" Mica called out in an excited voice.

"My, my, a map of the lost continent," Logan breathed as his attention stirred when his eyes fell upon it, "here is the ritual tree we had found near the outer banks ...and here is the route we must have taken to reach the river which led to the city of giants, and here is the Nida, the province of the Dwarves, as Allen put it," the professor stated as he turned to me with a smile.

"And there," I pointed, "is Asgard, where we are now!" I mentioned while noting the image of a white tree enclosed by a crystal spire.

There were several more outposts and castles lined alongside the eastern territories with but a few that were noted to the far west. Apparently, the high mountain range was an impassable barrier between the two lands during their era. Looking closely at the symbols etched upon the map, Logan went back to the model to reference the strange markings.

"Ah, this one here," the professor asserted as he examined the largest orb and the symbol marked upon it. Noting its design, Mica scoured the map and found it at the castle of Asga.

"Apparently, it's located here somewhere!" Mica uttered in excitement.

"That makes sense," Logan admitted as he rubbed his chin, "the great temple of Asgard was the most esteemed city in ancient legends and would be granted the largest of the orbs by its supreme position among its allies," he noted.

"This is a pretty big place, Doc," I mentioned, "Is there some sort of diagram around here which shows where it might be located within this complex?"

Searching around the chamber, we found nothing that hinted upon its position in or around the towers, but Mica logically assumed that we would likely find it under the foundation. Her conclusion made sense, as we had found the first one at the bottom of a deep tunnel under the sunken temple of the giants. That one was in a state of low power, as if on standby before we accidentally woke it from its long slumber. Our plan now was to disable the main globe, presuming it had an 'off' switch.

There was a rumble through the castle, and shards of ice broke free from its walls as we braced ourselves from the sudden tremor. We glanced at one another in worried shock, which slowly turned to a realization that the source of the quake was likely the activation of the geomagnetic conductor. As if on cue, the lower edge of the room lit up with power and several contraptions began to move at random; telling us the energy sphere located beneath this very fortress had awoken.

"Uh doc, just a question," I asked Logan as we steadied our feet after the tremor passed, "so what exactly happens when all six of these energy orbs are triggered, worst-case scenario?" I was afraid to ask.

"Hmm ...that's a question that my assistant can best explain," he responded as he motioned towards Mica. With a sharp look in her eyes, she tried to illustrate the effects. Looking around the room, she came to realize that although this ancient culture possessed an amazing level of technology, that they likely hadn't expanded into a space-faring race and had no global view of the Earth itself. Regardless; she used several bits of metal and odd items stacked about the tables to recreate the relative position of our continents on a rudimentary map.

"It is theorized that a polar shift merely flips the earth's magnetic poles," she offered with a glance my way to confirm I was following, so I gave her a nod that I understood, "the problems which arise during such an epic event, is that cosmic radiation and solar winds would have a devastating effect on plant and animal life during that time period when the veil of our planet's magnetic field is greatly weakened."

"How long does such an event take, and what could we do to counter it," I asked with a raised brow.

"Nobody knows the true span of time it takes; it could be months, years, or decades, or more ...it's just not known, but during that period of vulnerability, radiation bombarding us from space would very likely cause irreversible genetic damage to the flora and fauna of the entire ecosystem. Besides the point, that the levels of solar and galactic emissions we would suffer, would effectively crash every power grid and global communication network on the planet," she added in for spice.

"So ...that's bad," I responded.

"Oh, very bad," she quipped back, "human civilization itself would need to relocate underground in order to shield us from the catastrophic effects of the unfiltered solar winds. However, we're also talking about a significant depletion of the oxygen levels we are accustomed to, while our atmosphere would be stripped away into space. So yes, it's pretty bad."

"From the diagrams' Mica's predecessor has shared with me in the past," Logan interjected, "was that a warming of our climate would spike during such a polar shift. Given that over 40% of the world's population lives among continental shorelines, the death toll alone would be in the billions, however, the ripple effect from the aftermath upon our global infrastructure would collapse us back into the dark ages,"

"So ...it's *super* bad," I conceded with a lump in my throat while both Mica and Logan nodded in agreement as another aftershock from the tremor rattled the tower.

Hunted

As we were searching for a diagram of the tower in our effort to locate this alpha orb which was alleged to be present somewhere within the complex, we heard the sound of a scuffle and the racket of several items breaking on the level below us. The three of us glanced at one another with a look of concern as I took out my pistol and crept back down the staircase while I motioned for Logan and Mica to be as silent as possible. The commotion coming from below continued as I tiptoed down to the lower level. Once I arrived at the landing, I saw a shadow dash through the room as several artifacts went skidding across the floor in its wake.

Being a little jumpy as it was, I backed up the stairway to my companions and informed them that I had observed something large moving down there, and quickly suggested we should try to find a way out of the tower.

"What did you see?" Mica inquired with more of a spark of enthusiasm than the occasion called for.

"I'm not quite sure," I noted to her clear disappointment, "but it was big and fast," I answered, "it's best we not dally here and find a way higher up where we can get to a lockable door or create a blockade of some sort."

We had already been through encounters with giant bats, enormous spiders, and other strange creatures and I was trying to be vigilant about encountering something equally unfriendly. The level immediately above us in the research lab where we had been studying the models of the orbs was a large vaulted chamber which connected to a skywalk, bridging between several adjacent towers. Going for the doorway, we turned as we heard a strange high-pitched clatter coming from behind us on the landing; sounding eerily similar to a rattlesnake. Creeping slowly up over the last few steps, we saw a strange creature which appeared to be an oversized hound covered with white and gray patterns across its scaled hide, with thick tufts of fur riddled across its back, were there lifted several sharp erect needles from its bony spine when its eyes fell upon us.

I almost dropped my gun at the frightful sight of it, and Mica couldn't help but let out a stifled yelp of fear as the creature let out a horrific hiss from between the rows of sharply pointed tusks lining its jaw. It glared through crimson eyes, which shifted between the three of us like a predator sizing up its prey. I took a stance and fired a shot but missed in my haste. The ricochet caught the edge of a metal table nearby and the bullet zipped past its head. Instead of scaring it away, this act of aggression appeared to enrage the creature. Its spinal ridges stood erect and began to vibrate, causing the source of the quickened high-pitched rattle.

Logan and Mica stepped back against the far wall as I tried to steady my feet to take another shot but the beast seemed to anticipate my attack. Its blood-red eyes turned towards me alone as it singled me out as the immediate threat, and darted behind cover. The thing was quick, and its low profile made it hard to track as it crept among the pedestals and tables spread across the chamber.

Tom hadn't brought any extra bullets with his holster so I was trying to be conservative with the ammo, realizing I only had another handful of shots before we would be left helpless. The beast launched itself upon one of the tables to get a look at us, and just as quickly, jumped back down for cover as I turned towards it. Its gleaming lidless eyes were horrible to behold, giving it the soulless look of a serpent.

"Mica, go for the doorway and get out of here," I barked under my breath toward my two companions as I motioned for Logan to follow her.

They took several cautious steps towards the exit to reach the skywalk just as the beast began to turn my way. The door pivoted open on a central point as Mica edged her way through it, with Logan close behind while a gust of cold wind blew through the chamber from the open portal. The chilled air coursing through the room drew the creature's attention back towards my two companions, and the beast could see it's newly found meal was attempting to flee.

Once again, it pounced upon a nearby table to gain the high ground and turned toward Mica and the Professor as they made their escape. Positioned between us, I realized I couldn't take a shot while they were both in the line of fire, so I did something stupid and picked up a small sculpture lying upon a stand, and heaved it at the monstrosity.

Hitting it on its rump, the beast turned to hiss at me again in annoyance while its spines rattled. Its evil glare and its stance told me I was now considered first on the menu, so I retreated down the stairway just enough until I was sure I could turn my back and make a run for it. I had learned that predators were excited by the flight of prey, so I took the chance that this scaled hound would pursue me, rather than my friends. My bet paid off.

"Run for it!" I yelled over to Logan as he and Mica slipped out onto the bridge.

I scampered to the level below back into the chamber with the orbs and various contraptions, looking for a place to hide. I tripped and knocked over several items on a nearby table while trying to regain my balance; completely losing all initiative of cloaking my path. The creature cautiously made its way down the steps in pursuit, smelling the scent of my fear as it lingered in the stale air.

I tried as best as I could to be covert and as quiet as possible, but my heavy breath and racing heartbeat had become obstacles to achieving that end. I crouched behind a table attached to the back wall, only to realize that I had likely cornered myself. Peering around the edge of the counter, I sought another avenue to make my way past the lizard-like hound and back up the stairway. When I noticed the beasts long tail slink behind a nearby table, I quickly scurried back the way I came in.

It took only moments for the demon dog to notice I had fled once again, and it came scampering in hot pursuit as its talons slid upon the glassy floor. Dashing to reach the stairway, I blindly toppled several objects from the tables behind me in a vain attempt to slow the beast down. As I reached the top landing, I turned just in time to see the creature leap for my throat. In a flash, I tripped on the last step and came down hard on my back while the beast's sleek belly skimmed past my face as it missed its mark.

In a moment of dread, I realized that I had dropped the gun and reached out to grab it. Glancing back for but a split-second, the face of the creature filled my vision, its jagged sharp fangs clacking while its spine rattled as I lay there frozen in fear. Suddenly, the scaly mutt gave out a strange cry as its head jerked backward, so I took that opportunity to grab the pistol off the floor and scampered to my knees.

I looked up to see Mica, standing a meter away as the beast glared at her. There was a long metal lance sticking out of its backside which had partially crippled the beast. A pale look washed across her face in that frozen moment, and Mica could tell that she had only seconds to live as the creature turned its vengeful gaze towards her for the injury she had inflicted.

It crouched low preparing to pounce upon her, and before I knew it, I had fired two shots into its torso. The creature turned once to glare at me in dismay, as if surprised by the wounds it had received, and suddenly fell onto its side upon the table. Mica and I both stood there stunned for a breathless moment as we slowly approached its corpse; wondering what it was I had just killed. I was about to say something to her when the creature twitched. Out of a nervous reaction, I emptied another bullet into its body as I nearly jumped out of my skin in panic.

"I think it's dead now..." Mica whispered as she stepped over to calmly lower my trembling arm as I stood there aiming at it with the pistol.

"What the hell is this thing?" I asked, but knowing full well she had no clue either, "Where is Logan?"

"The walkway outside connects between three towers, and he's attempting to gain access into one of them now but I came back to see if you needed any help," she explained.

"Well ...ah, thanks," I stuttered, looking for the right words of gratitude but completely failing, "you saved my ass there."

"This is certainly a strange genetic mix," Mica noted as she dared to get closer to the animals' corpse to examine it, "it has the basic features of a large canine, yet has an extended snout like a crocodile, along with scaled plated skin like a reptile, yet it possesses hair like a mammal," she began to speculate as to how this creature could have evolved into such a complex monstrosity upon this isolated wasteland.

I pulled out the silver lance from the beasts limp body while noticing the fine etchings of ancient runes along its shaft, and remarked on its features and how sharp it was.

"Where did you find this nasty little toy?" I asked.

"There are two other spears just like this, set within the center of the bridge outside," Mica remarked, "and it was better than having nothing, so I grabbed one before I came back in."

"Huh, it might be a lightning rod of some sort, I would imagine," I speculated.

"Maybe so, several thousands of years in the past when the Antarctic landmass was near the equator but in our era, electrical storms are exceptionally rare here at the poles," she noted to my lack of education on the fact.

"Well, either way, it made a good pig-sticker," I returned with a raised brow as I admired the end of the bloody pike.

"We should get back to Logan and see if he found a way into the adjacent tower," Mica noted as I holstered my gun and took the pike with me in case any more of those things showed up.

Withdrawing through the pivoting door, we found the professor huddled near the recess of the opposite tower. It was obvious he wasn't having much luck trying to gain entry. We wandered up to his side to see what the problem was.

"Ah, is that beastie still running loose in there?" he inquired with a worried glance back towards the doorway.

"Allen shot it," Mica answered, not taking the glory for having saved my life, "...are both these doors jammed?"

"I tried the other one already, but they are both locked by some means, and I can't seem to figure out how they operate," the professor noted as he referred back to the door we had used as an egress onto the open bridge.

As he turned back around, he noticed the long silver lance I was carrying and snatched it from my hand. Returning back to the center point of the causeway, he began to inspect the other two rods which stood at the central circle. Observing the post-hole for the missing rod, he inserted the lance back into its original rest. Taking out his tuning fork, he struck one of the rods and all three of them began to twist in their sockets.

"Ah, now we're getting somewhere," the professor gloated as he waited patiently for the machinery of this advanced technology to reveal itself. I was guessing that he was hoping that the doors to the other towers would pop open to allow us entry, but instead, the sky bridge began to descend.

The fall of the bridge was wrought with snags, as the mechanisms which operated the lift had become blocked with ice as it ground harshly upon its set course to our discomfort, leaving us stumbling to keep steady upon our feet. Looking over the edge, I was praying that the thing wouldn't fail and plunge us to our deaths on the icy rocks below. The shallow rift at the bottom spun open just before we set down, leaving packs of snow to fall inward as we were showered with ice. The lift entered a shaft into the depths of the frozen glacier, in which this entire fortress was entombed.

The causeway suddenly came to a stop, leaving us stranded in darkness. Flipping on our flashlights, we took a look at our surroundings as light flakes of snow continued to drift down upon us from the opening far above. We heard the groan of ancient machinery trying to open a sliding panel along the wall of the landing but the deck was packed with chunks of ice that blocked its tracks.

"Come over and help me with this," I called to Logan in an effort to clear the seams around the doorway.

Mica grabbed one of the silver lances from the lift and began stabbing at the frozen debris. Realizing they made perfect ice picks, I followed in her lead and tossed Logan the third one from the bridge. After several minutes, we had chipped enough ice away for the door to allow it to function and the curved panel receded as far as it could. We lurched back in surprise when a draft of hot air spewed from the opening, turning itself into a thick mist around us as it hit the cold exterior air.

Making our way inward, we crossed a barrier of crystals lining the walls and floor which activated the panel door to secure itself once again; locking us inside. The temperature was far greater within this passage than anything we had experienced before and held an odd smell to it I found hard to identify. Mica distinguished its source, having gained her experience from many expeditions in the past during her career.

"It smells like rich soil, like the deep Amazon," she stated as we walked the wide curved path through the tunnel.

As we approached a bright light near its end, we started crossing several plants of vivid colors rooted amongst the floor. Their numbers increased as we approached their source as thickly wooded vines stretched out, clinging to the walls and ceiling of the corridor ahead. We shielded our eyes as we entered through the open portal, only to be amazed by what we saw before us. A vast chamber of crystal, now coated by a thin sheet of snow on its outer surface, was filled with rich plants growing wild, as one might imagine such a greenhouse to run amok after untold centuries.

There was loose soil here and thick moisture hanging in the air, rich with the fragrance of a living jungle. Mica couldn't help herself but to take samples and a few photos, while I stood there wondering how this vegetation could have survived unattended in the middle of this frozen wasteland.

"This was likely some type of arboretum or nursery at one point and time," she noted while referring to the clear crystal walls which allowed the sunlight in through the thin layer of ice and snow, "which seems to have survived from the decay of their own plant matter within this enclosed ecosystem."

"I have never seen such strains of vegetation before," Logan exclaimed as he looked through the various species of foliage.

"They likely evolved to survive in this environment, similar to many types of plants and wildlife species which find themselves trapped on isolated islands," Mica granted, "the decomposition of the plant matter creates methane and heat which can sustain itself in such a sealed biosphere," she added.

"Wait a moment," Logan announced as he held up his finger for us to be silent. We all stood there for a tense second while gripping our silver spears, wondering if he had heard another one of those lizard hounds creeping around.

"That sounds like running water," Mica responded after a moment, and we turned ourselves in the direction the sound was coming from. Trying to get packed snow and bits of ice to melt in our canteens had been an aggravating failure, and we were severely dehydrated despite being surrounded by an entire continent painted with a frozen ocean of water.

Pushing our way through the thick foliage, we stumbled across a creek, which we concluded upon closer scrutiny, had been artificially constructed. The waterway must have been a feeding system to the arboretum long ago, and still maintained that function to this day. Several vines had curled curtains of delicate roots over the gentle stream to gather moisture without blocking the course of the river that ran through the very center of the dome. Backtracking our way upriver, the source of the feed was coming from a large transparent sphere of churning liquid.

"Do you imagine this well is solar-powered, or perhaps fed by a natural spring?" Mica asked the professor.

"Hard to say," Logan noted as he gazed upon the behemoth sphere, "this civilization seemed to rely on harnessing naturally occurring geomagnetic energies, which wouldn't be affected by the amount of ice covering the fortress."

"Maybe the plants adapted themselves to the availability of sunlight," I suggested to them both as the obvious answer.

"Could be," Logan smiled my way for my quick thinking,

"The plant life on Earth has survived here a lot longer than any other species."

Mica tested the water for us with a meter from her specimen bag and declared it was safe for us to drink. After taking our fill, we followed the creek downstream where it fanned outward from the end of the dome, feeding out along its edges. It was there that we found a garden full of fruits, and nuts, and vegetables that were barely recognizable to what any of us had ever seen in a grocery market. The variety of plants we found was oddly colored and strangely shaped, making them appear quite alien.

"Do you think these are safe to eat?" I asked Mica, who also had a famished look on her face.

"Give me a few minutes to test these," she answered as she pulled out her kit and set it upon the soft ground.

I handed her a few large grape-like berries and shelled nuts from an overhanging tree. I also dug up some roots of various plants and other leafy bulbs which look like giant stalks of lettuce. I wasn't much of a gardener myself but these plants had somehow survived the catastrophe which befell the people who had built this orchard long ago.

Mica tested a few of the fruits and berries, along with checking them for acidity and toxicity embedded in their chemical proteins. She spat out a few of the portions she tried because of the unpleasant taste but eventually placed several of the samples I had dug up aside for us to try for ourselves.

"This white root here seems to be a species of carrot, I would assume," she stated while showing Logan and I the resulting specimens which passed her initial tests.

"And these berries?" I asked about the brightly colored red and blue grapes.

"They seem to be fine, though be careful of the thorny seeds," she warned while noting a certain strain of leafy greens which were also safe to consume. It wasn't exactly a salad bar but we were starving at this point, so we took a moment to rest and enjoy our exotic picnic.

"There is one thing which seems odd here," I noted while chewing on a root, "which is that I haven't noticed any bugs."

Looking around for a moment, Mica herself noted that anomaly. Greenhouses were meant to be pest free for the most part, but having gone unattended for this space of time any botanist might question how the plants achieved pollination without helpful insects to complete that task. It was a riddle that intrigued both of the scientists but they were happy enough just to get a fresh meal in their bellies.

I scouted the rest of the dome to make sure there weren't any unpleasant surprises waiting for us before we took a nap. It was nice to have a moment of peace, sitting there in the soft soil with the sound of the running water and the fragrance of the flora. The three of us settled down after our hastily devoured meal and we slept like babies. I awoke in the dark of night, roused by a low hum coming from the ground beneath us and a blinking blue light that was shining between a heavy layer of vines several meters from where we lay.

Without waking the others, I turned on my flashlight and strolled over to find the source of the illumination. Pulling off the overgrowth of vines and leaves, I discovered they had camouflaged a large oval doorway. There was a simple hand-print molded into the center of it; so like a curious idiot, I place my palm within its depression.

As I touched the door the blue light above me stopped flashing and turned stable, gleaming brightly like a cold sapphire, and the door folded inward. It was a fleeting moment that I had looking back and choosing between waking the others or satisfying this new inquisitive nature, which Mica had impressed upon me, so I dared to take a peek inside before telling them what I had found. Unfortunately, I never heard the door move as it silently shut itself behind me, sealing me in.

Within the dimly lit room, I crossed a strange circular stone that looked to be comprised of polished marble. Its cross-section was similar in shape to the large floating stone we had tripped upon beneath the first set of ruins below the dome. This stone, however, had been cut into several uneven sections which interlinked like a puzzle. Several pieces were of odd sizes that would only fit in certain configurations.

Daring to touch the contraption, I pushed the pieces into their allotted slots while I turned the stone block until the segments reached their correct position to interlock. Once it was whole, the ivory slab began to slowly spin on its own, appearing to be floating in midair. Having been dismantled and out of balance before, it now regained its former function. As it turned ever faster a bright row of crystals lit up the circular console which surrounded it, bathing the small room in a rainbow of colors.

I was surprised when the radio on my belt suddenly turned itself on and began to cycle through the static without my touching it. Taking it from its holster, I tried to see why it was malfunctioning, only to realize the dials weren't responding.

"Come in, can you hear me?" A garbled message cried, but the cycling static seemed to hone in on the transmission, "Walter to Logan team, can you hear me?"

"Yes, yes, is that you Mr. Humphrey? This is Allen, over," I called back.

"So glad to hear your voice ...I lost you there for a while, how is everyone?" Walter asked eagerly.

"We're doing well, considering. We had a few close calls but that story can wait for another time. We lost your signal before; were you able to trace our location?" I inquired with a pinch of hope seeping into my voice.

"I tried to triangulate your location via satellite but your transmission was buried by an atmospheric anomaly which made it impossible to pinpoint your position," Walter advised, while I noted that his signal became increasingly clearer as the errant static disappeared from the transmission.

"We are in an incredible structure comprised of some type of crystal," I tried to explain, but realized that it may look like any other clump of ice from a satellite image, "...but we're okay for now. Can you get a transport helicopter to return to the ship so you can scan the area for a visual on us?"

"About that," Walter responded with a hint of dejection in his voice, "we already have a helicopter here to conduct a rescue but we seemed to be experiencing a series of navigation problems here on the ship. Both the captain and the pilot said they can't rely on their equipment for guidance at the moment. Most of our electrical equipment seems to have gone a little wacky, and we can't get a bearing by any other means because of the cloud cover surrounding this storm."

"Well, we will see what we can do to locate some sort of landmark for the pilot to hone in on," I answered, reaching for a measure of hope and trusting they would not give up the search, "how are things going on the ship, Walt? I can imagine the rest of the crew is getting a little antsy to get back to port."

"Actually Allen," Walter interjected, "there has been a level of concern rising among the crew onboard since there was a great deal of seismic activity reported recently at the nearby Byrd Station, which appears to have been closely followed by an increase in reported quakes worldwide. Meteorological stations across the globe have started to light up, while nationwide emergencies have been declared in multiple countries over the past 24 hours alone," Walter mentioned with a touch of worry.

"What's going on?" I asked, but deep down I was concerned that what we did to that orb might be the cause of the global disruptions he was reporting.

"Seismologists are saying that the initial shockwave originated at the Antarctic, at an area not far from our landing site and that the continental shelves have begun drifting at an unprecedented pace. Nobody really knows at this stage but it looks as if the tectonic plates along the ring of fire are starting to flex," Walter stated, referring to the stretch of volcanoes along the continuous oceanic trench surrounding the Pacific Ocean. It appeared the mantle itself, was moving exactly as Mica had described it.

"Is there a way we could get the coast guard out here to sweep the area and find us?" I inquired, which seemed like the most logical choice in this emergency.

"I don't think you understand the situation here, Allen," Walter announced with a note of sympathy creeping into his voice, "Professor Logan made it quite clear that this private expedition was top secret, and we were not to contact any government agency for any reason whatsoever," he finished. Hearing him say that got me angry.

"Are you serious? Neither he nor Tom ever mentioned that to me before I signed on," I barked back, but my temper was starting to become chilled with the growing uncertainty of our rescue; which itself became even more dubious if they refused to call for outside help.

"Yes, I'm quite serious, Allen. Logan even had every crew-member of the ship sign confidentiality agreements. We are entirely on our own on this venture," Walter stated with bitter finality.

Understandably, I was upset to find out about this little quirk that might have been hidden in the fine print, which I admit, I never read in my haste when I was penning in my name on the employment contract in exchange for my first paycheck. There would be no international air-sea rescue coming to pluck our frosty asses out of this situation. I would certainly have to have a talk with the Professor about this matter at some point and make him realize that our chances for survival had dropped dramatically because of his paranoia.

"We can attempt a visual survey if we can possibly coordinate a signal at midnight for you to fire a beacon," Sir Walter suggested but unfortunately, we had used the last of our emergency flares.

"Ah, damn; that's not an option at the moment," I answered with a sigh, "but I'll try to check back at this time in 12 hours, Walt; but keep us updated," I pleaded.

"Certainly, Allen, just squawk me again when you have an open line. I've been on this channel for several hours straight trying to reach you," Walter mentioned to my confusion.

"But I didn't signal you, I was answering 'your' call, Walter," I answered to his surprise.

"But I thought you had, I received a radio burst on this

dedicated channel, so I answered the broadcast," he returned.

"I see..." I replied, trying to search for an answer to how that could have been true, "in any event, we'll check in twelve hours from now, over and out."

I knew I had drained a bunch of juice from the radio battery on that lengthy conversation, and felt strangely uneasy about how this crystal console had initiated a transmission from my radio without me handling it. I couldn't complain that it may have acted as an antenna to boost the signal for us to get in contact, but I had no idea how we could use that to our advantage if the ship couldn't appraise our position. It had become clear that we had triggered something awful that was screwing with the earth's magnetic field and we were the only ones in the position to correct it.

I started to make my way back to where the others were sleeping but suddenly realized I was now sealed within the small chamber. The hatch to the door was completely bare of any hand-print controls as I had used on its exterior side. Searching around the room, I couldn't spot any type of panel that might identify what these oddly shaped crystal rods might control. Banging loudly on the door came to no result, so I could only hope that Mica and the Professor would see the doorway I had unveiled and opened this rat-trap I had gotten myself into, and let me out.

I eventually gave up trying to yell through the thick hatch door and sat down to take a rest. After what seemed like several hours of waiting, I began to worry how much air this little chamber might be holding and feared I would suffocate to death. My concern for self-preservation eventually overcame my initial apprehension to mess around with the strange controls on the ringed console surrounding the spinning stone. I got up and looked through the several shades of crystals, having no clue as to what they were for. Eventually, I ended up testing several at random just to see what they might do in hopes of getting the door open.

After daring to pick a few of the crystal sticks out of their sockets on the console, I decided to interchange a few out of desperation. After a few random attempts, I noticed that the marble slab in the center of the device began to spin a little slower, so I tried to interchange one of the rods with an entirely different color. To my surprise, a small hidden slate with an embedded hand-print rose from the console at the center of the board, which I hoped was the same key I could use to escape my small cell.

Placing my hand upon the plate, I looked over my shoulder to see if the hatch to the door was opening. With a frown, I turned forward again to notice that the spinning slab had accelerated to a scary speed. Snatching my hand away, I suddenly felt the ground beneath me shake and all the lights in the room transformed into a dull orange hue. With a sigh of relief, I saw the hatch open behind me and I rushed outside just in time to come face to face with Logan and Mica as another small quake rumbled the atrium.

"Where did you disappear to?" Logan spouted with concern as his eyes wandered towards the closing door of the chamber I had popped out of.

"There's a room back there with a console, and I was able to reach the ship to talk to Walter. It must be some sort of antenna that allowed us to communicate," I replied, "but I, ah ...I may have accidentally set something off when I was trying to open the door to get out."

"This place is where the alpha orb is located, Allen," Mica snapped back, "if you assume it acted like an antenna, that might mean this is some type of transmission tower," she finished with a look of worry washing over her face. A sour sense of guilt sank into my stomach at hearing her words, while I wondered what I may have done to make our situation worse.

Shivers

There was little we could do to correct the mishap resulting from my reckless curiosity. Logan warned against reopening the vault I had entered, in the event that one or all of us might become entrapped as I had been. If that happened we would only be taking the chance of making the situation even worse. Mica grilled me on what I had seen in the small chamber, so I elaborated on the stone disk I had pieced together and the crystal shards I had experimented with in my efforts to get the door to open.

The truth was, I didn't quite remember which of the crystals I had replaced while I was fiddling around in there, so there was practically no chance that I could reverse what I had done to try and correct it. Logan surmised that even if we did, it was likely too late anyhow. The technology of this ancient society seemed to be triggered by manual controls with cascading aftereffects. Luckily, they didn't blame me for my clumsiness, since it could have easily happened to any one of us.

I promptly informed them of what Walter had said about the heightened earthquake activity which coincided with the general timeframe, whereby Mica had triggered the giant spinning orb we had found beneath the sunken city.

"Walter's mention of the recent seismic activity seems like too much of a coincidence, and only leans towards confirming Professor Rice's theories. The important thing is that we need to locate the alpha orb in this complex and attempt to disable it ...if we can," Logan noted with a shrug.

"What do you think that room I was in might have been used for?" I asked the professor, who had always seemed optimistic with the way he treated others.

"My assistant might have been correct in her assumption that this steeple acts as a transmission tower. If I was to guess, and I am making a wild assumption based on the situational facts here, mind you, is that they utilize those stone discs as a type of generator used in conjunction with the geomagnetic orbs that harness the natural energy fields of the earth," Logan stated as he gave me the long-winded version of his hypothesis, "and I wouldn't be surprised from the types of energies these devices tap, that it found some way to link with the crystal components within the wiring of your radio; which of course, is similar to the control shards you described."

The way the professor outlined his rationale of how this technology harnessed and redirected magnetic waves, and the way these ancient people had grown their own minerals in such a controlled fashion, it started to make a lick of sense. My radio had only turned itself on once I had gotten that stone flywheel going, which served to purge any errant static on the channel to reach Walter aboard our ship. Walter had stated that it was I who had first signaled him in that instance, which fit into Mica's theory that the console was a transmission center. The question was; what the hell was it broadcasting?

At first, we had thought that the arboretum was another dead end but the discovery of the small transmission chamber encouraged us to search the rest of the vine encrusted walls for something we might have missed. Once the morning light had lit up the dome, we fanned out and eventually found two separate exits not far from the transmission chamber I had stumbled upon the night before. Getting through the tangle of the trees and thick vines which had grown over the door panes was difficult and time-consuming, considering our lack of proper tools to be cutting through such dense foliage. When we were packing for this expedition nobody had thought they would have any need for a machete.

We had a hard time clearing one of the two exits, which resulted in our next route being chosen for us. We found the same indented hand-print upon the face of the doorway, which Logan himself was eager to try. The hinge cycled open and the pathway beyond it was lit by streaks of ambient daylight leaking through the thick crystal structure, giving the atmosphere within an almost mystical appearance. However, the stench coming up from the corridor below was anything but inviting.

Without a map to guide us, we felt like we were becoming ever more lost, but at least we had a source of warmth and food within the greenhouse should the arrival of a rescue party take longer than we anticipated. Logan was vocal about how confused he was about the basic architecture of the hallway we occupied, which contained several hairpin turns that eventually led us to a place directly beneath the arboretum where we had spent the night before.

The farther down we went, the thickening odor became so sharp that even the scarves wrapped around our faces were of little use to filter out the foul scent wafting up from below. Mica thought it might be methane, so we were extra careful not to do anything that might create a spark. After our path brought us several meters below the surface of the ice, we encountered a soft green light emanating from an opening at its end. What we saw in the chamber beyond was something out of a nightmare.

We found ourselves on the upper ledge of an enormous cavity riddled with some type of repugnant organic matter growing upon the walls; at its center stood a large circular glob of the material covered in the same muck that was splattered about the chamber. I was about to say something when Logan hushed me to be silent as he knelt down and gestured to the walls below.

"Look there," he whispered while he pointed, then moved his finger in yet another direction. As we stood there, our eyes began to pick up movement all around the chamber. We could make out several small cubs of those same horrid scaled hounds, which were crawling their way out of clustered egg sacks. This wasn't a refuse bin, but a breeding chamber for those vile creatures.

What caught Logan's attention was the large bulbous artifact at the center of this curved chamber, which was thickly spattered with pulsating cocoons. The eggs pale-green shade, gave them an even less appealing tone, as were the infant creatures that were covered in fetid slime as they hatched from their sticky buds.

"This must be their litter," Mica whispered back with wild astonishment, "I have never seen anything like it."

"It gives me the shivers," I blurted, "we barely survived one of those things and this is a whole god-damn colony!"

"*Shivers* ...that's a fitting title for them," Mica muttered back, "we have to give this new species a name, anyhow" she announced, keeping up with her academic principles.

"Fine, whatever," I rolled my eyes at her statement, "but I say that we leave these things here in peace and backtrack up to the greenhouse and permanently seal the goddamn door behind us!"

"And then what?" Mica shot back.

"Hell, try the other door, or climb back up the tower somehow," I reached for an excuse not to face a horde of these creatures ...these 'Shivers' as she liked to call them.

"That might not be an option," Logan interjected as we snapped at one another under our breath so as not to attract the nesting critters, "you see that opening across from us over there, parallel to ours," he indicated to the other side of the chamber as we nodded, "I would guess that is were the other doorway led. In my assumption, I would say that these two passages are part of an oversized valve release system to some type of purge tank," the professor pointed down into the massive chamber below us.

"You mean like a water overflow, or some type of air dissipation from the garden room?" Mica asked with interest.

"There was that odd giant glass tank in the center of the greenhouse," I added to help answer her question, "but I can't imagine what it contained," I finally admitted as I referred to the frothing liquid we had seen bubbling from within. The vat had been positioned directly above the source of the water channel as if it was some sort of reservoir, so I had assumed there was a connection between the two.

"Or, it could be a flow of gasses from this chamber which were being released up into the greenhouse," he countered, "which might explain the elaborate zigzag design of the passage," he pointed behind us, "Which was a way of cooling the air down between this point and the conservatory."

"For what purpose?" I blurted like an idiot, not being able to connect the dots, "There's nothing in here," I motioned into the cavernous room which had been turned into a breeding chamber for the Shiver beasts. The professor got a strange gleam in his eye and turned back towards me with a slight grin on his lips.

"I disagree, Allen. Take a closer look," he motioned back towards the center of the great chamber.

Mica and I turned our attention to the massive structure set within the middle of the room. A patchwork of organic matter, like that of a beehive, was stretched across the chamber from which the cocoons of the creatures young were suspended. The foul stench emanated from the steaming piles of dung and waste left pooling in the bottom below, not unlike a cave floor were bats might roost. After staring for a great while, the formation at the center began to take on a familiar shape.

"That, that's the alpha orb," Mica almost blurted aloud in her excitement, "encased beneath that nesting material!"

Logan's quaint smile for her assertive observation slowly turned into a frown. We might have found the alpha orb that controlled the others but there was no way to operate it with a huge nest of Shiver beasts choking the chamber.

"It doesn't look like that energy sphere is going into operation anytime soon, gunked up the way it is," I noted to Logan as we could clearly see it was tethered by tons of hive material anchoring it in place, "can't we just leave it be?"

Logan appeared to understand my point of view but had to clarify his thoughts for me so I could get a grasp of the situation. These geomagnetic orbs the ancients utilized to harness power were linked to one another; and this outer shell, the Alpha-Component, could conceivably control all the others in their succession. That was Logan's theory, one we would have to put into practice. That left us to deal with the Shivers, which had made a nest of the energy chamber.

Mica was glaring at something at the bottom of the room with interest and got Logan to take a look over her shoulder.

"Do you see that down there, just to the left of that clump of pods?" she inquired as she pointed down below us. Taking a peek beside them, I could see where she was directing us to look. There at the bottom, surrounded by organic material, was a console of some sort. However, it was what she saw sitting in the middle of it which had raised her interest.

"It's one of those ring keys, like the one you had before that activated the first sphere," Logan blurted aloud.

"We need to get that thing, and try to use it in the communication room Allen had found," she suggested.

"Sure ...and who's the lucky fool to attempt that reckless stunt?" I snorted at her in a condescending tone, since it was obviously a suicide mission. We could already see several dozen of those creatures roaming around the chamber.

"I'll do it," Mica answered bluntly after a moment's hesitation; realizing it was her own idea and she had no right to expect anyone else to risk themselves.

"You're nuts! Those things will tear you apart if you go down there," I spouted back at Mica, though realizing in that moment that I must have come across as a coward in her eyes.

"I wouldn't ask either of you to risk the danger. Besides, I'm smaller and quicker than you both," she snapped back with a measure of confidence, though I got the sense that she really didn't enjoy the idea of doing it either. The danger was very real and we had lost several of our dear associates recently. Mica wasn't a tender little flower, and she had spent a great deal of time out in the field. During her many years abroad, Mica made sure that her male counterparts would not treat her any differently than the rest of their crew and she had earned their respect by asserting herself.

Her selfless attitude made me feel like a jerk for having snapped at her as I had. Logan admitted that their chances would be improved if they had another such key to operate various devices within the fortress, and could use it to engage the lift outside the tower so they could reach another level within the citadel. With a bumbling apology, I tripped over my words as I offered to take her place, but at that point, Mica was adamant about doing the run herself.

We climbed our way back up to the greenhouse and made another meal for ourselves from the wild garden, after which we set about gathering vines to weave together a rope to lower Mica into the nest. Several hours later, we managed to tie enough creeper plants and bindings to make a cable strong enough to hold her weight. Logan took a few moments of his time to study the strange vat at the center of the dome, which appeared to process the water which fed the greenhouse, but his conclusions came up short. He did, however, discover a familiar inset there which the ring-key could fit into, that he had hoped might give him access to a console and reveal the basic functions of the giant cistern.

When we were ready, the three of us marched back down into the putrid bowels beneath the arboretum and quietly secured the strands into an anchor upon the lip of the vent, and took a measured breather to weigh the risks of what we were about to do. With an uneasy smile of confidence, Mica secured the vine to her belt and tied a loop at the bottom of the strand for her feet. After surveying the surrounding nest, with a nod from Logan's assistant, we began to lower her into the chamber.

Errant cries from the young creatures echoed off the distant walls, adding to the eerie atmosphere. Logan and I struggled to keep Mica's position steady as she gingerly picked her way down through the sticky material lining the walls. Even though our arms were exhausted by the time she reached the chamber floor below, we had to keep a vigilant eye on the roaming creatures to make sure she hadn't been seen.

The foulness of their lair was pretty ripe as it was, and Logan presumed that the overwhelming stench would help mask Mica's scent. If these feral beasts were busy tending to their young, then she could get in and out of there without being noticed. Mica had scouted her chosen path from above before she made her way down and there were few obstacles for her to cover from where she had landed. We observed her progress from above during the few wary moments Mica was forced to slink out of sight whenever a stray Shiver beast poked its fanged head out of the shadows. With our nerves on end, we watched as she eventually made it to her position at the encrusted console stationed at the foot of the enormous sphere surrounded by these dreadful creatures.

Scanning the area one last time, she stood upright and tried to grab the silver ring from its setting, only to find that it was encrusted with dried matter which had cemented it into place. Mild panic started to set in when she realized this risky jaunt would take more time than she had considered and that she would have to pry it from its mount. Looking around, she found a chip of stone to cut into the coating which had laminated the coil in place. Scraping into it created far more noise than she had wished to make and her efforts eventually began to draw unwanted attention.

Several of the creatures began to perk their heads up at the errant noise Mica was making at the console, but there was little we could do to warn her. Logan focused the beam of his light and began to flash it off and on in a vain attempt to get her attention but Mica was focused on getting the key-ring free of its fitting. One Shiver beast was inquisitive enough to crawl its way towards the console where Mica was positioned, and peered down upon her with its terrible crimson glare. Glancing upward, Mica's eyes widened and her heartbeat stopped in that frozen moment as cold panic set in.

The rigid spines along the creature's back slowly raised and began to rattle their awful sound. In that split second, Mica smashed the stone down hard upon the encrusted ring and broke it loose. The metallic key went tumbling to the ground and she dove for it the very moment the beast had crouched, preparing to pounce upon her. Around the chamber the angry rattle of their brood intensified as the pack honed in on their unwelcome guest.

The professor shouted out for Mica to run for it, as he motioned towards the lifeline of woven vines from where we had perched above. This action brought their attention towards Logan and myself, as the pack of Shivers began to sense there was more than a solitary intruder within their lair. Mica ran like a hare as she leaped through the spindles of cocoons while several more of the beasts concentrated around her as she fled. More than one of the Shiver hounds made a desperate vault to catch her, only to miss its mark as she skittered towards the awaiting line dangling against the wall.

"Go, go!" We shouted, bringing even more attention to ourselves as the chamber came alive with the sound of the agitated beasts and the rise of their hideous rattle.

She grabbed the line and we yanked up the vines as fast as we could; finding that doing so was much less graceful than we had anticipated. Jerking upon the rope, Mica lost the headlight she was wearing which went tumbling down into the nest of them. The beasts swarmed upon the bouncing light, nipping and snapping at the spinning flashlight as if it were a living thing.

One of the Shivers grabbed a hold of the stray end of the vine between its maw, and we almost lost Mica as the line was nearly ripped from our hands. The added weight of the beast was a burden we could barely carry. Seeing this uninvited passenger, Mica began to kick the animal in the snout with her booted heel. Eventually, the creature had enough of the abuse and lost its grip upon the vine between its jagged teeth.

Logan breathed a sigh of relief when we heaved his assistant over the lip, but the reprieve was short-lived. Shiver beasts were crawling their way up the surface of the blisters of nesting material to reach the inlet where the three of us stood gawking. Dropping the vine, we hustled our way back up the twisting corridor, losing our breath at the exertion of the steep climb.

"What the hell did all those things survive on out here in this wasteland?" I had to huff through tired breaths as we reached the last rise to the level of the greenhouse.

"Hard to say," Mica answered as she panted, "but since we

only saw them on the interior of the building, it's possible that these animals could have once been a species of domesticated pets that went feral after their masters died off, and they evolved to a point needed to survive this climate. There are likely many other species around here we haven't yet seen, which they could have hunted as prey, or they might even feed off of their own pack."

"You mean they are cannibalistic?" I blurted back as we jumped through the door, while turning around we could hear several of the creatures were making their way up the winding passage behind us.

"That may not have just been a breeding chamber," she noted, "it's not uncommon in such strained environments when food is scarce, that only the strongest of a pack survives and the runts are consumed."

"But for all we know, they could be omnivores," Logan added, "and there are likely other greenhouses like this that their brood has access to."

I tried to close the hatchway but Logan instead, placed a large dead branch in the way of it to keep it from sealing.

"What the hell are you doing? Those things will get into the dome!" I barked in confusion as to what he was attempting to accomplish.

"This is plan B," the professor mentioned as he wiped the sweat from his brow, "Mica, give me that ring," he ordered. His assistant handed Logan the silver key circlet and took off towards the second shaft to make sure it was also propped open.

"Plan B? What the hell is going on, why didn't either of you tell me about a plan B!" I cursed as I turned a nervous eye back towards the corridor as the rattling sound of the angry Shivers grew increasingly louder.

"Help Mica get that adjacent door open and get yourselves into that communications chamber," Logan advised as he started marching up towards the vat in the center of the greenhouse, but stalled with a slight paused to holler back to us, "and don't touch anything in there until I get back!" he snapped.

I just stood there for a brief second staring at him like a dolt as he left, but realized that Mica would need my help to prop open the other hatch. I caught up with her just as she had gotten the door partially opened since there were still matted roots thwarting her efforts, but we found another small log nearby to prop it ajar, which Logan had set up earlier for this eventuality.

Up at the churning basin at the center of the dome, Logan approached the control board and laid the ring into the seat upon the panel. Upon doing so, a spiral of blue lights lit up the board showing various rudimentary functions upon the diagram. Logan made the most logical decision based on his expertise and twisted the ring to the indicator on the controls. There was a brief moment of silence when the churning foam in the massive vat above him became still, before it began spinning with a bright yellowish tinge at a speed like a giant blender.

The piping surrounding it began to groan and complain about the function he had input, and Logan wasn't about to stand around and watch what was going to happen next. The professor grabbed the ring from its interface and raced back downhill along the path towards Allen and Mica, just as the blue light above the panel activated and they were able to open the door into the central chamber. Looking side to side, he saw several Shiver beasts forcing their way through the propped hatches, and were just moments away from being upon them. The professor grabbed us both by our arms and pulled us through into the darkened room.

"Close the hatch!" he demanded as he faced me, considering the proximity of the beasts clustering outside.

"I don't remember how," I blurted back in his same excited state, "I was just screwing around with different combinations," I admitted as I approached the circular console. The marble flywheel was still spinning before us but had reduced to a stable pace in its revolution. I looked around at the colored crystals in confusion, wondering what I should do.

"Here, take this!" Logan snapped as he handed the silver band to Mica, who handed it off to me in return.

I took the ring key and scanned the console for a place where it might fit, but only found the hand-print embedded at it center. I tried to place the ring into it, with no response, and found myself at a loss as to what to do next. Behind me, Logan was waiting at the door with one of the silver spears he had placed by the doorway; standing guard as the horde of Shiver hounds swarmed into the greenhouse and began to gather at our location. He stared out at the central vat which fed the watering system, watching as the large reservoir was now popping valves and bursting at the seams.

Thick yellow gas began to shoot out from hidden joints as the putrid steam tried to escape the building pressure within the sealed vat. One of the hounds got caught in the blast from the piping and screamed with a whine of pain. The creature's hindquarters began to corrode and frosted over as it froze into place. The sight of this did little to settle Logan's frantic mood.

"Allen! Hurry it up!" Logan cried out over his shoulder.

My eyes passed towards Mica who was preparing herself for the worst, but I caught a glimpse in her eyes as she motioned something to me. With her hands, she was making the gesture of placing the ring onto her wrist the way she had carried the first one she held. Following her lead, I slipped the thick pewter band onto my arm, then placed my palm back upon the depression once again.

Suddenly, the room turned a vivid blue and the hatchway sealed shut, just in time enough for Logan to shoo back several Shiver hounds with his pointed spear which had been nipping at his legs from the crack of the door. It wasn't a moment too soon, for less than a minute afterward, we felt an explosion rock the chamber as the vat outside ruptured and sent a stream of its acrid contents downstream towards the retaining wall and into the overflow vents at either side. Logan had set the tank to purge the system in a reverse flow.

"What was that?" I remarked with a look of surprise as we stood in the dim lighting of the chamber.

"The purification system for the water treatment already

appeared to be overloaded, which was logical considering the amount of time this automated system had been running," the professor answered, "so I devised a backup plan in case we ran into any trouble within the breeding chamber used by those vile beasts," he finished.

"Hold on, you intentionally rigged that thing to detonate?" I inquired with a note of shock.

"Well, not exactly," he admitted, "I was only intending to purge the vat to clear the passages in case we were followed by those creatures, but my guess is the system was so old that it couldn't handle the added pressure and it ruptured."

"You *guess*, huh?" I added sarcastically, "You do realize Doc, that you just blew up our only source of fresh rations we've found on this barren block of ice..." I added with a scowl.

"Hmm, I admit that I hadn't calculated such an outcome of this scale," Logan answered as he rubbed his chin in afterthought. I caught how Mica rolled her eyes as we now found ourselves in the same fix we had been in before. Who knows what we would find when we opened the hatchway again. From the sound of the boiling wreckage beyond the door, the entire dome outside had likely been destroyed.

The two scientists turned their attention back towards the central console and the crystal rods which controlled it. Mica set about resetting the crystal patterns to match the color sequence of a prism. Logan eventually located the specific rod which he presumed to control the hatchway door but I warned him that caustic slag from the water filtration vat might still come gushing into the chamber if he opened the door too soon. With that note of caution, Logan admitted to the logic of my advice and went on scrutinizing the floating flywheel while his assistant worked at the panel.

"May I?" Mica turned to me suddenly as I tried to shake the stress we had built up over recent events.

Holding out her hand in expectation, I removed the metal band from my wrist and offered it to her. She quickly slid it upon her own forearm and resumed adjusting the crystal rods, which now began to light up whenever she touched them with the hand upon which she wore the ring.

"How did you do that?" I inquired, wondering what it was that I had missed.

"Unlike the limited resources which our current society is addicted to, it recently became clear to the Professor and I that this ancient civilization relied heavily on naturally existing energies, and it was a simple conclusion that the color scheme here was also based on a sequence from the electromagnetic spectrum wavelength of light," Mica advised.

"And the band you're using acts as a key to allow the user full access," I added with a click in my mind.

"Exactly," Mica smiled, "now you're getting the hang of it," she granted as I was connecting the dots of how this ancient culture worked. After a minute, my radio clicked on again as the harmonics of the crystals within the panel synchronized with the internal workings of the radio.

"Allen, are you there?" Walter's excited voice came over the transmission. This time it only took a few moments for the line to clear up the static.

"Yes, Walter, you're coming in loud and clear," I answered, "Professor Logan, and Mica, are also here with me."

"Good to hear your voice, Walt, how are things on the ship?" Logan spat over the microphone as I handed him the radio.

"Ah, Logan, not so well actually, my old friend," Walter answered with a sigh of despair, "there have been several unusual weather systems popping up on global news reports along with increased earthquake activity, which has caused thousands of fatalities thus far across the globe. We also picked up information from wildlife biologists that migratory species appeared to be confused, and the Aurora Australis, the southern lights, was recently seen as far north as Brazil, and the Borealis itself was recently viewed as far south as Saudi Arabia." What he was relating in his report was visual evidence that the Earth's magnetic field had gone haywire.

Walter clarified that the crew of our vessel were becoming

concerned for their families back home on the mainland, but only agreed after much debate, that they would hold out for a few more days until a replacement rescue party could arrive. Logan had never mentioned to the ship's captain that there were actually no back-up plans for any type of recovery, even in such a dire emergency. This left the three of us in a dilemma. Walter had to locate us within the next 72 hours or the crew would turn the vessel back; leaving us stranded in this frozen wasteland. I took that bad news personally and clarified that we needed to get a visual signal to them of our current location.

After the noise died down outside, we waited an hour before daring to open the hatch again and we stepped outside to be greeted by a cold wind. The dome had collapsed at the area of detonation around the central container, which had destroyed much of the greenhouse. Whatever plants hadn't been destroyed in the initial blast would likely be dead by the next sunrise from the encroaching frost, as frigid air seeped in through the shattered enclosure. A long yellow stain now layered the rim along the surrounding walls, where the purged pollutants from the tank had surged onto the lower section, and were eventually drained through the elaborate system of pipes down into the cavernous chamber below.

We stepped outside into the debris field, finding everything which had been touched by the caustic foam had turned an eggshell white. Grasping at one of the dead plants with her gloves, the frail leaf snapped off in Mica's hands.

"They're all frozen solid..." she whispered aloud in wonder.

Logan could see that everything the toxic purge had touched had become brittle and layered with frost, as if it had been blasted with liquid nitrogen. The contents of the vat must have acted as some sort of coolant agent, he thought to himself as he stumbled across a few limp bodies of the Shiver beasts, which shattered like glass beneath the weight of his feet. The smooth outer walls of the collapsed dome were still too high to climb, so we cautiously made our way back down the twisting tunnel towards the core room to see what we would find.

Cycles of Change

It was the inner earth's magnetic dynamo reorganizing itself which was fueling this global disaster. How it actually worked was a mystery we had not yet solved but it may have been a subject of higher study by the enlightened minds of this advanced culture. They understood that this device they had acquired had the ability to tap into the natural fields surrounding our planet and could harness those forces for their own needs. From what Logan had seen in the lab back in the tower, was that their scholars had been on the verge of a breakthrough.

Discovering the true function of this mysterious device these ancient people had captured from the invading army those countless centuries ago, was one avenue to follow when the time came. Though for now, learning how it worked and understanding how it manipulated the earth's fields was our primary goal at the moment. Logan surmised that they may be able to reverse these waves and persuade the earth's core to enter its state of dormancy once again, but that strategy held far greater risks than anyone would be able to accurately predict. Inquiring further about his plans, I didn't like what I heard coming from the professor's mouth.

"Honestly, the mechanics of the earth's core isn't exactly known, but if it were to stop spinning, either by accident or by design, there is the chance our planet would become a sister to Mars," he explained.

"What the hell?" was all I could manage to utter, realizing the utter foolishness we were getting ourselves into by playing with such massive and mysterious powers within our own planet.

"Both Venus and Mars have a hardened core and virtually no magnetic field," Mica explained.

"So you're saying that screwing around with these devices might kill our planet?" I was forced to ask Logan.

"Truthfully, Allen, we're not quite sure," he granted, "to put it frankly, if a pole shift happens, it might take decades or centuries to complete its cycle as we explained before; leaving our planet and everyone on it at the mercy of the suns radiation and the solar winds until the field regenerates. However, I believe that these devices, these geomagnetic energy spheres we've discovered, could greatly reduce that interval with the proper application."

"And, what happens if you get your calculations wrong?" I inquired as to the shallow look in his eyes, which meant he hadn't told me everything.

"Well, if I'm wrong, we would effectively be throwing a wrench into the gears, as they say," he added with a shrug, "we could stop the polar shift in its tracks but that might stall the core, which may bear unforeseen consequences over time."

"How much time are we talking about?" I asked.

"On the grand scale, I would say a million years or less, most likely. The earth's outer crust would continue to spin of course, which might very well kick-start the core on its own, but there is the remote possibility that it might freeze up and our planet would slowly turn into a mirror of what Mars looks like today," the professor acknowledged.

"You're worried about that? Hell, I say we take the chance and cross that bridge a million years from now, Doc!" I blurted.

"But there's no guarantee, lad," Logan replied, "such a catastrophic suspension of the earth's natural cycle could cause all sorts of unprecedented consequences, such as a vast increase in energized electrical fields and magnetic eruptions or solar ions stripping away the atmosphere with a significant loss of its oxygen molecules. Our planet's surface could be exposed to a devastating level of ultraviolet light emissions and become far more susceptible to the effects of solar storms."

"You make it sound as if it's a lose-lose situation, Doc," I returned in rebuttal, "but you need to get your head out of the sand and realize that risking billions of people's lives for what might very well be a couple of decades, if not centuries, to suffer such lethal effects would destroy everything we know," I clarified as best I could, "and it would only make sense to give the human race time to address that situation in the distant future."

"So you agree that it's worth taking the risk?" Logan asked with a raised brow.

Nodding my head to him, I had to concede that the benefits outweighed the risks at this point despite the peril of likely condemning our little planet to an early death if we got it wrong. We just had to make sure we didn't screw things up. Unfortunately, we hadn't attained a reliable track record of accomplishing that over the past few days. By accident or not, we had started this scenario, so we might as well finish it.

We had been engaged in our sobering conversation during our walk down towards the nesting chamber. When we reached the core room, we found a mess of frost, and foam, and the tangled corpses of the Shiver beasts. Mica felt a larger sense of guilt about killing this breed which had survived here for countless ages, so I tried to console her that there were likely many more of these animals roaming around the crystal fortress. If and when we got out of here, she could send back an expedition team to collect live specimens, if she was so inclined.

We stood there on the ledge, gawking at the devastation we had wrought upon the creature's lair and left wondering how we could get back down to clear away the area around the console. Our only hope was that the control panel had remained undamaged, and while we were contemplating our next plan of action the room suddenly began to tremble. A dull vibration hummed through the chamber as the flash-frozen material caked around the sphere began to crack and burst apart. Thin blue lines of electricity began to finger their way through the tears that opened up until the giant orb started to move, breaking itself free from the brittle nesting material layered upon it. With a fiery spark, the arcs of light started to dance across its surface as the giant globe began to turn.

"It's been activated!" Logan breathed in astonishment.

"I'm confused, isn't that what you've been trying to get it to do all along?" I asked, bewildered by his reaction.

"There was residual power still present within this complex but from the models we found in the lab room in the tower, we believed this was the Alpha core, as it was the largest of the spheres," Mica explained, "however, while we were in the chamber where we took refuge, I attempted to synchronize the transmissions to the other five energy orbs located around the continent but hadn't initiated its operation."

The worried look on her face explained more than I was able to grasp in her answer. The professor himself, seemed just as upset at this turn of events. This occurrence put a kink in their hypothesis since they had hoped that the Alpha sphere would be able to control the smaller cores it was linked to. That idea, however, was now in question since it had clearly been triggered by some other means.

"The reason we came back down here was to turn the thing 'on' by using the power ring with that console down there, and attempt to manipulate its attunement with the geomagnetic frequencies of the earth's core," Logan explained to the confused look which had glazed across my face, "but obviously, it has activated itself, somehow, or one of the lower station spheres had stimulated its connection to the main sphere."

That made Logan and his assistant wonder if there was any chance of actually gaining control over the device, or if it was too late. The professor made it clear that this system was once used as a weapon, and no matter the outcome, the greatest fear he had was that a single country or government might get a hold of such a device for nefarious purposes.

Since it was already activated there was no reason to go below into the chamber, so we made our way up to the destroyed greenhouse and back to the bridge lift. This time, Mica was able to trigger the bridge with the ring-key, and she took us up to the first level above so that we could further explore the complex. Letting ourselves in through the portal doorway, we entered with a sense of caution, lest there be more of the Shiver beasts lurking about inside the complex.

"That was a pretty big explosion. Do you think there's a chance that Walter might have been able to spot the smoke from the greenhouse back there, Doc?" I asked the professor, but his thoughts on the subject phased into the shadow of a scowl.

"Maybe so Allen, but satellite updates take a full day to cycle, and there's always the chance that we are currently too far inland for them to make a visual confirmation from the coast. Regardless, any real-time satellite imagery would be from equipment owned by military entities," the professor admitted.

It still wasn't clear to me why the Professor and his assistant were so spooked by either military or government involvement in this epic project. And sure, I could understand his ethical dilemma of letting one country get a hold of such unique technology, which might taint his polished principles but he had to admit that things have gotten out of hand. Mica seemed to follow his lead, even when he failed to spell out his objectives from moment to moment, which made me uneasy about what it was they knew that I wasn't being told.

The entire deck of the level we had entered was brushed with silver foil along the floor and up along the lower walls, and oddly enough, the place seemed to be fairly clear of any dust and debris one might expect of such an ancient fortress. The temperature inside was a might chilly compared to what we had grown accustomed to back within the arboretum but there was little we could do to repair the amount of damage we had done to it. Mica circled the room and spotted something on a shelf upon the wall, and called us over.

There sat another sculpture of a broad tree made of the same crystalline material of the fortress. It looked to be nothing more than an art piece, until Mica pointed out what appeared to be embedded around its trunk. There above the grasp of the molded limbs was a duplicate ring key of the exact same size and shape of the one Mica was now wearing upon her wrist. This strange symbolism caused Logan to reflect on the many depictions he had researched about the icon of the World Tree, which he had seen in several historic volumes. In an epiphany, he came to the realization what the border ring surrounding all these images might have actually represented.

Of all the deities and idols these people might have held in worship in their ancient culture, they had instead chosen a symbol of nature as the most divine. The ring in its shape meant a cycle of life or representation of the earth itself; or as seen here, which combined both of these icons within the same motif. Crystals and harmonics, earth frequencies and the solar cycles, were all woven together in a graceful balance of being one with the world around them. Their era of technology was a place far removed from our modern civilization where we exploited our resources and engaged in great atrocities that poisoned our ecosystem. All of which, would be considered crude and ugly in comparison to their practiced philosophy.

The architecture I had seen here made me wonder how we had lost such knowledge and science during our evolution, and how a culture from the times of antiquity was able to create such grand accomplishments without all the mechanical devices we relied upon today.

"The way I see it," Mica answered my inquiry, "is that the people back then merely thought in an entirely different way."

"What do you mean?" I asked, truly curious about her statement.

"You need to understand, Allen, that the character and ethics of an individual is molded by their social environment," she began, "we could not find a qualified anthropologist to accompany us upon this expedition in the short time we had but Logan is doing his best to study the culture of these talented people who once lived upon this lost continent. In their day and age, there may have existed vastly different motivations for daily existence other than the petty accumulations of wealth or power, which drive the present formula of our own society."

I thought long and hard about her statement, and recognized that our modern world was rife with corruption from head to toe. Our governments and their regimes across the globe were infatuated with manipulating politics and power struggles, which usually turned the citizens they were meant to protect into pawns, who were exploited in every way imaginable. Modern-day slavery was disguised by forced acquisitions of land and property or endless taxation applied to everything under the sun. Hardly anyone opened their eyes wide enough to see it, because they had been groomed to believe that was just how things were supposed to be.

In this ancient culture, it appeared that energy was derived from a naturally occurring source and was used freely for the good of its inhabitants. But like most legends and tales of utopia, it was too good to last. I couldn't even imagine what kind of chaos this advanced technology would create in our modern society if an actual source of free energy was introduced into our civilization as a whole. Global economies based on fossil fuels would crash, and those who once controlled the taut strings of corporate power would suddenly find themselves swallowed by the vacuum of its absence.

In reality, it would spring war and bloody rivalries rather than sweep our civilization into a new age of discovery and invention. There was no room for charity in our era where greed and power were considered divine. We had been bred into believing that wealth was a badge of authority and to judge success with a dollar sign. Stepping back from that twisted perspective, I could see how bastardized and distorted the morals of our modern culture had become.

It made me wonder what type of place our world would be today if this ancient civilization had survived the polar shift. Logan and Mica were optimistic that our research in science, genetics, and written language, would have surpassed our wildest dreams if we hadn't been anchored by the pettiness and greed woven into our culture. Humanity had evolved into a selfish animal, unable to see past our own two feet. Witnessing such wonders as I had seen during this tour had taught me that my own sense of morals was exceptionally narrow-minded, and that I was in desperate need of a fresh perspective.

Logan picked up the small sculpture off the shelf and placed it on the silver counter next to us. When it touched the metal of the table, the tips of the roots and the limbs of the tree began to glow, and we watched in fascination as fingers of light formed around its circumference until they intertwined. The professor stood there gawking in astonishment as his eyes lit up when he realized what he was viewing.

"Do you see it?" Logan breathed aloud.

"Yes, we do..." I answered in confusion as to the baldness of his statement, but not quite understanding his point.

"Look, Mica," the professor pointed to the shower of lights from the small model of the tree which was now encapsulated by its own illumination. She observed that the lights seemed to be spinning in a vortex inward from the top canopy and out from the roots as the strings of light continued in their dance around the tiny icon.

"Is that a...?" She wondered aloud, not quite sure as to what she was seeing.

"Yes, yes! It's a torus," Logan exclaimed, "I never saw it before until now, but the iconic symbol of the tree of life is a representation of an energy torus."

The convex rotation of the lights was an illustration of the earth's own magnetic energy waves. The depiction of the world tree itself, was a striking image in two dimensions but in this active 3-dimensional model its true representation became clear. The balance displayed within its fanned branches as they connected to the spreading roots was no sheer accident of artistry but as a portrayal of the earth's energy fields in motion. This revelation opened a door to a fresh interpretation of this ancient image which has persevered throughout recorded history.

"This might mean that the iron tree we found was an ancient megalith, which was either an antenna or a receiver for these energy waves we have seen discharging across the globe," Logan suggested.

"But I thought that these giant orbs were the source," I

countered with a reply.

"Yes, they do in fact harness the natural earth's field," Mica answered, "think of them like a capacitor or a solar collector, but instead of sunlight they tap into geomagnetic radiation fields. The real problem now, is that they are out of alignment with the placement of where they need to be."

"You mean, like a solar panel that's facing the wrong way?" I offered my analogy.

"Exactly," Mica smiled, as she saw that I was using my imagination to work out the theoretical problem, "The continent of Antarctica is now several thousand kilometers from where it once rested along the geographic latitudes during the last polar shift, which creates several issues we may need to recalculate if we are going to succeed in dampening the current crisis."

The reality was that we just didn't have the equipment or manpower, nor hardware to get what we needed to get done. Logan refused all outside help in his efforts to hide this endeavor from the prying eyes of the government, which pretty much left us castrated from having any chance of success. When she saw that flustered look in my eye, Mica again reminded me that Logan would not budge from his stance regarding any outside interference. That only left us to scavenge what information we could find here within this glass fortress to make the required adjustments to the Alpha Orb, in order to stem the approach of what was promising to be a catastrophic event.

Logan wasn't sure that they could fully stop a polar shift entirely, although we might cripple or delay the onset of the impending crisis. We set about exploring the rest of the fortress with a due measure of caution so we wouldn't be caught alone in case we ran into any more of those Shiver beasts stalking the halls. When I asked him what it was we were looking for, Logan clarified that we were searching for anything that remotely resembled a console.

Roaming the chambers, we found the rooms disturbingly bare of any type of furniture or settings one might find in an abandoned structure. Mica suggested that such amenities might have long since decomposed, but that proposal was thwarted by the appearance that this crystal castle was sealed tight like a sarcophagus.

"Maybe it was raided sometime in the ancient past," I suggested offhand, "I've heard it often happened in Egyptian tombs and other such ruins around the world. Thieves and grave robbers run off with the goods in the middle of the night."

"It's always a possibility," Logan granted as we looked around, "hopefully they didn't scamper off with anything important."

Making our way farther into the building, we tripped across a strange arrangement of leveled platforms set in the middle of a chamber. There sat what appeared to be a set of outer and interior rings in the floor almost a full meter in height, but low enough where we could step-up upon the rise. Within its center, I noticed an inlaid image I had remembered seeing before but could not exactly place, so I assumed I was recollecting some glyph or rune I had seen somewhere over the previous days. When the professor climbed up to take a look at the central icon, I saw his expression changed into something unreadable.

"What is it Doc, you look like you've seen a ghost," I asked Logan, who had gone suddenly silent.

"It's ...it's nothing of concern, Allen," the professor mumbled as he looked around the raised dais in thought, "Mica, could you hand me that ring-key of yours, please," he asked his assistant, who removed it from her wrist and brought it to him.

Logan searched the central symbol and found an almost imperceptible indentation, and laid down the large ring within its setting. The moment he did so, the ring began to spin and quickly accelerated to incredible speeds. After witnessing this strange behavior, all three of us jumped back as the metal ring began to circle the outer edge of the dais border. Once it completed its circumference, the ring slipped to the next outer ring and continued rotating while the center platform rose out of the floor to a position far above our heads.

We backed away as the ring spun around and completed its

orbit of the 2nd platform, where it too, rose above the outermost ring. After the ring-key completed its third rotation of the exterior disc, it slowly stopped spinning and came to rest. Only then did Logan dare to pick it up again. Handing it back to Mica, the professor's attention was directed towards the center-most pillar which had risen beneath the emblem, where another glowing interface containing the full-body image of a woman now appeared.

We all glanced at one another in astonishment, realizing that this was just like the console with the reddish sphere we had found in the stone forest below the castle. Climbing our way up to it, the illuminated figure began to speak in a strange tongue, but we found no device for us to make physical contact with to allow it to connect with our thoughts. The glowing maiden stopped speaking for a moment, then resumed her speech in our language so that we could understand. Looking around him at his feet, Logan assumed the large round platform itself, was the channel for their connection.

"Welcome, visitors to our sanctum; may the light of the sacred tree fall upon you," she spoke in a whisper that penetrated our heads.

"Greetings..." Logan coughed, not really knowing if social etiquette was needed when communicating with the device, "there is a great deal we wish to ask you," he offered with a motion towards both myself and his associate.

"The Kish, hear and wish to share our knowledge," the woman offered in return; awaiting his request.

"The *Kish* you say?" Logan began, "I thought this was the domain of the Asgard?"

"Yes, the Kish are all men who dwell within our family, whether they are of large stature or small, being frail or hearty, or of any color or shade," she offered with grace, "and it is true that this is the citadel of the Asgardian lands."

"What happened to your civilization and its people?" Logan breathed with a tone of nostalgia seeping into his words as he addressed the glowing figure. However, there was a long wait of awkward silence when the device failed to respond and began to waver as though it were caught in a glitch. Eventually, it regained its function and responded to the Professors inquiry.

"A great many cycles have passed, and it is unknown where our people now reside," it answered curtly.

"Let me rephrase that question again," Logan offered to correct its misinterpretation, "a very long time ago there was a polar shift, a changing of the natural fields of the world, which resulted in this entire continent relocating to a new geographic position. What I meant to ask is, if any of your people, these 'Kish' as you call them, might have survive that cataclysm?"

"Your question cannot be answered," she returned, "for we have no way of tracing those who chose to leave this place," the image replied.

Logan realized that his current phase of questioning was just running them both in circles. It was obvious to him now that this fortress was a fixed point and that it could not provide further information on its citizens who had abandoned these frozen lands. Mica, however, stepped forward and put forth a question of her own.

"Tell us more about this crisis they suffered, before your people were forced to evacuate this region," Mica asked.

"From our great war with the Trinity, there also bloomed great strife," she began, "an artifact that was once a weapon of our enemy was transformed into an object of creation to benefit all those of the Kish. But there came a day when the stars did spin and a forever winter descended upon our green lands. This great weapon was parted into many, to help each of the six domains of the Kish to survive this change, but this resolution only brought sorrow, as each of these realms fell upon one another in their struggle to endure the bitter cold. The changes to our world and within our own social order, had been too great. Instead of combining forces in a joined effort to attain peace, the territories of the Kish withered from the civil storm brewing within our own walls, which destroyed our people more effectively than any fury a tempest could have wrought."

"So the polar shift must have happened *before* they split apart the energy orbs, which they did to assist each of the ruling kingdoms with their power requirements in order to keep their cities and their people alive through the frigid cold," Mica whispered to herself.

"Are these six orbs, these artifacts as you called them, can they be controlled to restore the natural energy fields of the world?" Mica inquired to the glowing maiden.

"The wise elders of the Kish attempted such a feat of which you speak, to spin the stars back where they once belonged, but in their effort in doing so, they had to link the split sections of the artifact once again into the former design of the weapon it once was," the woman answered.

Its words now clarified the contents of the mural we had seen back in the catacombs of the Dwarves, which were actually depicting the activation of the orbs towards their original purpose by reconnecting them to one another. Obviously, their efforts were unsuccessful but that fact didn't cause Logan to lose hope.

"So they tried, and it didn't work. Maybe it was because they had parted out the sphere and it needs to be recombined into the single configuration it once was," the professor surmised.

"You mean like taking the pieces of a bomb and putting it back together? Come on Doc, that's just nuts!" I blurted, "I thought you said that it would be a huge mistake to let any single government get a hold of this ancient technology, and now you're thinking about putting it back together in one bow-wrapped package for them?"

"You agreed it was worth the risk, Allen," Logan rebutted, "I will need to consult my associates as to the gravity of this situation," he turned back towards the image of the maiden and asked it another question, "How can we get these six individual source orbs to act as one?"

"By the hands of our Elders, the six sources of the separate realms have already joined together to act as one, and currently, only await the awakening of the prime," the figure answered.

"But the alpha sphere is already activated," Mica stated, as she was confused as to what it had meant by the prime source.

"Actually, *you* guys named it that, simply because it was the largest piece of the puzzle," I offered my opinion with a shrug, "did you ever stop to think that the outer shell wasn't what you thought it was, and maybe you got this backwards, and it was actually the innermost core within its center that was actually the controlling source?"

A stupefied look washed over Logan's face in a blank stare as he absorbed the simple logic of my words. Of course, the weapon the Kish spoke of would be designed like a planet, and the central core was the concentrated source which controlled all of its outer layers. They had gotten everything backward; but if that was so, that might very well mean they were in the wrong place to do any good. Mica, being attentive of the conversation, asked the woman the only viable question left she could muster.

"How do we awaken this ...this *prime source*, the core of the sphere weapon?" Mica asked.

"The knowledge of the Trinity who created the weapon was lost to us, and the only way the Elders knew of to awaken the heart of the device was to await a new cycle of change," the glowing images replied.

I turned to face Logan, who was torn between what he should do next. The Kish had somehow wired each of the six orbs together once again to make it functional, but apparently, it would take an active polar shift to kick start it into action. That meant we had to step into the eye of the storm before we could attempt to make it dissipate.

A World at War

Professor Logan managed to sway the ghostly interface of the Kish to direct him to another crystal console within the complex where we could once again contact our ship. We made our way to an adjacent chamber which appeared to be a duplicate control room to the one within the destroyed greenhouse, where we attempted to raise Walter on the communications channel. Within we found the disassembled sections of another flywheel, so I took a moment to fit the pieces together as I had done before. After it activated and began spinning, the crystal-lined console lit up and we attempted to reach our ship over the radio.

In our foresight, we had been wise enough to collect enough fruits and edibles from the garden and packed them in our bags, thereby leaving us with the relief of at least a few more days rations between us. After several hours of trying to reach Walter over the air, we gave up and finally got some much-needed rest. The three of us awoke just before the break of dawn the next day. Honestly, it was a beautiful sight to see the sunlight piercing through the clouds which lit up the crystal fortress with a spectrum of colors washing upon the walls. Mica came over to speak with me as I stretched and yawned while rousing from my uncomfortable bed on the hard floor.

"Carrot?" she offered as she pulled a large root out of her bag of plants we had gathered.

"Are you sure that's a carrot?" I uttered with doubt, looking at the tubular white root. Mica just shrugged and offered it again.

"I would hope so, at least it tastes like a carrot ...almost," she giggled as she turned away to view the morning sunlight gleaming in through the chamber as a rainbow of colors danced upon the walls, "It must have been truly beautiful here when the sun was higher overhead."

"What do you mean by that?" I asked, not catching her intent.

"When Antarctica was closer to the equator, the sun would

have been positioned almost straight overhead," she pointed up towards the high cathedral roof, "and I imagine the sunlight pouring in from above would have displayed this castle in all its majesty," she smiled again at the dream of it floating in her mind, "but now the sun barely makes it over the horizon here, even during this time of the year."

"I guess you're right," I answered while chewing on the strange vegetable, "it must have been a different world back then, covered in green forests and alive with life. It's hard to imagine now, looking out across this bleak frozen wasteland."

"Not for me," Mica replied as she brushed her hair aside, "doing what we do takes a lot of imagination; dreaming up worlds and the people that once lived, and you can't help but wonder about their hopes and dreams and how very different they must have been from our own," she finished with a distant look in her eyes. I could see that she was imagining it here in this moment and the past glory that this citadel once held.

I had to give it to her and the professor, for they made me view things from a different perspective, one far beyond my tiny and insignificant scope of the world of which I had been groomed to envision from our self-absorbed, social-media pushing society. We pretended to reach out and share ourselves, only to have far too many expectations about being accepted. It was if it was all some type of twisted psychological experiment to preen our population. I found it odd how so many people's lives centered on being popular with people they never actually knew or would ever meet. When I returned from my tour in the military and stepped outside of that narrow vision and took a moment to take an honest look at our culture in all of its flaws, it seemed pretty nuts that our society had been primed to be so entirely co-dependent that it could be seen as exceptionally unhealthy, or even downright dangerous.

I had only learned to be more self-dependent over the past few years while training during my various jobs in the field. I've worked as a private bodyguard and general security from time to time, but that type of self-defense discipline made me realize that there were far too many people who were entirely untrained for the realities of life outside of their own little bubble. It made me wonder how many of the citizens of the Kish, who dwelled within this advanced civilization, were left entirely unprepared for the chaos that befell them during the last polar shift which spun the earth on its edge.

I sat with Mica as we enjoyed the morning sunrise, while Logan got up and made his way back to the communications room to take another crack at getting in touch with the ship. He had previously borrowed my radio so he could open a channel. Fortunately, this console was placed out in the open so there was no chance of him getting himself sealed in. Once he returned back to the panel, Logan set down the radio and began adjusting the crystal rods on the control board.

"Logan expedition, this is Walter, come in team," a voice crackled over the radio. To Logan's excitement, he picked it up and responded in kind.

"Sir Walter, good to hear from you, old friend. We've been trying to reach you all night but to no avail," the professor breathed with a sigh of relief.

"Ah, Logan, I hope all is well. We were experiencing communication issues onboard here, and I have to report that there have been some complications regarding the escalating political tensions back on the mainland," Walter answered, "it's been a long night here on the ship with the entire crew in a panic, who are understandably worried about their families."

"I don't get your meaning. What's going on?" Logan remarked in confusion.

"There has been global pressure arising from the numerous earthquakes and hurricanes caused by the strange weather fronts which have been popping up over the last few days. Oceans waters have been receding from the coasts of Ireland up through Norway; and if the report I heard this morning is true, it actually snowed in Arabia last night!" Walter barked back as he related the shocking news, "These chaotic events have strained many national governments into declaring martial law in their desperate attempts to bring the rising discord among the population under control. Several nations have recently placed a majority of their naval forces out in open water while strengthening their land-based military presence among the civilian population, but they have met small pools of opposition by an unprecedented show of force while several communities worldwide have collapsed into anarchy."

Logan predicted something like this might happen but things were falling apart at the seams much faster than he could have imagined. Walter related that there were severe power outages that hit several major cities, which had drawn a significant military presence to regain civil order from looters; however, they encounter small pockets of dissidents who were opposed to their armed presence. He also reported that several provinces in Canada had experienced a collapse of their electrical grid during an especially intense aurora event overnight, as was also witnessed along the entire southern coastline of Australia. Minor conflicts in the Middle East had recently spread to adjacent territories, and there were talks of international war on nearly every news channel worldwide.

Walter went on to dictate that a great number of civil defense forces from rival nations were activated in an effort to secure their borders, and that tensions were escalating as civilians suddenly found themselves locked within areas of devastation, and were unable to escape to safety. The humanitarian crisis mounted when civil unrest began to spread from the lack of appropriate aid by the local government entities in their given districts. Civilians soon became disillusioned with the lack of integrity and response from the authorities who they had elected to protect them.

During his time teaching at the university, the professor had studied records of civilizations from around the world, spanning thousands of years. Logan had seen this type of development throughout history surrounding multiple cultures which had evolved around serving the upper elite who enjoyed the perks of status, while the servants and laborers who were the backbone of their society, were discarded and left abandoned when the empire faced any kind of calamity. Economic failure fell like a tidal wave upon those aristocratic survivors who had never worked a day in their life, and had no idea how to exist without someone serving their every need. Unfortunately, our own modern world had blurred the lines, by populating it with consumers to the point where the average person had no real clue as to how much they actually relied on others to provide for their daily existence.

The polar shifts might be just another natural cycle of our world, which our ancestors had experienced before but until now, the lack of evidence of their demise was brushed aside as a fanciful tale. The remnants of the Kish and their culture told another story; that humanity had been wiped out to but a handful of survivors who were left to repopulate the earth. Once again, mankind was witnessing an approaching shadow that promised to produce a radical thinning of the herd.

It did make the professor wonder if maybe the world was better off this way, since mankind had done so little to protect their environment and merely pursued its own selfish endeavors to pollute and destroy it. Perhaps this cycle of change was just Mother Nature's way of shaking off the parasitic fleas, which humanity had become. From his time within the forum of social studies at the academy, Logan had come to the conclusion that our present civilization, despite all of its technological advances, was the most synthetic and unworthy since the dawn of recorded time. It was the one single hypothesis he held that wasn't constructed from logic but from his own gut feeling.

Logan returned to where we sat after his conference with Walter on the ship, and enlightened us of the turbulent political atmosphere back home. We were shocked by what he said.

"The good news is, that Walter secured a satellite image of a heat burst in this region that was likely caused by the exploding dome, which he believes may pinpoint our location. They are double-checking the scans to make sure there were no other false readings. So we may know by tomorrow if they actually found us," Logan offered with a grim smile of hope.

I was praying that we hadn't traveled too far inland so that they could send a helicopter to retrieve us. Mica began to question why there were six spheres which comprised the original orb the Kish had referred to as a weapon. Logan explained how it may have been more than coincidence within the Sumerian culture itself, which had been lost to antiquity until its rediscovery in the 19th century, which operated by something called a sexagesimal system; which in fact, we still use today. I was surprised to hear that our world still utilized the same archaic science from ancient Mesopotamia, and their mathematical system for measuring time and geographical mapping, such as 60 seconds in our minutes and hours, and why there are 360 degrees in a circle, all which were based on their ancient calculations.

I found it to be an astounding revelation that the creation from the minds of a bygone culture could still have left such a fundamental impression in our modern world, which most people would never come to realize in their lifetime. That gave me a whole new perspective on Logan and his team of scientists whose hands drew the strings from humanities neglected past. In light of what we discovered of the Kish and the renewing cycles of the earth, it appears we had somehow stumbled upon our own forgotten future.

Logan returned to the raised dais to converse with the glowing icon of the woman who emerged from the ancient device. From their interaction, it became clear that this apparatus of the Kish had been asleep for countless centuries and was wholly unaware of the vast transition of time which had passed while it was lying dormant under layers of ice. The one thing that Logan was certain of, was that this ancient weapon and its six component spheres had begun to awaken from their long sleep, which once again began to harness the geomagnetic forces originating from deep within the earth. It had served as a warning device, but was it able to help us now?

"It is possible that the central core of the device can be accessed from this citadel but only once it becomes active," the glowing maiden related, "and once it does, you should be warned that its functions cannot be canceled until it completes its cycle."

That was troubling news, for we were hoping that we could define a measure of control over the device but the ancient artificial intelligence finally revealed that it had no clear notion of how much time had passed or even what global position the earth was currently in, which was vital data it required to assist us to that end. We had no way of merging their technology with our own since we had lost most of our equipment, including our GPS device, which Alexander had been carrying. We were stuck waiting for the inevitable, which is what influenced Professor Logan to have a change of heart about his plans for our rescue. I did not like what he had to say.

"We have to stay here..." he began with a sigh of defeat.

"What the hell are you talking about, Doc?" I snapped back, "We could get off this ice block by tomorrow, and you want to do what... play the hero?"

"Allen, please calm down. Unfortunately, he's right," Mica stepped forward to put a hand on my shoulder, "I don't like the idea of it either but it's our duty as scientists to see this through and be here to make the adjustments to the magnetic spheres when the time calls."

The steaming emotions I felt quickly dissolved after realizing how selfish and blind I was about our obligations. I was cold and tired, and stressed out about the news of the global meltdown, and I didn't want to spend the aftermath of it trapped on a slab of ice in the middle of nowhere. Logan suggested that we would be relatively safe here when the polar shift occurred but that revelation gave me little comfort.

"I just don't see why you need me here," I began, realizing I must have sounded like a coward as the words fell from my lips, "you could call in several more experts in this field to help you do ...whatever it is you're going to do," I barked.

Mica's eyes turned sad when I said that, while Logan's body language gave a weak sigh of resignation. I felt like a jerk just then, but I didn't like the fact that my life had been turned upside down since coming on this ill-fated expedition. I felt drained and scared, and didn't know how to deal with it other than running away. Whatever it was they held their loyalties to, I just didn't feel like I was of the same caliber. In reality, I just wanted an explanation as to why I should be forced to live up to their expectations.

"I'm sorry, Allen, that the prospects of this journey were not fully divulged to you in their entirety. I should have been more honest with you," Logan granted with a heavy heart, "when the time comes, I will have Walter send out a helicopter to drop off supplies and they can pick you up and take you back to the ship, where you will be provided with transport back to the mainland at the nearest convenience."

The hurtful look Mica turned my way, made me feel small. We had shared so much and I thought I was starting to see a new perspective, but maybe a tiger can't change its stripes. I had been groomed all my life to fit into a certain mold and when the stakes appeared too high, I had proven that I wasn't up to the task. Until this moment, I hadn't realized how weak of character I actually was, and my integrity suffered for it.

"Allen ...Allen, wait," Mica turned to follow me as I stormed away, more disgusted with myself at the moment than with our hopeless situation. I finally came to a stop as she caught up with me, but not knowing what to say. The scowl set on my face was from a mix of emotions I wasn't able to process.

"I, I just can't do this anymore," I yielded to her, "neither Thomas nor the Professor ever gave me the full scoop as to what we were doing here, and I feel like this whole thing was a mistake," I rambled on, "I know it's stupid, and that I would likely be somewhere else when all this ...*this bullshit* with the world turning upside down, but I don't see how we can do anything here without the right equipment and people who know what they are doing!"

"I understand Allen, I really do," Mica offered with a kind word as she leaned upon my back to put her arms around me, "but you *are* the right person, can't you see that?" Her words hit me like a rock.

"I don't know how you do it," I blurted like a baby with tears of embarrassment welling in my eyes, "the world is coming to an end, and we're stuck out here being chased by monsters, playing with magic rings, and giant stones, and whatnot," I stated as I touched the small metal circlet on her wrist she had recovered from the dais, "and I don't know what to believe in anymore!"

"I believe in you Allen," she muttered with a glint of kindness in her eyes, "but are you so afraid of losing everything, that you don't want to at least try to help save what we can?"

"But that's just it, Mica," I followed with an injured tone, "I don't have anything or anyone worth saving," I admitted. It was only at that moment that I realized how shallow my life had become. I had been scarred by failed relationships, living paycheck to paycheck, and running off to escape my regrets without having anything of real value to fight for. I felt hollow.

She kissed me just then. I didn't know why, because I had just bared myself as a whiny little coward who was so desperate to escape myself that I had chosen to abandon them. Somehow, all of that pain and anguish washed away within that fleeting moment she held me; it was if time itself had stopped so that I could appreciate that there was more to life than I was willing to see. I had been hurt before and trust wasn't something I gave away freely. I had become bias and jaded, which didn't make me a tougher person but someone far more brittle than I used to be. I lingered in that silent moment as Mica embraced me, recognizing what had been missing in my life for so long ...which was someone who actually believed in me.

It was a little awkward when we finally pulled away but all I could do was start with the stupid questions again.

"Why aren't you mad at me?" I spilled as I looked in her eyes while she wiped her lips.

"You needed reminding that there are people right here, right now, that need you, Allen," she muttered softly, and I couldn't fault her for her honesty.

"Well, Mica, I just..." I struggled as I searched for the words.

"If you want, I can drag the professor over here to kiss you too, if that will help change your mind?" She motioned towards Logan who was standing in the other chamber. Her slight smile soon turned into a giggle that became infectious.

"Hah, no, nah ...that won't be necessary," I grinned as I peered over her shoulder towards the professor who was conversing details with the interface.

"Time is short Allen, and we may not have much time to do what needs to be done. If you go back to the mainland you might end up just another casualty in what will eventually come," she noted with a raised brow, and I realized that she was probably right.

"But I'm not a scientist or possess any doctorate in this field. I've got no skill sets you guys need to accomplish this task. Hell, I accidentally locked myself in a room for Christ's sake!" I blurted.

"You've gotten us this far," Mica smiled back with a soft look as she gently took my hand to drag me back over to the platform where the professor was standing. I knew she meant them as words of kindness but they hit a soft spot when I thought of both Alex and Thomas, who we had lost along the way. The guilt of that still haunted me when I thought about it.

"Ah, there you two are. By asking several key questions, I've seemed to have gotten somewhere with this guide," Logan granted as he pointed to the illuminated ghost of the woman.

"Does this work by some sort of network that we can connect through to the other domains?" Mica inquired.

"Eh, not exactly a network per se, at least not in the way we think of it, but its more of an integration of knowledge which is unique among the other regions of Antarctica, which only share various select bits of information," Logan answered. His analogy left me a bit perplexed but that was nothing new.

"But, will we be able to adjust the connection of these six geomagnetic orbs once the polar shift begins, and align them accordingly?" Mica inquired.

"Yes, I believe we will. Apparently, there is a control tower at the upper level of this fortress where we can conduct the operation," the professor answered.

This was good news but we were still helpless to aid the global population suffering the brutal weather and earthquakes, which were devastating coastlines and rocking several regions around the world. From what Walter had reported, the death toll was climbing and putting governments on edge because their forces were being mobilized towards non-military endeavors during the course of conflicts between hostile countries. This left their borders vulnerable, and there were many rogue nations who would take advantage of such a desperate scenario. Even as we spoke, during this geographic crisis our civilization was tipping towards another world war.

Logan retrieved the information from the interface so he could draw a crude map of the fortress. From this data, he planned our route to reach the upper levels. Once we got inside the control room, we could manage the alignments of each of the orbs from that main control chamber. The only trick was that we would have to wait until the impending polar shift finally triggered the central core into operation. In the meantime, we only had a few days of raw vegetables to last us, but at least we had access to water from fresh snowfall drifting in from the shattered greenhouse dome.

We had to wait until late that evening until Logan could once again get the ship's crew back on the air to deliver an update. Unfortunately, Walter only delivered dire news that a handful of rival nations had already engaged in bloody conflicts in the midst of the ongoing natural disasters. Regions around the world were desperate for food and medicine; supplies which they had chosen to gain by use of force, rather than put down their arms and help one another. As always, the ugly side of human nature had shown its true colors.

As I gave a humble nod towards Logan, he let Walter know that the three of us would be staying onsite together until we completed our mission. Walter had already called in a helicopter but Logan informed them that instead of an extraction, they could refuel and load the chopper full of supplies and gear to drop off at our location. From the communications room, we weaved our way through the labyrinth of corridors and found ourselves in a maze that wasn't on Logan's detailed map.

"So, where are we at, Doc?" I asked with my hands on my hips as we looked about in confusion.

"That guide gave me directions, but they don't seem to correlate with what she, I mean, what *it*, said," he related while thumbing through his notes.

Mica stepped over to look at the rough map he had drawn and tried to make sense of it.

"I wish you would have let me helped you with this, Logan," she uttered with distress, "that's what an assistant is for, you know."

"Yes, yes, I know dear, just help me figure this out," he offered as he handed her a few loose papers from his pocketbook. The professor was still armed with one of the silver spikes from the lift, and he roamed about the open chamber while we continued to climb higher into the tower. However, according to his crude map, there was supposed to be a stairwell located at this intersection but there was nothing here.

"Are you sure you got the directions right?" I asked while taking a peek over Mica's shoulder, "There doesn't seem to be a way to get any higher. Maybe there is a hidden lift in the floor or something," I suggested offhand.

"I'm sure I got everything correct, Allen," he responded with a snort, "just help me look for an indentation for the bracelet key Mica is wearing and note anything else that looks out of place, would you?"

The three of us searched around both ends of the chamber but when we arrived to meet side by side, it finally dawned upon us that the doorway we had used to enter the room was no longer there. We suddenly found ourselves trapped inside a cell. Logan stepped back in contemplation as I began to feel an anxious churning in my stomach while wondering if we had walked into a trap.

"The corridor exit should be right here ...or here," Logan exclaimed as he pointed at one wall, then another several meters over, seeming a little unsure about his orientation.

"Well, this is unsettling," I blurted with a tone of anguish as we wandered around the large chamber, unsure as to what we should do next.

Mica, on the other hand, had a wild thought and removed the ring from her wrist, then placed it on the floor near the outer edge. Moving it around, she finally found a seam where the ring itself, began to rattle and spin. We had expected it to do something but after a while, it just sat there in place spinning slowly, and we had nary a clue as to what it was supposed to be doing.

"Considering how old this place is, maybe its internal workings have broken down," I suggested.

"I think you may be right, Allen," Logan answered as he scratched his head.

"Hold on a minute," Mica cut in, "Allen, give me your canteen," she ordered with her hand out.

"What, again?" I asked as I unstrapped the flask and handed it to her while referring to the trick she had pulled with the red sphere deep within the bowels of the fortress below.

Mica opened the canteen and gently poured out a stream of water into the center of the spinning ring while both Logan and I watched in amazement. Instead of creating a lubricating layer beneath the ring, the small amount of water she had poured into the circlet floated there and began to pool into a turbulent circle.

"Ah, it's creating a diamagnetic reaction. I should have known that the torus field would react to other natural elements," Logan exclaimed with mild surprise.

"Ah, I see ...but ah, what exactly does that mean?" I asked

bluntly, though failing in my efforts of trying not to appear so entirely naive as to what he was talking about.

"The technology of the Kish appears to be heavily reliant on magnetic fields, right?" She started to explain, and I just nodded my head in agreement like a dolt, "So the reason that this ring spins in this manner, is because it's inducing a small magnetic field."

"Ah, I see," I spat again, like an idiot repeating myself.

"So it's either generating, or responding to an electromagnetic induction, which creates..." Logan led off in thought as his assistant answered for him.

"An electric current," Mica finished his sentence.

"Yeah, it's a cute magician's trick, but what good does it do us?" I shrugged, not understanding why they were both getting so excited about it.

"These battery rings are not only magnetic keys, which are useful as locks and triggers, but they also create electric conductivity with the right element," she stated with a grin of satisfaction of what she had uncovered.

Mica had to explain to me that water itself was slightly magnetic, which was something I would have never guessed but that explained how it was floating there within the spinning ring. She quickly snatched the ring from where it was rotating and raised it, causing the field to collapse around the liquid, and in that instant, the blob of water lost cohesion and splashed to the floor. She then set the ring down in the same place and waited for it to begin revolving once again, until it reached its optimum speed. She then took the silver staff from Logan's grasp and slowly inserted it within the central axis of the rotating ring.

"Ah, this reminds me of an induction forge," Logan breathed.

"What exactly is that?" I asked without masking my dignity.

"It's a way to melt metal without direct heat from an ignitable source," the professor stated, although his explanation still left me in the dark, "which is actually used in our modern foundries and among many other applications using Faraday's law, but these sciences are not generally as well known to the public at large," Logan finished with a smile of satisfaction. I, however, was still at a complete loss.

"So, in short, it uses magnetism to heat the metal?" I blurted.

"Magnetic fields in rapid flux, yes," Logan shot back.

We stood there watching as the entire tip of the staff began to turn white-hot but it still did not seem to melt, making me consider that it was a type of special alloy. Within seconds, electrical arcs began to dance between the rod and the spinning ring, but Mica didn't let go of her grip. Apparently, the rod itself absorbed the voltage without passing it along to her.

"Do you think this staff we presumed was a lightning rod, might actually be another type of battery?" Logan inquired with astonishment to the cleverness of his assistant.

"I wasn't sure, but they both the ring and this shaft appear to be forged of the same type of alloy," she responded.

She lifted the rod out of the electrical vortex, then laid it down within the center of the room and backed away. Fingers of electricity emanated from where its heated tip touched the floor and the staff itself began to pivot in place. Like a needle in a compass, it began to spin, steering towards one section of the curved wall until it came to a stop pointing at one particular panel. Mica then grabbed the metal bracelet and placed it upon the floor at the edge of the room before it.

A jolt of electricity sparked from the coil and danced across the panel where the image of a tree suddenly appeared, surrounded by a thick border. This was the icon of the sacred tree the Kish so revered. Mica gently touched it while looking for a keyhole or depression where she could place the ring, but the walls surrounding us began to spin when she did. This took us all by surprise and left us disoriented while the walls twisted about us until they slowed to a stop. We could now see that several tree-formed designs of various styles were marked on each of the panels, appearing as though they had been created by different artisans.

Mica did the best she could to point towards the one that

originally appeared, although she wasn't quite sure because it all happened so fast. She put the ring back on her arm and touched the panel once again and it slid open, revealing that we had ascended to another level of the tower. Looking around, Logan recognized something he had recorded upon his hand-drawn map and claimed to know where we were. I picked the staff off the floor just as we left the room and the panel closed behind us, leaving us stranded in a pyramid-shaped room at the highest point of the citadel.

"Um, do you think I should have left this in there?" I asked Mica with a sense of guilt as I held up the silver spear.

"Well, it's too late to worry about that now," she noted with a shrug, "let's see if we can find that master control room Logan was talking about, shall we."

Making our way through the upper level, we crossed into a chamber which was unique, to say the least. A circular platform stood in the middle of an oval room, surrounded by half a dozen pedestals lining its circumference. Upon these podiums floated several clumps of what appeared to be different types of metal, each of them was shattered into a variety of pieces that moved independently from one another. Other settings contained shards of crystals levitating in midair, slowly rotating without any fixed point. Professor Logan strode up to the central platform and took his time inspecting the surface details.

Etched therein, were various images and symbols that lined its outer edge. He asked his assistant to hand over the battery ring, which he then used to frame several emblems upon the table. Mica assisted him from the other side as they searched for hieroglyphs that corresponded with one another. Marking them out, Logan was eventually able to get several of them activated.

The symbols began to glow a soft crimson color as one of the clumps of metal on a single pedestal began to snap together into its original form.

"Ah, progress..." Logan chimed as he offered a smile of satisfaction, "if I'm right, that sequence connected one of the power orbs to this console. Moving the ring key around the top of the table over each symbol to match them up, a separate clump of shattered crystals began to coalesce upon another stand; becoming one with its former structure.

"How the hell do you know what you're doing, Doc?" I asked, quite perplexed by the method he was using to control them.

"See here," Logan stated as he motioned for me to come over to his side, "this symbol is that of the Jotu, or the domain of the giants, where we activated the first orb, remember?" he asked, and I nodded, "and here is the one for the Nida, or the Dwarves, as you so quaintly called them, which was a predominant icon we saw branded upon their walls within the catacombs," he noted as he pointed to the crystal base which had joined itself into a single complete shard the moment before, "and this one represents the Asga, or Asgardians from the tall tales of the Norse mythology," Logan stated as he pointed towards that same symbol we had found embedded within the floor where the ghostly interface had emerged at the base of the tower.

I looked at it again, recognizing the symbol from before, but still not being able to place it from memory. I knew I had seen it somewhere and was irritated that I couldn't remember where it had been. Looking down to grab my flashlight, I unwittingly knocked aside Tom's boot knife which I had kept on my belt, and it fell to the floor. I peered at it closely as I picked it up, and noticed that the strange insignia cast within the hilt of the dagger was an exact replica as the one for this citadel which the professor had just shown me. I stood there stunned as I slowly turned the knife over to show it to Logan, wondering how the two images could possibly be the same.

Atlas Star

Although Logan appeared busy with the console, I couldn't help but bring attention to what I had discovered. Holding the hilt of the dagger up, I showed it to the professor.

"Why is the symbol of this ancient fortress on Tom's knife?" I demanded. I remembered now how Logan had reacted when we had first seen this same icon on the floor of the main chamber. He had also known this figure. Logan and Thomas had been associates for years and there was some history to this he was hiding.

"It would be too hard to explain at this point," Logan tried to shrug off my inquiry.

"Enough with the lies, Doc!" I grated with an unmistakable measure of anger in my voice.

"What is he talking about?" Mica asked Logan as she glanced at the dagger from across the table.

The professor stopped what he was doing and turned to me as he took the knife and placed it back in the sheath I had set upon the ledge. Logan had an odd look in his eyes as his thumb caressed the hilt across the symbol molded within its handle. He seemed distant at that moment as if lingering somewhere in the past. It was as though I had awoken a sour and unpleasant memory he seemed reluctant to recall.

"You may have heard of the Illuminati, the Skull & Bones, the Freemasons, the Knights Templar, Order of the Eastern Star, or of many other such secret backroom organizations and the conspiracies that surround them," Logan began, "which were all respected Orders of their given era, controlled by select groups of insightful men ...and women," he added with a modest nod towards his assistant so as to not forsake her gender, "they were self-appointed custodians who were seeking change in a social system which had fallen to the wayside; which in their eyes, had sunk to an ideology which seemed unfair to the common man. Their existence was twisted by slanderous whispers and tall tales that followed in their wake, which was merely the scripted disinformation that was fed to the public about these obscure societies, conceived by those who were in positions of authority at the time. As a result of their deceit and propaganda against these notorious groups, it was the very citizens themselves for which these organizations were created to protect, who in turn, began to fear them."

"But I thought those secret societies were intertwined with governments and monarchs, and other positions of control over the population," Mica announced with a look of surprise.

"Over time, some did eventually evolve into seats of power, seeking to press their own influence against the grain of their origin, but one must be reminded that many of these obscure societies evolved within timelines that stretched over centuries. What isn't common knowledge, is that many of those Orders derived from the roots of even older cults," Logan responded.

"So what does all that have to do with this?" I pointed at the symbol on the dagger, feeling that both Thomas and Logan were involved in something they had failed to tell the rest of us.

"Ever since I was a child, I had taken a keen interest in ancient cultures from the times of antiquity, and even in our most recent era of human societies where secret groups had arisen, whose real goals were to oppose superstition, deception, and overreaching religious influence on public life and its citizens, and especially so towards those that committed abuses of both state and administrative power," Logan answered, "Tom and I, along with Sir Walter and Alexander, as are many other scientists of ethical conscious, have been drawn together by a common theology that has been known by several names throughout recorded history."

"And what *exactly* is that?" I demanded with a suspicious glare towards Logan.

"It is known in many parts of the world as the Atlas Star, commonly seen as a crescent moon symbol below a rising star, though in reality, what most see as the icon of a moon is actually a representation of the Gaia, our own Earth, and the shining star itself, refers to creation," the professor revealed.

"But, Thomas wasn't a scientist," Mica pointed out.

"One need not be a scholar to join our cause," Logan corrected, "for it is based on a sense of ethics as a caretaker towards the Earth itself, and that all races of men should realize that we share this planet with many other forms of life," he added. This core doctrine struck me as strange because I never saw the Professor as a tree-hugging hippy.

"So what exactly does that mean? That members of this Atlas organization are all flower-power environmentalists?" I reached for an answer while trying to make sense of his wild statement.

"Far more than that, my friend, for we hold a common belief that mankind has lost balance with this world on which we live," Logan responded with the hint of a smile, "we are just common people who have awakened from the illusion of our modern societies and how these irrational, if not deranged, pursuits of greed and power have poisoned our civilization and stunted our growth as a whole," he finished.

"So you're what ...either feral hippies, or anarchists?" I began to struggle with his explanation.

"Or perhaps both, in a sense ...you might say," Logan granted with a slight grin, "and you may have seen the modern symbol for anarchists is actually a variance of a five-pointed star," he noted while gesturing towards the icon engraved upon the dagger, "within a circle, which represents the earth, and the 'A' is a modern update of the ancient symbol referring to the 'Atlas'. It's a fundamental translation, actually," he stated as he turned the dagger around so that the handle faced me to place the icon upright, "it was said that this symbol had once stood for *pacifism*, but its older meaning actually means; *purity*."

Mica came over and took the dagger and compared it to the symbol written in his notes, seeing the same vector of the archaic icon drawn within. Both Mica and I had no idea that Logan and his colleagues were all part of some secret brotherhood; and to her surprise, the professor took a moment to inform his assistant that her own mentor, Professor Rice, had also been a member of the same gentry.

"If that's true, why didn't he tell me about it?" Mica inquired.

"On many occasions, Vincent expressed to me that he had wished to disclose that information to you, dear, but only when the time was right," Logan offered as an answer.

"So what the hell does all this mean, what is your real agenda for coming out here, Doc?" I charged as Mica handed the small boot knife back to me.

"Our modern world has tipped hell-bent towards its own self-destruction ever since the turn of the industrial revolution," Logan stated as he regained his composure, "nonrenewable resources forged with toxins are polluting our ecosystem on a level far beyond what is being reported to the public; which due to our many types of global transportation, are no longer contained as localized problems to certain sections of the hemisphere," the professor admitted. This was, of course, all true, for we had seen such reports regarding toxic landfills and vast stretches of garbage floating in our oceans.

"Are ...are you actually trying to encourage this polar shift, Logan?" Mica dared to ask.

"No, no, my dear, you misunderstand the direction and the very purpose behind this expedition," the professor noted, "this ancient technology works in balance with the *natural* flow of energies without all the hazardous and permanent side effects of our current methods, which is something we are trying to understand to help us alleviate the damage we are doing."

"But why all the secrecy?" I asked brazenly, not seeing the two sides of the coin.

"Allen, my friend, governments aren't created for the good of the people; history has proven that they become self-appointed Shepard's wielding power over the common citizen, who are usually too blind to realize they have been corralled like cattle," Logan offered as an analogy, "and we need a free society where artisans and philosophers are allowed to flourish instead of being censored and silenced into a system of slavery. Though we stand here within the ancient ruins of these forgotten people, one might say that our own modern society, with all of its technological advances, is *actually* the Lost Civilization," he finished.

That was pretty heavy-duty psychology coming from the old man who surprised me with the deep conviction resounding in his words. He further revealed that there was a movement within this Order of the Atlas towards an open society where ideas and inventions were not tethered by petty greed but were shared for the benefit of everyone. That meant the end of corporations and their ruling conglomerates which supervised and swayed entire cultures and economies. In the simplest of terms, it was the vision for a better world.

I understood where Logan was coming from but couldn't contemplate if there was any basis of reality to what they were trying to accomplish. Frankly, the human race was a pretty fucked-up species. We killed without necessity, rather than pursuing peace and harmony. Mankind was warlike and selfish, while the Professor and his kind were putting a lot of faith in the poetic idea that it could all change. Even if these members of the Atlas ever achieved such an unrealistic goal ...how long would it last?

"For one, Allen, we're not an Order or a Cult, we are everyday people who were fed up with the lies and manipulation pressed upon us. We merely see that humanity can be better than what it is," Logan proclaimed with spirit.

"And, how were you drawn into all of this?" Mica inquired.

"Oh, I was just one of many such minds in the scientific community who saw that our skills were being swayed towards purposes we found both distasteful and offensive to our better senses," the professor explained, "my path eventually led me to join them, guided by the feeling of frustration I felt inside, like most members of the Atlas Star."

"So what do you do ...get a secret handshake, a ritual mask, or some sort of decoder ring?" I half-joked, "how did you join this *Atlas* movement?"

"By opening our eyes and seeing what was wrong with our world and actively doing something about it, Allen!" Logan snapped back with a stout touch of logic in his tone.

From what Logan revealed, there were millions of such members across the world who represented this same train of thought, and were willing to sacrifice everything to see it through. I could then grasp why they kept such a level of secrecy, for any government entity would see such a person as a dissident and their cause labeled as criminal, even if that was the farthest thing from the truth. By forging constant conflict, governments always had a convenient enemy to use as a culprit in order to sway the masses into their favor, even if such engagements were entirely fictitious. Theirs was a world of misdirection, and those who were of heart and mind of the Atlas could see through that deceptive veil.

"This technology here," Logan explained as he waved his hands over the console and its strange artifacts, "could be used towards the benefit of all mankind across the globe, and could terminate our dependence upon fossil fuels and nuclear power plants, and countless other industries which poison our world, but the powers that be would only suppress these advances, as they've always done."

I understood Logan's perspective well. There were always growing pockets of discord to be found among the civilian population, no matter what country you were in. As human history has shown, that rebellion was the natural reaction for those forced into a suppressed way of life, but today's society was blinded by trickery and deceit into living lives of indentured servitude. He was right, what the professor had told me before about the way our civilization had devolved into a culture of willful slaves began to make sense when you looked at it from outside of the box. The further I saw into it, the more that malformed crate began to resemble a coffin. Death and destruction became an infatuation with our species to a level of insanity. There had to be another way out!

"But there *is* a way for the world to escape this downward

spiral," Logan answered my plea.

"How so?" Mica replied.

"We must make every effort to keep this technology out of the hands of those who would abuse and control it, and make sure its resources are available to everyone," Logan replied, "our current political structure is merely a path towards regression. Once this ancient civilization and their advancements are revealed to the world, we must consider how it will affect future generations. The last thing we want is to make the same mistakes of our forefathers."

That said, the professor turned back towards the control board and began deciphering the symbols upon the console. Mica assisted on the opposite end while I looked on. They managed to activate another orb and connected it to the system.

"All that is left are the energy spheres from the Nif, the Alf and the Mu," Logan instructed his assistant as they concentrated on the board to coordinate their efforts.

"Which one do you presume is the location of the core?" Mica inquired as she looked over the specs.

"We already visited the realm of the Alf, or the Elves as they were known to be called, which was where we got separated in the vibrant forest and the flowing geysers," Logan replied, "the Nif was reputed as a frozen land, where even time itself was slowed. However, it is my deduction that the core may very well be in the domain of the Muspelheim, a realm of fire."

His reasoning seemed logical, if the energy orb was based on the model of the Earth itself. A solid core embraced in a bed of molten fire fit the common model accepted by the scientific community. Setting up the corresponding symbols, Logan and Mica activated the pedestal where the sections of a shredded plant assembled together before their eyes and began to glow with life once it was made whole again. Next, they concentrated on the realm of the Mu, and attempted to actuate the shattered remnants of a crimson gemstone, only to find that it refused to react. Logan appeared to be troubled at the situation that evolved.

"It's not working..." he mumbled at a loss to why he couldn't get the symbols to align.

"What if the earth's core isn't actually what we think it is," I mentioned with a shrug, "I mean, nobody really knows, right?"

They both knew I was correct. History had proven that conjecture among scientists and scholars had quite often ended with them being proven wrong.

"He may be onto something," Mica responded to my suggestion, "it's known that high heat can weaken and entirely impair the effects of magnetism, so it would be logical to consider that the innermost center of earth's core, if it is being used as a natural model for this ancient technology, might be far cooler than is commonly presumed," she offered.

"Hmm, an interesting theory," Logan set in deep thought as he rubbed his jaw, "it seems you're full of surprises Allen. All differences between us aside, I'm glad you were able to accompany us. Your unorthodox insight has proved to be quite beneficial," he exclaimed. Though I smiled, my curled brow revealed that I wasn't quite sure if the professor had just tossed me a veiled insult.

Mica offered to go back down to the lower level and question the sentinel interface to reveal the correct realm where they could find the central core, so as to avoid any mistakes, but a few moments later, she stormed back to the console in frustration since she was unable to get the doorway to open. Even by utilizing the ring and the tall rod as she had done before, there was still no reaction. This left Logan trying to access answers from the console itself, while we were left wondering if we were now trapped here. After much aggravation and little to no results to show for it, Logan yielded.

"Ah, well I have good news and bad news," he began with a look of surrender flowing over his face, "the bad news is, that it appears that there was a buried lock-down protocol for this control tower, which apparently engaged itself when we activated its systems. However, the good news is that there is a way to get a team member to one of the two realms left on the board."

"Well then, let's go," I suggested with encouragement.

"Ah, well there is a sour note to that course of action," he frowned, "as I mentioned, I only said 'a single' team member. The unfortunate side of this development is that only one of us will be able to transit to either realm and discover which one contains the central core," he confirmed, "from the information Mica and I are reading on this panel, is that there is something obstructing the link between the two last energy orbs somewhere within these particular domains, and unfortunately, we can't pinpoint what it is."

"Well, it would be prudent for either one of you to go, since you clearly know far more about this ancient crap than I do!" I blurted, stating the obvious as I motioned towards the console.

"We have to stay here and mind the control board, as it takes a minimum of two people to work this contraption," Logan noted, "so you will have to scout the area alone."

"But what will I be looking for?" I inquired.

"Actually, we aren't sure," Mica answered as her glance shifted towards the professor with a spark of innocence, "But you should know it when you see it."

Logan had activated a surplus escape pod, one which had been left behind since the time the fortress was abandoned all those ages ago. He led me to an inner wall where there appeared an ivory cylinder covered in thick crystalline sheets. Opening its hatch, he bade me to step inside.

"We're lucky this was here," Logan granted with a raised brow.

"Uh, are you sure this thing still works?" I asked with a shaky voice, noting the dismal condition of the interior of the craft.

"We'll find out soon enough. If it doesn't activate and send you off to the target area then we can think of something else," he muttered with fabricated confidence.

"And ...what if it just blows up?" I asked bluntly.

"Well, then *Mica and I* will think of something else," Logan abruptly squirmed out an answer, "did you have a personal preference which domain you wanted to search first?"

"You mean the Nif, or Mu, as you called it?" I inquired.

"Indeed, the realm of Muspelheim is likely to have volcanic activity, while Niflheim is reputed to consist of ice," Logan informed.

"Well, since I'm already dressed for cold weather and that's where the power core is most likely to be, then I guess I'll try that one first," I granted with mild hesitation.

"Ah, good, pertaining to your previous advice, that was the first set of coordinates I put in," Logan smiled as he looked over his shoulder and motioned towards Mica, who activated the control board before her, "oh, and here, take this, you might need it," he offered as he handed me the silver spear as I wiggled myself into the capsule container.

"What for?" I inquired with a hint of worry.

"The frozen realm of Nifleheim was also reputed as the home of a placed they called 'Hel' which was the legendary land of the dead," Logan answered as the ivory hatch slid shut.

"Hell? Wait ...what!" I stuttered loudly as the doorway sealed and the crystalline capsule began to shake. The whirring sound issuing from within the tight chamber helped me change my mind about this whole idea, and I began banging on the walls demanding to be let out. Apparently, they didn't hear me, for I felt my stomach sink as a pressure twisted down upon my shoulders from the abrupt acceleration; then there was suddenly nothing but the gentle wobble of the vehicle.

Within the tight cabin, I tried to rub off the grit from a narrow window but the glazed crystal contorted the view beyond. From what I could tell, I was now floating in the air high above the frozen terrain, drifting at the mercy of the dark storm clouds enveloping the horizon.

Gravity Storm

I awoke some time later, quite unaware how or when I had fallen asleep entombed within the capsule with both hands still gripping tightly onto the silver staff. The vehicle was floating through the air, drifting on invisible magnetic waves, leaving me cruising across the Antarctic badlands. My one worry, was that I was going to asphyxiate while trapped within the small chamber as the time passed but the air within seemed fresh as if it were being vented in by means I could not detect. Boredom set in as minutes turn into hours, while my crystal capsule rode upon the magnetic winds.

I perked up when I felt an abrupt drop in pressure and the craft began descending rapidly. Although I tried to see where I was, my view was still obscured by the nearly opaque material which comprised this strange chariot. Suddenly, the carrier picked up speed and shot through a deep crevice in the ice sheet, racing past chambers embedded within an enormous blue glacier riddled with hundreds of honeycomb structures. Deeper into the depths the capsule fell, like an arrow shot from an angry god. With a jolt, my curious ride came to a halt as the crystalline vehicle became embedded in a strange web-like structure, absorbing its deadly momentum as it bobbed and swayed until it came to a gentle stop.

Moments later, the hatch opened with a hiss of air, letting in a bittersweet fragrance I could not identify at first. Stepping out of the crystal container, the landscape of my surroundings was almost too overwhelming to absorb as I stood there speechless. Countless chambers lined the walls of the crevice where my ship had entered the vast fissure, the entire atmosphere within was saturated in a deep sapphire hue. Oddly enough, for being the realm of ice that Niffleheim was reputed to be from the legends of the Norsemen, it felt insulated from the bitterly cold winds howling across the surface high above.

After departing the ship, my first few steps sank into the strange sponge-like formations of fungus. It took me a moment to realize that the surface I was standing upon was precariously situated atop a giant mushroom. To either side of the fissure, I saw an entire forest of these turquoise mutations lining the bottom of the chasm, stretching out as far as I could see. The metallic staff Logan had bestowed, became necessary for me to use as a tool to keep a level footing while I climbed my way down to solid ground.

I was astonished to find a rolling forest of fungus in every tint of blue. The silence of this place was like a tomb yielding an eerie sense of timelessness. Picking a direction, I chose to head towards the section illuminated with the most light as my guiding beacon. Cutting a rough trail through the uneven carpet of cyan moss, I forced my way through several kilometers of the dense growth until I finally stumbled upon a bizarre city built over a frozen lake.

Streams of frost fell from the cavern ceiling, glittering like diamond waterfalls as they rained upon the surface of the lake. The suspended buildings appeared to be made from the ice itself, sculpted by nature as if they had somehow grown in their fantastical contours instead of constructed by mechanical means. It turned out to be more than just a tad difficult to find a way inside the structure because of its position above the lake, with no clear access to breach it. Crossing the outer bank, I came across several buildings of similar architecture but noted that there appeared to be nothing inside of them.

There were no vents nor plumbing or sources of light of any kind as we had seen in previous ruins which left these buildings strangely empty, appearing as if they had been used as containers for storage, rather than dwellings. With a sigh of fatigue, I finally discovered a narrow bridge spanning the distance from the shore to the main complex. The construct of it was slippery and hazardous, and I had to watch my footing lest a misstep sent me plummeting to the hard ice waiting below. Before I had departed the tower, Mica had instructed that I should find a similar interface located somewhere within the area.

I soon learned that the mega-structure itself was built like a labyrinth, with passages that led off into indistinct locations and blind alleys with unreachable floors high above. The more I searched, the less the layout of this compound made any logical sense in its design. It finally occurred to me that the reason this enormous metropolis was suspended above the frozen lake, was because that it actually wasn't a city at all. In all respects, it looked like some sort of exotically fashioned dam where a gravity-fed water flow from the surface might have once been used as a power source.

I realized that Logan had become infatuated with the idea that the Kish utilized the geomagnetic waves of the planet for their energy needs but it had not always been their only source of power. If this continent had once been located near our present equator then it was safe to assume that natural flowing water would have provided a vital alternative. That would certainly explain why there appeared to be thick ice formed around the entire facility, making it almost appear as if it was a natural formation. By luck, I stumbled upon an illuminated alcove, and by using the oversized silver pick, I managed to break my way past the wall of ice that encased it.

"Ah, yeah... not what I signed up for," I grumbled as I brushed off the chips of ice from my overzealous labor while trying to clear a passage.

Within the compartment, I found what Mica had briefed me to look for but I had counted my luck far too soon. The design of this interface was something I hadn't seen before. There were no crystals or segments of a flywheel to piece together; only the half section of a small sphere laying flat upon a pedestal, which left me perplexed.

"Ah dammit, of course it wouldn't be this easy," I blurted as I looked around for some sort of dimple in the console or a place to put the staff in an effort to get the thing to operate. Above the console, I found another half sphere, much larger in proportion than the first, which lit the interior of the room with a living light as if it were filled with a liquid flame. Turning back the way I had come, I couldn't find any other access to the rest of the chamber within which was riddled with chunks of solid ice. After wasting an hour chipping away at the debris, I found nothing concealed therein which would have been of any benefit towards my given dilemma.

Reluctantly, I backtracked and made my way back across the connecting bridge and took a seat upon the soft blue moss that littered the shoreline, so that I could contemplate the situation. Common sense told me that the enormous framework attached to the ceiling above the lake was some sort of down-spout and that the source of water could have been coming from a river that once resided on the surface far above. The only other option I had at the moment was to explore the path of the overflow and so I began tracing the banks of the frozen lake. Reaching the outer edge, I found the crest emptied into a colossal reservoir nearly half a kilometer deep. It was near this outlet that I came across several dozen capsules like the one I had arrived in, haphazardly stacked in a pile.

Apparently, a few survivors had made their way out here during those last days before the race of the Kish vanished from the earth. Searching for clues within the capsules, I stumbled upon a large pile of battery rings, similar to the one Mica carried upon her wrist. It was certainly a favorable find, but not knowing if any of them still worked, I decided to take as many as I could carry so that I could test them one at a time. The metal rings were uncomfortably cold and I couldn't fit more than a scant few over the cuff of my thick jacket, so in my ingenuity, I eventually stacked a dozen of the rings upon the tip of the staff in an effort to haul them easier. Having done so, I started my way back towards the bridge so I could try to activate the interface with one of them.

Carrying the staff in one hand as I made my way back towards the bridge, at first, I hadn't noticed the dancing sparks of static emanating from the stacked rings. I was circling the shoreline and was making my way across the bridge when I began to realize that each of the rings upon the staff were now spinning in place around the metal shaft.

"Uh-oh," I muttered aloud as I tried to tip the rod down to slide them off the staff, only to discover that they wouldn't budge from their fixed position.

In my cold-induced fatigue, I had entirely forgotten what had happened when Mica combined the ring she had with the staff to reveal the door panel back at the fortress, and realized it had probably been careless of me to stack so many rings that close together. As I tried to forcefully pull the rings off one at a time, I was rewarded with a painful shock as I tried to displace them. With a note of urgency, I scurried my way across the bridge as the entire length of the rod began to turn white-hot. With only a third of the way left to go, electrical arcs from the overpowered staff began to strike my arm with painful lashes.

Gritting my teeth in agonizing pain, I tried to hurry so that I could set down the staff on solid ground and try to figure what to do next but a powerful jolt from the energized staff stunned my arm and the nerves in my hand froze, releasing my grip. The staff and the spinning rings dropped to the floor of the narrow bridge and slipped over the side. Dancing arcs of electricity fingered their way into the air as if searching for a handhold to save itself. I dropped to my knees and peered over the edge, while biting my lip in remorse.

Brilliant arcs radiating from the staff reached out and touched the surface of the frozen lake before the sharp rod pierced the ice. I hadn't expected it to bite its way so deeply into the hardened surface as the electrical field reacted with the frozen water. Bright blue flashes raced out across the icy crust of the lake, followed by disturbing cracks as each tremor broke the serene silence of the cavern. Within moments, the lake below erupted with a massive upheaval as the energized staff reached critical mass at the apex of its violent reaction.

I looked from side to side, seeing that the bridge itself was cracking and beginning to collapse and got back onto my feet and started running for the central structure; nearly losing my footing as the narrow bridge crumbled beneath me. Jumping to the edge of the complex, the last remnants of the bridge broke free and fell away into the turbulent lake as plumes of broken ice erupted into the air from below. Great rifts opened up in the ice sheet as electricity clawed at the edges of its shattered surface. Deep within the frozen lake, a great deafening moan thundered through the air.

The cavern shook as blocks of stone and ice rained down into the turbulent waters which began to spout through the ice. Daring to peek once again over the edge towards the source of the clamor, and not quite believing what I was seeing, within the depths of the frozen waters an enormous orb, as black as death, was bristling with arcs of electricity. It took me only a moment to realize that I had really screwed this up, and swiftly fell into a state of panic.

Rushing back into the control room where the interface was located, I found that it was now illuminated by a ring of lights showing symbols upon its surface which had been hidden during my brief visit before. More bolts of electricity reached up from the churning lake to strike the overhanging structure while generating enough energy to spark the console to life. A concave pillar rose from its center and a familiar female face sprang from pins of light which floated within. After several moments it began to speak, though not in the fashion I had anticipated.

"Logan, it's on," the woman's voice stated, "it connected just now ...Allen, are you there, can you hear me?"

"Um, yeah it's me ...is that you Mica?" I answered to the device wearing the mask of the ancient guide.

"Yes, yes, we were worried about you," the sentinel image answered in its own voice, which was not Mica's; but merely repeating her words like an avatar, "we found a way to hack the interface so that we could communicate directly."

"That's great, but I, ah, have to tell you something..." I stuttered as another jolt of electricity sparked through the interface while I gripped onto the console to keep my balance as the structure shook violently beneath my feet.

"Were you able to locate the core?" she asked through the sentinel interface.

"Yeah, you could say that, but I did something foolish ...I mean, I kind of had a little accident," I quickly corrected, "I'm in a structure of some type hanging from a cavern roof, and the core is at the bottom of a frozen lake. Well, it's not really so frozen anymore," I admitted.

"We can try to control your interface there from our end once it becomes activated. Have you found anything that could have been blocking the connection to the fifth orb?" Mica asked.

"About that," I paused as the room shook momentarily, "are you sure that the main core can only be triggered by a polar shift? Because it seems a little feisty at the moment," I added for color as the groaning noise echoed in from outside the chamber.

"Are you saying it's active now?" the icon asked.

"I'm not positive, but it may have been awoken by an ample release of energy," I conceded with a shrug of guilt. My eyes turned towards the liquid light above me, which began to swirl with a strange rhythmic pulse similar to a heartbeat.

"How did that happen?" the interface responded.

"It had something to do with that rod and more than a few stacked power rings," I blurted quickly, "anyhow, I'm trapped inside this superstructure above the exploding lake. How the hell do I get out of here?"

A long uncomfortable pause made me wonder if the electrical interference had shorted out our connection but the interface finally responded with a sense of urgency in its tone.

"The Mu sphere just went online. I don't know how you did it, but good work!" the icon stated, although I wasn't sure if it was Mica or the Professor speaking.

"Yeah, that's great and all, but I would like to survive this, guys," I begged, "is there a way I can get out of here, like another ejection pod or something?"

"Wait a moment," the interface answered as the room shook violently, while I wondered if I actually *had* a moment left to spare, "we're going to disconnect from the interface at your location so you can ask it yourself, since our hack overrides its internal functions ...okay?"

"Sure, go for it," I spat, knowing I had no other choice in the matter. The face of the sentinel fizzled in and out several times until it finally began to respond once again.

"Welcome visitor, may the light of the sacred tree fall upon you..." the ancient device began to mumble its familiar introduction.

"...Of the sacred tree fall upon you," I repeated mockingly, "yeah, yeah, I don't really have time for pleasantries at the moment," I interrupted as the building shook once again, "is there any way to evacuate this facility to a safe distance?"

"There appears to be a disturbance in the base system, please wait while we access the situation," the interface responded as I stood there with my mouth open in shock at being placed on hold by this ancient form of customer service.

"Hey! Hello in there, this is kind of an emergency and I don't have a lot of time to wait," I yelled while I slapped the console, which began flashing erratically with flickering runes and blazing symbols I couldn't decipher. Aggravation got me nowhere as minutes passed while the jarring eruptions continued its violent escalation outside the complex.

"We have come to an assessment that this structure is in danger of collapse, please make your way to a pod and seek immediate departure," the device offered as an answer while I searched around in desperation, "correction, all of the pods seem to have been previously taken, you will need to find another route of escape," it amended to its suggested previous course of action.

"Aw fuck," I sighed, "is there anything else I can do from here?" I asked the console, praying for a miracle.

"This facility is utilized to provide coolant for the central nucleus," it answered, "it appears the core has recently awoken from dormancy prior to a terminal event."

I certainly didn't like the words it chose but I couldn't argue that things didn't look good for me at the moment. The interface addressed its concerns for my safety and directed me to enter a passage directly to the rear of the console, although it appeared entirely unaware that the passage was actually blocked by a wall of ice. It kept repeating its instructions to evacuate over and over until a final jolt of electricity coursed through the device, which appeared to short it out. Feeling like an idiot for getting myself into this situation, I ran back towards the entrance to see what was happening below.

Peering over the edge with a sense of dread, I saw the skin of the black sphere rolling with waves of electricity. Its surface was so dark that I couldn't tell if it was rotating as I had seen the other spheres operate before. I watched as it began to grow larger, though I didn't know how that was physically possible until I began to realize the sphere was actually rising towards me. I rushed back into the control room to see if I could possibly crack open the ice to the escape portal that was located within the back chamber, and tried in desperation to claw at the cracks and kick at the wall of ice that blocked my escape.

"The core sphere is now activated, anyone in the facility should withdraw to a safe distance," the interface popped back to life as it replicated its former warning.

"Why can't you just turn that god-damn weapon off!" I demanded while cursing through heavy breaths as I continued to beat at the wall of ice in vain.

"The prophets at this facility have concluded that the energy sphere was never meant to be used as a weapon," the interface revealed to my astonishment. I was so shocked that I ceased my antics to take a breath.

"What the hell do you mean?" I asked, "Everyone in the Kish said it was a weapon that was going to be used against them, but they captured it from an opposing army," I heaved as I remembered the knife sheathed on my belt and began to chip away at the ice with Tom's dagger.

"That was a misrepresentation of the truthful facts, which the prophets of this realm revealed from their research during the last era of our people," the interface answered, "a foreign force comprised of three races we called the Trinity, once visited our shores with a great device they wished to position upon our lands. However, these visitors were not invaders bent on conquering our region but had brought this mighty tool to help save both their world, and ours, from its untimely destruction."

At this revelation, I was left completely speechless. The shaking had subsided for the moment but the orb outside was growing ever closer to the superstructure situated directly above it. Asking the sentinel what it had meant by its statement, it divulged something the rest of the expedition team had overlooked entirely. The history of the Trinity and their defeat had been recorded with a certain bias, which was to make the Kish appear as victors of an unnecessary war. To hide their shame, their rulers had altered their recorded history to save face for a paramount mistake they could not otherwise erase.

The sentinel outlined how their own scientists they termed as 'prophets' had studied the core and learned its true purpose, which revealed that it was neither meant to be used as a weapon nor as an energy source which the rulers of the Kish had parted out to each of their clans, but rather acknowledged that the intended function of the particular device was to safely reset the natural cycle of the earth's polar shift. The Trinity had comprised of three diplomatic representatives from advanced cultures located across the globe, which needed to deliver the spheres to a specific geographic location on the planet in order to expedite the earth's natural shift, in an effort to minimize the catastrophic reactions of the earth's climate during the window when the planet's protective magnetic shield would subside. However, in their unfounded fears of these visitors who arrived upon their sacred lands, the Kish labeled these diplomats as intruders and seized the curious device they labeled as a great weapon for themselves, and in the process, they had unwittingly condemned their own civilization to its doom.

The people of the Kish stole this remarkable technology and divided it out among their domains in order to keep peace among their rivals but each of these realms manipulated the powerful apparatus to their own ends, provoking their downfall. They had done this to themselves. It appeared that mankind had carried the seeds of its own destruction by allowing greed and fear to persist in its culture over countless centuries. In the end, the earth was probably better off when the ways of the Kish were erased from history and their society had been left buried and forgotten.

"You also inquired about Hel," the interface declared as an afterthought to its long speech.

"Uh, what the hell are you saying?" I answered with a furrowed brow as electrical arcs from the rising orb began to penetrate the structure.

"Yes, we speak of Hel. The sub-domain of this facility," it answered bluntly. I recalled that Logan had mentioned it was the Kingdom of the Dead, or some such nonsense from his collection of myths and legends, "...which is currently your only route of salvation in this circumstance. Do we have your permission to transport you there?" the interface inquired.

"I uh, sure, whatever! Do it!" I stuttered with a note of apprehension as bolts of electricity surged through the structure, shattering the overhanging foundations.

In that aftershock, the wall of ice blocking my way split and fell to the side, opening a gap large enough for me to crawl through to the portal beyond. Finding only a small round chamber lined with dark crystalline panels within, I spun around in confusion. There were no vehicles or controls of any kind in the small room; it was just another dead end.

"You will be delivered to the suspension chamber, farewell visitor," the voice of the interface crackled before activating the apparatus.

The crystal panels flashed once, and I suddenly found myself enveloped in a type of composite glass, or ice, I wasn't sure which. I felt a sudden pressure as the clear block, which now encased my body, shot up through the roof and was jettisoned sideways out over the lake. As the block spun around midair, I could witness the massive orb crushing the suspended complex which had once fed the reservoir below; obliterating it entirely. My nerves struck a note of concern once I saw where I was heading, as my flight sent me over the edge of the banks of the shattered lake and down into the dark abyss waiting below.

Encased as I was, I couldn't move a muscle and was beginning to choke for lack of air. Feeling dizzy, I quickly blacked out. My last thoughts were wondering if this was how I was going to end my short and sorry life, by becoming a preserved specimen to be put on display in some archaic museum of oddities thousands of years from now. I certainly didn't like the idea of it.

                              *   *   *

Back at the crystal fortress, Mica and Logan were struggling to keep up with the chaos on the control console, which suddenly lit up around its entire perimeter in alarm. They were caught by surprise when a clear shard of crystal rose up out of the central platform, from which emerged a familiar voice.

"Is anyone out there?" It called, while the Professor and his assistant shared a shocked glance.

"Who was that?" Logan called over to Mica, though his query had been overheard by the crystal transmission.

"This is Alexander Beaumont with the Logan expedition," the voice stated.

"Alex, is that you?" Logan cried in wonder.

"Yes, of course, I just stated that fact. And to whom am I speaking?" Alex asked.

"This is Logan. Mica is here with ...well, Allen is away on assignment. Where are you?" the professor tried to fit his excitement into one sentence.

"After we got separated, I went back to the machine at the center of the quarry and managed to activate some sort of transportation track. It delivered me to a place which translates as the *Mu*, if that makes any sense?" Alexander offered.

"Yes, yes it does! The realm of Muspelheim," Logan responded. It made perfect sense that the domain of the Dwarves would be located near the fiery forges of the Mu.

"Anyways, I stumbled upon one of those giant spheres which they had locked down with an atrocious amount of clamps and chains. While searching around to try and find a way to open communications, I unwittingly released the sphere, which has just recently begun to power up. The good news is that it also activated the console here so that I could contact you," Alex granted with a sense of accomplishment.

Mica filled Alex in on the events that followed, including the balloon ride to the fortress of the Asgardians, and having sent off Allen to unlock the central core. Logan informed him they had also been able to reach Walter on the ship, and were able to locate their current position via satellite. With a little luck, they could also determine where to find Alex, unless there was a way he could travel to their location at the crystal spire.

Tapping into the main communications array, which Alex had initiated, they were able to contact Walter once again to get an update on the global situation. Things had only gone from bad to worse. Allen's accidental activation of the main core had seemed to coincide with the reported violent increases of seismic activity worldwide, which led to several ruptures throughout the pacific basin. Several countries had tipped towards the brink of a 3rd world war, threatening either hostile invasion or armed retaliation as the borders of many nations were overrun by great numbers of the population seeking sanctuary from local disasters during the great exodus.

Of noted concern, they were unable to reach Allen after he had released the core. Logan attempted to hack the sentinel once again at his location but found the system would not respond. Presuming the worst, they advised Walter on board the ship, to send out a supply run to their location and possibly send a search and rescue party out for Alexander and Allen on their return trip. Professor Logan gave Walt a list of things he would need so they could resume their work with the orbs, and hopefully, assist them to escape the confines of the control room if they were unable to access a way out.

Several hundred kilometers away, a giant black orb broke its way through the ice, sending tremors throughout the area. The dark sphere sat floating in place as it hovered like a specter of death above the horizon, having risen from its watery grave. Deep below the earth's crust, the inner core began to tear at the surface, sending shock waves through the mantle as it wrenched violently against the gravitational pull of the moon. Sea levels rose and swelled to heights never recorded; feeding raging storms that battered the coastlines across the hemisphere.

While the catastrophe unfolded, the colossal black orb, poised above the frigid wastes of Antarctica, began to turn, adjusting to the invisible magnetic currents streaming from the Earth's core. Thick clouds surrounding the frozen continent began to amass and swirl about the black orb positioned at the eye of the storm; drawn into its vortex. The frozen shelf entombing the continent of ice began to crack and shatter, breaking free from the ground beneath. Small fragments of ice first began to rise into the air, soon followed by enormous broken blocks floating above the fractured surface of its windswept plains.

Unseen for ages upon the Earth, a gravity storm manifested above the surface of Antarctica, displacing several thousand kilometers of ice. Loose debris from snow-capped mountains to its icy shores hung suspended in the air as the energies emitted from the six giant orbs fanned across the continent, generating a cyclone of magnetic waves. The ancient device of the Trinity was never designed to operate in this fashion, and the distances between the parted fragments created a colossal gravitational anomaly within the void between them.

"What is happening?" Mica uttered in panic as she saw enormous boulders of ice and snow lifting into the air around the fortress. Looking through the crystal walls of the spire, it was obvious something remarkable was happening. Logan left the console to stand beside her, as he too, was left gawking in numb bewilderment.

"I have no idea ...could it be the central core is causing this reaction?" he muttered to himself.

"We have to reach Allen and find out what is happening in the region of the Nif.

Trying as they could, Logan and his assistant attempted to initiate the original hack they had made into the Sentinels interface so they could try to reach Allen again, and find their lost colleague.

*   *   *

Luckily for Allen, the gravity storm surrounding the active core, which was now suspended above the surface, had caught his suspension capsule in mid-flight and gradually lowered it into the depths below into an area where an eddy of magnetic streams converged. Allen's capsule came gently to rest at the bottom of a great chasm where the overflow from the frozen lake above had once drained. Among an island of crystalline cylinders littering the small isle, Allen found himself the newest addition to the collection of the overfilled suspension chamber. A single crack in its casing had been aggravated by the unstable gravitational stresses during his descent, and with a creak, the capsule broke asunder as it settled.

Allen's limp body rolled out onto the ground. After several moments he began to cough and gasp for breath, having nearly died from suffocation while sealed within the transport cylinder. The black haze lifted from his eyes, and with a faint sigh, Allen struggled to sit upright and surveyed his strange surroundings. Peering overhead, he realized he was now at the bottom of the gorge he had seen from the edge of the lake stationed above.

"That ...that's just great," I sighed with a dense feeling of hopelessness sinking into my stomach, knowing that there was no way that I could scale that impossible height back to the level of the frozen lake. Even if I was able to, there was nothing left of the complex regardless, as the inner sphere had destroyed everything in its path when it penetrated its way to the surface. I had screwed up royally, and there was nobody else to blame but myself.

Gathering my energy to get up and survey my surroundings, it was clear that this place was a dumping ground for thousands of suspension capsules. The real question was; what were they for? Brushing off the layers of frost from the large cylinders that were haphazardly toppled together in piles, I noticed there appeared to be an odd assortment of containers sealed within every one of them. I remembered that the interface called this place Hel, which apparently was a suspension repository. Could it be that during the last days of their civilization, that the Kish had begun to collect a massive stockpile of remnants from their culture?

It was the only conclusion I could think of, but there was no clear reason why they would have them encased within these thick glass-like shells. It was almost as if they wanted to preserve them individually rather than in some large library or buried crypt. Perhaps this was a depository for keeping their society's secrets, or maybe it was just a type of sealed disposal for dangerous waste. Every conclusion that Logan had conceived suggested that the Kish had chosen to utilize only natural non-invasive methods in their style of technology, so it didn't make sense if this was poisonous or radioactive debris.

The thought of that made me worry. For regardless of any unforeseen danger, I didn't wish to stay here any longer than necessary. I had expected a place titled as the 'Kingdom of the Dead' to be more impressive; however, this was just a colossal trash bin for countless cylinders. It did make me wonder what the true purpose was of the enormous drainage apparatus which had graced the roof above the lake. The only logical conclusion was that it was meant as a cooling bed for the central core for lack of any other answer I could think of.

I was a little startled to see pebbles and chips of ice floating around me, which were gently rising into the air on their own accord. I took a closer look through the fissure the large orb had created in its violent departure from the cold lake and saw the swirling chunks of ice and rock orbiting around it in the sky high above. It was as if someone had turned off the gravity near the orb, and thought perhaps I could use that to my advantage.

Looking through the graveyard of containers, I found a few that were cracked open like my own. Of those few, the thick crystalline material was mostly intact. With luck, I finally found one that had been entirely breached by the failure of the casing. Daring to reach inside, I removed several tablets composed of both glass and stone.

I was perplexed. These certainly didn't appear dangerous, nor did they have the appearance of mere garbage, which would be discarded into this massive junkyard. The stone tablets were etched with the same Sumerian scratches that I had seen Logan deciphering before. The glass panels themselves, appeared to be made of some sort of fabricated crystal but instead of etchings like their stone counterparts, they contained colored bars embedded within them. Having no clue as to what they were for or what they said, I chose a few tablets at random and placed them in my coat pocket before wandering off towards the edge of the funnel to check for a route out of this place.

I turned around to peer across the wide chasm toward the sound of a rising pitch. A thin beam of light began to emerge from the far wall, partially hidden behind thick layers of ice that had formed over the previous millennia. Once the source of light hit the top of the embedded structure, I felt a vibration in my feet and the ice surrounding it shattered and fell away, raining down a deadly shower of frozen debris. Hidden behind this veil of ice was a doorway more than a dozen stories high, which slowly folded open and slid back into its own recess. Stepping from the murky darkness beyond its breach, emerged a single mysterious figure.

Revelations

The lone figure materialized from the gloom and began to slowly approach my position from the far side of the fissure. Curious as to who or what this person was, I pushed myself forward to meet this stranger halfway across the broken field of capsules scattered between us. As we grew closer, I could see that this unusual being was wearing a curious set of robes consisting of bronze metal plates, with a piece of headgear that obstructed its face. It raised its hand as if to greet me, so I timidly mirrored the gesture while standing there in shock as I faced this strange visitor from a long-forgotten past.

It tried to say something in words I couldn't recognize, presumably speaking some ancient tongue. Like an idiot, I shook my head and shrugged as if that was the universal gesture for not understanding. The strange being stepped forward aggressively, and I was taken aback by its change of demeanor as I stumbled and fell while backing away in defense. It loomed over me while I laid there on the ground with my arms up to protect myself, when it suddenly reached for its shoulders and pressed a clamp to remove its armored headpiece.

As its helmet came off, I saw a blackened figure underneath, wearing a pair of cracked bifocals.

"Sorry lad, I didn't realize you couldn't hear me through the helmet. I've been wearing it so long that I had forgotten I had it on. It's quite comfortable actually," Alex muttered as he stepped forward to take my shaking hand as he helped me up to my feet.

"...Alexander?" I mumbled, not believing my eyes. His face was covered in black soot, looking as if he had walked through a smelter, "How did you get here?" I stammered in surprise.

"Ah, well, after we got separated, I found this suit in one of the storage chambers of the Nida, you know, that Dwarven crypt we came across. Anyhow, their race is much smaller than the average Joe; even for my size it was a tight fit, but adequate," Alex answered, referring to his shorter height, "I couldn't find a way to reopen the doorway where we parted, so I used this neck-piece here to access the machinery we found in that mineral farm, which activated some sort of transport container," he stated while tapping the ornamental bronze mantle covering his shoulders.

"Well, I'm glad to see you're alive, my friend," I shook myself back to the reality of our situation, "but we're in a real dilemma here." I pointed upward past the edge of the frozen lake towards the large broken rift now open the surface where dark storm clouds were swirling with giant chunks of ice suspended midair.

"Oh, well now, that *is* quite astonishing," Alex admitted as he looked up in wonder at the incredible sight.

"Logan and Mica are at a citadel he called Asgard..." I began until Alex interrupted.

"Yes, I know. I was able to reach them through a crystal apparatus. They told me you were here," he smiled through the grime covering his face, "the transport I found sent me from the mineral farm to another location rife with active lava tubes, where I discovered an enormous forge filled with remnants of all sorts of devices made from interesting alloy metals. After exploring a bit, I ran into some sort of holographic guide that gave me the locations to each of the territories we had yet to discover, and I freed a shackled energy orb in order to get one of those control boards to work again. It was all quite an adventure!" Alex spouted with a grin.

"Well, your little adventure isn't quite over. We still have to get out of here. Do you know a way back ...and what the hell is that you are wearing?" I inquired while distracted by his oddly plated outfit.

"Oh, this ...as I had lost my thermal jacket a while back, so I put this thing on to stay warm, but it actually acted as vital insulation to protect me from the searing heat of the forge," he uttered with a sigh of relief as if he was reliving the hellish nightmare, "that place was hot, I tell you!"

"But, can you get us back to the others at the fortress?" I begged him once again.

"Ah, well I'm still working on that little crux. At this moment, I would have to say, *no*," he uttered with a half-guilty glance towards me, "however, it would appear that being anywhere else is better than here," Alex announced as he visually scanned the piles of capsules scattered about as far as we could see.

"Do you know what this place is?" I asked, noting Alexander's primed interest in the blocks and what was contained within them.

"The holographic guide stated this place was a suspension repository," Alex responded, "where they stored bits of genetic material and technical information, from what I gathered."

Making our way back into the cleft from where Alex emerged, we boarded a narrow horizontal lift which lowered us farther into the depths; revealing just how deep the stack of capsules was set within the fissure.

"This will take us down into the complex of the Nif," Alex advised as he bent down before a panel, which appeared to connect with his bronze mantle.

"I thought that region was on the lake above us," I replied.

"No, not at all, I believe the area above was merely a convection bowl for the main core where they once used freshwater as a type of lubricant for its function. The energized water would be purified and delivered to the bottom of this repository tank where it was used to activate a series of buried cells deep beneath the crust, like some giant battery. It was actually quite a genius feat of engineering, if I say so myself," Alex noted with a hint of admiration in his tone.

The bottom of the lift opened up into a massive chamber, where fresh ionized water was now seeping in from portions of the melting lake above for the first time in centuries. Whirlpools quickly condensed the flows which were redirected into several separate channels. Each one was large enough to swallow an entire aircraft carrier. It was all quite impressive, to say the least. The size of the facility itself, appeared as though it could accommodate a hundred thousand people, or more.

Alexander led me to the interface he had used to locate the repository and grabbed a single crystal shard from several laying scattered upon the ground, to show me how he could hack their systems in order to establish communication. He placed the shard on the interface board and stood before it.

"Apparently this device also works by proximity to the magnetic locks within this neck-piece as we had discovered before. These crystals focus the audio transmissions to their sister consoles across the continent. It was a little trial and error at first but I finally got it to work so that I could reach the professor," Alex advised as he turned to look at me before activating the console. As he did so, the familiar glowing hologram of the female guide sprang to life before us and offered its customary introduction.

"Logan, Mica, can you read me? Is anyone there?" Alex tested the transmission band. After several anxious moments, he was able to connect with them.

"Alex, is that you old pal?" the glowing maiden repeated in the sentinels' feminine voice.

"Yes, I made it to the Nif, and found Allen," Alex responded.

"That's fantastic, we thought we had lost him too," the console related his response, "we are detecting a gravitational anomaly at your location, can you verify?" Logan asked.

"Yeah, we can verify it all right," I responded over Alex's shoulder as he stood at the control board, "the central core has released itself from a frozen lake, which was used as some sort of holding tank, but has since drifted to the surface above ground."

"Astonishing," Logan repeated over the interface, "we had a supply shipment inbound but it had to turn back because of the adverse weather conditions created by the cyclone. We got a hold of Walter back on the ship, but he warned us that in light of the approaching catastrophe that our fellow scientists have forwarded their dire forecasts to the authorities and executive branches, revealing that we were facing an extinction-level event of such a scale that several governments have abandoned aid to their citizens and began maneuvers for self-preservation." This situation had turned upside down in a heartbeat. Regimes worldwide had started to evacuate to their underground shelters to preserve the continuance of government. Like the cowards they were, they had chosen to hide in their bunkers so they could survive the calamity by deserting their own citizens. It was a sad revelation that those in authority we so trusted, chose instead to save their own necks, rather than fulfill their sworn obligations; not just for their own people, but had forsaken the humanitarian crisis in its entirety.

"*Wow* ...what bastards," I blurted out loud.

"Bastards, indeed! I would certainly agree," the interface repeated Logan's words but in the voice of the female sentinel, which almost made the remark comical.

Walter had also related that the Government-imposed martial law had begun to wane, and led toward a chaotic breakdown of society as people ransacked cities and looted supplies in their desperate struggle for survival. On a troublesome note, he let Logan know that there was a naval vessel currently approaching their location by sea. Apparently, this carrier had intercepted the communications between Logan's party and their ship, and was sent out to investigate.

Walter and the captain weren't sure what to do. If they tried to evade the military vessel, it would likely send them too far from the flight range of the supply helicopter they had waiting on the pad. If that happened, their team might be left abandoned with little chance of return. That made me wonder how long we could survive out here if we were left on our own.

Alex said that after his rations ran out, that he had sustained himself by consuming lichen and fungus, and even harvested peculiar bugs as a source of nutrition. I hadn't realized that the little fellow was such a hardcore survivalist, which left me partially impressed. The small red beetles he had found established their colonies near the active lava tubes. I declined his offer to try one when he pulled a few of the dead insects out of his pocket.

Cool water started gushing in from the rift below as melting ice poured in from the fractured lake and began to shower into the overspill tank. Unfortunately for us, the tubes leading to the buried batteries were already choked with solid ice, since the waterworks weren't designed to operate at this temperature and the level quickly began to overflow the surrounding banks. There was no time to delay, as Alex and I scrambled for higher ground within the complex to escape from the rising water, forcing us to withdraw from the communications console. Out of desperation, we breached a venting system and followed it through its winding labyrinth, fighting the drafts of heated air coursing within.

"Ah, I need a rest, this suit is really heavy," Alex complained as he plopped down in the vent passage.

"Do you know where we are heading?" I asked.

"This architecture looks familiar," Alex remarked as he patted the ventilation housing, "so it's my guess that this network of vents leads back to the lava chambers which feed into the giant forge," he conceded while supporting his hypothesis by the heated air coming from the direction ahead of us.

His immediate worry was that if the water level rose high enough to back-flush through these vents, then we could end up either drowned, or the volatile reaction of the ice water hitting the exposed lava tubes would create a steam pressure reaction, which would cause the whole area to blow. Unfortunately, that was the very direction in which we were heading and Alex also pointed out that I didn't have a protective thermal suit to shield me from the intense heat. These were all possibilities which I had not considered, and none of them were very pretty.

"Alex, we might die down here," I blurted with weariness.

"Yes, that's ah... a high probability, but we might make it out... if we're lucky," he added as he gasped for air while taking a breather from the exertion.

"But if the world gets destroyed and we all end up trapped on this ice rock, why should we even bother trying? I mean, what exactly would we be surviving for if the world fell into ruin?" I asked innocently. It was a fundamental question for anyone facing similar scenarios across the world at that very moment. There were so many people clawing hand and foot while struggling to survive; what were they so desperately fighting for when nothing familiar would be left but a life of hardship?

"Allen, there are but a handful of people who view life itself, in a far different context than most of our society," Alex started with a solemn note, "instead of seeing the world as to what affects only them, there are those of us who find a greater calling, and question instead, how they can contribute towards everyone and our society as a whole. I, for one, fell into this field because I was captivated by the history of all those people who came before me, and what they had to offer which I could add upon; and I thought it would be a terrible loss if their tribute to humanity, no matter how small that might be, was simply forgotten," Alex confessed, "so when you ask, *why we should even bother trying*? I must answer ...why not? If you can understand my perspective that owing the effort to survive for *yourself* alone, would be immeasurably selfish on every level, but owing it to our ancestors and those we share this world with right here, right now, would be the right thing to do. With all due respect, I would say to choose life."

Alexander's words caught me off guard as to how deeply philosophical he actually was, having not seen him in that color of light before. It made me wonder how many people who were currently knee-deep in the unfolding catastrophe around our globe were either committing suicide because they could not stand the change or face the suffering, or were running away while mindlessly searching to escape their fate without any given consideration for others. Those empty and selfish souls who were seeking deliverance merely to survive another day, now seemed like an appalling waste. I could see now that Alexander, Mica and Logan, and their lot were trying to make the world a better place; for it was what they believed in.

At the given moment, I didn't feel a sense of guilt for my

heartless question or depressing demeanor as I once would have, for I could now contemplate the angle Alexander was presenting. We were trapped in an epic situation with the world falling apart around us, which would make anyone lose their mind but he and the others remained focused. His desire was to make the world a better place, not for what it once was but for what will be to come. I could now see why he and Logan had become good friends.

After our brief rest, we pushed our way through the ventilation corridors and found ourselves on the edge of a track which appeared to be a footpath. Trailing beside it was a single rail we found attached to the sidewall, though neither of us had any idea what it was for. Advancing for nearly an hour, the corridor dipped into a funnel that was encrusted with dark volcanic glass. I didn't like the idea of being in here without a suit but Alex noted he hadn't actually found any similar gear since he left the mineral farm near the crypts.

"Hold on ...do you hear that?" I stopped Alex in his tracks so that we could get a bearing of our surroundings. Listening intently, he stated he couldn't.

"Why ...what is it?" he whispered.

"I swore I could hear something like a..." I began to answer as I perked my ears, realizing there was some sort of ambient noise in the background growing progressively louder.

Suddenly, a gushing wave of glacier water spewed into the funnel from the path above where we had been standing just moments before, making us fight for our footing. Falling here would be a deadly mistake, as the sharp volcanic glass could tear us to shreds while we were at the mercy of the raging waters. To make things worse, the glass began to shatter and break under the weight of the barrage pouring in and pockets of the black shards began to crack beneath us; revealing a void below our feet.

Alex and I turned toward one another with a glaze of panic brushed in our eyes when the entire flooring gave way, and we fell into the chasm below. We came to rest on a shallow ledge several meters down while being drenched from the cascade pouring in from the chute above. Both of us looked below, and could see that we were situated on the edge of an active lava tube that had encrusted upon the lower chute.

"Well, I think we just found out where all the hot air was coming from," Alex stated nervously as he scooted away from the ledge.

The chasm was alive with flowing red rivers, glowing from the heat of the molten rock. Within minutes, the pressure of the current went from a meager downpour to a torrent surging over our heads. Alexander and I were fully expecting the explosive reaction that followed as the natural chamber filled with scalding steam. Alex was well insulated within his plated suit but I was sweltering in my arctic gear.

The deafening hiss of steam rose through the cavern as the molten rock began to harden from the sudden cooling. Expecting the worst, Alex and I nearly embraced in a hug. We glanced at each other awkwardly as the stream of gushing water subsided for a brief moment, until a sudden deluge washed us from our perch and down onto the hardening lava tubes below. The torrent swept us out along the steaming crust as we slid across its glassy surface and fell into a hollow lava tube; all the while, I could feel the boiling water begin to burn through my apparel.

It was an unpleasant ride as we were swept through tight hissing chambers as if it were some hellish waterslide. My backside felt cooked as did the rest of my body as we were propelled through the heated funnel. Flung about as we were at the mercy of the torrential waters, I felt a gust of cold air wash over me, then another, as we shot through the underground current. Finally, we toppled down onto a graveled shore where I was momentarily disoriented by the blinding light.

Stumbling out from the steaming sulfuric soup pouring upon my back, I called out to Alex, and I eventually found him several meters away lying on his back like an upturned tortoise; trying but unable to stand while he was weighed down by his drenched metallic suit.

"How are you feeling? Any broken bones?" I asked, though feeling a little bruised and beaten myself.

"Oh, my," he stalled as he looked around, "no, no, I think my armored outfit took the brunt of it," Alexander bubbled as he spat out a mouthful of rancid water; "...oh, that's got a nasty taste to it. Where are my glasses!" Alex felt at his face in a sudden panic.

Looking around in haste, I found his spectacles half-buried in a spot of snow, but they were now in far worse condition. I handed them to him as he put them on, only to realize one of the lenses was entirely missing and the frame itself was bent out of shape. He didn't seem to mind as much about the damage for he was just thankful to be alive. We stepped further away from the geyser spout where we had been ejected as another burst of steam and acrid water came spewing out.

Looking around to get our bearings, we found we were in the presence of a looming cliff reaching far above us towards the stormy sky. Peering out towards a vast ice shelf, Alex made a guess as to where we were.

"I do say, I believe we're at the rim of the transatlantic mountain range, which would explain this geothermal activity," Alexander exclaimed.

Apparently, we had been dumped somewhere upon the lower range of west Antarctica. This left us in a bind, being left stuck in the middle of nowhere in our water-drenched attire. I was expecting symptoms of hypothermia to set in at any moment but the hot steam from the geyser kept the temperature fairly tolerant. The area around us had melted away the ice and the black pebbled shore of the beach stretched out towards an enormous ice plain as far as the eye could see.

Pointing out an odd feature rising above the white plain, Alexander and I marched our way to what turned out to be an old abandoned drilling station. The battered sign on the edge of the building read 'Loner Station-1978', which seemed like a fitting title for the solitary site. We let ourselves in as there was no lock on the door, and I was elated to see that it had been recently used and left restocked with supplies. Alexander was merely glad to get his hands on some real food.

We scoured the place for emergency equipment and found a radio. Since the solar panel outside the building had been covered in snow, I had to gas up the generator, which took some effort to get the contraption running. Once we had some power pumping through the station, Alexander jumped on the radio to contact our ship. Bearing on our frequency channel, we picked up an enormous amount of static, which was likely due to the storm cluster generated by the active core at the center of the cyclone which had engulfed the entire skyline.

"Anyone on board, do you read?" Alexander chattered on the line while feeding himself with his fingers on a freshly opened can of tuna fish.

"Please identify yourself," a voice cut over the radio, barely breaking through the static.

"This is Alexander and Allen from the Logan expedition, trying to reach our ship. Is that you Walter?" Alex asked, trying to listen over the noise.

"Yes, Alexander! I thought you were lost, and you found Allen, that's amazing! I will have to inform the others," Walter chimed, though most of his speech was broken because of the erratic interference, "what are your coordinates ...are you two safe at the moment?"

Both Alex and I quickly rifled through the station to find a chart and found our location upon a map, and provided it to Water so that he could send out a rescue party; though he confessed that it would take some time to reach us. After we went off the air, Alex and I spent a greater part of the evening sitting next to a heater drying out our clothes, and with a little hunting, we found an extra thermal coat for Alexander to wear stuffed in the meager storage bins left at the campsite. After dusk, the night sky was ablaze with shimmering curtains of an immense aurora which stretched across the horizon, alive with dancing colors while dark storm clouds orbited the hovering sphere beneath their flickering glow. The rainbows of glittering lights made the Antarctic appear as though we were standing upon some alien world.

The next day, we awoke to the constant drum of thunder disturbing the peaceful serenity of the icy plains. As dawn lit up the sky, we could see that a large portion of the colossal storm front had dissipated, and was now replaced by a swirling mass of rock and ice, appearing like a giant ring surrounding a tiny dark planet. We were desperate for information on the others and what had happened but the radio static was raging at points that were nearly deafening, as relentless feedback screeched through the speakers. It wasn't until several days had passed that we finally received a response to our hails.

"This is Walter, calling Alex or Allen. Over," Walter radioed in over the radio. Jumping to the microphone, we tried to tune in the frequency.

"This is Alexander. We read you. What is the situation?"

"Take a look out your six, old friend," Walter answered as Alex gave me a dumbfounded look while I rushed to the door.

Stepping outside in nothing but my thermal underwear, I squinted my eyes against the morning sunlight breaking over the horizon to glimpse several snowmobiles approaching us over the ice shelf. I was so shocked that I stood there like an idiot, forgetting that I wasn't even dressed. Alex came outside to join me and we waved in unison while Walter arrived as a passenger clinging onto the back of one of the sleds. Several members of the ship's crew had ridden out to pick us up from where they had moored the ship the night before.

"Ah, it's good to see you two!" Walter remarked as he raised one arm to give us a hug; still tendering his healing arm in its sling, "Let's get you back to the ship. We already sent out a transport helicopter to pick up the Professor and his assistant."

"What, already?" I blurted, "I thought that they were going to stay at the control tower at the fortress until the danger was over?" I asked in dismay, as the black orb could still be seen poised above the horizon with its haunting ring of ice and rock orbiting around it.

"Ah, about that, there's quite a lot that's happened over the past few days you need to catch up on," Walter confessed as he ushered us to grab our gear. Retrieving my clothes and packing Alexander's extraordinary metal suit, we hopped on the back of the sleds and made our way across the ice field towards the ship. The captain had relocated our vessel to the western shore as they set out to evade the approaching naval ship. However, after the eruption of the gravitational storm, the military ship abruptly broke off its pursuit. I was glad to be back in a warm bed and it had been a long time since I had a hot cup of coffee, but I found the inner strength not to add a spot of Gin from the bottle sitting at the table for us to share.

We ran outside in expectation when the helicopter arrived back at the ship later that day but discovered that neither Mica nor Logan were aboard. The pilot stated that they had requested to be dropped off back at our original rally site at the iron tree, for reasons they didn't disclose.   However, he relayed their message, asking the three of us to join them. Within the hour, we had prepped ourselves as the aircraft was refueled while Walter, Alex, and I, boarded for our departure.

The flight back inland was an incredible sight; having a birds-eye view of the gravity storm lingering above the icy plateau. During our flight out, the pilot even remarked over the intercom, *"That's something you don't see every day,"* which was certainly an understatement.   The mega-structure of spinning stones slowly orbiting its black nucleus cast strange and ominous shadows in the fading light. It was a tense ride the entire time it took to get there until we finally came within sight of the old camp at the base of the colossal tree.

Setting us down in the open field, the men pulled out a few supply crates and helped set up our monitoring equipment around the encampment where several tents had been erected. The sun was falling fast, so we tromped our way through the thawing snow towards the clearing around the great tree, while noticing that the avalanche of ice and snow, which had previously blocked the stone doorway, had entirely melted away. The scene was illuminated by several lamps posted around the exposed roots winding through the bedrock. Though Logan stood up first upon seeing our arrival, it was Mica who came running to greet us as she jumped into my arms, smiling.

"I'm glad you're alright," she whispered into my ear as we walked into the camp and took a seat next to Logan.

"Ah, Alexander. We're pleased you could join us," the professor offered with a kind grin towards his friend, happy to see him alive and well. Alexander shook his hand gently with solemn forgiveness for having been left abandoned during the expedition, for which he held no blame.

"I thought you were going to stay at the fortress to oversee the transition of the polar shift," I asked with mild curiosity, considering what had transpired since we last spoke.

"After you had prematurely activated the core, we attempted to harmonize the magnetic emissions connected through the spheres. However, during our effort to fine-tune them, we discovered that the induction fields had managed to balance themselves on their own," Logan answered.

"Uh, yeah, how about repeating that in layman's terms, Doc," I responded with a foolish smile.

"Somehow, the network of energy spheres had aligned themselves without our aid," Mica offered as a blunt, if not fully clarified, explanation.

"But, I thought you said triggering the sphere too early would be disastrous if you tried to stall the core," I barked, "so has everything on the mainland gone back to normal?"

"Ah, well, that's an interesting question," Logan answered, "It appears nothing will truly be the same again for many nations. But then, I guess we can place that burden on this ancient weapon," he added as he pointed up towards the dark mass of swirling ice and rock glinting in the falling sunset.

We sat together in the lamplight, catching up on recent events as they filled me in. Logan was surprised upon hearing my side of the story but gave a nod of understanding when I told him what it was I had learned from the sentinel interface, that this 'great weapon' the Kish so feared, wasn't a device forged towards their destruction, but one which had been designed for their salvation. The Professor had a surprising confession of his own, while Walter confirmed his shocking words as he monitored incoming radio chatter from across the globe.

Logan had ultimately achieved his goal to ease the polar shift, if either by accident or by design, as the ancient technology of the Trinity had ultimately served the function for which it was created those countless eons ago. In coordination with his fellow scientists of the Atlas, whose professional expertise was relied upon to advise the entrenched militaries and governments worldwide; by an artful sleight of hand, they had manipulated the pretense of a deadly apocalypse to feed their governing officials. Needless to say, the devastation suffered in the precursor of the polar shift was real enough, and only served to stoke the fears of world leaders. In their craven eagerness to save themselves, nearly every branch of authority across the Earth had retreated into deep underground bunkers and fortifications as they abandoned the very people who relied upon them for direction; leaving them to perish in the approaching cataclysm. These forsaken victims had found commonality and kinship, and forged a bond with the spreading fellowship of the Atlas.

As the governing elitists, who solely valued their own lives, sought to hide deep within their secured bunkers, the discarded civilians revolted and sealed them within their fortified vaults. Over the past several days, a massive undertaking of citizens from around the globe rose up, and arrived with bulldozers, and machinery of every type, combining their efforts to welding shut the bunker doors and buried those cowardly and corrupted authorities who abused their positions, imprisoning them within the very vaults where they had sought shelter. All the politicians and their military regimes who wore a badge of power suddenly found their shelters covered with meters of cement and earthen debris, and all the self-serving rulers and leaders, dignitaries, and dictators now found themselves permanently entombed. They had gathered in their sealed fortifications to preserve themselves and protect their positions of power, and in the end, they got their new world order, but it was one that didn't include them or their kind.

The act of burying these crippled minds who ruled our lives and so eagerly suppressed human expression and our freedoms had, in turn, unified populations of every race from around the globe against them. There were now only those scattered few left who fought against this fresh change, which ushered in an era where the human race could begin anew. Being so close to utter annihilation, the ragged survivors who had helped one another began to recognize that the struggle for wealth and power they had been so groomed to pursue, had poisoned mankind's true path. So they buried the worst of humanity in the darkness where they had gathered, and stood united to embrace a brighter future for the generations to come.

For a brief moment, it made me wonder how our society as a whole and our global economy could possibly function without governments around to manipulate them, but whatever doubts I held yielded to an unspoken sense of relief. With a glance into Mica's eyes at my side, I realized that the world was now free to start afresh, and it felt good to be unchained. In my curiosity, I had to ask Logan how he had managed to get so many of his academic colleagues to conduct their coordinated deception on such a grand scale. Logan laughed, and gave me a word of clever advice which I would never forget.

"In this field, digging through the lives of people long past, I have learned a few things, my boy, and one of them is to remember, that *Life isn't fair* ...so I suggest that you cheat whenever you get the chance!"

The laughter that followed echoed through the limbs of the giant tree above us as iridescent strings of shimmering light unfolded from its branches, like a great glowing willow. We sat there gazing at this wondrous sight under the strange arctic sky, while the southern aurora danced in the heavens above;

enveloped by the prismatic glow radiating from this ancient symbol of life which had endured through untold ages. Mica reached out to hold my hand and rested her head gently upon my shoulder, and as she held me, I felt a curious sense of comfort at that moment, a sense of inner peace which would last me the rest of my days.

About the Author

Michel Savage has been devoted to writing throughout his career. If one reads between the lines they will find his novels revolve around the reminder that we are only borrowing our small place in nature but for a brief period of time, and to take responsibility for the environment, for one another, and all other living creatures with which we share this world; and hopefully planting a seed in our conscience of the importance to preserve what is left of the wilds, our untainted woodlands and ever-dwindling rainforests.

He has had the blessing of sharing his stories and artwork around the globe, which is a gift in itself, and would encourage others not to waste too much of their lives chasing someone else's dreams but to follow their own.

One of the most valuable lessons he has learned in his years is that there are far more important things in life than power and money, such as kindness, compassion, and consideration towards others.

...share that thought if you will.

Enter the Grey Forest

www.GreyForest.com

Also by
Michel Savage

Broken Mirror

Hurtling through space was an enormous tumbling rock known as MN4 our astronomers affectionately named after an ancient Egyptian god of destruction. Asteroid Apophis was the talk of the year that every scientific community on Earth was aware of, though its flyby in April 2029 was to be nothing more than a spectacular celestial event; but as warring nations were locked in global conflict, our civilization was unprepared for the devastation that followed in its wake.

Several years after governments fell and society dissolved a ragged pack of survivors stumble upon the buried truth, revealing what circumstances had led to the aftermath that ensued; leaving them to question their struggle to salvage what few splintered shards were left of our world that would forever define our bitter legacy.

Outlaws of Europa

The 2nd moon of Jupiter has been turned into a prison planet where for several generations, robot drone ships have been dumping the scum of the universe and are patrolled by a ring of advanced security satellites that would destroy any vessel attempting to land. After a century of research, old core samples from the ice reveal that the frozen oceans of Europa held the base element of an immortality drug that can extend the human lifespan several-fold. Now greedy military corporations race for the new fountain of youth, only to discover they can't disable the orbiting sentry which was programmed to protect itself at all costs.

It appears the Confederation has a problem. How do they get past a self-evolving AI that has appointed itself as Warden, and furthermore, retake a planet roaming with Earth's worst criminals who might well be immortal themselves.

Hellbot – Battle Planet

Tranquility was one of those out of the way planets in a system far out of reach from the normal space lanes. Loners, dreamers ...whoever they were, chose to colonize this world. Thirty cycles ago something went terribly wrong. It was rumored their terraformer reactor went critical, and few escaped the chain reaction that clouded the atmosphere with a planet-wide sand storm. A decade of hard labor evaporated overnight. What wasn't buried under the ocean of sand was left to fry under the twin suns.

Human explorers began to wander back into the forgotten zone. No one knew of the machines that had evolved, or the war that raged beyond the edge of the universe ...where mankind did not belong.

Witchwood
The Harvesting

Every day around the world hundreds of people go missing without a trace. Year after year their numbers add up to millions of lost souls who are never to be seen again; and their numbers keep climbing ...this is where many of them went.

Project EVE

In the late 1940s after the 2nd World War, a classified government program was created in order to explore the military use of psychics to gain an advantage for their soldiers during armed conflict. At a remote laboratory in the mountains, a secret compound comprised of several hundred test subjects were trained to enhance their abilities with the goal of achieving the skills of telepathy and mind control. Assigned to investigate this covert project, Walter Grant found himself entangled in a web of conspiracy and deceit when he discovered that the residents of the colony were being held captive by the scientists who had hidden the ugly truth behind their dangerous experiments.

At the heart of the project was a girl named Eve, whose extraordinary mind held the key, a child who would prove to them why humanity could not handle such power.

Shadoworld
Veil of Shadows

Ash was an orphaned street urchin who grew up in the gutters of a desolate medieval city; his bitter youth spent picking pockets and snatching trinkets from the wealthy to survive.

Over the years his art for stealth and sharpened skills had drawn the attention of the Thieves Guild who took him into their folds. Little did they know that the boys tragic past would one day find itself woven within the treacherous schemes of a mysterious spider cult.

As of late, a series of chilling murders had befallen several nobles within the privileged upper districts. Their gruesome deaths had appeared to be centered around an ancient cursed skull, which had recently found its way into the hands of a rich collector. There were few who would trespass upon the strange realms of witchcraft and dark magic ...but a master thief does not fear those who dwell in darkness, for he is one with the shadows.

Shadoworld
Shadows Gate

Asra found himself alone in the middle of the barren sands, unable to remember who he was or how he had gotten there. Saved by a caravan of traveling gypsies, he entered into an exotic world of dancing acrobats, fortune tellers, and mystics who performed their skills for cheering crowds across the desert empires.

However, his destiny would change the day he stumbled upon a forbidden shrine to find a mythical creature entombed beneath its shattered ruins.

Promises were whispered and a dark pact was made with the ancient demon; a bond of magic that would lead him on a perilous journey to reveal his forgotten past.